'Daryl Sahli served in the Rhodesian Army as a National Serviceman in 4 Independent Company, Rhodesian African Rifles. The novel he has written, whilst fiction, is based on true events. A great deal of effort has gone into ensuring that details of weapons and military procedure are factually correct. Where this book stands out from other Rhodesian war accounts is that it is written through the eyes of a National Serviceman serving in a unit run by regular officers and senior NCOs who had little respect for part-time soldiers. These nineteen year-old men were expected to perform against the enemy as professionals and in most cases they did exactly that. Many of the characters in this book did exist and for someone who was there, it makes for a good read.

... Daryl Sahli`s novel is a great action thriller and an authentic account of a war, now forgotten and unknown to many. This book is as enthralling as any war novel I have read.'

- Ian Livingston-Blevins

Althea ('Ma Farran')

My very best wishes...

A SKIRMISH IN AFRICA

DARYL SAHLI

You see ... some of us can
Read & write!

Daryl

MyStory
PUBLISHING

Northlands Business Consultants Pty Ltd
ABN 75 091 308 146 Trading As

MyStory Publishing
P.O. Box 5336, West End, QLD, 4101, Australia

National Library of Austrlia Cataloguing-in-Publication data:

Sahli, Daryl
A skirmish in Africa / Daryl Sahli ; photograph by Jason Sahli

ISBN: 9780987156402 (pbk.)

Rhodesia. Army. Rhodesian African Rifles - - Fiction.
Civil war - - Africa - - Fiction.
Zimbabwe - - History - - Chimurenga War, 1966-1980 - - Fiction.
Africa - - Fiction
Sahli, Jason
A823.4

This book is a work of fiction. Names, characters, places and incidents are either the product of the author's imagination or are used fictitiously and any resemblance to actual persons, living or dead, business establishments, events or locales is entirely coincidental.

Cover design by Despina Papamanolis
Maps & Contact Diagrams by Daryl Sahli and Despina Papamanolis
Author photograph by Jason Sahli
Typeset in 11 / 13.2pt Palatino
Printed and bound in Australia by Griffin Press
70gsm Book Cream

MIX
Paper from
responsible sources
FSC® C009448

The paper this book is printed on is certified against the Forest Stewardship Council® Standards. Griffin Press holds FSC chain of custody certification SGS-COC-005088. FSC promotes environmentally responsible, socially beneficial and economically viable management of the world's forests.

In memory of 2nd Lieutenant A. J. (Gus) Du Toit,
3 Independent Company, Rhodesian African Rifles,
killed in action.

It is true what they say; '… *only the good die young*'.

My very special thanks to my wife Karen for providing the inspiration to write this book and for her unstinting support throughout the project. My thanks to Ian & Marjie for providing the spark; to Phil, Rob & Pat, Tom & Carol, Jeremy and my daughter Megan for proof reading and providing valuable input. A very special thank you to James Knox and John Bucknell who joined in my enthusiasm for this project and helped enormously with editing and advice.

Map 1: Southern Africa 1975
Country names (colonial names) [year of independence]

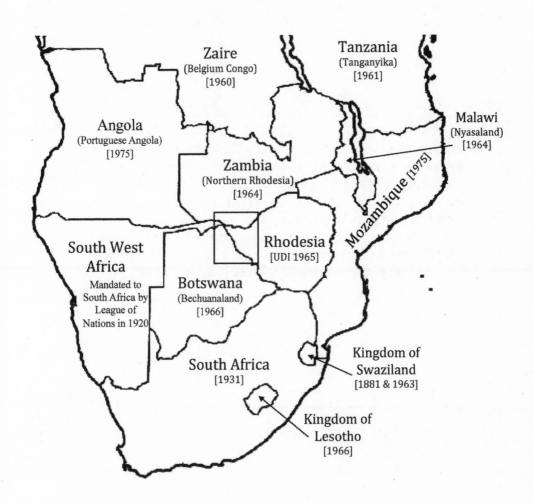

Map 2: Operational Areas for Rhodesian Forces and the Patriotic Front (ZIPRA, ZANLA)

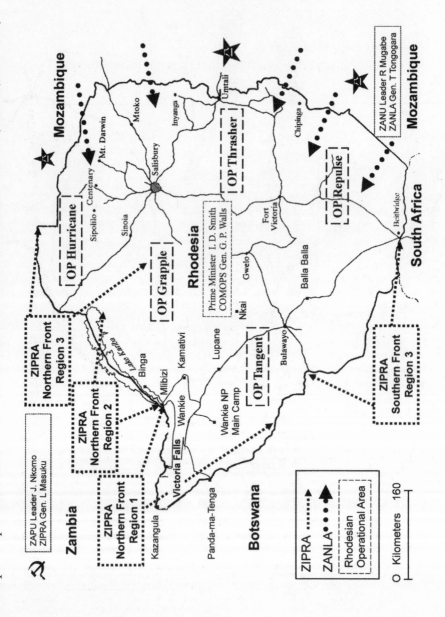

Map 3: Northwest Rhodesia where this story unfolds

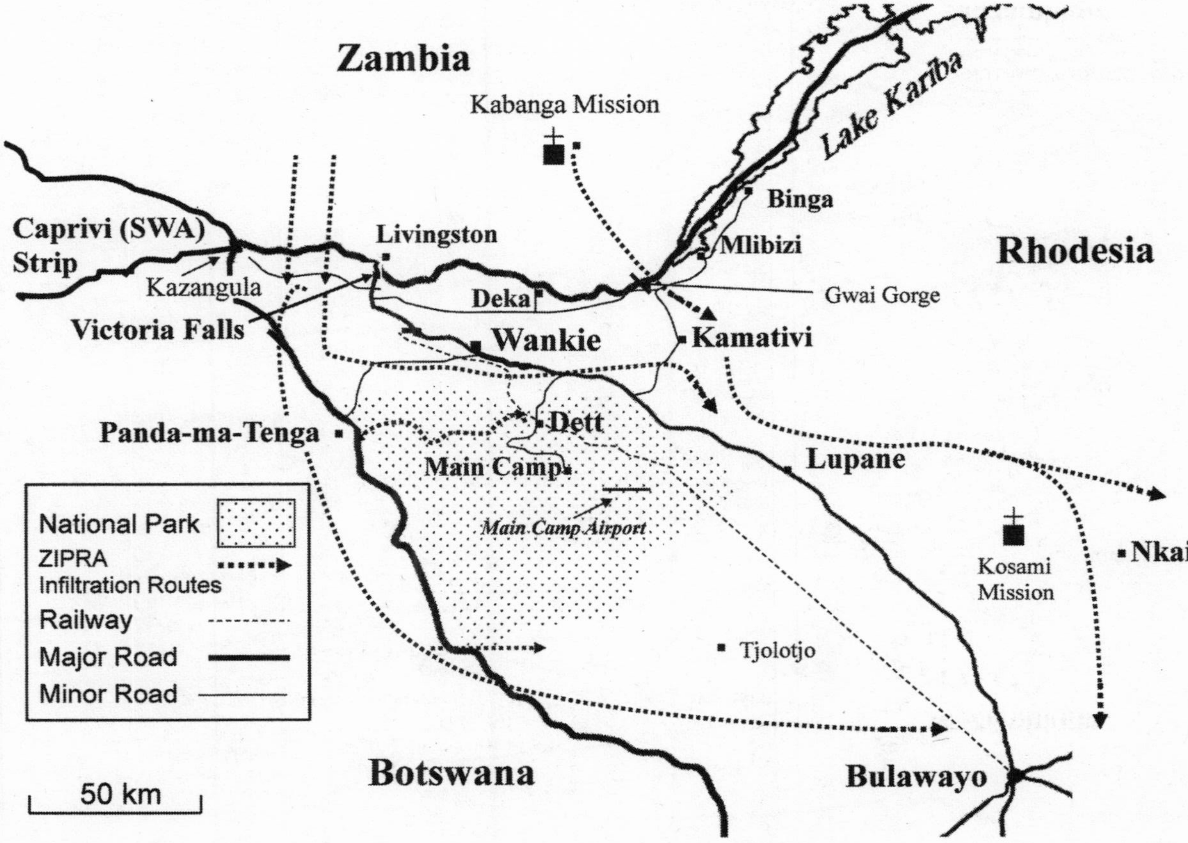

Zambia

Rhodesia

Lake Kariba

Kabanga Mission

Binga

Mlibizi

Gwai Gorge

Kamativi

Livingston

Deka

Wankie

Nkai

Kosami Mission

Lupane

Tjolotjo

Dett

Main Camp

Main Camp Airport

Bulawayo

Capfivi (SWA) Strip

Kazangula

Victoria Falls

Panda-ma-Tenga

Botswana

National Park

ZIPRA Infiltration Routes

Railway

Major Road

Minor Road

50 km

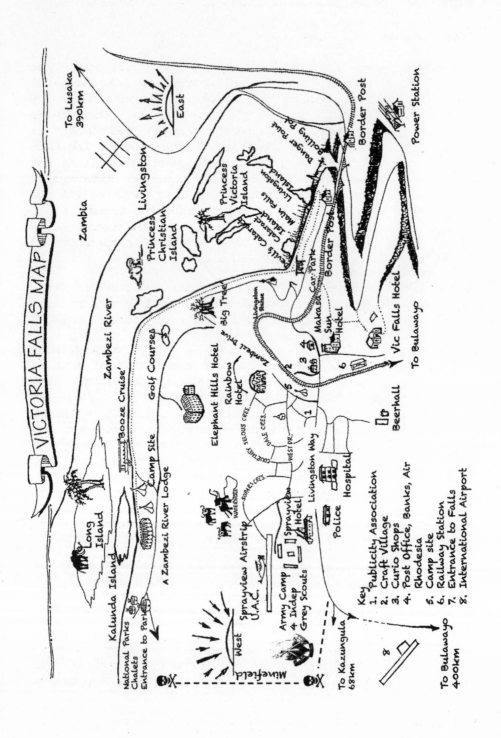

Extract from the *Rhodesian Army Counter-Insurgency Manual (1975)*.

[Definitions:

Insurgent: An indigenous or foreign national not recognized as a belligerent by International law, aiming to overthrow a government by force. In revolutionary War the terms "guerrilla", "revolutionary," "terrorist" or "insurgent" are used on occasion to indicate differences in the opposition. When it is not necessary to indicate specific differences, however, "insurgent" is used to cover all the roles implied by the foregoing terms. It is also taken to include such additional terms as "saboteur," "enemy" "insurrectionist" or "rebel," where applicable.

Terrorist: A supporter of a dissident faction (in fact, an insurgent), who is trained for or resorts to organized violence for political ends.

Insurgency: A form of rebellion in which a dissident faction instigates the commission of acts of civil disobedience, sabotage and terrorism, and wages irregular warfare in order to overthrow a government. In its ultimate stages it could escalate to a conflict on conventional lines. Although insurgency often starts internally, it has seldom been known to succeed without outside assistance, support and encouragement.

Counter-insurgency (COIN): All measures, both civil and military, undertaken by a government, independently or with the assistance of friendly nations, to prevent or defeat insurgency. (Refers to the Rhodesian Security Forces)

Counter-insurgency operations (COIN Ops): Counter-insurgency operations are the military aspects of counter-insurgency. These consist of: Anti-terrorist operations (ATOPS), Psychological operations (PSYOPS), operations in support of civil authorities (OSCA).

Anti-terrorist operations (ATOPS): Any military operation against terrorists.]

Glossary

1 Brigade	Brady Barracks in Bulawayo, also JOC Tangent Headquarters
AK47	AK47, (or Kalashnikov), Soviet Union, selective fire, gas operated, magazine of 30 rounds, 7.62×39mm assault rifle.
ANC	African Nation Congress (South Africa)
BDF	Botswana Defence Force
Call-sign, c/sign	Rhodesian voice procedure, the name or number given to a unit, large or small. Personnel issued with a radio would automatically be allocated a c/sign.
CASEVAC	Casualty Evacuation.
CT	Charlie Tango, Communist Terrorist, voice procedure using C and T from the phonetic alphabet.
Chimurenga	The liberation war. ZIPRA called the First Chimurenga the Matabele Rebellion of 1890, ZANLA referred to the First Chimurenga as the Shona Rebellion of 1893, while the Second Chimurenga is believed to have started, by both ZIPRA and ZANLA, with the battle of Sinoia on 28 April 1966 in which 21 Freedom Fighters were intercepted by Rhodesian Forces and killed.
Click/s	Rhodesian slang, kilometres.
Combined Operations (COMOPS)	The organisation set up to co-ordinate the activities of Air Force, Police and Army. COMOPS were also responsible for planning and executing external raids.
Cordon Sanitaire	Border minefield. These were laid in a number of places around the country. In the Op Tangent area the minefield surrounded Victoria Falls and stretched from the gorges below the falls to Binga on Lake Kariba.
FAF 1	Forward Airfield, FAF 1 was at Wankie (Hwange)
Fireforce	Quick reaction force usually manned by men of the regular Battalions of the Rhodesian Light Infantry (RLI) or the Rhodesian African Rifles (RAR). Fireforce was both heli-borne and para-borne, made up helicopter gunships and troop carriers, plus close air-support aircraft.
FN	Fabrique Nationale (Belgium), self-loading rifle, magazine 20 rounds, 7.62×51mm (NATO) round.
G-car	Aerospatiale Alouette III, 'G' for General Duties, helicopter troop carrier, 4 fully equipped soldiers, plus pilot and technician/gunner, twin .303in Browning MkII machineguns mounted on the left, cyclic rate of fire 1,200 rounds per minute. The first Alouette IIIs were purchased in 1962.

Glossary

Gomo	Shona, hill or mountain.
Grey Scouts	1 Grey Scouts Regiment, Mounted Infantry, specialised in fast follow-up.
Ground Coverage BSAP	Specialised police intelligence gathering unit. British South Africa Police was the name of the Rhodesian Police Force, name stems from the pioneer column of the 1890s when the British South Africa Company supplied the police force.
Indep Co	Independent Company, six in all, units of the Rhodesian African Rifles. Located at Beitbridge (1), Kariba (2), Umtali (3)(5), Vic Falls/Wankie (4), and Inyanga (6).
Intaf	Department of Internal Affairs, Administered the system of Protected Villages.
Jesse	Thick thorn scrub.
JOC, sub-JOC	Joint Operations Command, the JOC for Operation Tangent in Matabeleland was located at Brady Barracks in Bulawayo. Wankie (Hwange) was designated as a sub-JOC.
K-car	Aerospatiale Alouette III, 'K' for Killer, helicopter gunship, Fireforce (K-car) Commander seated next to pilot facing rearwards, plus pilot and technician/gunner, mounting one French Matra MG 151 20mm cannon on the left, cyclic rate of fire reduced to 350 rounds per minute, high-explosive incendiary shells. Cannon sights calibrated for an altitude of 800ft AGL.
Kopie	Afrikaans, hill.
Locals	Local villagers, tribes-people.
Lynx	Reims-Cessna FTB 337G, (Military version used in Vietnam as the O2 Skymaster) twin-engined, push-pull aircraft, used for close air support, carried mini-golf bombs, 37mm SNEB rockets, frantan canisters and twin roof mounted .303 Browning machineguns. These aircraft were smuggled into Rhodesia from France in 1975.
LZ	Landing Zone
MAG	Fabrique Nationale (Belgium), matirueurs a gas, 7.62×51mm (NATO) round, belt-fed machinegun, cyclic rate of fire 650 rounds per minute
Mujiba	Shona, civilian youth, running with and supporting insurgent operations, the 'eyes and ears'.

Masodja	Shona derivation of the word "soldier'. The connotation is that to be referred to as a Masodja, one had to be blooded in battle; the title had to be earned.
NS	National Service, ranged from one to two years depending on manpower needs and changing policy.
RAR	Rhodesian African Rifles, two regular airborne battalions, six infantry independent companies, an HQ and a Depot training establishment. Some of the officers in the unit were foreign volunteers from the Commonwealth Countries (United Kingdom, Australia, New Zealand and Canada).
RIC	Rhodesian Intelligence Corps
River, The River	The Zambezi River. Its size and prominence of this river on the northern border made it 'The River'.
RLI	Rhodesian Light Infantry, one regular battalion, made of four airborne commandos including a Support Commando, HQ and Training Troop. The unit exclusively white specialising in Fireforce operations and major external raids, mostly regular soldiers but in later years included national servicemen to boost numbers. The unit included many foreign volunteers from the Commonwealth Countries (United Kingdom, Australia, New Zealand and Canada) but also South Africa, France, USA (Vietnam veterans), Holland and Germany.
RPD	A light machinegun, Soviet Union, 100 round segmented belt in a drum container, 7.62×39mm cartridge, cyclical rate of fire 650 rounds per minute.
RPG	Rocket Propelled Grenade, RPG7, Soviet Union, hand-held, shoulder-launched anti-tank weapon capable of firing an unguided rocket equipped with an explosive warhead, fired both anti-tank and high explosive/fragmentation warheads.
RR	Rhodesia Regiment, four brigades, ten territorial infantry battalions and a training depot. The Rhodesia Regiment fought in the First and Second World Wars.
SB	Police Special Branch
SF	Rhodesian Security Forces
SInf	School of Infantry, Gwelo (Gweru), also called Hooters, Hooterville, College of Knowledge.

Glossary

Stick	A team of 4 men, a stick commander, two rifleman and a MAG gunner, the maximum number that could be carried in a fully loaded Alouette III troop-carrying helicopter, G-car.
SWAPO	South West African People's Organisation
Tangent, Op Tangent	Operational Area – most of the Province of Matabeleland
The Falls	The Victoria Falls
TTL	Tribal Trust Land
Umkomto-we-Sizwe	Military wing of South Africa's African National Congress (ANC).
Vlei	Afrikaans, marshy, low-lying area.
ZANLA	Zimbabwe African National Liberation Army, military wing of ZANU
ZANU – (PF)	Zimbabwe African National Union – (Patriotic Front alliance after 1972), Robert Mugabe became the leader of ZANU after the death of Herbert Chitepo in 1975.
ZAPU – (PF)	Zimbabwe African People's Union – (Patriotic Front alliance after 1972), Joshua Nkomo was the leader of ZAPU from its inception in 1961.
ZIPRA	Zimbabwean People's Revolutionary Army, military wing of ZAPU.

Foreword

A Skirmish in Africa is a story set in the time of the civil war in Rhodesia (now Zimbabwe) in the mid-1970s. The 'Bush War' between the liberation movements and the Rhodesian regime started in 1966 and ended with the independence of the new Zimbabwe in 1981.

This was a time of considerable upheaval in post-colonial Southern Africa with liberation struggles taking place in South West Africa (Namibia), Rhodesia and South Africa. In addition, there were superpower-sponsored civil wars taking place in the ex-Portuguese colonies of Mozambique and Angola and in the Belgian Congo (Zaire). The liberation struggles provided fertile ground for the extension of Cold War influence by the major powers. China was supporting regimes in Tanzania and Mozambique while the Soviet Union, together with its communist ally Cuba, were active in Angola, Zambia and South West Africa. The USA were supporting opposition movements in Angola and Congo and providing tacit support for South Africa in its war against the South West African People's Organisation (SWAPO) and the Cubans in Angola.

Britain, as the ex-colonial power in Rhodesia, maintained economic sanctions and an arms and oil embargo. Sanctions were a response to the Unilateral Declaration of Independence (UDI) declared in 1965 by the Rhodesian Government led by Ian Smith. Britain was anxious to ensure a path to black majority rule in Rhodesia but was strongly resisted by the white 'rebel' government. Feeble post-UDI British foreign policy regarding its rebellious colony, plus internal pressure caused by the war in Northern Ireland, a struggling economy, labour strike action and the oil crisis, left a political vacuum where the so-called 'Rhodesia Question' became a Page 5 story. During the crucial 1974 – 1979 period, weak Labour Governments under Harold Wilson and then James Callaghan made half-hearted attempts to negotiate a settlement between the opposing parties, all failed. The longer the war went on the more polarised the respective positions became.

The liberation movement in Rhodesia, called the Patriotic Front, consisted of two very different organisations; the liberation movement led by Joshua Nkomo, the Zimbabwe African People's Union (ZAPU) and the movement led by Robert Mugabe, the Zimbabwe African National Union (ZANU).

The Soviet Union had taken the decision to support the liberation movement led by Joshua Nkomo, ZAPU. The Soviets trained freedom fighters in bases in Zambia, Tanzania and Angola and the most promising black leaders were sent to the Soviet Union for training. Considerable philosophical and tribal differences existed between

Soviet-supported Joshua Nkomo, ZAPU, and the movement led by Chinese-supported Robert Mugabe, ZANU. Joshua Nkomo drew his support predominantly from the Matabele tribe in the south, while Robert Mugabe's support was drawn virtually exclusively from members of the Shona tribe in the north. The differences in supporter base had resulted in open warfare between the competing liberation movements with a series of leadership purges. The alliance between Nkomo and Mugabe, however, allowed the two movements to suppress their differences to focus instead on the common enemy, the white minority government.

While the two communist superpowers jockeyed for greater influence, the leaders of the 'Front Line States', Samora Machel of Mozambique, Julius Nyerere of Tanzania and Kenneth Kaunda of Zambia, had their own agendas. They too were seeking to influence the outcome of the liberation struggle to their respective advantage.

On the opposite side of the political divide lay Ian Smith and the white Rhodesian electorate. Smith made a number of secret approaches to Joshua Nkomo, his preferred partner, to negotiate a settlement. All were rebuffed. Realising that a political settlement was vital, Smith commenced a negotiation with internally based black leaders, the so-called 'internal settlement'. The prospect of an internal settlement, which had the potential to be internationally recognised, spurred the Patriotic Front to even greater violence.

The apartheid regime in South Africa was desperately trying to prop up their position in South West Africa and Rhodesia, the 'Buffer States'. The South Africans supplied Rhodesia with weaponry including military helicopters and pilots, but as importantly, they kept the lifeblood of the country, oil and fuel supplies flowing north. Thus the rivalries between the super-powers and the leaders of the Southern African states added to a dangerous mix which intensified the war to the extent that it escalated into the neighbouring countries. Rhodesian forces, in an attempt to staunch the flow of insurgents into the country, intensified raids into Zambia and Mozambique attacking training camps and military bases but also destroying vital infrastructure such as roads and bridges.

In this story, I have attempted to give the reader a snapshot of what the war was like for both sides together with an idea of the many contradictions that faced the warring parties. This story is based in the province of Matabeleland, but more directly to the area around the famous Victoria Falls.

On the Rhodesian side this story relates to a sub-unit of the Rhodesian African Rifles, 4 Independent Company, made up of young white national service officers and NCOs and black riflemen and NCOs seconded from the regular 1st and 2nd Battalions RAR. The RAR fought in Burma during the Second World War; post-war it served with Commonwealth forces during the Suez Crisis in Egypt (1951-1952) and fought in the Malayan Emergency (1956-1958).

On the Freedom Fighter side, the story includes a Brigade of Zimbabwean People's Revolutionary Army (ZIPRA), the military wing of ZAPU, and their charismatic leader.

The detail on military tactics and weapons is authentic and will appeal to a reader interested in military history and the subject of counter-insurgency. As is inevitable I have drawn from my own experience as a nineteen-year-old national serviceman in the Rhodesian Army.

In the end, soldiers fulfil the bidding of their political masters. Consideration of concepts such as 'right' and 'wrong' become blurred but that does not detract from the bravery and commitment of the men in the thick of battle. Their sacrifices were no less trivial and no less tragic.

*

'Our votes must go together with our guns. After all, any vote we shall have, shall have been the product of the gun. The gun which produces the vote should remain its security officer, its guarantor. The people's votes and the people's guns are always inseparable twins.'

Robert Mugabe (1924 -), a leader of the Zimbabwe African National Union (ZANU) speaking in 1976.

1

The mining town of Kamativi, northeast Rhodesia (Late -1970s)

'CONTACT … CONTACT … CONTACT… 42 … 42 … 42, this is 43 do you read?' The voice on the radio in the hot cramped police station hissed and spluttered, as if a thousand miles distant.

'43 this is 42 … go.'

'42 … Contact … Approximately one hundred Charlie Tangos … I am about eight clicks northwest of your loc.' The urgent, metallic voice was tainted with a hint of panic. Heavy gunfire could be heard in the background through the static.

43 was the c/sign for 2nd Lt Charlie Williams, commander of 3 Platoon, 4 Independent Company, RAR. He had been following a group of communist insurgents, for two days, all the way from the *Cordon Sanitaire* minefield at the Gwai Gorge on the Zambezi River about 40km to the north. The Army Engineers had picked up the spoor[1] on the dirt road between Mlibizi and Victoria Falls.

Williams' follow-up[2] group had steadily closed on the enemy during the day, calling in when the trackers updated the age of the spoor… 3 hours, 2 hours, 1 hour … 30 minutes. Williams had reported that he had seen fresh urine only minutes before making contact. The enemy were heavily loaded, moving slowly, a re-supply group heading for Lupane TTL 120km to the south.

Williams had only twenty-six men with him.

42, the c/sign for 2nd Lt. James Gibbs, OC[3] of 2 Platoon 4 Indep, looked across at his 2IC[4] Sergeant Mike Smith standing anxiously at the door, no need to give any instructions, he had heard. The two policemen in the room watched in silence. Gibbs was about 6ft 2", lean; his blue eyes peered out from a blackened face, covered in thick sticky camo-cream.

2 Platoon had been waiting expectantly all day, listening. When Williams radioed, '30 minutes', the tension in the air became palpable, a taste in the back of the throat. There was a smell of nervous sweat … nobody spoke.

'Hello 2 … Hello 2… this is 42,' Gibbs had grabbed the hand-piece for the Police HF radio. 2 was the c/sign for the sub-JOC at Wankie, some 50km to the east.

'42 … 2 reading you fives, go,' came the instant response.

---

1 Tracks
2 The process of tracking and following insurgent groups.
3 Officer Commanding.
4 Second-in-Command.

'Roger, 43 has made contact at grid reference … One hundred Charlie Tangos we are responding. Can you send air support? …Over.'

'42, copied, we are scrambling a Lynx, Echo Tango Alpha your loc … sixteen minutes.'

'42 copied … out.'

Gibbs hurriedly folded his 1:50,000 map that he had spread on the table, then looked up at Smith standing in the door. 'Smithy let's get down to the helicopters,' he said confidently, trying to disguise his own nervousness. The Sergeant nodded, swallowing hard, this would be Mike Smith's first contact with the enemy.

Sgt Mike Smith, c/sign 42Alpha, was at least four inches shorter than Gibbs, green eyes, more solidly built; he too was covered in camo-cream, now streaky from sweat. Smith turned, hoisted his webbing then walked out into the late afternoon sunlight. He called out to the two sticks of men waiting in the shade of a tall Msasa tree.

'43 has contact, maybe a hundred … put on your kit and double down to the helicopters,' he shouted loudly, certain that his voice belied his own apprehension.

The sudden realisation of the time of day hit Mike Smith as he jogged down the road from the police station to the waiting helicopters, *Shit it's 4:30 already, we have only an hour or so of daylight! This is not good.*

Two Alouette III G-cars were parked one behind the other on the cricket pitch at the sports club at Kamativi tin mine. They had flown down from Wankie that morning in anticipation of the contact. The pilots had heard the contact report on their radios and they were already winding up the turbines. The blades began to spin throwing up dust and bits of cut grass.

'Smithy you take Stop 2 … I am Stop 1[5],' shouted Gibbs over the whining engines. The Alouette III G-car could only carry four troops plus the door-gunner and pilot. The door-gunner doubled as the 'tech' or maintenance technician. As the engines spun up the tech could be seen fussing over the twin .303 Brownings mounted on the left of the helicopter.

The two sticks led by Gibbs and Smith ran through the stinging dust to the front of the helicopters, crouched down, waiting for the pilot to signal for them to load. *Not much of a cricket pitch, more dirt than anything else* Smith thought to himself as he covered his nose and mouth with his hat, *you wouldn't want to be diving for the ball on the midwicket boundary.*

---

5 The break down of the traditional infantry section into smaller four man teams called Stops. The name derived from the term used to describe a group of men used to block the escape of insurgents after a contact. In a Fireforce, Stops were numbered Stop 1, Stop 2, Stop 3 etc. A Stop Group could be made up of more than one c/sign and more than one Stop, as in the case of troops deployed by parachute.

The helicopter engines reached full power with the blades spinning in a blur. The pilot gave the thumbs up to show he was ready. Smith glanced back at his stick, Dube the MAG machine gunner, festooned in belts for 500 rounds, the 'Gun' his pride and joy, Moyo and Fauguneze the other two riflemen squatted behind him, their faces etched in concentration. As he ran forward to the helicopter, bent almost double out of the way of the blades, Smith felt the blood drain from his head; this was also his first deployment from helicopters, *a hundred Gooks[6] only eight of us! … Shit!*

The Alouettes skidded over the trees in line astern, buffeted by the hot afternoon thermals. It was still over 36°C on the ground. The tech leaned over and passed Smith a headset, which he slipped over his head. He could hear the two pilots talking to each other. The tech in Smith's chopper gave a short test burst with the twin Brownings; a spent casing missed the capture bag and bounced onto the floor of the helicopter. The loud shuddering of the machine guns vibrated through the whole helicopter. Smith watched the casing as it rolled back and forth, his mind trying to come to grips with the reality of what was rapidly unfolding. *This scene[7] is going down.* His stomach twitched with an empty, sick feeling; he had no idea what to expect.

It took only a few minutes to find the contact area. Thick clouds of black smoke hung over the trees, a bush fire had started, probably caused by white phosphorous grenades or tracer bullets.

'42 … 42 … where the fuck are you? …. I am taking serious concentrated fire … they are assaulting our position …' there was clear desperation in Williams' voice.

Smith sat anxiously staring at the smoke ahead. *The shit has hit the fan big time.*

'43 this is Blue 1, do you read,' the pilot of Gibbs' chopper called on the radio, a controlled, unemotional voice.

'Blue 1 … I can hear your engines … I can't see … I am in thick smoke.'

'43 … I am going to fly directly over your smoke tell me whether I am on your left or right.'

The pilot clawed for more altitude and flew directly over the smoke cloud.

Smith caught a glimpse of green tracer snaking up from the trees below as the helicopter ahead disappeared into the smoke. Shock! *Fuck! The CTs are shooting at the helicopters!*

'Roger Blue 1 you are over my position, roll left … roll left.'

---

6 American slang from Vietnam, adopted by Rhodesians to describe communist insurgents.
7 Rhodesian slang, a contact with the enemy, a battle.

'43 … mark FLOT[8]!' called the pilot, his voice remarkably calm and steady.

'Roger. I am marking FLOT … NOW … green smoke,' responded Williams instantly.

A puff of green smoke drifted up over the trees below.

'43, I have you visual … standby.'

The techs in both helicopters saw the green smoke marking Williams' position and directed a barrage of fire into the trees below. As the helicopter banked violently Smith looked down at the trees flashing by. It was difficult to see the ground through the trees but in the few open patches it was possible to see CTs running in all directions.

'Blue 2, Blue 1, the Charlie Tangos are starting to break off, … we need to get these stops on the ground, try to find an LZ to the south, I am going to the east.'

'Blue 2 … copied,' came the clipped response from Smith's pilot.

The pilot looked back at Smith, his gloved forefinger pointing down. Smith nodded. The helicopter broke out of its orbit to the south.

'Captain I have a clearing for LZ … roll left,' the tech called out to the pilot on the intercom. Smith caught a glimpse of a village below, a small cluster of huts.

'Roger I see it.'

The pilot glanced back at Smith again, pointing down vigorously, descending rapidly. *What can we expect when we hit the ground?*

As the helicopter banked into the LZ a CT appeared in the village clearing, carrying a RPG rocket launcher. Smith stared in disbelief as the man lifted the launcher to his shoulder. *I am going to die!* The tech tried to swing the Brownings around to bear on the CT, firing all the time, trying to 'walk' the bullet strikes towards the target. The back-blast was clearly visible as the rocket ignited. The pilot slipped the chopper to the right desperately trying to get out of the way. Smith watched in horror as the deadly rocket passed inches in front of the canopy … the helicopter hit the ground hard, dust swirling in red clouds, visibility suddenly reduced to nil.

Dube, to Smith's right was first out firing the MAG as he went. Smith leapt after him, forgetting the headset, which tore off his head as he jumped. The helicopter, suddenly released from its load, lifted as the pilot reapplied full power. Moyo and Fauguneze hesitated for a split second too long, and then jumped to the left; the aircraft was already too far off the ground. Fauguneze landed awkwardly, snapping his ankle cleanly sending him tumbling in the dust, rolling over in agony.

---

8 Forward Line of Own Troops, the line demarcated with smoke grenades, white phosphorous grenades or mini-flares to mark the position of ground forces to allow for safe air strikes.

Smith looked up, the chopper was gone. He was completely exposed in the centre of the clearing. He glanced over at Fauguneze, the man writhing in pain. *Fuck …what am I going to do now?* His mind screamed as he tried to get a grip of the situation. Dube hadn't stopped firing. The CT with the RPG had disappeared. Dust began to settle.

Smith got to his feet and ran over to where Fauguneze lay curled up clutching his ankle. He grabbed Fauguneze by the shoulder straps on his webbing, dragging him across the clearing to the shade of a village hut. The foot hung limply at an awkward angle, bouncing over the uneven ground. Fauguneze made no sound.

Smith turned up the squelch on his A76 VHF radio[9] so he could hear the communication around him. It hissed loudly in his ear.

'Blue 2, Blue 2, Stop 2 … CASEVAC, CASEVAC … Over,' called Smith frantically to the helicopter. He waited a few seconds. Tried again. No Reply.

Smith could hear the pilots talking to each other, trying to provide support for Williams, who was now completely silent on the radio.

'Stop 2, Stop 2, Stop 1 … do you copy,' called Gibbs. He had been dropped to the east.

'Stop 2 go.'

'What is the problem?'

'One of my stick has broken his leg … he is US[10].'

A momentary hesitation, 'Copied, hide him in thick bush. We will come back for him later, we need to get to 43's loc ASAP.'

'Roger, Stop 2 out.'

Smith and his stick hurriedly carried Fauguneze out of the village in the direction of the contact to the north. Despite his obvious agony, Fauguneze remained silent, uncomplaining. They found an overgrown thicket and pushed him in under the thorn bush. Smith then stuck an ampoule of morphine into him.

'Fauguneze I have to leave you … don't shoot at any Gooks, stay completely still'.

Fauguneze nodded and smiled. They all carried three day's rats[11] and four water bottles so Fauguneze could last on his own for a while.

'Get some Gooks *Seg*[12],' Fauguneze looked up at him with a weak smile. The morphine was taking effect. Smith slapped him on the shoulder.

---

9 Small VHF radio, carried by Section and Stick commanders. Also referred to as the 'small-means'.

10 Unserviceable, most often applied to faulty equipment but also applied to sick or injured soldiers.

11 Rations, ration packs. These were designated AS African Soldier and ES European Soldier to cope with dietary preferences.

12 Sarge, Sergeant, the black accent pronounced 'a' as a soft 'e'.

'*Sala kahle*, stay well,' Smith called back as he and the others made off towards the sound of gunfire.

The noise intensified as they hurried forward. Heavy, sustained MAG fire rolled through the bush, grenade explosions and the rattle of .303 rounds from the helicopters filled the air as they flew overhead, one behind the other.

Lt Gibbs with Stop 1 was rapidly closing from the east. His progress suddenly halted by a stream of CTs as they exited the contact area directly into his path.

The arrival of the helicopters had been enough for the enemy to break off the action.

'Stop 2, Stop 2 ... this is Stop 1 do you copy?'

'Stop 2 ... go.'

'We have to RV[13], I cannot move forward fast enough ... I have too many Gooks to my front,' called Gibbs, frustration etched in his voice.

It was standard procedure in a helicopter deployment for one of the pilots to direct the ground troops, this was not happening.

The Lynx suddenly burst overhead. Its engines at full power were racing, the engine note changing as the pilot banked to look at the battle below. The scene was out of control. Williams had stopped calling on the radio and there was no response from any of the other 43 c/signs. The two choppers continued to orbit the contact area at low level, shooting at targets of opportunity. Still no instructions were being relayed to the ground forces to direct them onto CT positions. Smith found out later that these were South African pilots who had only recently been transferred to Rhodesia. This was their first scene.

The Lynx pilot tried to take charge.

'43, 43, this is Blue Leader do you read?'

Silence ... Williams made no response.

'43, 43, 43 this is Blue Leader do you read,' called the Lynx pilot, concern now in his voice. *Still no reply ... where the fuck is Williams?*

Then, a faint crackle, 'Blue Leader ... this ... is ... 43Alpha.' It was Sgt Iz Kennedy, 2IC of 3 Platoon.

'43Alpha can you see me?' called the Lynx pilot urgently.

'Negative ... I am lying on my face ... I am hit ...'

'Standby ...' the Lynx pilot hesitated, trying to assimilate the chaotic situation below him.

'This is Blue Leader ... who else is down there?' he called, his voice more insistent.

Smith and Gibbs both replied giving their respective positions. They could both see the Lynx as it orbited at 2,000ft.

'Blue Leader, Stop 1, I am pinned down ... I have CTs to my front

13 Rendezvous.

and left,' called Gibbs anxiously.

The staccato of a Soviet RPD machinegun and rifle fire was clearly audible to Smith's right. He moved his stick towards the sound of the gunfire, hoping to flank the CTs shooting at Gibbs. The silence from Williams was disconcerting. *Maybe his radio is US*, Smith thought.

'Stop 1, Blue Leader, copied, call me in,' replied the Lynx pilot.

The Lynx banked tightly while at the same time losing altitude. Gibbs directed the Lynx around to fly over his position, giving corrections, 'go left', 'go right'. He then marked FLOT with a red smoke canister.

'Stop 1, I have you visual, confirm CTs in rocks to your west.'

'Affirmative ... Charlie Tango's in rocks to my west, one hundred metres.'

'Stop 1 ... standby ... I am going to throw fran[14].'

The Lynx banked right, then, with engines howling, it dived at the rocky outcrop, at right angles to Gibbs' position. The pilot opened up with the .303s mounted above the wing and didn't stop shooting all the way down. The Lynx was virtually touching the trees when the pilot released a fran canister. It tumbled momentarily, exploding on impact, blanketing the rocky outcrop in superheated gas, a deadly, bright orange petroleum cloud.

Smith watched the Lynx strike while sweeping forward towards Gibbs' position, Moyo and Dube next to him. CTs suddenly appearing in the bush ahead, looking back over their shoulders at the Lynx. Smith stopped, lifted his rifle trying to get the peep site on target and then he double-tapped, CRACK, CRACK. The FN rifle bucked in his shoulder.

The movement in front of him seemed to suddenly click into slow motion. *Keep your aim down. Look through the bush ... not at the bush.* He fired round after round, TAP, TAP ... TAP, TAP; trying desperately to see the bullet strikes.

The magazine emptied. *Shit ... out of ammo ... change magazine ... fumble with the chest webbing ... fire and movement ... fire and move ... fire and move! ... keep moving or die.* The voices of his training instructors blaring in his head as he tried vainly to implement what he had been taught.

As Smith and his stick ran forward they could hear blood-curdling screams. The frantan, made from a petroleum gel, incinerated everything in one massive burst of flame. A CT broke cover, his chest and back charred. The man ran a few metres and stopped. He looked over towards Smith, his AK47 hanging from his hand, his eyes wild, staring. He shouted something in siNdebele; Moyo shot him. No further gunfire came from the outcrop, a thick cloud of smoke hung in the air; the stench of burned flesh mixed with fuel frantan filled the air.

14 Frangible tank napalm bomb.

More CTs appeared, firing wildly, not aiming, just holding the trigger down on fully automatic, bullets spraying into the trees. Dube gave a short burst with the MAG from the hip. Dust lifted up in front of the escaping men but the panicked and bewildered CTs kept running, not knowing where the gunfire was coming from.

'Shoot the fuckers, AIM … SHOOT LOW!' yelled Smith, 'Watch my tracer!'[15] Adrenalin was now pumping through his veins, making the picture in front of him suddenly vividly clear, as if illuminated by a spotlight.

The three of them blasted away … red tracer streaking through the air. Smith had loaded the first three rounds of each magazine with tracer as this helped to mark target, to show the other rifleman where he wanted them to shoot. The CTs just kept on running, seemingly oblivious to the gunfire being directed at them.

'For fuck sakes KILL THEM,' Smith bellowed again. Not one CT fell; they disappeared into the thick bush, running like the wind. Smith looked across at Dube and Moyo they had manic grins on their faces, eyes wide.

The bushfire, ignited by the airstrike, had taken hold. Muffled explosions erupted as the ammunition, grenades, mines and explosives, in the abandoned CT backpacks started to burn off.

The gunfire stopped abruptly. A strange silence descended over the bush, broken only by the crackle of flames as the fire spread.

It was rapidly getting dark. Smith and Gibbs arrived at the centre of the contact site simultaneously. The members of 3 Platoon crept out of the cover they had taken, looking shaken. Smith marvelled at the men as they called out and joked with each other. They thrived on *hondo*[16] it was in their blood.

The soldiers gathered together, all trying to talk at the same time.

'Keep quiet,' Gibbs had to shout to get the men's attention.

'All of you … get down in all-round defence. There may still be Gooks in the area. Smithy get the lads organised,' yelled Gibbs.

Smith organised the men into a wide circle, pointing out fields of fire[17] into the surrounding bush. The excited chatter subsided into hushed whispers. The terrorists were known to regroup in the contact area once they thought the soldiers had left. The surrounding villagers would also come looking for spoils left behind. There were two slightly wounded soldiers, but nothing looked particularly bad. Smith ordered Moyo, who had some very basic medic training, to see what he could

---

15 The FN tracer round was red. The AK47 tracer round was green.
16 Shona, war, conflict.
17 Field of fire or arc of fire is a term used to describe the siting of weapons so as to give mutual support.

do for them.

The air force had gone back to Wankie for a beer. Smith looked up at the sky, *Blue Jobs[18], Lucky Pricks!*

'Has anybody seen Lieutenant Williams and Sergeant Kennedy,' Gibbs whispered to the 3 Platoon men around him.

'They were up the *gomo[19]* further *Ishe[20],*' a rifleman pointed back up the hill where the fire had burnt everything to a crisp.

The contact had taken place on the side of an undulation, not very steep, but clearly Williams had the higher ground. Smith looked up the hill. *Maybe that's what saved their bacon.*

'Fuck!' Gibbs said under his breath. 'Mike, can you take two men and walk up the hill … see if you can find Williams and Kennedy. Get back here in fifteen minutes, it will be dark very soon.'

Thick smoke filled the air, a sickly sweet smell of burnt explosive. It was almost impossible to see anything in the rapidly fading light. Smoke continued to swirl in clouds across the contact area as a faint evening breeze began to disturb the rancid atmosphere. Smith crept gingerly through the smoke up the blackened hill. Rifle ammunition was going off like fire crackers somewhere to the left. A loud explosion sent them diving into the still smouldering ashes, a TM46 landmine[21] in a backpack.

'Ishe over here,' one of the riflemen pointed.

Sgt Kennedy was lying on his side propped up against a tree, his head lolling to one side. Smith ran forward and knelt down next to his friend. He shook Kennedy's shoulder.

'Iz … are you Okay?'

Kennedy looked up, his eyes glazed. 'I got hit man … in the arse … fuck it hurts,' he groaned, winching as he tried to move.

Smith moved around to have a better look at the wound. Kennedy's combat pants were completely soaked in blood. It oozed out through the pants leg. Smith took his penknife and cut the pants open from the ankle upwards. He looked down in horror at the exit wound in the back of the leg. The bullet had passed right through exposing the bone.

'Iz … they got you in the leg not your arse, you don't know your arse from you elbow … How the hell did you play Nuffield Cricket[22]?

---

18 Rhodesian slang for air force, army was referred to as 'Brown Jobs'. The term Blue Job was taken from a song written by John Edmonds, a Rhodesian folk singer, *I wish I was a Blue Job up in the sky, I wouldn't have to walk if I could fly.*
19 Shona, hill or mountain
20 Shona, loosely 'Sir', pronounced *'eeshare'* was a sign of respect used by RAR soldiers for officers and senior NCOs.
21 TM46 landmine, Soviet origin, total weight 8.6kg, 5.7kg of TNT.
22 Nuffield Schools Cricket Week is a provincial schools cricket competition conducted each year in South Africa; the Rhodesian Schools Cricket Team was invited to play

It's nothing more than a scratch man … you dumb bastard.'

'Smithy they got Charlie Williams.'

Kennedy pointed with shaking arm out to his right.

Smith looked in the direction Kennedy was pointing. He slowly crept over a few metres to the clump of thick grass where Williams lay. He was lying on his back, his chest covered in a mass of blood; his nose and ears were still bleeding.

'Lieutenant Williams are you okay Sir?' whispered Smith, touching the man's hand. Williams lay deathly still, his skin felt cold and clammy. Smith put his finger to Williams' neck to feel for a pulse, there was nothing. *Charlie Williams is dead!*

Smith sat back in disbelief. He felt nauseous as his head began to spin, a combination of shock and the aftereffects of the adrenalin high. Williams had a strangely peaceful expression on his face, his eyes clear, staring almost questioningly into the fading blue sky. His radio still hissing static, he was holding the handset to his ear. *He had been listening to the radio right to the end.*

Feeling tears prick at his eyes, Smith turned away. *I cannot let the men see.* He looked back to where Kennedy lay, his face now hidden in shadow.

'They came up the hill at us … I could hear them talking, they made a frontal assault man! … I tried to flank to the left but they got me as I broke cover … the bloke who got Charlie was a honky Smithy.'

'The Gooks don't have any whites with them Iz,' replied Smith gently.

'He was a fucking *mukiwa!*[23] I could see him clearly … he was over there … he had camo-cream on but I could see his blonde hair.'

Kennedy's head fell back as he passed out from loss of blood.

Darkness closed in, the fires raged all around.

Mama take this badge from me
I can't use it anymore
It's getting dark too dark to see
Feels like I'm knockin' on heaven's door

Knock-knock-knockin' on heaven's door[24]

---

against the South African provinces.
23 Shona, white person
24 1st Verse, *Knockin' on Heaven's Door*, Copyright © 1973, 1974 Ram's Horn Music. Sung by Bob Dylan for the Motion Picture *Pat Garrett & Billy the Kid*.

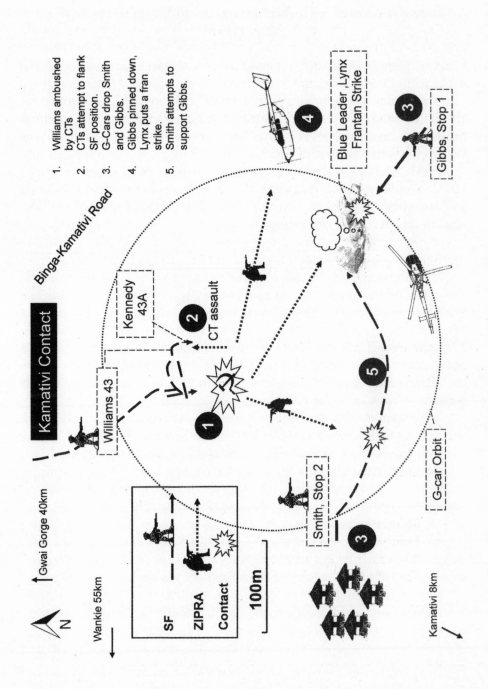

1. Williams ambushed by CTs
2. CTs attempt to flank SF position.
3. G-Cars drop Smith and Gibbs.
4. Gibbs pinned down, Lynx puts a fran strike.
5. Smith attempts to support Gibbs.

Binga-Kamativi Road

Kamativi Contact

Williams 43

Kennedy 43A

CT assault

Blue Leader, Lynx Frantan Strike

Gibbs, Stop 1

G-car Orbit

Smith, Stop 2

SF

ZIPRA

Contact

100m

Gwai Gorge 40km

Wankie 55km

N

Kamativi 8km

2

Operations Room, 4 Independent Company (RAR), Sprayview airfield, Victoria Falls

'Combined Operations[25] regret to announce the deaths in action of Second Lieutenant Charles Edward Williams of Bulawayo and Rifleman Sipho Fauguneze of Gwanda. Security forces attacked a large group of terrorists in the northwest of the country and succeeded in killing ten and capturing a large quantity of arms and ammunition, follow-up operations are continuing…

In other news the British Government has announced increased measures to tighten the oil embargo on Rhodesia …' Joy Cameron-Dow, the Rhodesian Broadcasting Corporation (RBC) newsreader continued on in her smooth, almost reassuring voice, seemingly detached from the dreadful news she was reading.

Sgt Mike Smith and 2nd Lt James Gibbs sat in the Ops Room at the 4 Independent Company base on the edge of Sprayview airstrip, outside the town of Victoria Falls, in the northwest corner of Rhodesia. The walls were covered in large-scale maps of their Operational Area from Kazangula in the west to Binga in the east then south to Lupane, an area well over 2,000 square kilometres, including the Zambezi, Victoria Falls and Wankie National Parks. Comprising just over a hundred men including 'cooks and bottle-washers', 4 Independent Company (RAR) was the only permanently stationed army infantry unit in the area.

Despite the uniforms and the neatly positioned berets, the two men looked like schoolboys waiting to see the headmaster. Both had the fresh faces of youth, faces that did not need the razor very often. Their skins were tanned but smooth and unblemished save for a few pimples brought out by the clogging camo-cream. Mike Smith had a troubled expression on his face, the sort of expression illustrating the uncertainty of not knowing the severity of a pending reprimand. James Gibbs, on the other hand, studied the map on the wall in front of him with deep intent, as if trying to memorise each detail for future reference. Concentration was etched on his face as his eyes flashed left and right.

The drone of the 'Flight of the Angels' could be heard in the distance, taking tourists for flights over the Falls. Sightseeing aircraft that took off and landed throughout the day used Sprayview airstrip. Normalcy was just across the airstrip, no more than 200 metres away. *Might as well*

---

25 The military organisation set up to co-ordinate the activities of Air Force, Police and Army. COMOPS were also responsible for planning and executing external raids and commanded the Special Forces Units including the Rhodesian Special Air Service and the Selous Scouts.

have been a 1,000 miles, Smith thought as he sat in quiet contemplation.

The air was thick and it was hot, hot like only the Zambezi Valley can get. Smith and Gibbs sat in sweat soaked uniforms in quiet reflection, each alone with his thoughts. In all the time that they had worked together in 2 Platoon, the hours on patrol, the hours in ambush and the lonely OPs, most of the time was spent separated. Each ran a section of the Platoon, most often patrolling many kilometres apart, only speaking during daily sitreps[26]. It was important that they were comfortable with their own company since talking to the black troops in English, even at the most basic level, was virtually impossible. They didn't teach black languages at school in a country where the white population was about 200,000 and the black population over 7 million. In a British Colony it was up to the natives to learn English, that was just the way it was.

Smith shuffled in his seat. The ceiling fan slowly rotated, making an intermittent scraping sound, like a dog scratching at the door.

Three days had passed since the contact at Kamativi. 1 Platoon had been deployed on follow-up, they had picked up a few wounded CTs but the trail had run cold. Smith had found Sipho Fauguneze, still under the thorn bush he had been hiding under, four CT bodies were recovered from around his position; Fauguneze had put up a hell of a fight. Smith was convinced that Fauguneze had shot the first CT he saw, then, after he had shot two or three, the others took him out. Fauguneze had accounted for more CTs than the rest of 3 Platoon and 2 Platoon combined. Smith had asked Gibbs whether Fauguneze should get a medal or something. Gibbs said he would look into it. Fauguneze was a popular member of the platoon and very close friends with Bukhosi Dube and Emerson Moyo as they came from neighbouring villages. There was a deep feeling of loss amongst the men that Smith felt powerless to deal with.

The Independent Company system was a strange beast. There were six Independent Companies in all, made up of regular professional black soldiers, regular, almost exclusively white, senior officers and warrant officers with national service platoon commanders with a few national service platoon NCOs. The regular soldiers' attitude towards the national servicemen ranged from condescension to utter contempt. The national servicemen's attitude toward the regular soldiers ranged from pity to disgust. At a platoon level the relationships between the predominantly white national service leadership and the regular black riflemen and junior NCOs was good, at least workable. The rotation of national servicemen through the company every twelve months was difficult for most of the black soldiers to cope with which meant that

26 Situation Report, daily report of activities made by every deployed c/sign.

13

they avoided any form of attachment or camaraderie. It was certainly far from an ideal situation.

Major Reginald Peacock, the CO of 4 Indep, strode into the room, breaking their reverie. Both men scrambled to their feet. Peacock made no attempt to sit down, but instead walked around behind his desk, standing feet apart, hands clasped behind his back, at parade rest. Without any greeting, he launched at them.

'You people have been part of the worst scene I have ever heard of. I can't believe how you fucked it up like this. … For Christ sake over a hundred Gooks and you got ten! The Lynx accounted for at least five of those.'

Peacock's name was pretty descriptive of the type of bloke he was. He was ex-British army, commissioned into The Queen's Own Buffs, The Royal Kent Regiment, later to become the The Queen's Regiment, which he reminded people of at every opportunity. He was a real ponsi-pretentious prick, in his mid-thirties. He was tall, walked ramrod straight and cultivated a handlebar moustache, which he twirled vigorously when deep in thought. His accent was all English Public School, hot potato in his mouth. Peacock told the story that he had decided to resign his commission in the British Army after his battalion's second deployment to Northern Ireland where, as he stated, he 'collected a bullet and a wife - both equally painful'. His wife and kids were in an army house in Wankie, while his twenty-five year old mistress, the manager of the UTC[27] branch at Vic Falls, was ensconced in a flat in the town.

Smith studied the man intently. *Someone said that they had kicked him out of the RLI - who knows? What the fuck is this prick doing here anyway? The bloody Poms got us into this shit in the first place!* Smith looked across at Gibbs whose face remained completely devoid of emotion but his eyes belied his feelings.

'Sir … the G-car pilots did not attempt to co-ordinate our attack, they just dropped us and, for all intents and purposes, disappeared,' ventured Gibbs in a vain attempt to provide an explanation.

'I am sick of listening to your NS bullshit excuses,' spluttered Peacock, his chin thrust forward. When he got upset Peacock's face glowed bright red, which coupled with a slight twitch to the moustache added to the distraction, making him difficult to take seriously. Not interested in any debate, Peacock continued, 'SB[28] are coming over to debrief you two and sub-JOC are sending someone over to prepare

27 United Touring Company
28 Police Special Branch, specialised in intelligence gathering and maintained a network of informers. SB collected details of every terrorist captured or killed including ballistics analysis.

a report on the two deaths … Make yourselves available.' He waved dismissively towards the door. Then, as if an after-thought he addressed Smith, 'Sergeant Smith … take a group of eight men to Bulawayo to attend Williams' funeral. The family don't want a full military funeral but they have agreed to the Last Post and pallbearers from the company… collect your orders from the CSM[29].'

'Excuse me Sir ... I knew Williams well, he went to Milton ... I played rugby against him, I know his parents and his sister, I don't know if I can handle it,' Smith lamented. They had also been in the same NS intake and together with Gibbs and the 1 Platoon OC, 2nd Lt Paul Rice, had been at the School of Infantry together.

'I cannot believe you people … there is a bloody war on, pull yourself together man and get on with it,' spat Peacock, starting to shuffle papers on his desk.

Smith swallowed hard, blushing fiercely from the reprimand.

The Major moved his gaze across to Gibbs who stood rigidly behind his chair staring at a point above the Major's head.

'… and you Gibbs will take over 3 Platoon until we can find a replacement. There is an NS course coming out of the School of Inf in a few weeks, maybe we can get one of them. Be ready to redeploy onto the River in twenty-four hours. Until then, you and Sergeant Smith sort it out … that will be all,' instructed Peacock, pointing towards the door dismissively.

The two national servicemen stood to attention, saluted, about faced and smartly retired. There was no further mention of Charlie Williams, Sipho Fauguneze, Iz Kennedy, or any of the other wounded soldiers. Kennedy would be lucky to keep his leg. Fortunately the bullet had exited so the risk of infection was a lot less. Opening the batting for Rhodesia now seemed a very long way off. Gibbs, Smith and the remains of 3 Platoon had been forced to spend the night in the contact area and despite pumping four drips into Kennedy, with plenty of morphine, his condition was very poor by the time they had got him out on a truck. It didn't help that they couldn't get a helicopter casevac the next morning; apparently all the helicopters had been sent on an 'external[30]'. Priorities were clearly elsewhere.

Nobody seemed to care about Sipho Fauguneze's heroic effort. When Gibbs raised it with Major Peacock he dismissed it out of hand as simply a soldier doing his job and dying in the process.

Smith had talked to Gibbs about what Iz Kennedy had said about seeing a 'White' Gook, they both concluded that keeping quiet was the

29 Company Sergeant Major, Warrant Officer 2nd Class.
30 An attack outside the country. Rhodesia raided insurgent training and logistical bases in all neighbouring states, even as far as Angola and Tanzania.

best policy. *What difference would it make, Iz was delirious anyway ... it can't possibly be true.* The thought played on Smith's mind as he relived the contact over and over. *Where could such a person come from if it was true?*

As the two men walked out into the heat of the day, the CSM shouted across from his office.

'So here we have the two steely-eyed killers from the sky.' The CSM's voice dripped with sarcasm.

Smith's opinion was that CSM Swanepoel was undoubtedly the biggest arsehole that God had ever put breath into. He was about forty, over-weight, an ex-RLI regular, hated the RAR, hated officers and particularly hated national servicemen. In fact he hated everything except beer and poaching, those he loved in limitless quantities. He saw his posting to 4 Indep as the worst possible form of punishment. It may very well have been. Word had it that he had raped a girl out the back of Club Tomorrow nightclub in Salisbury. Being stationed on the edge of two of the most prolific game reserves in the world, Zambezi and Wankie, Swanepoel had unlimited poaching opportunities, some small compensation for his 'punishment' posting to 4 Indep.

What has this prick got in mind now? Smith had never before had to face the disturbing emotion of disliking a person so much that they could make him feel physically ill. The CSM knew exactly how to get under his skin. Smith had passed out of the School of Infantry Officer's Course as a Sergeant. This was a bitter disappointment; he had enormous difficulty coming to terms with it. The worst consequence of his failure was the effect on his self-confidence. No matter how hard he tried Smith was plagued by uncertainty and self-doubt. He felt awkward with making decisions and shied away from asserting himself. The CSM was all too aware of this fact, rubbing it in mercilessly at every opportunity. 'So you weren't good enough Smith?' he would say, with a smirk on his face. This comment by the CSM stabbed like a knife, making Smith want to scream in frustration. The feeling of being completely powerless in face of this bully was confronting.

Swanepoel's attitude towards Smith and the other national service NCOs was made worse by the stagnation of his own career. He had taken nearly ten years in the RLI to make Sergeant so it niggled him that these young whippersnappers arrived on the scene after six months training with a 'Sergeant's' rank - *The officers didn't matter ... everybody knew they were useless, but Sergeant! ... For fuck sakes!*

The CSM marched purposefully across the quad, calling out as he approached, 'A successful contact Sir, ten dead, you only missed ninety ... bloody good show!'

'Sarcasm is the lowest form of wit, CSM,' replied Gibbs, his A-level

English coming to the fore.

Gibbs' standard form of defence was baiting the CSM with witty comments and leg-pulling most of which the CSM didn't get, not being the sharpest tool in the shed. The CSM came to a halt, his pace stick wedged under his arm. Gibbs stopped in front of the CSM.

'Thank you CSM for those few kind words … once more into the breach and all that.' Then, in a sudden rush of blood to the head, Gibbs saluted the CSM smartly, throwing his hand up rigidly in position.

Swanepoel blinked up at him in surprise. This was highly irregular. Junior officers are not in a position to lord it over senior NCOs. Realising that he was obliged to return the salute, Swanepoel looked about, a few soldiers had stopped a small way off to observe the banter. Gibbs stood straight-backed, his salute parade-ground perfect. Smith came rigidly to attention. The two national servicemen stood together, braced up. There was no way out. Swanepoel shuffled to attention throwing a begrudging salute, his hand quivering, his face flushed with his contempt.

Gibbs held the salute another punishing second, then smartly came back to attention.

'As you were CSM,' said Gibbs, effectively dismissing the CSM. He then turned smartly on his heel, walking away briskly as if he had other far more important things to do. Smith trailed behind, dreading the likely devastating consequence of this seemingly minor altercation.

The CSM's eyes followed them, blazing, 'What the fuck are you looking at?' he screamed at the few soldiers that had stopped to watch.

2nd Lt James Gibbs and Sergeant Mike Smith had yet to celebrate their 19th birthdays!

*

Carpark of The Anglican Cathedral, Bulawayo

Sgt Smith took Dube and Moyo with him to Bulawayo together with six others from 3 Platoon including Corporals Ndlovu and Ncube who were in Charlie Williams' section. Most of them were from Bulawayo, so the opportunity to spend two days at home after the funeral was gratefully received.

Dismissing the funeral contingent at 1 Brigade HQ at Brady Barracks in Bulawayo, Smith issued strict orders to report the next day at 08:30hrs, with clean uniforms, berets, and boots polished. They had not been issued RAR No1 Dress Uniform so they were going to wear their camouflage uniform with berets and stable belts.

The funeral detachment had spent a few hours practising carrying a makeshift 'coffin' using empty mortar boxes strapped together. The CSM had played merry hell with 2 Platoon, as retribution for Gibbs' smart-arse comments, insisting on barrack room inspections, kit inspections, forcing Smith to do a full inventory of his armoury, weapons, ammunition and equipment. It had taken hours. While the CSM couldn't do much about 2nd Lt Gibbs, Sgt Smith, on the other hand, was fair game. He had also cancelled the platoon's evening passes which was seen by the troops as the most excessive, cruel punishment. Many had wives and girlfriends in the local township that they did not see very often. By the time he left Vic Falls for the funeral, Smith could quite happily have walked over to the CSM's office and shot him. His humiliation at the hands of the CSM was absolutely shattering. The feeling of being at someone else's complete mercy was utterly demoralising. Smith felt alone and isolated. The rest of the platoon had had enough, they too were contemplating homicide.

St John's Anglican Cathedral in Bulawayo is an impressive building made of huge granite blocks, set in manicured gardens, and beautiful, towering jacaranda trees that were just coming into bloom. The sweet bouquet of Jacaranda blossom permeated the air. Smith stood self-consciously together with his small detachment under a tree close to the Church entrance. He really had no idea what to do. Depot RAR had sent a Bugler up from Shaw Barracks at Balla Balla, dressed impressively in his No 1s, slouch hat and ostrich feathers.

Williams' death had a terrible effect on Mike Smith. He couldn't get it out of his mind. It was all he could think about. *That could so easily have been me!* He didn't know Williams that well, they were not close friends and yet he still felt distressed. He wasn't sure what the appropriate emotional reaction should be. Was he to behave distant and aloof, could he show his feelings to the family, would he be able to control his emotions when the time came? *I just feel so shit!* Smith's parents had wanted to attend the funeral to give him support but he had insisted that they didn't.

Waiting in the oppressive heat was uncomfortable; Smith felt the sweat running down his back made worse by his nervousness. People started arriving in dribs and drabs. They stopped to chat at the door before going in. A group of schoolboys from Milton School arrived, dressed neatly in blazers, white shirts and grey trousers. They looked across at the army detachment under the tree with envious eyes. *My turn will come soon ... I will get my chance to slot[31] a few Gooks.*

It looked like it was going to be a big turn out. Mr Williams was a

31 Rhodesian slang for shoot or kill.

respected member of the community. He owned a large steel fabrication business and was Captain of Bulawayo Golf Club.

Finally the hearse arrived with the family. Smith looked across as they climbed out of the car. *Oh Shit here we go.*

Smith whispered to the detachment to form up on the tar forecourt. The men shuffled over and formed up - this was a white man's funeral, new to them. Their faces were sombre; the importance of the ritual of laying a person to rest was deeply ingrained in their culture.

'Squad … Squad … ATTENTION!' Smith shouted as loud as he could; he needed to make a good show of it.

'On my command squad will turn to the right, march to the back of the hearse, and halt …' he instructed. Then at the top of his voice, 'Squad, SQUAD … RIGHT… TURN, by the left, QUICK … MARCH!'

They marched to the hearse and came to a halt in perfect time, driving their boots into the tar with a loud crunch.

'Remove your berets,' Smith commanded, they were hastily removed and tucked into epaulettes.

Smith was relieved the family was inside because they then made a complete hash of removing the coffin from the hearse, almost dropping it. 'Come on, concentrate' he hissed at the soldiers.

Six of the men were designated as pallbearers while Cpl Ndlovu was to walk behind carrying Williams' beret; the extra man carried a folded 'Green and White' Rhodesian flag. The contingent managed to shuffle around to face the door, holding the coffin by the handles.

Smith did not know the command to lift the coffin so he whispered, 'put the coffin on your shoulders.' He was now sweating profusely.

' … Squad … funeral … MARCH,' Smith blushed horribly, sweat burning his eyes, he couldn't think of anything else to say. The pallbearers held the coffin on their shoulders; arms linked underneath, miraculously figuring it out themselves. They carefully negotiated the stairs and entered the church in good order. As they entered the vestibule the organ burst into a stirring hymn.

Mine eyes have seen the glory of the coming of the Lord;
He is trampling out the vintage where the grapes of wrath are stored;
He hath loosed the fateful lightning of his terrible swift sword;
His truth is marching on.
Glory, glory hallelujah! Glory, glory hallelujah!
Glory, glory hallelujah! His truth is marching on.

Smith followed the coffin four or so paces behind, slow marching, arms rigidly by his side, head fixed straight ahead, not daring to glance left or right. The place was packed. There was a large group of black people too, Williams' domestic servants and workers from the steel factory. The Hymn ended with its thumping crescendo.

Our God is marching on.
Glory, glory hallelujah! Glory, glory hallelujah!
Glory, glory hallelujah! Our God is marching on.

The black women began to cry; they called out and ululated, almost at a scream. That set off all the white women, who in seconds turned the church into uncontrolled sobbing.

Smith was having difficulty keeping it together, the church was bathed in sorrow, permeating his soul. Eyes on fire, chest tight, Smith felt he could hardly breathe - *Just keep on going, don't break down, they are depending on you.* The squad reached the coffin's plinth, turned smartly and gently set the coffin in place. Cpl Ndlovu placed the folded flag on the coffin with Williams' beret neatly on top of it. They then turned on some silent command, independent of Smith, and marched slowly to the back of the church. Smith did a neat about turn and followed, his men silhouetted against the bright sunshine outside the church entrance. He had learned from experience that his troops would always figure what he was doing wrong and then compensate by doing it their own way. They had probably already saved his life a few times as a result.

The funeral service flashed past in a blur. The Headmaster of the school gave a short eulogy regarding William's achievements, about what an all-round good bloke he was. The Minister then described the unnecessary loss of a young life, cut short, too soon, but reconciled the death on the basis that he died bravely, defending his country against the forces of evil. He had done his duty and made the ultimate sacrifice. The Minister finished the service motioning to Smith to fetch the coffin. The organist began the final hymn.

Be Thou my Vision, O Lord of my heart;
Naught be all else to me, save that Thou art.
Thou my best Thought, by day or by night,
Waking or sleeping, Thy presence my light.

The funeral party once again marched slowly down the aisle.

Be Thou my battle Shield, Sword for the fight;
Be Thou my Dignity, Thou my Delight;

Smith marched past the coffin and turned to face the back of the church. It was then that he saw Mrs Williams and her daughter Jane in the front row. They both looked up at him, eyes with deep black rings, tears were streaming down their faces. He had only met Jane once before, at the passing out parade at the School of Infantry. Despite her obvious distress, Jane gave him a fleeting smile. Mr Williams sat bolt upright staring ahead, not flinching. All that Smith could think of was, *what would my family be doing if it was me?*

Heart of my own heart, whatever befall,
Still be my Vision, O Ruler of all.

In the sudden silence after the hymn, the six pallbearers stood facing each other, Ndlovu reached forward to retrieve the beret and flag, his boots scraping on the parquet floor.

The Bugler burst out the opening bars of the Last Post. The sound filled the Church bouncing off the high rafters, resonating off the walls. Smith felt tears prick his eyes, he was going to pieces fast - *this so easily could have been me!*

The Bugler ended, as the Last Post does in soft mournful tones. The Church fell silent once again, a few stifled sobs carried through the cloisters, an expectant shifting of feet.

Moyo glanced at his Sergeant. Seeing the distress etched on Smith's face, he began to chant.

' *A,B,C,D, Supportie, Headyquartas*	*A,B,C,D, Support Headquarters*
Siyakutengera sweet banana….'	*I will buy you a sweet banana*

It was the RAR Regimental Song, *Sweet Banana*[32]. Moyo's deep sonorous voice echoed through the Church. The soldiers responded, spontaneously lifting the coffin to their shoulders in perfect order, singing out the chorus, their voices harmonising,

'A, B, C, D, Supportie Headyquartas
Siyakutengera sweet banana….
Banana, Banana, Banana
Siyakutengera sweet banana'

Moyo continued with the next verse,

---

32 The title of the Regimental March of the RAR, originally written in 1942 as part of a competition by members of the RAR band. The song evolved over time to include changes and events that the Regiment experienced.

'Nhowo, pfumo, ne tsvimbo   Shield, spear and knobkerrie
Ndiyo RAR, muhondo ne runyararo   That's RAR in war and peace
Ndichakutenga sweet banana'   I will buy you a sweet banana

They shuffled slowly to the door of the church, the brilliant sunlight framing the small group.

'Burma, Egypt ne Malaya   Burma, Egypt and Malaya
Takarwa tikakunda ...'   We fought we conquered ...

Smith sang at the top of his voice, his heart soaring. The pallbearers continued the song, out into the hot Rhodesian sun, a small crowd had gathered in the street. They turned and gently laid the coffin on the wheeled stand behind the hearse.

'Banana, Banana, Banana
Siyakutengera sweet banana ...'

The detachment fell silent, facing each other over the coffin. For what seemed an age there was no sound, not even traffic in the street. Nobody moved, Smith looked down at the Jacaranda blossoms carpeting the driveway, *serenity mingled with such desperate sadness.*

Lifting his head, Smith called out, 'Squad ...Squad will retire ... Squad about turn, ...leeeft... right, left ...right, left.' They turned smartly, marched fifteen paces, their boots crunching loudly as they halted, driven into the tarmac, bringing finality ...

The congregation had assembled on the steps of the church, standing respectfully, watching as the small funeral party marched off. Ndlovu passed the flag and beret to Smith who marched smartly back to the base of the steps where the family had gathered. He saluted, then handed Mrs Williams her son's beret and the folded flag. He then stepped back, saluted again, spun on his heel and marched away to stand under the shade of a tree to wait for the hearse to leave. The congregation started to break up, people speaking in hushed tones, paying their respects to the family.

Mr and Mrs Williams and their daughter Jane walked over towards where Smith was standing. He saw them coming, not sure what to say or do.

'Mike thank you for coming we really appreciate it,' said Mrs Williams in a shaky voice.

'It's no problem Maam,' replied Smith respectfully, not knowing what else to say.

'Were you there when Charles died?' she asked removing her

sunglasses, looking up at him straight in the eyes. The directness of the question brought no escape. She tilted her head, seeking an answer. Smith, still searching for the correct words, glanced across at Mr Williams; he too looked at him expectantly.

'I was there soon after Maam ... we were too late, Charlie was already dead Maam ... he had fought at his best ... he was heavily outnumbered ... he saved his platoon,' stammered Smith, completely lost for words.

She stretched out, taking his hand in both of hers, squeezing it hard. Smith looked into her eyes, the pain was so desperately clear, so deep. He tried frantically to think of something to say, something more helpful, something supportive, but no words would come. He just stood rigidly in front of her feeling hopelessly inadequate.

'Thank you so very much for coming,' she said dropping her hands to her side, tears again running down her cheeks, then adding 'I shall thank your mother when I see her again ...' Mrs Williams took another moment, then taking his hand again, she said with intense sincerity, 'Mike please look after yourself.'

'It's a pleasure ... thank you Maam, I will,' murmured Smith in reply, instantly regretting it. *It's a pleasure! Are you mad, what a bloody stupid thing to say!*

He glanced across at Jane, she seemed to be studying his face. She smiled faintly. He smiled back, trying his best to stay in control.

Mr Williams shook his hand mumbling something inaudible, his voice cracked with emotion. The three lonely figures then turned to walk back into the church. Jane hesitated and ran back to where Smith was standing.

'Mike, can I write to you?' she asked quietly.

'Sure ... Sure you can ... that would be great, ... Thank you,' he whispered, embarrassed that he had not been able to say anything to help, to ease the pain. Jane smiled up at him and ran back to her parents.

*

Depot RAR, St Stephens College, Balla Balla

The contrast between the funerals for Charlie Williams and Sipho Fauguneze could not have been more stark. Fauguneze's family had been brought up by truck to Balla Balla from his home village near Gwanda. The RAR had taken over the grounds of St Stephens School that had to be closed down because of the war. A military funeral in Fauguneze's home village would be difficult with a contingent of RAR present. The local villagers and tribesmen were already the subject of terrorist intimidation and violence, so conducting a military funeral near the village was out of the question.

By the time Smith and his small contingent arrived at Depot RAR in Balla Balla the funeral rites were well underway. A tent had been set up on one of the disused cricket fields where the family mourned their lost son. The body had been wrapped in a cowhide blanket and sat upright on a grass mat in the middle of the tent. The family sat around it in a circle. The relations, including Fauguneze's sisters, cried out in sorrow, throwing their hands above their heads. The crying and ululation was important to show Fauguneze's spirit that they cared deeply for him. Wives and girlfriends of the soldiers based at the Depot had also joined the funeral, swelling the numbers in the tent to well over a hundred. Dube's own wife was amongst the mourners as she lived in the married quarters next to the base.

As Mike Smith had been present at the time of Fauguneze's death it was important for him to sit amongst the family. This was explained to him in hushed tones by Moyo who ushered him to a place in the circle of mourners. Dube and Moyo then sat down next to him as witnesses to the departure of Fauguneze's spirit from amongst the living to join the ancestors.

The Matabele conceive a person as made up of three aspects, the material and two spiritual beings. They believe that from birth to death, a person lives with a spirit, which looks after him and could bring good fortune or misfortune to him. This spirit was called *Idlozi* and a fine line of distinction existed between this spirit and the one that passed onto the ancestral world. The *Amadlozi* is the very powerful spirit that passes on to the next world. It is this spirit that must be respected above all else because it takes an active interest in the welfare of it's living relatives. The *Amadlozi* requires the living to maintain proper relationships with it and disrespect or irreverence could sometimes result in severe punishment or even death. The *Amadlozi* spirit also secures their relatives from witchcraft and harmful magic. As Fauguneze's father was the headman of his village, the family *Amadlozi* had higher status. This was added to by the fact that Sipho had died in battle as a brave and fearless warrior.

Smith watched in total fascination as the cleansing process, the *Ukuhlanziswa*, began. The people in the circle passed a calabash full of traditional sorghum beer from one person to the next. The Matabele believe that death brings a bad omen to the nearest living relatives of the deceased and such an omen could be passed on to neighbors, so it was necessary for the family to be cleansed. A man, the *Sangoma* or spirit medium, stood up to call to Fauguneze's *Amadlozi*, to assure him of the families commitment to his spirit. The man had a high-pitched voice that sent a shiver down Smith's spine. The mourners repeated the man's words in slow deliberate tones and the crying abruptly stopped as the *Sangoma* determined that Fauguneze's *Amadlozi* had heard their calls.

A message was sent to the contingent of RAR men who formed the funeral guard of honour. The RAR band struck up with a hymn sung in siNdebele that was taken up by the mourners. The sound of the harmonising voices struck Smith profoundly and he felt the same lump in his throat that he experienced during Williams' funeral. The family, including Smith, Moyo and Dube, watched patiently as the army conducted their ancient ritual of laying a soldier to rest. Two goats were presented to the family by the army, to be slaughtered once Fauguneze was finally buried outside his home village.

The body, still wrapped in cowhide, was collected by the family and the lonely procession walked slowly across the field towards where the trucks waited to take them home. The mourners continued to sing, clapping their hands at the same time, the sound building as the guard of honour, formed up across the field, joined in. The sound of the singing seemed to permeate the body and Smith felt caught up in the crescendo of all the voices in natural harmony.

As the sound of the singing slowly abated, Smith took the opportunity to pay his respects to Fauguneze's mother and father. Both were very old and bent and they nodded politely as he spoke to them in English. The feeling of complete inadequacy returned as he tried to express his regret at the loss of their eldest son. He had no way of knowing whether they understood what he said but Dube had stood by and spoke to them gently in siNdebele. The mother listened carefully to what Dube had said and then slowly stretched out a withered hand to touch Smith on the arm, as if to reassure him. She then spoke to him in a soft voice in her own language, her eyes looking up into his, they showed an inner strength borne from a life of hardship.

Mike Smith turned away from her, tears welling in his eyes, overwhelmed by the emotion of the occasion.

3

Lupane TTL, northwest Matabeleland

Captain Vladimir Gregori Benkov, late of Alfa Group or Group A, part of a Spetsnaz (special forces) OSNAZ unit attached to the KGB, sat on a large granite rock under the cover of tall Mopani trees. Captain Benkov was in his early thirties, a very tall, solitary man, with classic east-European features, a chiseled face, pale blonde hair, and almost transparent ice blue eyes. His most disturbing feature was his eyes. They were completely vacant, lifeless; he had the habit of fixing people with his gaze which made being in his company uncomfortable, most often forcing others to avert their eyes away. He seldom smiled.

The Soviet soldier was dressed in the East German, 'Rain' or 'Strichtarn' camouflage pattern, referred to by the Rhodesians as 'Reisfleck'. By his side was a folding-butt AKM[33], he carried Spetsnaz chest webbing with eight magazines, two rifle grenades, two percussion grenades and two fragmentation grenades. A large Spetsnaz knife in a scabbard was attached to his webbing belt.

Vladimir Benkov was, in many ways, a prisoner of his hopeless and abused childhood. His father had been part of the defense of Stalingrad where the horror of the experience had effectively ended his life at the age of eighteen. Juri Benkov, Hero of the Revolution, could not maintain any relationship with his family and could not hold down a job. Alcohol and drug abuse provided his only refuge. He had descended into the abyss of depression. Vladimir never spoke about the alcohol induced beatings that both he and his mother endured, the seemingly endless terror locked up in the broom cupboard - the beatings, the beatings, they were the worst. The father's death on the icy tracks of the Moscow Metro came too late to save the son. The young Vladimir really had no chance; his mind was a twisted mess by the age of sixteen which made the only possible outcome, other than death or jail, a career in the military.

A tortured mind and violent mood swings meant that Benkov was unsuited to the traditional airborne military he was drafted into. He began his service with the 171st Independent Communications Brigade, *Medvezhi Ozera* Moscow Military District, stationed close to his home town south of Moscow. He was never a team player, quite happy to beat his fellow recruits to a pulp for no apparent reason. His instructors had noticed his penchant for inflicting pain, his seeming lack of emotion, coupled with supreme physical strength and endurance. His

---

33 An upgraded version of the Soviet AK47 assault rifle.

unbridled violence ensured his transfer to the Spetsnaz. Alpha Group was a very special part of this elite unit. Alpha Group specialised in deep infiltration and intelligence gathering, often acting alone or in small groups. This made Alpha Group a great source of advisors and instructors for the many Soviet-sponsored wars in the Third World. Benkov was the perfect, highly trained, psychopathic killing machine. A lethal loner, completely self-reliant, Benkov was happiest in his own company.

The young captain had come to the attention of Colonel Lev Kononov, the head of the Soviet advisory delegation to Joshua Nkomo's Zimbabwe African People's Union and its military wing the Zimbabwean People's Revolutionary Army (ZIPRA). Colonel Kononov was the instrument of the Soviet 'Bridge across Central Africa' policy to train Freedom Fighters for the various liberation struggles underway. The Portuguese had long since abandoned their colonies of Angola and Mozambique. These newly independent countries now provided the logistical platform for the liberation movements in South West Africa (Namibia), Rhodesia and South Africa. A network of ZIPRA bases was built in Zambia and Angola for this purpose. Military training for ZIPRA and the other liberation armies took place in various places in Africa, mainly Libya, East Germany and the Soviet Union. ZIPRA was primarily supported by the Soviet Union, its main military and logistical base being in Zambia.

Training Freedom Fighters was a very interesting diversion for Benkov. He had previous experience with training Viet Cong in North Vietnam and Cambodia. The result was a speciality in planning and executing insurgency operations. He had worked in Africa in the past. As a young officer he had been sent as an observer to support the Cuban expedition to the Congo. The leader of the force was the legendary Ernesto 'Che' Guevara who chose to support the Marxist Simba movement, as well as Laurent Kabila, a rebel leader in Katanga Province, both fighting the regime of the 'Western Puppet', Joseph Mobutu. Benkov had formed a low opinion of Che Guevara who he thought was too idealistic, hesitant to make the hard military decisions that were needed and much too focused on political education. The Guevara expedition failed and Benkov learned the most important truth, *the rebels must be trained in such a way that they do not shy away from performing the atrocities necessary to terrorise the local population into providing unconditional support.*

While there were large numbers of volunteers for the freedom struggle in Rhodesia, many of the young cadres had been effectively kidnapped by ZIPRA forces as part of an aggressive recruitment drive. In some cases, this entailed a degree of 'persuasion' as many did not see the fight for freedom in the correct light. Benkov found that most of the recruits got the picture rather quickly minus a few teeth and stitches. He took great pride in beating the reluctant converts to within an inch of their lives. A few never adapted to the re-education process and unfortunately perished from their wounds, mostly deep knife wounds. *The price of freedom is high.*

Benkov was waiting for the daily flash radio message which was transmitted from the Soviet base in Lusaka. This was a coded message using a one-time message pad system where both sender and recipient used copies of the same code-key pad system to encode/decode a single message. The message pad was then destroyed and a different code used for the next message. These messages were made more difficult to monitor because the flash messages were transmitted at different times of the day. The Rhodesians could not break the code without the message pad which they did not have. By way of contrast, the daily 'Shackle' and 'Button' codes used by the Rhodesians were in the hands of ZIPRA within hours of issue through a network of spies and informants.

As he sat on the rock Benkov reflected on his recent eventful arrival in Lupane. He had left the training base near Kabanga Mission about 120km northeast of Livingston a week earlier. They had travelled by truck to the Zambezi River opposite the confluence with the Gwai, part of the deep set of gorges cut by the Zambezi below Victoria Falls. They had crossed the river in relays using rubber inflatable boats, ferrying the hundred or so ZIPRA cadres and all their equipment. The heavy rains in northern Zambia had swollen the river making the gorge a raging, terrifying torrent. It had taken the whole night to get the men and equipment across. Miraculously only one load of cadres was lost, weighed down by their equipment and without lifejackets they had no chance of survival. Even if they had known how to swim, the gorge teemed with crocodiles. Once across, the band of insurgents climbed into the Gwai gorge with its massive rock strewn bed. Benkov had rested the group for a full day at one of the frequently used base camps in the gorge before crossing through the *cordon sanitaire* minefield.

Traversing the minefield went remarkably well with only four men lost when they triggered a 'plough-shear' anti-personnel mine. The device was particularly horrific, a plough-shear erected on a tree, the convex area packed with explosive mixed with metal fragments, nails and ball bearings. The blast effectively shredded the four men standing in front of the mine, spreading blood and gore over a wide area. The explosion was heard at the Army Engineer's camp not far away. With such a large band it was almost certain that their trail would be discovered. The leaders of the liberation movement expected casualties of at least fifty percent. *The price of freedom is truly very high.*

Once through the minefield Benkov set a course directly for Lupane, figuring that the Rhodesians would take a day to get organised before they would try to track his group down. Being followed did not, in itself, create any concern in his mind as the intelligence reports showed there was no RLI or RAR Fireforce[34] at Wankie or Victoria Falls. He also knew that a large 'external' raid was going on in Mozambique at that time which normally sucked up all the available helicopters and other air support. He knew he would face either the under-manned and under-trained Army Engineers or the inexperienced Independent Company. So it was.

Doubling back at the end of the first day Benkov established how far the follow-up group was behind him. He counted the twenty-six men of 3 Platoon and their leader resplendent with white face and A76 radio aerial. Watching their careful but noisy progress, he plotted their demise.

It was not necessary to inform the whole ZIPRA band of what he saw, but instead he confided in his two interpreters and the HQ team made up of three RPD gunners who he had trained personally. They would be ready when the time came. He had enjoyed the satisfaction of shooting the wounded officer in the chest, but it was the arrival of the helicopters and then the Lynx that prevented him from wiping out the whole SF follow-up group. His band's casualties were very light indeed, ten dead, fifteen or so wounded, all the wounded had since died. Benkov was impressed by the accuracy of the frantan strike by the Lynx. *That needs to be remembered!*

The mission given to Benkov was to seek out the main routes for a potential conventional ZIPRA attack across the Zambezi west of Victoria Falls to drive east through Lupane to Que Que. Once that was achieved the capital, Salisbury, would be sealed off and in so doing, split the country in two. The Soviet military planners determined this mission as being of vital importance, which was why they needed to infiltrate their own reconnaissance specialist. This was the 'official' version of the mission as it was explained to the Nkomo leadership team. The truth was somewhat different.

Colonel Kononov himself had conducted Benkov's briefing, in the presence of the Soviet Ambassador to Zambia, Professor Vassily Solodovnikov. The detailed briefing took place at the Soviet Embassy

---

34 Quick reaction force usually manned by men of the regular Battalions of the Rhodesian Light Infantry (RLI) or the Rhodesian African Rifles (RAR). Fireforce was both heli-borne and para-borne made up of Alouette III helicopter gun-ships and troop carriers, plus a Lynx and a Paradak (Dakota). Fireforces could also call in Hunter and Canberra air support during large attacks.

instead of the ZIPRA War Council Headquarters called 'The Rock' located in the western outskirts of Lusaka. Prof Solodovnikov had a very close working relationship with the leader Joshua Nkomo, and was largely responsible for planning troop levels and training requirements in the various camps in Zambia. Solodovnikov also requisitioned and facilitated Soviet arms shipments including the build-up of a conventional war capability, tanks, armoured personnel carriers, artillery, anti-aircraft guns and missiles.

It had impressed Benkov that he had been selected for this mission that required infiltration into 'Zimbabwe', as the liberation movement called the country.

Infiltration by Soviet Spetsnaz into Zimbabwe had previously been undertaken very rarely but as Prof Solodovnikov had said, 'The liberation war is now entering a new phase.' The Professor had leaned across his desk to impress his point, 'Comrade Benkov ... we are concerned about our allies in this war being persuaded by the West to negotiate with the oppressive colonial regime. Comrade Nkomo is coming under increasing pressure to seek a settlement; this cannot be allowed to happen!'

Col Kononov then added, 'Benkov, we are concerned about the fighting spirit that exists on the ground. We suspect that Nkomo and ZIPRA are focussed more on a holding plan instead of attacking the enemy. They seem to be waiting for our conventional assault that we are presently planning. This is having the effect of passing the military initiative to Robert Mugabe and his ZANLA forces. You are to make this assessment and impress upon the local commanders that they need to lift the operational tempo.'

The Colonel had been deliberately vague on the methods that Benkov should adopt.

'You may need to shake things up a bit Comrade,' said Kononov with a laugh, knowing the Captain would use a broad interpretation of these instructions.

Prof Solodovnikov, at the end of the briefing, made the most startling revelation, 'Captain, you are aware of our support for Comrade Nkomo, this has been freely given since 1961, but we are concerned about the Chinese and North Korean influence on their friend Comrade Mugabe. We need to ensure that Comrade Nkomo comes to power when the struggle is over. At the moment the lack of results by ZIPRA is playing into Mugabe's hands. You will turn this around for us! We cannot end up backing the wrong horse!' The Professor finished with a flourish, emphasising his point by punching his fist into his hand.

The three men stood up at the end of the briefing and shook hands. '... You will not discuss this mission with anyone Vladimir,' Kononov reminded him, deliberately using Benkov's first name to emphasise his trust in the abilities this very special soldier.

'You can have faith in me Comrade Colonel, I will not let you down,' replied Benkov, standing to leave. He braced to salute, then he realised he was in civilian clothing, instead bowing his head respectfully to the two men.

'Good luck Comrade Benkov, *Do svidaniya!* Till our next meeting!' Kononov showed the young captain to the door, patting him on the shoulder as they parted.

Benkov's base for the next three months was a small village about 20kms to the east of the village of Lupane on the main road between Bulawayo and Wankie. The base was in heavily wooded Mopani country, surrounded by low hills. The good news was that there were no SF elements in the area and ZIPRA had infiltrated the best part of a battalion of cadres. They were spread out in a 10km radius, mainly in the protected riverbed of a tributary of the Bubi River. Nobody could come or go from the area without ZIPRA being informed … or so they thought.

If the Spetsnaz officer had one weakness, it was the fact that he enjoyed the company of young girls, very young girls. He had to be discreet with this activity at home in Russia but the missions to Vietnam, Congo and now Zambia had provided him with a steady supply of young girls. The colonial wars in Third World countries placed few restrictions on deviant behaviour. He was in his own personal heaven, young girls and the potential for as much violence and killing as he liked. Benkov's only real concern was his relationship with the local ZIPRA Brigade Commander, Tongerai Chabanga.

As the receive light lit up on the radio, the messages from Lusaka started to come in. Message pad ready, Benkov began writing down the code as it arrived. Once the message was decoded, he was startled by the new information and the alterations to the orders he had received - *Comrade Chabanga will not be pleased.* Benkov looked across lovingly at the three SAM-7 'Strela' heat-seeking, ground-to-air missiles propped up against a tree. They provided a few interesting possibilities.

*

ZIPRA Base Camp, Lupane TTL, northern Matabeleland

Brigadier Tongerai Chabanga was the commander on the ground of the ZIPRA operational area designated Northern Front Region 1.

This area encompassed most of the northwest of the country with the two major towns being Wankie and Victoria Falls. Comrade Chabanga would not have described himself as a fanatic, but in the sense that he lived and breathed the freedom struggle, consuming his every thought, he most definitely was. He also would never admit to being short, but he certainly was, about 5ft 4", very slightly built with a wiry, sinewy body. His diminutive stature gave the impression that he was much younger than his thirty years. He had bright brown eyes, a ready smile and a pleasant disposition that drew people to him. He compensated for his smallish stature with boundless energy and enthusiasm, but most effectively, with a supreme intellect. Tongerai Chabanga was also a modest man, achieving his rank through dedication and commitment, not relying on political patronage and intrigue.

Chabanga had been recruited by ZAPU while studying law at university in Zambia, identified for his deep and abiding hatred of the white 'Invaders' of his country. Chabanga had been born and brought up in a village just north of the town of Nkai in Matabeleland and educated at the local Catholic mission school. He had escaped from the country at his first opportunity. Despite his hatred for the 'Settlers', that is not to say that he hated all white people. That was not true. 'We are fighting against a system' he would say, 'not white people'. What he hated was the fact that his people were denied their political rights, first by the British colonial power and, thereafter, by the ridiculous Unilateral Declaration of Independence by the Smith regime. In his mind the natural outcome of a democratic process in the country would result in black people holding power. It was the injustice of the situation that Chabanga hated; it gnawed away at him, like throbbing pain, deep in his gut.

The Brigadier remembered how excited he was when he was selected for military training in the Soviet Union. The fact that Mugabe had courted the Chinese meant that the Soviets had made the only decision possible, to provide their complete, unequivocal support to Joshua Nkomo and ZAPU. The excitement of being sent to the USSR quickly turned to disillusion when the white Russian students, also studying in Tbilisi in Georgia, subjected him and his comrades to racial attacks. The situation became so bad that the young freedom fighters had to be moved from Tbilisi to the Northern Training Centre near Moscow. Despite the better treatment in Moscow, Chabanga always felt that racism in the Soviet Union was just below the surface. The fact that the Soviets were using the Freedom Struggle as a way of projecting their power and influence disturbed him, but he had reconciled with himself that once the struggle was over the Soviets could be dispensed with.

Chabanga quickly became fluent in Russian, as he had concluded that that was the fastest way of earning recognition and thereby separation from the rank and file. The Zimbabweans, as they called themselves, shared the training centre with members of the Palestine Liberation Organisation (PLO) where Chabanga befriended the future leaders. His proficiency in Russian gave him entrance to Patrice Lumumba University in Moscow. As part of the learning experience, he visited PLO camps in Libya where he was trained with leaders from other liberation movements. These included the Irish Republican Army (IRA), the Red Army Faction in West Germany and the Basque Fatherland and Liberty (ETA) in Spain. Chabanga reflected on what a happy time that had been, being caught up in the excitement of making a real difference in the world, fighting capitalism, Zionism, injustice and colonial exploitation.

Once the academic aspects of his training were complete, Chabanga went to the liberation movement training camp set up by the Soviets in Perevalnoye in the Crimea, near the city of Simferopol. This camp was also used for training freedom fighters from Angola, *Umkomto-we-Sizwe* from South Africa and SWAPO from South West Africa. In Perevalnoye Chabanga was trained by World War II Crimean guerrillas, who had operated in the mountains, forest and bush, in terrain not very different from Southern Africa. 'General Fyodor', Major-General Fyodor Fedorenko, an ex-World War II guerrilla commander in the Crimea, headed the training of African freedom fighters. Chabanga recalled the time when Colonel Fyodor showed him World War II trenches and hideouts when he came to tour the camp and check on the progress of the training.

The military training course covered many subjects including communications, insurgency, surveillance, secret writing, secret meetings, photography, military management, ambush, attack and small arms. Chabanga took willingly to the promise of a socialist state where all the valuable assets and resources of the country would be placed in the hands of the 'People'. This is what he believed the People wanted.

The only aspect of the training in the USSR that Chabanga resented was the continual emphasis by the Soviets on promoting their ideology. Lecturers from the Institute of Social Sciences tried to indoctrinate the African freedom fighters with their form of Marxism; he remembered one particular lecture breaking up with the Zimbabweans standing on their desks chanting in Russian, 'Screw your Marxism' over and over again. As one of his comrades said at the time, 'I have come here to learn how to shoot and blow up things, not to learn about Marxist Communism.'

When he had finally returned to Zambia to begin his operational duties, Chabanga was appalled by the conditions he found in the training camps. Squalor, disease and complete lack of discipline pervaded the camps. This was in the time before the Patriotic Front alliance had been formed and the two rival political movements, ZAPU and ZANU, were at open war against each other in the training camps and many were killed when the Zambian Army was called in to quell the fighting. It was at this time that Chabanga realised the full enormity of the philosophical and tribal split between Mugabe and Nkomo.

Mugabe's ZANU was unashamedly focused on forwarding the interests of the Shona tribe, while Nkomo's ZAPU had always been a multi-ethnic organisation, although more recently the leadership was mostly Matabele. Despite the formation of the Patriotic Front by both parties to promote the war together, united, Chabanga had an abiding distrust, bordering on hatred, for the ZANU leadership, in particular Robert Mugabe.

While he was grateful for the much-needed support provided by the USSR, Chabanga resented the interference of the Soviet advisors in Nkomo's war strategy and the influence they had over his political leadership team. It was clear to him that his leaders were being manipulated, in particular with the ridiculous idea of a conventional assault against Rhodesia across the Zambezi. Chabanga had made it clear that any thought of a conventional assault across the Zambezi was ludicrous while South Africa was still under the yoke of the apartheid regime. Chabanga had studied the tactical options closely. The South African conventional war capability was massive; he had remonstrated with his superiors, *had the South Africans not swept the Cubans in Angola aside? Would they not intervene? Absolutely they would! Are they not already in the country, supplying equipment, helicopters and pilots? Were Mirage F1s not flying top-cover for Rhodesian attacks into Mozambique?* He had heard reports of South African Puma[35] helicopters flying over the south of the country.

In Chabanga's mind, victory was to be based on convincing the United States, British and Commonwealth Governments of the legitimacy of Joshua Nkomo's claim to the leadership of Zimbabwe. This was to be promoted ahead of any internal settlement that Ian Smith was trying to organise. If this were done correctly, Britain would hand power to Nkomo once the war was won. The important thing was that Nkomo provided the new political leadership when that time came. He knew that Mugabe and his forces would never agree to the

---

35 *Aérospatiale* Puma, four-bladed, twin-engined medium transport/utility helicopter, SA 330C, operated by the South African Air Force.

leadership of Nkomo, for this reason they would need to be crushed. As Chabanga had argued with his compatriots, *the defeat of Mugabe was when conventional forces would be needed!*

While Chabanga was an educated man, enlightened to the politics of the world, he was still a Matabele at heart, with the same blood as the Zulus from the south.

The one person in the world that Tongerai Chabanga respected, hero-worshipped, was the supreme military commander, General Lookout Masuku. Masuku was a true leader with hard-won experience in the liberation struggle. He too had been trained by the Soviets and had field experience with the North Vietnamese Army of General Vo Nguyen Giap. Masuku was a proponent of the 'conventional war scenario' but had objected to the detailed reconnaissance to be undertaken by Benkov. The Soviets had put pressure on Nkomo to allow the reconnaissance to take place threatening a reduction in their support if it was not done. This information had all been fed back to Chabanga who felt deeply betrayed. *Who was in charge of our struggle anyway?*

There was a celebration with the arrival of such a large re-supply group, with all the news from comrades in Zambia. Chabanga had met Benkov rather coolly.

'You are not welcome here Comrade,' he said in perfect Russian as he strode forward to meet the Soviet Captain.

He looked up at the giant of a man who towered over him and without waiting for a reply said 'What will be the consequence of you being killed, or worse … captured … Comrade?'

'I am a humble soldier following orders Comrade Brigadier,' ventured Benkov respectfully.

'How am I going to keep your presence here a secret? Look around you … we are in the middle of a densely populated area,' Chabanga waved his arms expansively.

'I will stay hidden Comrade … I have camouflage paint. I will complete my mission as quickly as possible and leave,' said Benkov deliberately choosing to take a submissive stance as he was in unknown territory with no support.

Chabanga pressed his point, 'Exactly what is your mission comrade? With your satellites you can study the terrain; you don't need a physical reconnaissance.'

'It is always important to assess the enemy's capability first hand Comrade Brigadier,' replied Benkov, starting to get irritated at Chabanga's line of questioning, thinking - *this is none of your business!*

Chabanga sensed the change in the Russian's mood, thought about pushing him further, but decided to back off for the moment.

'Very well Comrade Benkov, we will discuss this further some other time,' he half turned to leave; then added brusquely, '... you will keep me informed of your every movement ... every minute of every day ... is that clear Comrade?'

'It is clear Comrade Brigadier,' replied Benkov, standing with fists clenched, trying his best to hold his temper in check.

'Very well then ... you may refer to me by my name Comrade, rank is of little consequence here,' added Chabanga, his inherent civility and manners coming to the fore, he offered his hand to the Russian. Benkov shook the little man's hand, surprised at the strength in his grip.

He watched as the diminutive commander strode purposefully away - *Chabanga could be a formidable adversary - he will need to be watched.*

4

4 Independent Company (RAR) base camp, Sprayview airfield, Victoria Falls

When Sgt Smith returned to Victoria Falls after the funerals, he found that 2nd Lt Gibbs with 2 and 3 Platoons were still deployed on the River. 1 Platoon remained on follow-up south of Kamativi. Smith's own section was on camp guard duty, and hating every second of it. Under normal circumstances a platoon bush trip would last eight days, with two days out to replenish and re-supply, followed by a further eight days and so on, for six weeks. At the end of six weeks the Platoon were allowed to return home for a week of R&R[36].

Smith snuck into camp in the late afternoon hoping to avoid the CSM or any other person in authority. He planned to get into town for a few sundowners[37], *Shumbas*[38], preferably at the Victoria Falls Hotel.

'Sergeant Smith, so good to see you!' came the flamboyant call. Smith turned to see the Company 2IC, Captain Ian Fullerton BCR[39], striding purposefully towards him. Fullerton was a professional soldier in every sense of the word. About the same height as Smith, twenty-six years old, dark brown eyes, long shaggy black hair, a reputation with the women, and a serious thirst. He had been promoted and transferred from D Company, 1RAR with a glittering record. *A real player*, who loved his job, loved the Regiment, loved his soldiers and loved the war! Fullerton was the sort of bloke who was larger than life, who really only either loved something or hated it. Nothing he did was in half measures. He loved everything about the army, with the exception of Major Peacock, who he hated, passionately and unreservedly. The feeling was completely mutual.

Fullerton's only disappointment at 4 Indep was that they were not a designated or trained Fireforce. Acting as a Fireforce was only possible for 4 Indep when absolutely no one else was available. The regular battalions of 1RAR and 2RAR together with the RLI manned the Fireforces around the country. These units were also parachute-trained. Fullerton wore his parachute wings proudly on his shoulder, regaling audiences with graphic 'war stories' of jumping into firefights[40], made more colourful after a few beers or *jimboolies*, as they were often called.

---

36 Rest and recreation / recuperation.

37 Drinks at sunset, traditional colonial gin and tonic, more likely a few beers watching the sun go down.

38 Shona, lion, used to describe Lion Lager beer

39 Bronze Cross of Rhodesia, awarded for valour in the face of the enemy.

40 A battle, a contact with the enemy.

It was the intense Fireforce action that Fullerton missed desperately; he needed, therefore, to find other forms of distraction.

Fullerton needed equal measures of, women, liquor and *hondo*. Denied any of these pursuits for any prolonged period of time, made the Captain grumpy, very grumpy indeed. Captain Fullerton was presently short on *hondo*, a problem he proposed fixing at his earliest convenience. The Captain had earned the nickname *Ingwe* or Leopard, from the black troops, for his bravery and aggression, a title he was enormously proud of. He was happy to be addressed as *Ingwe* in substitution for 'Sir'.

'Sergeant Smith, you are going to drive me into town for a beer, I am going to get pissed, I am then going to try to get lucky with a German tourist, and tomorrow you and I are going to Jambezi to slot a few Gooks,' stated Fullerton with a disarming smile. Jambezi was a Protected Village in the Wankie TTL about 50kms to the east.

Smith knew better than to make an excuse when invited for a beer, plus he really enjoyed Fullerton's company. He had not had the opportunity to join a Fullerton 'bush trip' thus far, but he had shared a few beers in the mess and transported a few of the Captain's stray damsels back to their hotels in the dead of night. He was particularly grateful that Fullerton did not mention or discuss with him the fact that he had passed out of the School of Infantry as a 'Sergeant'. While he had to put up with the constant jibes from the CSM, the fact that Fullerton treated him the same as the other national servicemen provided some relief. Fullerton was a close friend of Smith's Course Officer, Captain Walker and he felt sure that they must have spoken.

The opportunity of deploying with the legendary Captain seemed an exciting prospect but the same nagging uncertainty sat in the back of his mind. *At least I have finally had a contact. But am I good enough – will I screw up?*

Smith washed up, put on a clean uniform complete with stable belt and beret, and drew a Two-Five[41] from the MT[42]. He loved driving the Two-Five, 16 forward and 16 reverse gears, enormous power, a go-anywhere anytime kind of vehicle. The drive into town was no more than a few kilometres; Fullerton's favourite haunt was the casino at the famous Victoria Falls Hotel. Smith pulled up in the car park outside the main entrance to the hotel. The Two-Five was a lot wider than civilian vehicles and so occupied two parking spaces.

'*KANJANI INGWE!* HELLO!' came the loud, boisterous welcome. Over rushed Nyika, the 'Admiral', the celebrated Vic Falls' Hotel doorman and concierge, resplendent in a sea captain's cap, a bright

41 Mercedes Benz Unimog, 2.5 tons
42 Motor Transport (yard).

red tailored coat, black sash and a chest full of badges and medals. All the staff at the hotel knew Fullerton from his womanising exploits but also his military reputation through talking to the RAR soldiers in the nearby townships and beerhalls.

'*Kanjan, Nyika*' replied Fullerton who was also fluent in Shona. They exchanged pleasantries including Nyika giving a summary of the status of his various children and wives. Smith couldn't be certain but he was sure that Nyika was giving Fullerton a comprehensive summary of the available 'talent' including descriptions of approximate age coupled with room numbers. While Nyika was Matabele, he, like virtually all black people in the country, spoke both major languages seShona and siNdebele fluently.

'*Tatenda*, thank you, Nyika' Fullerton leapt to the ground, 'Sergeant Smith let me buy you a beer, then make yourself scarce until I come looking for you.'

Both men carried their rifles, as this was still an operational area, the hotel had been revved[43] on two occasions. The hotel had made arrangements for the many soldiers that visited. At the entrance, the old porter's lodge had been converted to an armoury where Nyika carefully checked in their weapons, issuing them each a receipt.

The two soldiers in their smart camouflage uniforms walked through the hotel entrance, a magnificent Edwardian-style colonial building, five-star, built in 1904, with a majestic courtyard split by two reflecting pools surrounded by mango trees. When the mangoes were in season, the trees would be alive with Vervet Monkeys, squawking and squealing. Heads turned as the two men in uniform walked purposefully through the courtyard; men in uniform were always impressive. Smith braced up a little, feeling good walking next to his Captain.

Through the courtyard was the main part of the hotel built in a stately arc to allow all the rooms a view of the Falls, the spray clearly visible about 3kms distant. In front of the hotel was a large veranda about half the length of the front section and in front of that, an open patio with hundreds of chairs and tables set up for breakfast and dinner. Giant wild fig trees dominated the patio; birds filled the air with sound, chattering incessantly. Walking out onto the front veranda, bathed in the late afternoon sunlight, *Ingwe* stopped, standing hands on hips, scanning the occupants. Not seeing an obvious target, he chose a table with a view of the arched front entrance so that he could make an adequate 'appreciation' of any possibilities that might arise. The hotel was very busy; most of the tables were taken by holidaymakers from various parts of the world. 'War' and 'Holiday' were such close

43 Rhodesian slang, attacked or shot at, also applied to being shelled or mortared.

bedfellows at Victoria Falls. The two soldiers drew the attention of those nearby; whispers and smiles passed in their direction. Smith felt obliged to smile back.

A smiling waiter approached in starched white uniform, black sash with tassels, a red fez on his head, '*Masikati Ingwe*, good afternoon Ingwe.'

'*Masikati, maswera sei*? Afternoon, had a good day?' replied Fullerton, smiling back in his disarming fashion. He ordered a round of beers, *Shumbas*, and sat back to look at the splendid view. In the background the lounge singer began Don Maclean's *American Pie*.

> *A long, long time ago...*
> *I can still remember*
> *How that music used to make me smile*[44].

'Captain Fullerton - good to see you!' a young Lieutenant dressed in light khaki dress uniform approached, threading through the closely packed tables.

'Lieutenant bloody Dawson ... how the hell are you,' Fullerton stood to welcome the new arrival. Lt Robert 'Dick' Dawson, commander of 3 Troop, 1Grey Scouts, shared the RAR base camp at Sprayview airstrip. Dawson was immaculate with the distinctive light grey beret, lanyard and grey and maroon stable belt.

'You look like you are on the hunt tonight, you useless bloody donkey-walloper, you.'

Fullerton and Dawson were good drinking buddies both had shared a bit of female action. Dawson was supposed to be dating one of the croupiers from the casino.

> *Them good old boys were drinkin' whiskey and rye*
> *And singin', this'll be the day that I die.*
> *this'll be the day that I die."*

'Good to see you Ian,' replied Dawson with an officer's informality. He turned to Smith, 'How are you Mike, sorry about ...' Dawson hesitated, changing tack, '... did you hear that I have signed up Regular? They have offered me Captain in a month or two.'

Dawson was two years ahead of Smith at school, and he had attended Milton School in Bulawayo with Charlie Williams. Smith had played golf with Dawson and his younger brother Jeff as juniors at Harry Allen Golf Club.

'Good to see you too ... Sir ... Congratulations! You look like you

---

44 *American Pie*, Don Mclean, 1971

mean business tonight,' Smith stood to shake Dawson's hand. He had always liked him, they had been good friends and Dawson had a seriously hot sister, Amanda. The gulf between them, 'Sergeant' to 'Lieutenant', felt like an impenetrable barrier. The army seemed to suspend their friendship. Smith was grateful that Dawson had never enquired about how he failed the course at the School of Infantry. But that just seemed to make the gulf between them all the greater.

They smashed down three beers in quick succession, the conversation covering a lot of ground rapidly. A short clipped comment was made on the death of Charlie Williams, *no need dwelling on the dead; focus on the moment, on the living*. Smith was asked to recount his perspectives on the contact in which Williams had died. He found the opportunity to talk about it strangely relieving. The two officers listened respectfully to his account intently without interruption, not asking any questions or making comments. With a nod from Fullerton the officers adjourned to the casino and Smith went to chat to a few Grey Scout troopers that he knew from school.

About three hours later Fullerton reappeared, 'Smithy I need some help, I have a small problemo.'

The officer, not waiting for an answer, steered off towards the hotel entrance listing very slightly to port. Smith followed him, also feeling unsteady on his feet after a good many beers.

The scene that presented itself at the hotel entrance jolted Smith somewhat. Shaking his head in amazement Smith observed the Two-Five embedded in the cab of the Military Police (MP) Land Rover. Fullerton had successfully 'targeted' an attractive tourist who now sat in the back of the open Two-Five looking slightly perplexed. Fullerton had attempted to reverse the Two-Five, which was left-hand drive, out of the parking but this requires a swift switch of the gearbox from forward to reverse. This is accomplished with two levers that essentially switch all sixteen forward gears simultaneously. Unfortunately Fullerton missed the switch and the truck, in neutral, had rolled back into the Land Rover.

'You need to get me back to camp so that I can do a bit of *skirmishing*,' whispered Fullerton with a poorly disguised wink indicating the very attractive young lady sitting in the back of the truck. 'Let me introduce you to Francine ... she is French, not too good on the lingo ... but she certainly seems to understand slap and tickle.' Fullerton winked again his eyelid moving in slow motion as if recovering from anaesthetic.

'*C'est qui, ton ami?*' the woman asked, presumably of Fullerton. Smith looked up at her, having no idea what she had said. She was absolutely stunning, mid-twenties, long jet-black hair, accentuated by the dress which was full length and pearly white. The bodice was cut low. Smith's eyes seemed to fix themselves on the delicate cleft, mesmerised by the gentle movement below.

'She is really hot… Cher,' volunteered Smith in support of his Officer, his eyes still fastened on the white dress and the promise beneath.

'*Est-ce que vous pouvez parler français Sergent?*' the girl asked. Smith caught 'Sergent', which had to be him, but he couldn't be sure.

'Yesh … Maam,' Smith replied, not sure what else to say.

'Quick Smithy, before we get in shit with the MPs,' interjected Fullerton urgently, at the same time unceremoniously ripping a page out of the vehicle logbook.

'Okay … Cher, back to camp,' said Smith, climbing unsteadily into the driver's seat.

The girl giggled, she also had a few drinks under the belt, '*Allons-y plus vite mon Capitaine.*'

Smith leaned back, trying to focus, 'Does she speak any English … Cher? … Does she understand what you have in mind … Cher?'

'I understand *perfectement Sergent*,' said the girl demurely in thickly accented English. She quite obviously understood everything that had been said. Smith, now embarrassed, dragged his eyes away, returning to the task at hand. Fullerton sat in the back, his arm draped over the girl's shoulders, more for support than anything else.

'Jesus Smithy, I might be able to buy a few more helicopters!' exclaimed Fullerton as his addled brain contemplated the possibilities, '… the Alouettes are French built after all.'

'Yes … Cher … good idea Cher … we need more helicopters.'

Smith struggled to get the Two-Five into gear then jerkily tried to extract the tail from the Land Rover. The tow hook had snared the roof of the Land Rover dragging the much smaller vehicle behind it, causing a high-pitched scrapping sound.

'For fuck sakes Smithy, don't make so much noise,' called Fullerton from the back, his arm still around the French heiress. She giggled again, enjoying the adventure. The Land Rover put up a sterling fight, grinding behind the Two-Five for a good twenty metres before surrendering. It stood forlornly across the driveway its cab all but ripped off its mountings.

Racing out of the hotel grounds, Smith turned left onto the main road then over the railway line, gunning the vehicle back up the hill towards camp. The cool night air provided no sobering effect whatsoever, instead causing his head to begin a slow and deliberate spin.

The entrance to the camp was a narrow dirt road on the southern end of the Sprayview airstrip. Negotiating the dirt road, Smith was vaguely aware of the approach of an on-coming vehicle. It was difficult to see over to the right, as the Two-Five was left-hand-drive and high off the ground. As the headlights drew closer and closer, Smith tried desperately to remain on his side of the narrow road, then suddenly, CRUNCH.

'Don't stop Smithy, keep going, it's just a small bump, nothing serious,' cajoled Fullerton anxiously from the back; he seriously wanted to make 'contact'. The girl laughed loudly, obviously enjoying herself immensely.

Smith didn't give the matter another thought. He pulled the vehicle into the pitch dark MT, he greeted the guard on duty and staggered to bed with a rapidly oncoming hangover. Fullerton went on to further international relations and helicopter purchases.

As he jumped down from the truck, Smith overheard Francine ask Fullerton, '*Pour quoi avez-vous besoin d'acheter des hélicoptères Capitaine?*'

*

The next morning dawned to the customary military morning activity, confined mostly to the duty sections and camp guards. Smith managed to stagger to breakfast, still sporting a serious hangover and then mustered his section for pre-deployment inspection. Smith had two lance corporals in his section, Tovakare and Nkai, who were also the other stick commanders. Each section was made up of three sticks with four men in each. Each platoon was made up of three sections, making a full platoon complement of thirty-six men.

Smith stood in his full combat kit, his FN, zeroed to 100m, chest webbing with eight magazines of eighteen rounds each. The magazines were old so placing a full twenty round load into the magazine was too much for the spring creating the risk of stoppages. All webbing for magazine storage was designed to enable quick magazine replacement. The first two rounds of his magazine load were tracer, with a tracer every third round thereafter. He loaded consecutive tracers as the final two rounds to indicate the end of supply. The first two tracer rounds would most often be used for marking target, '*watch my tracer!*'

Under the left arm pouch in his chest webbing, Smith carried one white phosphorus grenade, under the right arm one shrapnel grenade, an M962[45], and two smoke grenades of different colours. Blue smoke was used to indicate a c/sign requiring a casevac of a wounded soldier. Smoke grenades were essential for marking FLOT to aircraft or for rapidly identifying the stick's position to other c/signs. In the centre pouch of his chest webbing he carried pens and pencils, a protractor, a mini-flare projector with six flares, a converted small photo album

45 Fragmentation grenade.

with mission briefing notes in the plastic sleeves, and his copy of the 'AIDE-MEMOIRE for PLATOON/SECTION COMMANDER'S ORDERS and APPRECIATIONS'. His maps, in a clear plastic sleeve, were always stuffed down the inside of his chest webbing so he could reach for them easily. His compass hung around his neck on a leather cord over a face-veil that was indispensible for wiping away sweat and as a cover for nose and mouth when travelling on dusty roads. Another piece of vital equipment was a mosquito-netting headpiece, not standard issue, that could be slipped over the head as protection from Mopani flies, Tsetse flies and mosquitoes. On his web-belt Smith carried two water bottles, just behind his hips, with a single kidney pouch that carried his medical kit, catheters, saline drips, drugs and bandages. His pack was small, lightweight on a metal frame with two additional water bottles in pouches on each side. In the pack was his A76 radio, two spare batteries, rifle cleaning kit, a belt of 50 rounds for the MAG, rations 'rats' for five days, with his sleeping bag strapped to the bottom of the pack. The radio hand-piece was clipped to a toggle on his chest webbing harness inches from his left ear. A few loose potatoes and onions were stuffed into the pack to try to make cooked rat-pack meals a little more appetizing.

Smith wore a short-sleeved camo-combat shirt and combat pants. He had on occasion run through thick thorn scrub that cut his legs to ribbons therefore he resolved that thick combat pants were a better option than shorts, despite the heat. This dress was different to other NS members of the company who often wore green T-shirts and shorts under their webbing. The dress code for combat was flexible for most units where men wore what made them feel most comfortable. Smith figured that because his men wore combat shirts and pants he would look too conspicuous with his white legs and arms exposed, *maybe that is what had happened to Charlie Williams*. He still had to administer camo-cream to his arms and face.

The black RAR soldiers preferred to use a standard webbing arrangement having magazine pouches and water bottles mounted on the web-belt, with the web-belt attached to an over-shoulder harness to help bear the load. They also preferred the large standard issue backpack to carry extra food and water. Headwear was the standard combat cap with the RAR badge, the shield crossed by spear and knobkerrie. Smith preferred his canvas camo-floppy hat. He wore commercially purchased 'light-weight' ankle high boots, made from soft leather with a rubber sole. He preferred these to the standard army issue boots that were much heavier, or to the canvas 'clandestine' boots with a smooth sole for anti-tracking purposes but dangerous on wet surfaces.

The kit inspection required each man to lay out his equipment on top of his plastic bivy. Smith was busy checking through the kit and inspecting rifles when he became aware of someone approaching from behind.

'Where is your section Sergeant Smith?' called Fullerton, marching up purposefully, looking as fresh as a daisy.

'This is my section Sir!' replied Smith, somewhat perplexed by the question, uncertainty etched on his face.

'I only see nine soldiers in front of me Sergeant, sections have at least twelve soldiers in them,' stated Fullerton condescendingly.

'Sir, this is all I have. … I have one KIA[46], I have one on long leave, one sick with malaria, one with tick-bite fever and I have two on light duties with VD[47],' responded Smith carefully counting off using his fingers.

Fullerton nodded, 'Be ready to deploy in an hour.' He turned smartly and walked back to the Ops Room making no further comment on the status of the depleted section.

Smith returned to his men lined up in front of their barrack room. The hustle and bustle of camp activities continued around them. The Grey Scouts were preparing to mount-up to exercise their horses. Smith's attention was drawn to a vehicle approaching on the entrance road, spinning red dust lifting in its wake. He stood perfectly still, glued to the spot; a sudden feeling of foreboding passed over him … someone behind him laughed.

The MP Land Rover passed by, the driver leaning out from under the squashed roof, precariously hanging onto the steering wheel, his only way of staying in the vehicle. The passenger manned the gearstick, lying flat on the bench seat following gear-change instructions from the driver. Hanging out of the vehicle as he was, the driver could only just reach the clutch pedal. The severely damaged Land Rover jerked to a halt as the driver stalled, the passenger having missed the instruction to change into neutral. As the dust settled around the vehicle all heads turned in surprise. Then the camp dissolved into spontaneous laughter.

Unfolding himself from the passenger seat an MP Staff Sergeant emerged. His face puce, the MP screaming across the quad, spitting pure vitriol, 'Sergeant Smith I want you and that fucking Two-Five log book … NOW! You are going to regret you every stepped foot into this Army, you fucking NS wanker!'

A crowd gathered around the Land Rover marvelling at the driver's calisthenics. The young MP driver stood next to the vehicle impressed with all the attention, a beaming smile on his face.

Smith reluctantly walked over to where the MP Staff Sergeant

46 Killed In Action
47 Venereal disease, sexually transmitted disease, e.g. gonorrhea, 'the Clap'.

stood, his section trailing behind.

'I am sorry Staff ... I am not sure what you mean,' he said innocently, his face blushed crimson.

'You will go to DB[48] for this you little shit,' shouted the MP pointing at the forlorn Land Rover.

The MP then turned and bellowed at his driver, 'Private Jones, go to the MT and get me all the Two-Five log books ... DOUBLE AWAY ... you stay right here Smith!' The MP grabbed for Smith's sleeve but he stepped back out the way.

The crowd continued to grow, the troop of Grey Scouts, now mounted on their horses, sat in their saddles, passing comments.

'Staff, would you like to borrow a horse?' asked one.

'Jeeeze Staff, you can make your wheels into a coupe,' said another. The troop broke into raucous laughter as each trooper tried to outdo the other.

The MP whipped around, 'Fucking shut up you people ... you useless donkey wallopers ... I will charge the lot of you.' The MP was fast losing his cool as he cast about looking for some support, '... where is CSM Swanepoel?'

'He is in Wankie,' someone said.

'Now, now Staff, what appears to be the problem.' Captain Fullerton appeared, surveying the Land Rover. '... You seem to be the victim of an unfortunate accident Staff?' He walked up to the MP looking intimidating in full combat kit, A76 radio, rifle, webbing and camo-cream. The camo-cream had the effect of hiding Fullerton's facial expression causing the MP to peer up at him quizzically.

'This is no accident Sir! This is malicious damage to property ... Sir,' said the MP importantly, still looking carefully into Fullerton's face.

The young MP Private could be seen doubling back across the camp clutching the four Two-Five log books. The MP Staff Sergeant stormed towards the approaching man, snatching the logbooks, turned and strode back shaking them above his head.

'This will do it!' he cried out victoriously, '... your NS Sergeant is in for the high-jump Sir.' He stopped in front of Fullerton feverishly flicking through the logbooks. The hastily torn out page was quickly discovered ... *the incriminating evidence had been tampered with.*

In disbelief, the MP rounded on Smith, spittle flying from his mouth, he spluttered, 'What the fuck is this?' Thrusting the defaced document under Smith's nose he screamed, '... You little prick you have torn the page out ... you... little ... you are going to DB so help me.'

The MP turned to his young driver, 'ARREST this man,' he screeched, his voice cracking into falsetto. Standing pompously, his

48 Detention Barracks, located at Brady Barracks, Bulawayo.

head held back, his arm outstretched, the MP's shaking finger pointed at his victim, *victory was at hand … a close run thing.*

It was at precisely this juncture that another cloud of dust appeared on the service road, a bright red, 1972 Alfa Romeo Giulia 1600 Super, hove into view. As it drew closer it seemed to be crabbing a little. Everyone turned to look at the new arrival, which halted in its own cloud of dust next to the first, flat-roofed, victim. The Alfa driver's side, front and rear doors were a crumpled mess bound together with galvanised wire. The crowd now pretty much included the entire camp plus the cooks who had run across from the kitchen to witness the excitement.

Major Peacock extracted himself through the passenger side door, his height making this impossible to achieve in a dignified manner. He straightened up, visibly shaking, beside himself with rage.

Turning to the MP, with as much control as he could, Peacock asked, 'Staff who was driving that Two-Five last night?' The car was his pride and joy, one of very few of that model in the country. Unfortunately he had not been driving the vehicle himself, he had been having a night with the young UTC Manager and he had asked the CQMS[49] to drive it around to her flat.

'I am absolutely positive that it was Sergeant Smith Sir, absolutely convinced … Sir,' stated the MP officiously, still clutching the logbook, still pointing accusingly at the alleged perpetrator.

'Now hang on just a minute Staff, that logbook is incomplete, you cannot accuse a brave young soldier of such an offence without absolute proof … We have a war on, we are about to deploy against the enemy,' interceded Fullerton helpfully.

Major Peacock burst out in frustration, 'I don't give a fuck about logbooks!' he hissed. Turning menacingly on Smith he demanded, '… did you drive that vehicle last night Sergeant Smith?' The Major's face was bright red, his eyes almost bulging from their sockets, his moustache twitching wildly.

Smith stood perfectly to attention with the full knowledge that his next words were going to make a potentially catastrophic difference to the rest of his life.

'I … I can't remember Sir.'

Memory is such a fickle thing. Smith relied on two of the most important rules in the army: 1st Rule, never volunteer for anything; 2nd Rule, never admit to anything.

'You can't remember! … YOU CAN'T REMEMBER! … You little turd, you imbecile you … you …' Peacock became completely lost for words, his voice trailed off, his composure, the 'stiff-upper-lip', had

49 Company Quarter Master Stores.

deserted him.

The crowd pressed in expectantly.

Fullerton, seeing the potential for the situation to escalate out of control interjected, 'That logbook is incomplete; I think that someone else may have used the vehicle last night.' Then addressing Peacock directly he said, 'Sir, I fear we may never know the answer.'

Fullerton, his face as black as the ace of spades and completely expressionless, then resorted to the oldest military tactic in the book … a diversion.

'Why weren't you driving your car last night Sir?' he asked quietly, respectfully.

The whole camp knew the answer.

The Major stared at him, lost for words. There was absolute silence.

Not waiting for a response Fullerton continued, his tone lifting enthusiastically, 'If you will excuse me Sir, Sergeant Smith and I must deploy immediately to Jambezi, a Police call-sign believes CTs are about to attack the Keep[50].' With that he turned away, calling over his shoulder, 'Sergeant Smith I want your section on your vehicle, NOW, we are needed elsewhere.'

'Mon Capitaine… Mon Capitaine,' a woman's voice called out. Francine stood waving from the centre of the quad, her full length white dress revealing an alluring silhouette, high heels held in one hand, her long black hair wafting gently in the breeze. The large crowd of men turned to look at the spectacularly beautiful woman standing in their midst, dumbstruck.

Fullerton disguised in his camo-cream, stepped towards her.

She looked across at him, then with sudden recognition, *'Mon dieu Capitaine, qu'est ce qui s'est passé? Vous êtes completement noir!'* Her tone no different to calling a friend in a café in Montparnasse.

'What is she saying?' someone asked.

'Who cares, she is HOT!'

Standing in the middle of a military parade ground in Africa, surrounded by a large body of admiring men, Francine was completely unfazed, *'Mon Capitaine, vous pouvez me rammener à l'hôtel ?'*

'I think Francine wants to be taken back to her hotel, Sir' said Smith helpfully.

The MP Staff Sergeant stood holding the logbooks, his eyes firmly on the French Vision in front of him, the wind now having left his sails. 'Sir you can't let them go … I need to make a full investigation,' he urged. The MP and the Major remained riveted, both looking at the <u>French woman</u> before them, defeat now at hand, the incongruity of the

50 Protected Village, PV.

situation their mutual undoing.

'Carry on please Staff,' snapped Peacock resignedly, clutching to regain control, '… we will leave this matter for the moment.' The Major pushed through the crowd of men to get to his office. He marched past Fullerton, ignoring Francine completely.

The MP, shaking his head despondently, stalked back to the Land Rover, then taking the gearstick, assumed his position on the bench seat.

'First gear please Staff,' asked the driver politely.

'Staff … it was Colonel Mustard, in the library … with the candlestick!' called out a Grey Scout wit from the saddle.

5

The Road to Jambezi Keep, west of Victoria Falls

The road to Jambezi was heavily corrugated. The almost white sandy surface was like talcum powder and after only a few kilometres the back of the truck and all of its occupants were covered in a light film of white dust. It stuck to Smith's sweaty, blackened, face making him look like a member of the Minstrel Scandals[51].

Rifleman Bukhosi Dube, MAG gunner, sat in the back of the bouncing Four-Five[52], contemplating the loss of his close friend Sipho Fauguneze. Dube was a Matabele with warrior blood going back many generations, Zulu blood. In his veins flowed the blood of Lobengula, son of Mzilikazi the first King of the Matabele Tribe, son of Matshobana, son of Mangete, son of Ngululu, son of Langa, son of Zimangele; all descendants of the Zulu Khumalo Dynasty. Mzilikazi had incurred the wrath of the powerful King of the Zulus, Shaka; he had been forced to flee his native land near the Black Mfolozi River in Zululand, South Africa, in 1821. Mzilikazi took his clan north, eventually settling in the area know as Matabeleland, north of the Limpopo River, where he set about building his kingdom by subjugating the indigenous Shona population.

Dube's great-grandfather, Veremu, was the illegitimate son of King Lobengula. Veremu's aggressive fighting spirit had earned him a command in the elite Mbizo Regiment. Veremu had fought to free the Matabele Kingdom from white settlers who had occupied the land in 1890. He had been present at the destruction of Alan Wilson's Shangani Patrol in 1893, but had also witnessed the annihilation of the last of the Mbizo by maxim guns at Bembesi in the same year.

Dube's grandfather, Lwazi, had served with the predecessor to the RAR, the Rhodesian Native Regiment. Lwazi had fought at the Battle of Songea against the German Askaris in German East Africa, Tanganyika, in 1917. Dube's father, Ndumiso, carried the Bren gun at Taungup in the jungles of Burma in 1945 against the Japanese. His Uncle, Qubhekani, fell at the battle of Tanlwe Chaung in the same year. Ndumiso, as CSM of C Company 1RAR, was despatched to Malaya during the Emergency in 1956.

Yes, Dube was a warrior; he carried *The Gun*, the MAG, in the same way that his father had carried the Bren gun. His life was intertwined

---

51 Minstrel Scandals 1971, EMI Records, musical theatre production, male members of the cast had blackened faces.
52 Mercedes Benz 4.5 ton 4×4 chassis with a steel, V-shaped, armoured body for mine and ambush protection.

with the Regiment; he had earned the title *Masodja*[53]. Dube, although not a tall man, was as broad as he was tall. His arms were like tightly woven rope, bulging biceps, promising enormous strength. The Gun was like a toy in his hands, he was one of the few men who had the strength to fire the machinegun with one arm, from the hip. He could also lift *The Gun*, aim and fire it from the shoulder, almost as accurately as others could with a rifle. He was a man with simple needs, he loved bully beef, *sadza*[54] and gravy, chillies, *Chibuku*[55]; payday; he also enjoyed fighting; on trains, in beerhalls, in barrack rooms, pretty much anywhere and, of course, he loved women. He disliked CSM Swanepoel; in fact he disliked all warrant officers, Mopani flies, snakes, lions and buffalo beans[56]. Some would have described Dube as surly, possibly because when deep in thought he had a pronounced frown that made him seem taciturn, intractable and unapproachable. In fact, those three words described Dube precisely, taciturn, intractable and unapproachable. He was a man of few words, seldom smiled, while his strength and brooding detachment projected an aura that demanded respect. The junior NCOs in the Company knew better than to issue Dube unnecessary orders, or to try to discipline him, as he was not above issuing a few firm slaps to the head after a skin-full of *Chibuku*.

Dube was given a wide berth by all except his closest friends. He did not have many friends but the few he did have were treasured above all else. To these few men he was generous to a fault, supporting them through thick and thin with his whole being. He counted amongst his friends Sipho Fauguneze and Emerson Moyo who had been in his stick since they left Depot RAR with the result that the death of Fauguneze had affected him very deeply.

The war was not a subject that Bukhosi Dube dwelt upon much. He had sworn allegiance to Rhodesia and to the RAR, but he did not see this in a political sense. The Regiment was a way of life, it had provided for his family for nearly fifty years. If the Regiment went to war then Dube went to war, it was part of his heritage. In his home village near Gwanda, to the south of Bulawayo, many of his school friends had left to join the freedom struggle, seeking a better life, with the promise of riches when the land was retaken from the whites. Dube knew that the day might come when he would have to face his friends in battle; brother against brother; that was the way life had worked out. He knew

---

53 Shona derivation of the word 'soldier'. The connotation is that to be referred to as a *Masodja*, one had to be blooded in battle; the title had to be earned.
54 Cooked Mealie (maize, corn) meal, part of the staple diet of the black population.
55 Opaque traditional sorghum beer.
56 A stinging nettle common in the Zambezi valley, brushing up against the nettle would result in the most excruciating rash that could literally drive a man mad in pain and discomfort.

that some of these friends had infiltrated back into the bush around their home village, their families continuing to support them. They did not interfere with the Dube family, they had respect, but they were intimidating the surrounding villagers and subverting the youth. This situation made returning to his home village for R&R difficult. Dube had been forced to move his young wife and son, for their protection, to an army house bordering Depot RAR, at the old St Stephens School at Balla Balla.

Sitting in the back of the jolting truck, Dube contemplated in his mind being transferred to 4 Independent Company from C Company, 1RAR. C Company had been as close to him as his own family. At first he enjoyed the informality created by the NS NCOs and Officers, their lack of discipline and their mostly slack attitude had been refreshing. They were much more considerate, going out of their way to make things as easy as possible. Sgt Smith and Lt Gibbs didn't have an air of superiority and seemed genuinely interested in their troops' welfare. He had been impressed with the way Sgt Smith had handled himself at his friend Fauguneze's funeral. The fact that Smith had broken down in front of the family showed to Dube that this man cared deeply about his men. That counted for something. Dube had decided begrudgingly that he liked Sgt Smith; although he would never show it, and would absolutely never say it. The young sergeant's inexperience provided a great deal of risk for the men in his section that meant he had to be watched like a hawk in the bush. Both Dube and Moyo and assured the others that they had matters in hand and they would guide the green Sergeant as best they could.

The issue that was bothering Dube greatly was that so many soldiers were dying. He had lost four close friends in the past year. This was more than he had lost in the previous three years in C Company.

The truck gave a sudden lurch to the left as the driver tried to avoid a gaping hole in the road. The driver skidded in the dust along the shoulder of the road, wrestling the heavy vehicle to a halt. Up ahead a wisp of black smoke twirled high into the air.

'Standby ... free your weapons ... standby for an ambush,' shouted Fullerton excitedly. The dust from the sudden stop drifted slowly over the occupants of the truck. The soft click could be heard as the FN's safety was pushed to 'Fire'. The diesel engine continued to idle loudly making the truck rattle and vibrate. Each occupant in the back was strapped in. In front of each outward-facing seat was a steel flap that could be dropped to allow the rifle to be pushed through. The flaps clanked loudly as they were unhitched.

'Driver! ... Reverse the vehicle; put it in the middle of the road,' called Fullerton urgently.

The Four-Five is open-topped, only the driver and passenger part of the cab is covered with a steel hatch to allow for an observer or gunner. Fullerton unstrapped himself and stood up to look out, performing a rapid 360°. If the ambush was going to be initiated it would have happened already. The vehicle inched backwards into the road the engine revving loudly.

Fullerton, sheltering his eyes from the sun, stared further down the road, scanning both sides.

'Fuck! … A Police Land Rover has hit a tin[57]. … It looks like a boosted tin.'

Smith also stood up, gazing out in the direction Fullerton was pointing; the gaping crater in front of them looked about a metre deep. The dirt around the hole was blackened by the blast; bits of twisted metal lay in the road.

'Sergeant Smith see if you can raise Jambezi on the radio … we are only about ten clicks away.' He then turned to face the men sitting in the back of the truck, 'Right we are going to exit out the back in single file … you will walk out along the tracks of our vehicle … *Chenjerai!* … Watch Out! The Gooks often lay APs[58] around a tin … *handei!* … Let's go!'

Gingerly the section exited the back of the truck moving back about fifty metres along the tracks in the road, then split into two groups, covering each side of the road.

'Sir, Jambezi reports that one of their POs[59] is due back from Vic Falls,' Smith called out.

'OK, Sergeant Smith take half your section twenty metres into the bush and walk up parallel with the road until we get level with the police vehicle. Go slowly.'

Fullerton took the other half of the section on the left hand side of the road while Smith went up the right. They advanced about fifty metres before the wrecked vehicle came into sight. The Land Rover had been vapourised from behind the cab; it had been a rear wheel detonation. The Police Land Rovers were built with a heavy-duty roll-cage, with steel plate on the floor of the cab; the occupants could strap themselves in. The Land Rover travelling at about 80km/h would have been lifted off the ground rear first, then bounced end over end maybe four times before coming to rest. Debris was spread along the road, the rear-differential lying nearly eighty metres from the site of the detonation.

'Sergeant Smith I want you to cover me, I am coming out into the

---

57 Landmine, can be boosted with two landmines place one on top of the other.
58 Anti-personnel mines.
59 Patrol Officer

road,' Fullerton called from the opposite side. Smith watched Fullerton walk out towards the vehicle cab, then stooping to look inside.

'Jesus … there are three of them in the front seat,' he shouted, pushing closer leaning inside. 'One of them has definitely had it … the other two look like they are breathing … it's a massive fucking mess! Smith come across and help me, the rest of you stay alert.'

The problem with mine detonations in the middle of a densely populated TTL was that the CTs might have heard the explosion and be tempted to come and have a look at their handiwork.

Fullerton and Smith worked quickly to get the two survivors out of the cab and off the road into the bush. They were very banged up, both unconscious. The blast had burst their eardrums; blood ran out of their noses and ears trickling down their cheeks. Their faces were swollen from the force of the blast making them almost unrecognisable, both had legs and arms broken. Smith administered morphine and put drips into both policemen. They worked as fast as they could to splint legs and arms to stop any further movement.

'There is no chance of a helicopter casevac out here,' stated Fullerton resignedly. He stood and shouted into the bush, 'Corporal Tovakare!'

'*Yebo Ishe.*' Tovakare came jogging into the road.

' … I want you to take two men and drive these people back to Vic Falls to the hospital.'

Tovakare nodded his understanding and shouted the names of two men who quickly joined them in the road. They carefully loaded the injured policemen into the back of the Four-Five, then zipped their dead colleague into a body bag and tied him onto the bench seat. Cpl Tovakare then left with instructions to return to the Jambezi Keep before nightfall.

'Well Sergeant Smith, we need to take a small ten click hike to the keep. Give them a call and tell them to expect us,' ordered Fullerton, back in control as if the horrible business of the landmine explosion was already a distant memory. He took out his map and compass and plotted a course.

The detachment now numbered seven in total. Fullerton followed by Dube the gunner with Smith in the rear. Standard patrol formation was single-file; this was the easiest to manage, reducing potential confusion, particularly in thick bush. Smith noted the relaxed attitude of the troops. Fullerton imbued confidence; the men obviously enjoyed his presence and leadership. *I should learn a few things here today*, Smith thought to himself. He had never been on a patrol with a senior officer before.

They had gone no more than two hundred metres when Fullerton raised his fist in the air to stop. The patrol knelt down facing alternately left and right. Fullerton made his way back down the line to where Smith was kneeling.

'Listen here you little Fuckwit, you are making too much noise,' hissed Fullerton loudly into Smith's ear. '… If you make any more noise you can go back to the road and wait for the truck. If you want to be a fucking amateur you will end up a dead amateur … you can get killed on your own time. *Wa nzwa nyere*? Do you understand?'

Smith blushed brightly with embarrassment, the rest of the section were watching the exchange. Fullerton had deliberated pulled the Sergeant up in front of his men as a way of demonstrating to them that he understood their concerns about being led by raw national servicemen. The familiar desperate feeling of complete isolation washed over Smith, the humiliation stabbed him like a knife, turning his mind into mush. He could not bear to reply or apologise, instead staring off into the middle distance. Satisfied that he had made his point, Fullerton stalked off to the front of the line.

Yes, it's a full time job keeping the young sergeant alive, thought Dube, as he glanced across at his friend Emerson Moyo who nodded back knowingly.

*

Bulawayo Road, 80km south of Wankie

Captain Vladimir Benkov, 'Comrade Vladimir' to his cadres, was observing the main tar road, the A8 between Bulawayo and Wankie. The time was approaching midday and the convoy from Bulawayo was due at any time. Not just any convoy, a heavy vehicle convoy, which included the most important heavy vehicles of all, petrol tankers.

Benkov had a stand-up disagreement with Chabanga about his plans to ambush a road convoy. Chabanga could not believe that the Soviet could suggest such a stupid thing.

'Have you any idea of the level of response? We will have a Territorial Company or worse an RAR Company in here in no time,' Chabanga had yelled.

'I need stability in this area to build my forces, to protect my arms caches. I cannot face a Rhodesian sweep[60],' objected Chabanga aggressively.

'You are a field commander in a war Comrade! Your duty is to prosecute the war to the greatest extent possible,' Benkov had suggested, taking the 'coaching' posture recommended by his superiors.

60 The process used by Rhodesian forces of spreading out attacking troops in line-abreast to flush out insurgents, sometimes in thick bush.

'Our mission is to win the support of the local population, to build our forces for the final thrust,' Chabanga retorted, in a condescending fashion.

Chabanga's superior attitude was starting to get under Benkov's skin.

'Comrade Chabanga, why are you afraid?' he asked as politely as possible for what was the most veiled of insults.

Chabanga carried the blood of the Matabele, descended from the Zulu, the Mzilikazi clan. Nobody accused him of cowardice. Nobody!

'… Don't you pretend to lecture me on the prosecution of our struggle! You are impudent! You have no idea of our pain or our hardship. How dare you insult me in this way!'

Chabanga shook his fist in the face of the Soviet, tempted to shoot him then and there. The argument, conducted in Russian, attracted the attention of the young cadres who looked on with concern.

Benkov, realising that he was skating on thin ice, replied respectfully, 'Alright Comrade Brigadier … but my orders are clear, we need to be seen to be aggressive in this area. What are your suggestions? You don't want to be outdone by ZANLA … by Mugabe, do you?'

That comment won the day. Chabanga avoided any discussion on his erstwhile allies. He did not trust Mugabe; the memories of ZANLA's brutality in the camps in Zambia still haunted him.

Benkov compromised on his plan by promising to spring the ambush further north of Lupane, then to make his exit to the west so the Rhodesians would think that they had infiltrated from the Botswana border and were returning there.

The Rhodesians had a system of convoys on all major roads. There were civilian convoys for passenger vehicles, there were convoys for caravans and cars with trailers, and there were the heavy vehicle convoys. At holiday time the convoys could count as many as two hundred vehicles. Police, mainly police reservists, who were mostly too old to be on the 'active' list, always escorted the convoys. The convoy escort comprised three, four or even five vehicles depending on the size of the convoy. The escort vehicles were Mazda pick-ups with a round roofless turret mounted in the middle of the rear tray. The turret was made of a thick steel wire overlapping mesh that was supposed to be bulletproof, though not necessarily RPG7-proof. Inside the turret was a single Browning .303 machinegun. The gunner, normally wearing a motorcycle helmet and goggles, could rotate the turret with his feet, pushing left and right. Some of the escort crews, driver, observer and gunner, could be in their seventies, old enough to have manned the turrets of 44 (Rhodesian) Squadron RAF Lancasters over Germany. The vehicles were not protected in any other way and relied on travelling at speed, over 120km/hr, to stay out of trouble. But of course, the heavy vehicles couldn't go much faster than 80km/hr even down hill.

Convoys were regularly attacked by ZIPRA but it was generally a haphazard affair with a few magazines expended on fully automatic, then a rapid departure. There were incidents of trucks and tankers being successfully attacked with RPG-7s but shooting from the side of the road at moving vehicles had proved to be difficult. *Today was going to be different* - Benkov had decided on a degree of experimentation. The spot he had chosen was a steep hill section with good cover provided by large granite rocks on the both sides of the road. The road followed a set of undulations, deep enough to provide dead ground when travelling in the interceding valleys.

The approaching convoy could be heard long before they saw it. Benkov nestled the RPG launcher in his arms, the missile already fixed in place. He had his fifteen freedom fighters stretched out in the rocks along the crest of the steepest undulation. They had all been briefed carefully via his interpreters. *Hopefully they all understand* – Benkov contemplated as he took up his position. This was the first premeditated ambush action for all the cadres in this band. They were all nervous but excited, flushed with the exuberance of youth, all shuffled in their positions.

Exactly on schedule the first escort vehicle appeared, followed by four horse and trailers all travelling at about 80km/h. It was possible to hear the drivers change down, double de-clutching, as they revved the engines to take on each steep rise. The freedom fighters watched as the front escort followed by the first five vehicles passed by. Then the 'target' appeared, three petrol tankers struggling up the hill, engines labouring. The vehicles ahead of the tankers rapidly gathered speed as they started down the other side, rapidly widening the gap to the first fuel tanker now half a kilometre behind.

Benkov stepped confidently into the road just behind the crest of the hill; the first tanker driver could not see him. The Soviet slowly and methodically lifted the launcher to his shoulder, taking aim roughly where he expected the truck to materialise in front of him. He took a deep breath to relax his body, slowly breathed out while striding forward to the crest of the hill. Pulling the trigger the booster fired and the expanding gasses exploded the projectile out of the tube with a thudding whoosh at 117m/sec. After 0.1sec the solid-fuel rocket fired sending heat washing over Benkov's face, increasing the speed of the projectile to 294m/sec. To the trained eye the launching flash and whitish blue-gray smoke provides a clear indication of an RPG launch. No such warning came to the driver of the tanker as the projectile entered the centre of the windscreen, travelled through the cab into 20,000 litres of petrol-blend[61]. The whole unit convulsed into bright yellow flame lifting in a churning cloud into the sky, followed instantly by black acrid smoke.

A cadre rushed into the road handing Benkov another loaded rocket launcher. The second tanker was only thirty metres behind the first, Benkov strode to the side of the road to get an angle on the second truck; it too disappeared in a mountain of smoke and flame, leaping hundreds of metres into the air, billowing and churning. The thick choking stench of burning diesel attacked the senses. The third tanker jerked to a halt, the driver jumped from the cab, hit the ground, turned and ran for his life down the hill. The ZIPRA cadres hidden in the rocks let rip with AK47, RPD and SKS[62], a hail of lead and green tracer raced down the hill in the direction of the rear escort vehicle that had skidded to a stop behind the third tanker. Dirt sprayed in the air around the vehicle as bullet strikes hit the compacted shoulder of the road.

Benkov was enjoying himself; he strode down the hill with his AKM now in his hands, no thought of seeking cover. He lifted his rifle to the shoulder, taking careful aim at the cab of the stricken escort vehicle, double tapping rounds down the hill.

The gunner in the turret of the escort vehicle recovered from the initial shock of the explosions in front of him. He opened up with the .303 Browning, shots flying high, trying desperately to bring the gun to bear on his attackers. The driver slammed the van into reverse speeding backwards completely undoing his gunner's aim. In seconds the concentrated fire turned the cab of the police escort vehicle into a bloody mess. The driver died with his foot flat on the accelerator with the van careening across the road, ploughing backwards into a tree. The lone .303 gunner fired bravely, swinging his turret wildly from side to side, hopelessly seeking his tormentors, terrified out of his wits.

Benkov considered killing the Browning gunner with another RPG round but his thoughts were interrupted by the return of the first two escort vehicles. Alerted by the violent explosions, they came hurtling back over the hill, firing blindly, their path blocked by the burning vehicles. The asphalt had been set alight by the intense heat, melting, running down the road in rivulets. The heat was so intense that some of the trees closer to the road spontaneously burst into flames.

Still standing in the road, Benkov casually signalled to his men, the attack group melted into the thick bush ... casualties nil. The cadres

---

61 The petrol in Rhodesia was blended with ethanol (alcohol) to extend the volume and lift the octane level. During the period of the oil embargo Rhodesians pioneered alternative fuel technology converting sugar cane into ethanol.
62 Semi-automatic carbine, Soviet Union, 10 round internal box magazine, 7.62x39mm

howled with delight, jumping up and down embracing each other then braking into raucous song as they marched off in single file. The police Browning's continued to fire forlornly into the bush behind. A good ten minutes passed before the third tanker exploded, ignited by the burning tar. The plume of rapidly rising smoke from the burning tankers lifted high into the sky, visible for miles in all directions.

The whole attack had lasted a single minute.

Just as expected, the next morning a platoon of territorials from 9th Battalion RR, on their six-week call-up, arrived at the ambush site. They followed-up for a day travelling due west, then lost the spoor after crossing a dirt road. 9RR searched up and down the road for four hours, checking for any sign. The CTs had simply vanished into thin air.

Mission accomplished.

6

Wankie TTL, near the Protected Village of Jambezi, 50km east of Victoria Falls

Ingwe Fullerton, together with Mike Smith and 2 Section, 2 Platoon, 4 Indep, continued his steady progress towards the Keep at Jambezi. The system of Protected Villages or 'Keeps' followed the same idea developed by the British in Malaya during the 1948 Emergency and the US Strategic Hamlet Program in Vietnam during the 1960's. The theory was to deny the terrorists access to food and information by providing the local population a haven from threats and intimidation. The PVs were places that provided schooling, medical services and accommodation if the need arose. The protected village system was administered by the Department of Internal Affairs (Intaf). The police also used PVs as bases. The program, while based on sound counter-insurgency principle, was deeply flawed. The freedom fighters called them 'concentration camps'; the local people hated them because of the forced removal, often far from their home villages, livestock and crops. Most often the promised services were not available and disease spread in the cramped conditions. For these reasons the PV system was a major freedom fighter target, plus an excellent source of propaganda.

The going was slow for the Fullerton detachment heading for Jambezi. The bush in the TTL was very sparse from drought and over-grazing. The terrain was mostly flat but with virtually no cover at all except for a few tufts of grass and small clumps of withered trees almost devoid of foliage. The ground was criss-crossed with paths and cattle trails leading every which way. The surface of the ground was bone dry, cracked; a few blades of grass eluded the constantly foraging goats and cattle. Resourceful and intelligent goats browsed low hanging branches by standing up on their hind legs or even climbed into trees. The result is that all the trees looked like they had been neatly pruned at the height of a two-legged goat.

The whole area looked like it had been swept with a giant straw broom. The villages were round pole-and-dagga (mud) huts interspersed with livestock kraals[63] made of thorn thicket. The villages and kraals were built close to each other in many cases only a few hundred metres apart. People wandered around doing their daily chores completely oblivious to the presence of the SF patrol. There was no sign of concern;

---

63 Afrikaans, animal pen or corral, it was important for livestock to be penned up at night to protect them from wild animals and theft. Thorn scrub provided the best building material as once it was wound and twined together it made an impenetrable barrier for man or animal.

many children ran up to look at the soldiers as they walked past, some waved. The black soldiers laughed and joked with them.

Fullerton stopped and scanned every open *vlei*[64] and cleared paddock before crossing. This was done either by skirting around or by spreading out in a sweep line, crossing at the trot. *You don't want to get caught in the open.*

Someway up ahead a band of freedom fighters had heard about the successful detonation of the mine from their informers. There were five in this small ZIPRA band. They had been living in the area for nearly two years and knew the area like the back of their hands. When they laid the mine they had instructed a few *mujibas*[65] to sit on the side of the road to warn any busses that came along. They did not want to draw too much attention to themselves as they enjoyed the freedom of living in the area, not wanting to deal with a SF sweep. The locals had looked after them really well and they had formed romantic relationships with the womenfolk. A message had been relayed to them by the area Political Commissar that they had better get more involved in 'The Struggle' or else, hence the begrudging laying of the mine. Their only mistake thus far, if that was what it was, had been the rape of a young girl who had rejected the advances of the group leader. She had informed her parents, who in turn informed the village Headman, who in turn had discussed it with the local Chief, who had agreed that punishment should be dispensed. The freedom fighters were, of course, oblivious to this.

The five freedom fighters, overcome with curiosity at the outcome of their handiwork, strolled along in the direction of the explosion without a care in the world, AKs and SKSs over the shoulder, talking loudly. They had trained a network of *mujibas* in the area and no reports of SF had been made; the message that three policemen had been killed arrived via bush-telegraph[66]. Unfortunately for them after the explosion the *mujibas* had all gone home for a rest during the heat of the day and did not see 4 Indep arrive.

Ingwe Fullerton saw them first, lifted his fist, the section instantly knelt down, facing alternatively left and right.

'42Alpha, I have five Charlie Tangos visual about five hundred metres to my front,' he whispered into the A76 mouthpiece strapped to his shoulder. Fullerton had to use the radio, as he could not call out to Smith or easily communicate with him, as he was a good 30m behind.

'Roger ... 44,' Smith replied trying to hide his sudden shock at being

---

64 Afrikaans, marshy, low-lying area.
65 Shona, civilian youth, running with and supporting insurgent operations, the "eyes and ears" of the insurgents normally aged between ten and sixteen.
66 A system of relay runners.

called on the radio.

'Right … I want you to carefully come up next to me, leopard-crawl … don't make a noise.'

Fullerton signalled the presence of enemy by lifting his fist, pointing his thumb down, and then showing five fingers. Using his forefinger and index finger pointing to his eyes to show that he had 'enemy visual', he stretched his arm out horizontally in the direction of the enemy with his hand fully extended vertically. To indicate the fact that he wanted the men to crawl up to his position he cupped his fingers inverted on the top of his head, the signal for 'come to me'. Slowly the patrol took to the ground; each man carefully crawled up level with Fullerton. It took what seemed an age for the men to crawl up into an extended line. They lay on the edge of a village with absolutely no cover other than the buildings themselves. Any attempt to run for cover would have alerted the CTs ahead. The period taken to crawl into position meant the CTs were now much closer. Fortunately none of the locals were close by to raise the alarm or panic.

Fullerton whispered into Smith's ear reassuringly, 'Ok, these Fuckers are going to cross ahead of us, to our left probably on the other side of the village. Just stay cool, this is going to be just fine.' He could see Smith was a little flushed.

Fullerton then lent over and tapped Dube on the shoulder pointing to a broken tree stump on the edge of the village about 50m in front to the left. That was the point at which he wanted him to open fire, the rest were to follow. He lifted one finger to Dube pointing once again to his own eyes, *You take the number one in the line.* Dube nodded his understanding, pulling the MAG, now supported on its bipod, into his shoulder. Looking back towards Smith, Fullerton showed three fingers with the same instruction. The sudden realisation, *Shit … number three is mine!*

The CTs came on, the last seconds of their lives ticking away. The leader stopped in a clearing ahead, well short of the designated stump. Smith's eyes were glued to the man's every movement. *What is he doing? Come on you prick, don't stop now.* Every man in the sweepline had a CT in his sights; they held their collective breath, still a little too far away for the perfect kill.

The CT leader scanned the village ahead, looking straight at the patrol's position. His eyes seemed to hesitate for a split second. He turned his head, unsure of what he had seen. At that instant a young woman emerged from the nearest hut, carrying a young child on her hip. She saw the sweepline of soldiers only metres away and screamed in fright. The CT whipped his head back to look at the disturbance, his eyes never focused; Dube unzipped him with a sustained burst. The patrol followed, the CTs were just over a hundred metres away, not an easy shot when lying prone. Smith thought he got his CT with the second double tap; the man seemed to spin around. Fullerton dropped number two where he stood. The rest of the CTs took off into the bush. The dust from the bullet strikes began to lift into a thick haze, hiding their rapid departure.

Fullerton leapt to his feet shouting, 'Come on … *KAJIMA*, run … let's go … sweep in line.' Charging off at a sprint Fullerton rapidly left the rest behind. They struggled to keep up … running past two dead CTs, chasing after the other three. Bullets ripped overhead, the crack and thump; one of the CTs was shooting back over his shoulder.

'To your right,' yelled Fullerton, pointing into the distance.

Smith, sucking for air tried to correct the angle of his run, lost his footing, tripped and sprawled into the dust. The dirt entered his eyes, nose and throat, in an agonising rush. The sweepline disappeared into the bush ahead. Rolling over trying to regain his feet Smith rubbed to clear his eyes of dirt, only succeeded in making it worse. *I can't see!* The dust was in his throat, making him break into a convulsive cough. Feeling he was about to suffocate he panicked. *I can't breath!* Blind fear gripped him as he struggled to get to his feet, the bulk of his pack and webbing weighing him down. Eventually he hauled himself onto his knees using his rifle as a crutch. His chest heaved judderingly, spit and saliva running down his chin. Still coughing violently, air just would not come, his lungs burned. *I am going to die!* Holding his eyes tightly shut, his head spun wickedly. Still blinded, his eyes misted in tears mixed with the dust, created an excruciating irritation.

Slowly getting to his feet, Smith felt the air returning to his lungs in short gulps, his chest still heaving from the shock of the fall. He tried to call out but no sound would come from his raw throat. His vision still blurred, the radio hand-piece hung dangling from its cord. Still flustered, he grabbed a water bottle from his waist pouch; pouring water into his throat, the relief was painfully slow. He held his head back, spreading water over his face to clear his eyes, shaking his head at the same time. Still disorientated, he spun around looking for signs of the sweepline. There was nobody in sight … listening carefully, there was no sound, and then making a decision, he began to trot forward. A few isolated shots rang out from up ahead, *difficult to know how far*.

Movement up ahead … Smith stopped in his tracks, a CT had been hiding in an ant-bear[67] hole. Not seeing Smith's approach, the CT had waited for the sweepline to pass and was now looking around to make his escape. Smith stepped behind a tree, slowly lifting his rifle, aiming at the mound; he could only see the top of the man's head. *Keep both*

67 Aardvark.

eyes open look down the sights. He double tapped … two dusty strikes … *missed … Fuck!*

He began to run, his legs taking over his body, everything seemed to slow down, in slow motion, legs pumping, and no sound, just legs pumping, pumping … rifle shooting. *Fire and movement … Fire and movement … Move or you die …* his training ringing in his ears.

The CT dived out of the hole, rolled onto his feet, digging for traction in the dust. Smith was closing on him fast, trying to aim his rifle; firing again, it was no use, he missed. The man was fast, the distance between them rapidly increased. Smith reached the edge of a wide *donga*[68] then he spotted the man running down the sandy bottom. The bank was too steep to climb down, too high to jump. Choosing to run along the top he could see the CT ahead of him, the man still gaining distance. Smith stopped to take aim at the fleeting figure, fired twice watching bullet strikes in the dust. The CT made a mistake, he looked back, not seeing the tangle of tree roots ahead, he tripped and fell. Smith saw his opportunity, fired again, the magazine emptied - *Fuck!* - the frustration was punishing. His brain drenched in adrenaline, he dropped the empty magazine in the dirt, clawed for a replacement in his chest webbing - *Please don't let him get away*. The man was getting back to his feet. Clip, cock, fire … TAP … TAP. The CT was hit in the small of his back, his body seemed to be thrown forward, rolling him over. The man writhed in the dust trying to grab at the pain, the impact of the FN round was devastating, unforgiving, the damage too great. The man's body slowed its gyration as his life began to depart. Smith kept firing, emptying the magazine, the body jerking with every strike until the man lay still.

All was suddenly quiet. A bird called in the distance. Smith stood on the top of the bank looking down at his victim, breathing hard … trying to comprehend what had just happened. His mind was a churning jumble of thoughts and emotions, none making any sense. His whole body seemed to be shaking from a combination of shock, exertion and the adrenalin rush.

Ingwe Fullerton and the rest of the patrol appeared on the opposite side of the *donga*.

'Well fuck me gently if our little NS wanker has not slotted himself a Gook? Absolutely fucking amazing!' He turned to the rest of the group of soldiers and pointed expansively across the *donga* towards where

---

68 Eroded river or stream, normally dry but a rushing torrent after a thunderstorm, often steep sided and boulder strewn with sometimes very thick vegetation along the banks.

Smith was standing.

'MASODJA,' he shouted.

'MASODJA' came the reply in unison.

Mike Smith looked down into the gully where the dead man lay. He had taken a life this day. Thankful that his men could not see his shaking hands ... he didn't know whether to laugh or cry.

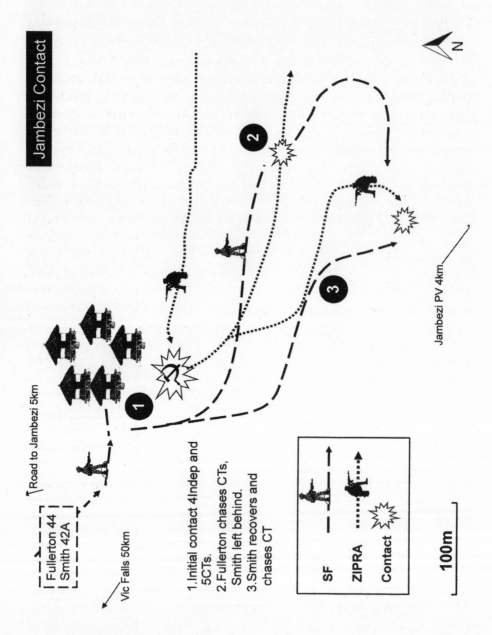

Jambezi Contact

Road to Jambezi 5km

Fullerton 44
Smith 42A

Vic Falls 50km

1. Initial contact 4Indep and 5CTs.
2. Fullerton chases CTs, Smith left behind.
3. Smith recovers and chases CT

Jambezi PV 4km

N

SF
ZIPRA
Contact

100m

7

ZIPRA Base Camp, Lupane TTL, north Matabeleland

Benkov and his group returned to the base camp at Lupane to a tumultuous welcome. The camp and local villages were alive with the news of the destroyed convoy. The bus drivers passing through had given a graphic account of the devastation. Such a successful attack had not happened on this scale before. Chabanga was seething inside. He welcomed the group back for appearances sake but he was desperately concerned. Not only could this Soviet soldier undermine his authority, but he could also make him look ridiculous in front of his own men.

Chabanga knew that power was based on a combination of personal strength and controlled brutality. Chabanga ruled his forces by fear. They needed to fear him more than they did the enemy. This same principle applied to the local population, but the power needed to be tempered with respect. Chabanga recalled the words of Lookout Masuku, 'only if you treat the population with respect do you find it easier to fight the enemy. We are fighting for the liberation of these people. If we kill them, who are we going to rule?' The local population needed to understand that his was absolute power. No opposition was to be tolerated and unstinting support was demanded. Masuku's orders were also clear regarding informers. He had ordered that all informers were to be summarily executed. 'An informer is more dangerous than someone who is carrying a gun,' he had said.

Chabanga had made a few examples when he first took over control of Northern Front Region 1. Some local Headmen had refused to provide assistance, defying his instructions, wishing instead to maintain the old ways. In the new socialist order there was no room for tribal and clan loyalties. These needed to be broken down so that the government of the people by the people could be managed centrally. *This is what the People wanted*. Chabanga was surprised as to how many Chiefs and Headmen he had to kill to get the message across. In fact, simple killings had not been enough, he had been forced to resort to torture in some cases. He left the bodies in places where there could be no doubt as to what had transpired. *It had to be done, the sacrifice of the few for the good of the many*. That was all in the past the people were now good supporters of the new Nkomo regime.

If Chabanga had erred in his leadership it was in the area of military aggression. He interpreted his orders as being simply to subdue and control his area. He was to build up his forces through continued infiltration and to recruit from the local population, to be sent back over the border to be trained. He had built up a considerable supply of arms and ammunition, housed in a network of arms caches. This was all in readiness for the eventual political capitulation of the illegitimate Rhodesian regime at the hands of the British. The real battles in the country were to come when Nkomo, through his military instrument, ZIPRA, was to take control of the country to make sure that Mugabe and the Shonas did not assume power. This was precisely why ZIPRA had focused on building up conventional forces, tanks, heavy guns, aircraft and logistical support. Some men were even being trained to fly MIG-21s in East Germany. *Nkomo and his ZIPRA forces will crush Mugabe when the time comes.*

Despite his present military role, Chabanga harboured political aspirations. For this reason, exposing himself to risk of injury or death in battle was to be avoided. *What purpose would my untimely death serve? To deprive the nation of such a gifted leader would be a needless waste.* Chabanga often contemplated the future, his rise to political office, the power and the glory. *What was the use of power, of the struggle, if the trappings of victory did not follow. The People will reward me with land, houses, and many cattle. I will choose the farm I want, it will be taken from the white settlers.*

In Chabanga's mind there was little point in taking on the Rhodesians at what they did best, counter-insurgency operations. This would result in the loss of too many trained men who were going to be needed in the future. For this reason he deliberately did not undertake large-scale attacks on infrastructure and the local white farmers. Attacks were only undertaken when the opportunity was right, with little chance of casualties. He also made sure that the attacks, if they were made, were well away from his base in Lupane. He authorised these attacks every few weeks just to keep his men involved and motivated. Chabanga also enjoyed his monthly trip to Bulawayo by bus to see his family and talk to his own local informers. Things had been running very smoothly indeed.

Now Chabanga had this white Soviet in his midst who did not respect his authority, inspiring the newly arrived cadres with his attack on the convoy. Chabanga's other problem was he did not want this Russian getting captured, that would be disastrous. He contemplated the options, *Maybe a death in the night is a solution? That is how my forefathers dealt with such difficulties, the assegai or poison, it matters not which.*

'Comrade Chabanga,' called Benkov, in his respectful way. 'I wish to discuss with you some ideas I have for another attack, we can cause even greater damage.'

Chabanga could not believe his ears. *Another attack so soon! You must be mad!*

'By all means Comrade Benkov, I would be delighted to hear of your plan,' Chabanga replied with poorly disguised surprise. A deep feeling of foreboding washed over him.

*

At that very moment walking down a dirt road to the north of the village of Lupane was, Sgt Cephas Ngwenya, 3 Group, Selous Scouts[69]. The Selous Scouts were an elite unit trained in long-term infiltration of enemy held areas, internally and outside of the country, coupled with highly developed observation skills. They were the supreme masters of intelligence-gathering through observation. Both white and black soldiers manned the unit; the black soldiers were drawn mainly from the RAR but included policemen drawn from Police Special Branch and Ground Coverage. Sgt Ngwenya had originally been a member of 1 Troop, Selous Scouts, part of the original group of men that formed the unit. He had transferred to 3 Group when it was formed to operate amongst his own Matabele people.

The Selous Scouts were trained in so-called 'pseudo' operations where they were taught to pose as insurgents, to infiltrate the enemy organisation. They were taught how to approach a village, how to approach a band of terrorists in the field, passwords, pass signs, liberation songs and how to collect food from the local population. The skills the Scouts were taught included 'turning' captured terrorists; the unit had recruited a good many 'converts' who now fought against their previous comrades.

Ngwenya was not a physically imposing man despite his family name, *Ngwenya* meaning 'crocodile' in siNdebele. He was slightly built but he had the hunting instinct of a crocodile; silence, patience, speed, then the attack, vicious and deadly. He knew the Lupane area well having been brought up not far to the south in a region called Tjolotjo. Dressed like a poor peasant subsistence farmer, his posture and demeanour reinforced that impression.

Sgt Ngwenya was the single-man advance party for a Selous Scout operation in Lupane. The briefing he had received indicated that the operation was going to take at least three weeks, maybe longer. It would appear that the destruction of the road convoy to the north had attracted somebody's attention. For the local freedom fighters, these

---

69 3 Group, Selous Scouts was set up by the commander of the Selous Scouts to specialise in operations against ZIPRA in Matabeleland. This was necessary because of the very different command and control structure and strategy of ZIPRA when compared with ZANLA in other parts of the country.

were definitely the wrong sort of people.

Ngwenya walked down the dirt road comfortable with what lay ahead. He needed to establish the terrorist presence and identify the area in which they were based. Once he had refined the general location of the terrorists through talking to the local people, he would call for the rest of his team waiting in Wankie. He had hidden his weapon, radio and kit in a warthog burrow, to be retrieved later.

8

Jambezi Protected Village, east of Victoria Falls

Captain Fullerton and Sergeant Smith stood in front of the gates of the Keep at Jambezi. Someone on top of the earth wall gave a shout and the gates slowly opened. Standing in the entrance was a young Police Section Officer who was in command. The policeman was wearing a torn light blue T-shirt under his chest webbing. The T-shirt had the words 'Cheers Gook' emblazoned below a skull and crossbones clutching a beer. He had an FN by his side, green shorts, and black smooth-soled 'clandestine' 'takkies', really old style hockey boots but with smooth, trackless soles. The only indication that he was a policeman was his cap, which was the same 'best dress' police cap he would have worn if he manned a speed-trap in downtown Bulawayo. The Section Officer gave them a warm welcome, introducing them to his two Patrol Officers, his Senior Constable and three Intaf personnel.

'Welcome to Jambezi Captain Fullerton! It seems you have had a busy day,' said the PO with a manic smile floating across his face. His eyes flicking left and right, taking in the number of RAR soldiers that had arrived.

'Yes, nothing like a bit of killing to brighten up a dull afternoon,' replied Fullerton with a broad smile, quite relaxed after the excitement of the day.

Smith was taken aback at the friendliness with which they were received; he detected signs of relief on their faces. *Why are these people so pleased to see us?*

It was virtually dark by the time they entered the PV; the stars could already be seen clearly in the evening sky. Smith stood in the middle of the keep and looked around. The protected village was rectangular, the outer perimeter was a steel-mesh fence topped with barbed wire. Inside of that was a compacted earth wall that had been pushed up by bulldozers, leaving a shallow 'moat' all the way around. The moat was dry dirt, the walls too steep to climb. The flat-topped earth wall stood at about five metres. The top was about two metres wide and easy to walk along. At each corner was a machinegun emplacement with a steel-framed corrugated iron roof topped with sandbags. Inside the keep were a number of buildings, school, clinic, administrative buildings and barrack accommodation. There was also a large ablution block and a canteen. A steel water tank on a high steel lattice frame dominated the centre of the Keep that doubled as an OP[70]. The earth walls had rooms

---

70 Observation Post or Observation Position.

built into them all the way around making them cool and comfortable. In addition, there was a system of slit trenches connected to a mortar pit, and a few underground trenches and bunkers covered by concrete slabs.

As they entered the Keep preparations were underway for the evening with an 81mm mortar being mounted in its pit, mortar rounds were being placed at the ready and the MAGs on tripods on fixed lines placed in the four gun emplacements. At rough count Smith figured there were about fifteen policemen and Intaf personnel. The water tower had two men on it and it looked like two men in each of the four gun emplacements.

Through the discussion with Smith and Fullerton, the policeman managed to ascertain that the man who had died in the landmine explosion, was a young NS police officer. He had only been with them for a week. There was a momentary silence as the group of policemen absorbed the information. The Section Officer agreed that they would go out the next day to collect the bodies of the dead CTs and talk to the locals. They also needed to establish whether the CTs in the contact were the same as those described by their informants.

An important evening routine for each SF c/sign on deployment was to send a sitrep (situation report), including their grid reference location, through to their respective bases. The combined sitreps for all c/signs in the unit were then aggregated and forwarded to the JOC, which in the case of Op Tangent[71], the operational area for most of Matabeland, was 1 Brigade HQ at Brady Barracks in Bulawayo. When contacts had been made or other important information gleaned, this was then sent on to the HQ of Combined Operations, COMOPS, in Salisbury, via Army HQ. The whole analysis and transfer of information was co-ordinated by the Rhodesian Intelligence Corps (RIC). All dead and captured CTs were transferred to the police Special Branch (SB). The dead were photographed and fingerprinted and their weapons' ballistics were analysed to try and trace their historic activities. The living 'captures' were then subjected to interrogation.

Smith completed his sitrep for c/sign 42Alpha, giving a brief description of their contact, which was duly transmitted by 4 Indep to sub-JOC Wankie, then JOC Tangent in Bulawayo. In the RIC Ops room at 1 Brigade a middle-aged Staff Sergeant tore the telex message off the machine and cast his eye rapidly down the list of c/signs. *Oh no ... Mike has been in another contact!* The Staff Sergeant was Mike Smith's father, Henry, doing his regular weekly duty-night in the RIC Ops room. He took up a few coloured pins from the desk, wrote the c/signs on small

71 Operational Area – most of the Province of Matabeleland

slips of paper and jammed them into the large scale map of the Op Tangent area, he hesitated when he got to 42Alpha, held the pin in his hand for a few seconds thinking about his son, then carefully put it in place. *What am I going to tell Helen when I get home?*

After the last light 'stand-to', the 4 Indep soldiers were shown to various empty rooms mainly located in the sides of the earth wall. Fullerton and Smith were duly invited to dine with the Section Officer, quick to point out that they had a good stock of cold beer. They clearly did not get too many visitors. Smith felt comfortable although it did seem a bit confined, not being able to see out to the horizon. He was so used to sleeping on the ground in the bush that sleeping in a small room felt claustrophobic.

Smith dismissed his men to their quarters, listening for a few moments to their banter with the policemen manning the gun emplacements. He wished he could understand all that they said. Moyo was laughing loudly at a joke somebody had made.

The hot showers and the opportunity to put on clean clothing were greatly appreciated. The troops took the opportunity to wash their uniforms and clean their rifles and equipment. Dube strolled over to the police cook to ensure that he was on top of his game. He carried various ingredients contributed by the men to the evening meal. Smith detected a few clear instructions being issued, food was one of the few subjects that Dube was prepared to discuss.

The Keep had a public address system with large conical speakers attached to the water tower directed to the four points of the compass. The policemen had connected the speakers to a stereo turntable. As Smith stepped into the shower the sound of Uriah Heap's, *Easy Living*[72], boomed out,

This is a thing I've never known before
It's called easy livin'
This is a place I've never seen before
And I've been forgiven

Easy livin' and I've been forgiven
Since you've taken your place in my heart

The keyboard belting out, Smith sang along at the top of his voice at the same time playing the air-guitar.

Somewhere along the lonely road
I had tried to find you

72 *Easy Livin*, Ken Hensley, © EMI Music Publishing. 1972

Day after day on that windy road
I had walked behind you

Easy livin' and I've been forgiven
Since you've taken your place in my heart

Smith suspected that the local villagers knew the words to the song off-by-heart, probably forced to listen to the LP *Demons & Wizards* all too often. Some would argue that this would be a form of torture in itself.

Fullerton and Smith presented themselves for dinner in green army issue vests, shorts and their combat boots, their rifles in one hand and their chest webbing in the other. What followed was a meal of steak, roast potatoes and vegetables, cooked for all occupants of the Keep. The black soldiers preferred *sadza* instead of potatoes. Fullerton and Smith threw down a few beers, deciding not to over do it … *who knows what the next day could bring?* The SO and his staff, on the other hand, were keen for a serious drinking session, drowning their sorrows after the death of one of their compatriots. At about 9pm Smith and Fullerton excused themselves preparing to retire to bed. The policemen drank well into the night, the music collection getting a good hearing. As Smith suspected, the record collection reflected the enigmatic tastes of the SO. He went to sleep to the blaring sounds of Uriah Heap, Status Quo's *On the Level*, and Jethro Tull's *Aqualung*.

*

A characteristic of mortars is that they can be fired from a good distance from the target. The Soviet 82mm mortar has a range of around four kilometres. The problem with operating mortars is that the crew have to know the range and bearing for the shot to be accurate. The other thing is that mortars are heavy to carry, the tube, the base plate and the ammunition. If the crew cannot be directed onto the target, without an accurate range and bearing, then the crew must be able to see the target and the fall of shot. Another thing to consider is if the crew fire from one place for too long, the enemy will figure out where they are and fire back. This was the predicament that the band of freedom fighters faced when they decided to mortar Jambezi Keep on this particular night. What they also could not possibly have known was that *Ingwe* Fullerton had taken up residence in the Keep for the night.

When a mortar fires it makes a distinctive, loud, thudding

Piv..v..v..v..vt sound. This was the sound that Fullerton heard when he was taking a leak on the way to bed. The sound is so distinctive, so terrifying, he instantly screamed 'MORTAAAAR', running out into the open quad, shouting on the top of his voice. The first bomb had reached the apex of its trajectory and was on its way down. Piv..v..v..v..vt, another bomb was on its way. Fullerton dashed to the ladder at the base of the water tower. The first bomb exploded just short of the western facing earth wall.

Wrapped in his sleeping bag, Smith sat bolt upright, trying to comprehend the noise. He had never been mortared before. The second bomb hit, this time on the top of the earth wall. Smith fell off the wooden cot he was sleeping on, trapped in the sleeping bag, kicking wildly to get out, … The third bomb hit just on the inside of the earth wall, a deafening explosion rumbling over the camp … Feeling around on the floor for his combat boots … the fourth bomb hit the middle of the compound. Crawling in the darkness Smith was vaguely aware of Fullerton bawling instructions. *Is he calling me?* The fifth bomb struck, just outside the entrance to Smith's dugout. Dirt fell from the roof; dust swirled into the room setting Smith off on another coughing fit.

Boots on … chest webbing… rifle … Smith crawled to the door and looked outside. A sixth bomb hit the concrete roof of the ablution block just as the MAG on the western wall opened up in the direction of the mortar flashes. The MAG on fixed lines, attached to a tripod, has a cyclic rate of fire of close to 1,000 rounds per minute over a range of 1,200 metres. They were probably not effective but the red tracer rounds made for an impressive show.

The vibration from the last mortar round must have bumped the record player, because the air suddenly exploded with an opening guitar riff, and then,

> *Get down deeper … and down*
> *Down down deeper … and down*
> *Down down deeper… and down*
> *Get down deeper and down*

Not wanting to run out into the open, Smith looked across the centre of the Keep. The police Section Officer was in the mortar pit with one of his constables. Another bomb struck the earth wall. They both seemed completely calm, almost relaxed, as if discussing a fuel requisition, the policeman was naked except for his police cap and his white 'jockey' underpants with a cigarette trapped between his lips.

Want all the world to see
To see you're laughing
And you're laughing at me

The constable stood next to the tube holding a projectile. The policeman looked up from the site and bellowed loudly, 'FIRE' as if calling shot at El Alamein, the constable, standing right next to him, dropped the bomb down the tube, then another, then another, as fast as he could, Pvvvssst ... Pvvvvvvst ... Pvvvvvst.

I have all the ways you see
To keep you guessing
Stop your messing with me

Get down deeper ... and down

Fullerton by this time had climbed on top of the water tower watching the fall of shot and calling down corrections. He was really making no difference at all, drowned out by the booming Status Quo, *Down Down*[73],

Down down deeper and down
Down down deeper and down

The MAG gunners in the gun emplacement on the western wall had called out the name for the CT firing position, 'ELECTRIC CIRCUUUUSSSS'. With the police sense of humour, they had named all the prearranged targets after nightclubs in Bulawayo and Salisbury. As it transpired, they were quite used to being mortared and had a set of co-ordinates already worked out for each of the most popular CT firing positions. As the attack was coming from the west, the policemen knew that there were only two positions where the CTs could see the fall of shot and fire at the same time. It took four rounds for the SO to get onto the Electric Circus target and he then dropped a para-illuminating round. The area to the west lit up like daylight ... he then dropped another eight bombs, lifting fire slightly with every shot. *The Gooks would be on the move.*

I have found out you see
I know what you're doing
What you're doing to me

73 *Down Down*, Francis Rossi and Bob Young, 1974, Vertigo Records

Down down deeper and down

The song finished, the crackle of the record player as the turntable continued to turn, the needle sending out a loud, scrape … scrape … scrape.

The attack stopped as quickly as it started, the CTs had dropped ten bombs onto the Keep from a range of +-1,500 metres. The return fire from the police had not been deadly accurate but enough to encourage the CTs to call it a night. One CT got winged with a slight flesh wound; his was the only injury on either side.

The night returned, once again, to its peaceful quiet. The crickets started up their noisy buzzing … a cow bellowed in the distance.

The poor bastard doing a dump in the ablution block pulled the chain … *Man what a shit that would have been?*

*

Fullerton was up at first light; he looked in on Smith in his dugout, then nonchalantly observed, 'We are going to look for those Gooks that mortared us last night … then we are going to find the Gook we missed yesterday.'

Smith mumbled an acknowledgement. He had slept fitfully after the shock of the mortar attack. The contact of the previous day also played over and over in his mind, the sight of the CT he had shot falling to the ground, twitching in death. The others seemed to take it all in their stride.

Nobody was hurt in the mortar attack, getting revved at Jambezi was simply a part of the natural scheme of things. To Smith's astonishment Fullerton was completely unfazed, almost as if he had enjoyed the experience, he joked loudly with the policemen. His confidence was infectious.

'… Was that your first mortar stonking Smithy?' Fullerton enquired over breakfast.

The policemen all looked across at Smith waiting for an answer.

'Yes Sir, it was,' he replied trying to sound blasé.

'I remember a bush trip to Vila Salazar on the Mozambique border … we were mortared most nights … you get used to it,' added Fullerton encouragingly.

The policemen all nodded their agreement … *Ja getting stonked by mortars is not so bad!*

Part B of the day's plan was already taken care of. When the Keep gates were opened, a lone CT, quite dead, was sitting propped against a tree. His AK and his webbing lay next to him. It would appear that the local Chief, concerned that justice had not been meted out successfully by the army the previous day, had dispensed a bit of 'rough' justice for himself. The CT's throat was cut from ear to ear.

Fullerton showed the policemen where the contact had taken place on the map, giving accurate directions to the bodies. The police drove off through the bush in their Land Rover and Fullerton and Smith went off to inspect the CT mortar position. They found the position without too much difficulty, the imprint left by the 82mm mortar base plate very clear in the hard ground. The pounding had driven the base plate deep into the soft soil. The CTs had abandoned a backpack used for carrying the mortar bombs. Their escape was clearly to the southeast. Fullerton bent down to examine the *spoor* and the rest of the section did the same.

'I think there were seven,' stated Fullerton authoritatively.

'*Hayi Ingwe,*' replied Dube, 'No, I think there are nine.'

Dube took a twig and carefully circled each footprint, showing the differences, like instructing a young child, he explained his conclusion. The practice of 'reading' the ground is instilled in young tribesmen from the time they can walk. In areas where communication is difficult, being able to tell who is about and which direction they are walking in is important. In this way, in the context of a village for example, if a child needs to know where his mother is, he simply reads the ground. He can tell whether she is visiting neighbours, working in the fields or fetching water. More importantly, if a stranger is in the area, the local people reading the ground can tell where the person has walked, how long ago, and from the *spoor*, roughly how old, male or female, injured or healthy. For Dube and the others this was second nature. Access to this ability, to read the ground and the rural environment, was the supreme advantage for a *mukiwa* posted to the RAR.

'*Tatenda,* thank you, well done Dube, does everyone agree?' enquired Fullerton, to a general nodding of heads and mumbled consent.

'Right, Sergeant Smith … call up the Keep and tell them what we have found and that we will begin follow-up immediately. … Also tell them to call sub-JOC in Wankie on the big-means[74] to inform them of the new developments. We may need some help later in the day.'

What help is he talking about? We have no Fireforce in the area; the nearest help is two hours away by truck … for fuck sakes! The feeling of uncertainty and foreboding returned. Smith's stomach seemed to be holding a flock of vicious butterflies.

74 TR48, HF radio.

The routine for follow-up started in the same way as it did the day before. Smith was now wide-awake, as he did not want to get another ear bashing. Within a few minutes, Fullerton called a halt and gestured for Smith to come forward. He pointed to the ground; there was clear evidence of a pool of blood that had dried in the sandy soil.

'Looks like a Gook got hit by a mortar; he is not bleeding too badly … probably just a flesh wound. This could be our lucky day.'

Smith tried not to show his feelings; he did not trust himself to speak, simply nodding his agreement, stomach already in a knot … *Our Lucky Day??!!*

As the morning progressed, it was clear the wounded CT had not been successful in stopping the bleeding as every five or six metres a telltale drop of blood could be seen in the dirt. The CTs changed the direction of their escape more to the north. This was a heavily populated TTL, the follow-up team passed through village after village, endless cultivated fields. The rains had yet to begin so nothing had been planted.

Both Smith and Fullerton had their radios turned on but set on low volume so as not to be too distracting, the sense of hearing was absolutely vital in the bush.

'Hello 44 … this is Yellow 2, do you read … Over?'

Both radios came to life. Fullerton's personal c/sign was 44.

'Yellow 2 this is 44 I have you fives,' he replied.

Who is Yellow 2? Smith thought. The answer came immediately.

'Roger 44 … we are Arty from Vic Falls, we heard you might need some help … over.'

Artillery! Smith had been careful to relay Fullerton's message via the Keep in full. 4 Indep had clearly interpreted the message that help was actually required!

'Bloody hell Smithy, we have a troop of guns at our disposal,' said Fullerton with renewed excitement.

'Yellow 2, exactly where are you … Over,' he enquired.

'44 … we are on the main drag[75], at the turn off to the Keep … Over.'

'Roger, Yellow 2 we are about eight clicks to your east. We are following nine CTs in a north-easterly … direction, *spoor* is approximately ten hours old … Stand-by.'

Fullerton stopped, took out his map and quickly worked out the grid reference. He then transmitted the reference in the 'clear', that is, without the use of shackle and button codes.

'Copied 44 we have your loc, standing-by … Yellow 2, out.'

---

75 Road, dirt roads were sometimes dragged by a vehicle towing chained together tyres. This helped to detect the tracks of insurgents crossing the road. The road from Victoria Falls to Kazangula had a 'drag' on each side of the main tar road for this purpose.

What could Arty possibly do to help our follow-up? Smith thought to himself incredulously.

The day got progressively hotter making the going slow and exhausting. This area was supposed to be crawling with CTs so Fullerton wanted to be as careful as possible.

Up ahead, the CT mortar team had once again buried their mortar in an abandoned prospecting trench, covered the arms cache with dirt and cut branches, then gone off to catch a bit of sleep. Their base was a large granite *kopje* complex that had a commanding view of the surrounding bush. The last thing on their minds was an RAR follow-up group so close.

The patrol reached the place where the CTs had buried their mortar at about four in the afternoon. Fullerton carefully marked the spot on his map, he was careful not to disturb the area, not wanting the CTs to think that the arms cache had been discovered. He called the section together.

'Okay, it looks like our Gooks have buried the mortar over there,' he said pointing to the newly cut branches. 'This means that they are likely to be very close. … It looks like they have moved off in that direction,' he added gesturing towards a heavily wooded area dominated by a large granite *kopje*. Looking at the map, it was a large complex probably four or five kopies, heavily broken by granite boulders with very large trees growing through the rocks.

Smith studied the thick bush ahead with the massive granite rock formations, he paled at the thought - *You could hide a Battalion in there! Please don't say you want us to go there.*

'Smithy we are going to have a little fun this afternoon,' said Fullerton with a broad smile on his face.

'Yellow 2 this is 44 do you read, Over'.

The radio connection was made with the artillery. Fullerton established that Yellow 2 had two guns with him.

'Roger Yellow 2 … Fire Mission.'

Fullerton read out the map reference which was the closest *kopje*, then the references for the other four marked on the map. Smith had learned about calling in an artillery fire mission when at SInf[76], but never thought he would actually do it. The whole country only had two batteries of guns.

'Copied 44, we will fire one round to range, talk us onto the target.'

The old World War II 25-pounders had a range of a maximum of 13,000m; here they were firing at a range of about 10,000m. Their rate of fire was between six to eight rounds per minute depending on the gun crews. Fullerton's plan, which he quickly explained to the waiting

76 School of Infantry, Gwelo (Gweru)

section, was to stonk the kopje, and in so doing; flush out the CTs who they would then shoot. *Sounded pretty straightforward.* He then spread the section out in a line well short of the *kopje* but with a good field of fire.

The first round came screaming over, a high-pitched SSSSHHHHFFFFGGG, landing just at the base of the *kopje* with a huge explosion of dust and debris.

'Add one hundred,' called Fullerton into the radio. This gave the gunners a very good idea of how well they had laid their guns. Another round came over landing right on top of the *kopje*, shattering a large tree.

'On target,' Fullerton called excitedly.

'Target ident confirmed ... standby... Ready,' came the Arty gunner's reply.

'Shot!' called Fullerton into the radio.

What followed was a sight to behold. The gunners put six shells onto each of the targets. The explosions gave a deafening thump as they impacted deep in the rocky outcrop. The impact on the granite rocks was spectacular as the rock fragments turned into the worst type of shrapnel. Smoke and dust lifted into the late afternoon sky. The sound of the shells as they passed overhead was chilling. *You don't want to be on the other end of that.*

Sure enough, about half way through the shelling, two CTs came sprinting out from the base of the *kopie.* They were really moving, looking back at the devastation behind them. The section opened up from about two hundred metres, they both went down in a hail of bullets.

The Fire Mission was completed and Fullerton congratulated the artillery on 'good shooting'. He confirmed the two kills.

'Yellow 2 can you pick my c/sign up on the main drag, I need a lift back to 4s loc[77].' *Thank goodness for that.* The men were exhausted. Smith felt like he could curl up and sleep where he stood.

All the members of 42Alpha smiled broadly and slapped each other on the back. *Man are we gonna get pissed tonight.* Clearly Ingwe Fullerton had satiated his requirement for 'hondo' for the time being, he now wanted to address his other two major interests,.

---

77 4 was the c/sign for 4 Indep at Victoria Falls. Voice procedure was not to talk about locations by their name but rather by their c/sign.

9

4 Independent Company (RAR) base camp, Sprayview airfield, Victoria Falls

The ageing telex machine in the Radio Room at 4 Indep clattered into life. The duty NCO watched as the machine finished printing its message marked TOP SECRET, Major Peacock's eyes only. The NCO ripped the message off the machine and strode purposefully into Maj Peacock's office.

He saluted smartly, 'Message from 1 Brigade Sir', then handed over the message, turned and left. Very few of the soldiers in 4 Indep referred to Maj Peacock by the customary *Ishe*. Peacock had also made no attempt to learn any of the local black languages; his superior pommie[78] attitude was always too obvious.

It would appear that the camp was to receive some important visitors. The message informed Peacock that a SADF[79] delegation would be visiting him the next day and he was to render any assistance that they may require. Major Peacock was the highest-ranking regular officer in the area.

Anybody who was not infantry in the army was referred to as either 'wankers' or 'jam-stealers'. This was an old army reference inferring that those in the rear echelon always got first access to the jam, thus denying the Infantry their share. Artillery took the cake as 'wankers'; they were in permanently based fixed firing positions, they could not drive on dirt roads for fear of landmines and needed an escort wherever they went. The gunners sat around all day waiting for instructions to fire, which would be highly unlikely, got pissed every night and had first crack at any *punda*[80] living in the Vic Falls village or on holiday. Their camp at the Elephant Hills Hotel was a paradise. The hotel had been burnt down after a Katyusha rocket, fired from Zambia, had hit it some years before. It was a 5-Star hotel, with squash courts, pool, pub and many of the old hotel rooms were undamaged. This was by far the cushiest number in the army.

The problem with the 'wankers' and 'jam-stealers' at Victoria Falls was that there were far too many of them. They provided competition. The soldiers at 4 Indep, black and white, resented their presence to a greater or lesser extent. The black soldiers, with wives and girlfriends

---

78 Colonial slang, person from England (UK), can be both a term of endearment and derogatory, believed to derive from Prisoner of Mother England - convicts transported to Australia.
79 South African Defence Force.
80 Rhodesian Slang, women.

in the local township, were on constant alert to any advances made towards their women. A network of informers had been recruited by the Company to ensure that any such information was relayed back. Any jam-stealer caught making advances on 4 Indep women were dealt with accordingly. It was a constant subject of discussion amongst the troops during deployments.

The artillery troop dropped Smith and 2 Section off at their camp at about 7pm that evening. Fullerton addressed the men with a few clipped words in seShona. Judging by their reaction Smith figured that the men were happy with what he had to say. Fullerton then brought the men smartly to attention and dismissed them to the showers. Smith turned to leave.

'Just a minute Sergeant Smith,' said Fullerton lightly.

'Yes Sir?' replied Smith, bracing up, dreading another dressing down.

'Not a bad performance Smith, your bush-craft needs some more work but you showed good aggression when it was needed. Am I right, that was your first Gook?'

Smith nodded, swallowed hard, this was the first positive feedback he had received since joining the unit. He studied Fullerton's face carefully but it was clear that the comment had been sincere. *He really thinks I did okay!*

'Thank you Sir,' was all he could manage. He suddenly felt elated; the nagging doubts were momentarily relieved. He braced up, then turned and headed for the showers and the pub. *Shit … bloody fantastic!*

There was still no sign of 2nd Lt Gibbs with the rest of 2 and 3 Platoons; he was still on deployment on the River. 1 Platoon had gone on R&R. Fullerton went in search of Lt Dawson of the Grey Scouts and headed into town for a 'piss-up'.

Smith was delighted to see Troop or 'Colour' Sergeant Bruce O'Connell of the Grey Scouts. Colour O'Connell was the 2IC of 3 Troop and had just returned from a course in Salisbury. He was tall, well over 6ft 3', about thirty-five years old, with a weathered darkly tanned skin and bright blue eyes. He was Australian.

'G'day Maaate,' O'Connell called, 'Heee ya goin?'

O'Connell was great fun, a real character, always ready with a smile and a bad joke. Smith really enjoyed his company and their long animated conversations. Not surprisingly O'Connell also enjoyed a beer and a song. He treated everybody exactly the same, black, white, officer, NCO and trooper. He had absolutely no airs and graces, he was just an all round good bloke. The result was that his troop would follow him to the end of the Earth and back again. He got on really well with

Lt Dawson that made for a very motivated and happy troop. He was called 'Ozzie' by his peers, 'Colour' by everyone else.

O'Connell hailed from a place called Bedourie in far Western Queensland. He tried to explain where that was but nobody really ever got the idea. Describing the town as 'the furthest place a man could go from anywhere', he recounted the key features as, 'horses, cattle, snakes, dust, beer and flies'. The two things in short supply were, 'water and Sheilas'. He had been born and brought up on a 'Station' that sounded like it was the size of Matabeleland. He had worked as a 'drover' or stockman from the day he had been old enough to stay in the saddle. He was as much at home in a saddle as he was on his feet, probably more so. O'Connell had been conscripted into the Australian Army, serving with the 1st Armoured Personnel Carrier Squadron in Vietnam. He told stories of his experiences when his squadron had been part of the rescue of the Australian forces in the Battle of Long Tan in 1966. If given any encouragement at all, he would regale his audiences with graphic accounts of the other actions he had been involved in. He served two tours in Vietnam but after eventually returning home, couldn't live with the naked contempt the Australian public had for Vietnam veterans. His decision to come out to Rhodesia was made partly for his love of adventure and the military life and partly because he wanted to be in a place where he would be more appreciated. His natural affinity for horses and riding made his choice to join the Grey Scouts an easy one.

Very few things upset O'Connell; he was not a disciplinarian, rare for a Troop Sergeant. The one area, however, where there was no compromise, was looking after and grooming the horses. Here his passion bordered on fanatical. While in camp he had his troop up every morning at first light, feeding, watering, brushing and trimming. This was routine for the first two hours of every morning. The horses would then be saddled and the troop would go through a series of maneuvers. The daily exercise of the horses was great spectator value for the rest of the camp, in particular the black soldiers, who would cheer and clap whenever a movement was successfully completed. This routine earned the troop the nickname 'Household Cavalry', which was as much for the impressive way they performed as it was pulling their legs. The RAR soldiers gave O'Connell the name *Bhiza*, meaning Horse, quite literally a man named 'Horse'.

O'Connell loved a party, anywhere, anytime. A few beers would inevitably result in a song or two. It was not uncommon for his troop, or part thereof, to be found formed up in a pub somewhere in Vic Falls, giving a full-voiced rendition of *Waltzing Matilda* or *Wild Colonial Boy* to the rousing applause of those present. Smith had watched in awe as O'Connell, standing to attention on top of the Long Bar at the Victoria Falls Hotel, gave an emotional rendition of Banjo Paterson's *Man from Snowy River*. Tears streaming down his cheeks O'Connell recited all thirteen verses in a booming animated voice. The audience was captivated, spellbound, breaking into tumultuous applause when he finished.

O'Connell's closest companion was his horse, a mare he named 'Sheila'. She was not the biggest horse in the world, made to look quite small under O'Connell's tall frame. She was definitely not the best looking horse either, her coat of thick wiry hair was patchy and she bore the scars of many a fight. O'Connell, using the same words from Paterson's poem described her proudly:

> *She was hard and tough and wiry - just the sort that won't say die -*
> *There was courage in her quick impatient tread;*
> *And she bore the badge of gameness in her quick and fiery eye,*
> *And the proud and lofty carriage of her head.*

Yes, O'Connell had a feel for exaggeration and melodrama, his Irish blood no doubt contributed to that. All Smith could see in his mind's eye when O'Connell described Sheila was the meanest, most bad tempered, ugly horse he had ever seen. Her eyes reminded Smith of Jack Nicolson's in the movie *One Flew Over the Cuckoo's Nest*, wild and demented. She had the run of the camp refusing to be confined to the horse lines. Wandering around the camp she took great joy in trying to bite and kick anyone she disliked. This included pretty much anybody who wasn't a Grey Scout. She was also quite clearly the leader of the other horses in the troop and was not above biting and kicking them as well. She would respond immediately to her name or a soft whistle when called by O'Connell but ignored everyone else. He talked to her continuously in a kind and gentle way when working with her, just as if she was a cherished younger sister. She, in turn would nicker softly whenever she saw him. Smith marvelled at their attachment. He, as with most other people, was terrified of Sheila. She too had a name given to her by the black soldiers, *Murwisi,* meaning, *a person that starts an argument or fight by attacking first*. That described Sheila perfectly. The soldiers would watch her stalking unsuspecting visitors to the camp, then howl with laughter as she bit and chased them about.

The only way for anyone to ingratiate themselves with Murwisi was to feed her, preferably carrots or apples, her favourites. This meant that her real 'mates' in the camp were the cooks who always fed her a few carrots when she put her head through the kitchen window. She recognised the cooks as people to be respected and went out of her way to run up to them when she saw any of them walking around the camp. This was disconcerting for most, as seeing a horse charging in your direction, then skidding to a halt with a slobbery muzzle thrust in the face, takes a bit of getting used to. Smith tried feeding her a carrot on only one occasion but nearly lost a finger as she bit down hard to get the whole thing at once. He had yelped and jumped around in agony, shaking his hand in pain, to the obvious delight of O'Connell.

'I think she likes you mate,' O'Connell chuckled.

Smith and O'Connell plus a few other NCOs, sat in the mess and drank beers while Smith related his experiences over the preceding two days. Talking about the contacts seemed to help, it was a relief to be able to talk about it.

'*Fair Dinkum* Mate, if you carry on like this you should go for SAS[81] selection,' said O'Connell with a laugh. They adjourned to bed early, Smith felt absolutely drained, *SAS ... you have got to be bloody joking*!

*

The next day those in camp were drawn up on the edge of the airstrip at 8:00am sharp in clean uniforms, berets and stable belts. A parade of the Company was seldom called; the only previous occasion was when the Head of COMOPS came to visit. *So much for 'Top Secret', the whole town will know in minutes,* Smith thought. The duty NCO had given him the run down on the signal the night before. The Grey Scout troop trotted into position behind the formed-up RAR contingent. Peacock had a feel for pomp and ceremony, his experiences in 'The Queen's Regiment' not forgotten. Someone had said that Peacock had threatened Lt Dawson with a bunch of horrible things to get him to agree to be part of the 'Parade'. The Household Cavalry were not impressed. Smith stood smartly behind the formed-up soldiers, in line with the other sergeants. There was no sign of Fullerton, parades not being part of his tripartite list of interests.

Out in the distance the drone of an approaching aircraft could be heard. The aircraft, a Britten Norman Islander, appeared overhead. Smith watched as the aircraft circled the airfield once before turning onto its final approach. It gently touched down and taxied on to the hard standing at the end of the runway. The engines were shut down then a short delay ensued as those inside got ready to disembark.

The door opened and six smartly dressed officers stepped out onto the tarmac. Major Peacock marched over to meet them. There was a

---

81 Special Air Service, Rhodesia had a squadron of SAS referred to as C Squadron when the unit was expanded after World War II. To this day, the British SAS leave the 'C' vacant as a sign of respect for the Rhodesian SAS.

short exchange of pleasantries, nodding of heads, shaking of hands. Smith watched as Peacock gestured across at the waiting troops, clearly indicating their availability for inspection. The senior officer could be seen accepting the offer, bracing up enthusiastically, an enormous man with a massive barrel chest, sporting a waistline that indicated a penchant for beer and rich food. He, Peacock, and another officer, who must have been the adjutant, came marching over.

'Parade… Parade, ATTEEEENSHUN!' barked the CSM, wanting to put on a good show. The men came smartly to attention.

'Parade … Parade will present… PRESEEENT ARMS!' the men slapped their rifles loudly, stamping in the dirt.

'Who are these pricks?' a Grey Scout trooper enquired from behind where Smith was standing.

'Fuck knows … they look like Slopies[82],' someone volunteered.

'Shut-up in the ranks,' spat Dawson.

The South Africans were dressed in a light brown, desert-type uniform, smartly ironed shirts, lanyards, medal ribbons, and the badges of rank in orange and yellow on the epaulettes. They wore combat pants and smartly polished black combat boots. All of the officers wore berets but it was not possible to see their insignia.

The guard of honour was drawn up on the dirt surround of the airstrip, their boots already covered in dust. The inspection party walked through the three ranks, the South African officer making a few comments here and there but Smith could not hear what he was saying. The reviewing party then came across to the four NCOs standing behind the drawn-up ranks. Smith then got a closer look at the officers. As the contingent approached Smith heard the senior officer ask Peacock a question, he then laughed loudly slapping the Major on the shoulder, Smith only heard the words '… Majuba Hill'[83].

The tall Brigadier, whose nametag read 'Jooste', stopped in front of Smith. Looking down at him he addressed Smith in his thick Afrikaans accent, 'you are the only white soldier here *Sersant*, how can that be?'

Smith was flabbergasted, he looked across at Maj Peacock for support but clearly he had not heard the question.

'I beg your pardon Sir?' questioned Smith politely.

'I said … where are all the white soldiers?' asked the Brigadier more loudly, speaking slowly and deliberately as if talking to a young child.

Smith stumbled for an answer, 'We are the RAR … Sir.'

82 Referring to the derogatory idea of a 'sloped' forehead caused by repeated slapping as a non-too-smart South African tried to understand something, i.e. the sudden realisation, … slap on the forehead, hence a 'sloped' forehead, thus the singular 'slope', diminutive 'slopie', plural 'slopies'.

83 Reference to the 1st Boer War battle in February 1881 where the Boers defeated a British force made up of the 58th Regiment and the 92nd (Gordon) Highlanders.

That answer clearly did not register with the Brigadier who barrelled on, ' ... but how can you fight your war with only 'black' soldiers *Sersant*?' he said with strong emphasis on the word 'black'.

Smith was now convinced the Brigadier was 'taking the micky'. *Maybe I should laugh*, Smith thought.

'We are all the same colour ... Sir, I wear camo-cream ... Sir,' answered Smith confidently ... *that should bring the house down*.

The Brigadier merely shook his head, muttering to himself, then with a perplexed look on his face marched off to inspect the Grey Scouts. As Peacock walked past he glared at Smith, trying to fathom what had just been said as he had only heard the last sentence.

The Grey Scouts were mostly white troops, which seemed to impress the Brigadier more. The inspecting party walked across the front of the rank of horses. Farmers in South Africa, particularly in the Matatiele district of Natal, had donated a good many of the Grey Scout horses. Matatiele is at the base of the mountains bordering the Kingdom of Lesotho. The horses had the genetics of the tough and rugged Basutho ponies, celebrated for their stamina. The Brigadier appeared pleased calling up to the mounted troops with various questions.

O'Connell was drawn up in the middle of the formation, Sheila fidgety as always. Parades were not her thing. As the inspecting party walked past, Sheila, *Murwisi,* decided for some reason that she did not like the young South African adjutant. Her head shot forward and bit into his shoulder. The adjutant jumped out of his skin, screamed in shock, grabbing for the horse's halter with his free hand. She wouldn't let go, shaking her head from side to side flopping the man about like a rag-doll. He was howling blue murder in Afrikaans. O'Connell yanked on the reins and tried to back out of line. This only succeeded in dragging the officer after him. The man's screams became more urgent. Terrified, he lost his footing, his free arm flailing about trying to regain balance. Suspended in Sheila's clamped jaws his limp body jerked up and down with the excited movement of her head.

'Let go Sheila!' instructed O'Connell, smashing down on her head between the ears with the flash-hider of his FN. That was no good either she just wouldn't let go.

The Brigadier turned to see what had happened. Being an experienced horseman himself, he strode back, trying to grab Sheila by the noseband. She twisted her head away, still refusing to let go. As the man leaned forward again Sheila turned her head further away, dragging the adjutant around with her, pushing her flank in the way of the Brigadier. The Brigadier then made a fateful mistake; he hit her hard on the shoulder with his baton. That infuriated Sheila, she whinnied through her teeth. Still holding the adjutant, she kicked out at the Brigadier with her front hooves. She hit him square on the right knee, taking him down as if in a rugby tackle from Willie-John McBride[84]. The Brigadier rolled in the dust clutching his knee in agony, yelling loudly, spraying Afrikaans swear words, some of which Smith thought he recognised. In the process of kicking the Brigadier, Sheila also clipped the luckless adjutant with a flying hoof, making him shriek even louder.

The soldiers who had all turned to see what was going on broke out into uncontrolled, convulsive, laughter. Some merely sat in the dirt, their bodies gripped by paroxysms of laughter, tears steaming down their cheeks. The CSM bellowed at the men to get back into ranks, his calls lost in the tumult.

The Grey Scout formation broke up as the other horses took fright. The rider immediately to the left of O'Connell was thrown, landing in a heap in the dust; his horse took off for the lines chased by two other troopers. The rest of the troop began milling around, kicking up dust, the riders fighting for control. Sheila resolutely maintained her grip on the adjutant, the smart brown South African uniform eventually giving way with the shoulder epaulette ripped off together with most of the right sleeve. Sheila squealed with delight, shaking her head, waving the shredded sleeve from side to side, like a trophy at a cup final. She lifted her head, neighing in victory, lifting her front hooves up off the ground, pawing the air. O'Connell, struggling to get her under control, swore loudly. The unfortunate adjutant sank to his knees, his shoulder now exposed and bleeding with his beret awry, shirt covered in horse saliva, his left leg paralysed from the violent kick.

Peacock was struggling to help the Brigadier to his feet. He was not strong enough to lift the mountain of a man. The Brigadier's knee was unable to carry his weight. Kneeling down, Peacock put his shoulder under the man's arm, put in a massive effort, but instead toppled over on top of him. The Brigadier swore loudly in Afrikaans, pushing to get out from under the Major.

The inspection was over. The legend of *Murwisi* grew. She trotted back to the lines, head held high, still clutching the torn shirt in her mouth.

*

The rest of the day saw three other aircraft arrive at Sprayview, depositing very important looking officers who made their way purposefully to the Ops room. No more thought of guards of honour for

---

84 The Irish lock who toured South Africa in 1974 as captain of the British Lions. The most successful Lions tour ever defeating the Springboks 3-0.

them. Something big was happening. Smith was asked to boost the size of the guard on the perimeter of the camp and he placed a rifleman on each corner of the Ops room complex. He then spent the day checking with each guard, ensuring a changing of the guard every two hours. No vehicles were allowed in or out of the camp. Half way through the day Smith saw Fullerton being summoned into the meeting.

At about 5pm the meeting started to break up and the various parties returned to their aircraft to fly out. The South Africans had decided to stay overnight and went off into the Falls with Maj Peacock for dinner. The Brigadier's mood seemed slightly improved with the help of painkillers and strapping on the knee. The young adjutant, still looking much worse for wear followed along in a clean shirt, his arm wrapped in a sling, limping painfully.

Sheila, whinnying forlornly, had been tied to a tree for punishment. There was no greater castigation for her than being tied up. The CSM, who also hated horses and Australians, had threatened to shoot Sheila on the pretext that she must have rabies or something ... he even cocked his rifle to make his point. A stand-up argument ensued where O'Connell was heard to threaten instant death if a hair on his horse was harmed.

'Your fucking stupid CO insisted on a parade, you useless fat fucker,' squawked O'Connell.

Smith had never seen him in such a temper. O'Connell continued with a stream of expletives, out-matching the CSM who was a bit slower verbally and also a little lost with the Aussie accent.

The CSM did, however, manage, 'You bloody useless, sheep-shagging, donkey walloping ... convict', which impressed the crowd.

Lt Dawson, seeing the altercation, ran over, inserting himself between the two men.

'That is quite enough! CSM there will be no further talk of convicts or shooting horses.' Then with the faintest glimmer of a smile, he turned to O'Connell ' Colour O'Connell, there will be no further references to people's weight or their mother's sexual preferences.'

The two protagonists stood their ground glaring at each other. O'Connell was visibly shaking. Dawson pushed each man away, forcing them to back off.

Sheila bellowed from the horse lines as if giving her opinion on the matter. O'Connell went over to speak to her but she was inconsolable, turning her back, even aiming a kick in his direction. *Heaven has no rage like love to hatred turned, Nor hell a fury like a woman scorned*[85].

Smith hit the sack early that evening, the sight of Sheila destroying

85 William Congreve (1670 – 1729), *The Mourning Bride* (1697) spoken by Zara in Act 3, Scene 2. The phrase in common parlance 'Hell hath no fury as a woman scorned'.

the parade bringing a smile to his face, this was definitely one for the books … *I must remember to tell Gibbs all about this.*

*

'*Ishe … Ishe!* The police have called, they need you urgently at the beerhall in the township, there is some trouble,' urged the duty NCO shaking Smith vigorously. Still half asleep, Smith looked at his watch … *midnight … Fuck! … What is going on? This is bullshit!*

Dragging himself out of bed Smith dressed and called for the duty NCO to organise a driver. He strapped on his chest webbing, grabbed his rifle from under his bed and set off. As the Two-Five approached the beerhall, Smith could see three police Land Rovers and a large crowd had gathered outside. There was a loud hubbub, with people pointing and shaking their fists. Smith climbed down from the vehicle then he and the driver pushed through the crowd at the entrance to the beerhall. The scene that presented itself was as astounding as it was familiar. Along the left wall of the beerhall was his 2 Section, in the middle were at least five people being ministered to by the police and medics while on the opposite wall was a motley collection of Artillery, Engineers and Services personnel, clearly distinguishable by their stable belts.

Smith walked to the centre of the hall where a young police Patrol Officer was writing down names.

'What is going on here PO?' enquired Smith politely.

The Patrol Officer, who appeared extremely agitated, turned and pointed towards the members of 2 Section standing against the wall. 'Your blokes have been knocking ten colours of shit out of them,' he said, waving in the direction of the soldiers drawn up on the opposite wall.

'I have five injured, including one of my constables who tried to intervene, … 4 Indep are in for the high jump this time Sergeant Smith, it's bullshit! … This happens every weekend with your lot.'

'Who started it PO?' asked Smith, trying to appear helpful.

'Who fucking knows? … All I know is that whenever we have a disturbance it's your Company involved - every time a coconut!'

'… are you going to charge anybody PO?' asked Smith as delicately as possible, not wanting to enflame the situation any further.

The policeman rounded on Smith, his face flushed with anger, pointing accusingly across the room towards the RAR soldiers.

'That man there! The one shaped like a prop.' He was pointing at Dube who was taking a sudden interest in the ceiling.

'He … He is a bloody menace. He's a raving lunatic. It took three of my men to pull him off. So help me, if we hadn't intervened he would have killed somebody.'

The black soldiers did not adhere to the 'Queensbury Rules' in a fight. Anything goes, including the very real possibility of death for the opponents. The whole scenario was made increasingly dangerous by the addition of large quantities of alcohol.

Clearly 4 Indep had the better of the fight. Dube's right eye was swollen shut. Moyo, still clutching a Chibuku, had a blood-nose, LCpl Nkai a few cuts and a bleeding ear. The rest had minor injuries; droplets of blood were dripping on the floor where they stood. They were all extremely drunk, some having difficulty keeping upright, wavering and wobbling about, totally legless.

Smith walked across to where his troops were standing, he didn't have to say anything.

Nkai, being the senior rank, immediately stepped forward on his uncertain legs.

'*Ishe* … that man was sleeping with Moyo's woman.' Nkai indicated a man lying on the floor, his face a bloody pulp.

'What do you mean? Moyo's wife lives in Bulawayo!' replied Smith, looking across at Moyo who would not meet his eye.

'*Ishe* Moyo has a girlfriend … these people know he has a girlfriend. … They know not to sleep with her,' continued LCpl Nkai earnestly. 'Moyo came to the beerhall for beer with us and he found out which one it was and then he beat him. The others then attacked us and we defended ourselves.' Nkai then turned and pointed menacingly at the other soldiers across the room, 'It is them *Ishe!*'

The perverse logic was impossible to argue against. Smith could only stand and listen, each man taking a turn to embellish the story still further.

While Smith's pointless interrogation was going on an ambulance wailed outside, the worst of the injured were loaded in the back and sent off to the hospital.

The PO made a careful note of the names of the offenders on both sides, their respective stories and then admonished them all in fluent siNdebele.

'A report will be sent to your commanding officers for punishment,' stated the Policeman loudly so that all the locals heard him. He had to be seen to be doing something. The PO made it clear their behaviour was childish and unacceptable and that if he ever caught anyone of them fighting again he would put them in the cells. Everybody nodded and mumbled their acceptance. All then went their separate ways, just like naughty schoolboys caught smoking behind the bicycle sheds.

Smith loaded his men onto the back of the Two-Five and decided to give his own lecture.

'You have brought disgrace on the RAR, you have brought disgrace on 2 Platoon and you have brought disgrace on me,' he said reprovingly. 'If the police make a report to the Company you may be charged. How can I go out to war without you?'

LCpl Nkai, speaking for the others, replied, 'We are sorry *Ishe*, it won't happen again.' The others nodded their assent; a few mumbled their apologies.

Smith looked across at them knowing that this attempted contrition was rubbish.

'We won the fight did we not?'

'*Yebo Ishe!*' they called out in unison, broad smiles breaking out across their faces. The jam-stealers would think twice next time!

10

Lupane TTL, north Matabeleland

Sgt Cephas Ngwenya, Selous Scout, had completed his reconnaissance in Lupane TTL. The rumours of a large, well-organised, force in Lupane were accurate. They were more than likely responsible for the attack on the heavy vehicle convoy. The local tribesmen were quite free with this information, as they did not suspect that Ngwenya was a member of the Rhodesian security forces, quite the contrary, he had given them the very strong impression that he was seeking to join the terrorists as a recruit. Dressed as he was as a local peasant farmer it did not take long for him to make contact with a small group of ZIPRA terrorists. As part of his cover, Ngwenya had made enquiries on how to get to a training camp in Zambia. He was welcomed with open arms, the information he needed was freely given.

Now sitting in his OP position, high on a hilltop overlooking the Lupane TTL, Ngwenya studied the surrounding countryside. He was part of a team of eight Selous Scouts from 3 Group, divided into two sticks of four. They had taken up their positions on two hills, separated by a few kilometres, but clearly visible one to the other. The choice of OP was based on the reconnaissance work that Ngwenya had done in the previous week. They were prepared for a long stay, maybe as long as two weeks. This would not the longest OP Ngwenya had manned, not by a long chalk; he had spent four weeks on one occasion in Tete Province in Mozambique. In that case they were tasked to ambush a terrorist leader, he took all of four weeks to arrive ... they got him then.

Ngwenya was twenty-eight, an ex-policeman, trained by Special Branch in intelligence gathering and counter-insurgency. He had been part of the original 'pilot' pseudo scheme set up by the police.[86] While Ngwenya was a Matabele and, therefore, a siNdebele speaker, he spoke seShona fluently; this allowed him to operate freely in Mashonaland. When Major Ron Reid-Daly formed the Selous Scouts in late 1973, Ngwenya volunteered for selection, primarily because he had heard that the pay would be more than double what he had been earning in the police. That had proved not to be completely correct but the danger and excitement provided by the Scouts had compensated to some degree. More importantly, he enjoyed the informality of the unit and the freedom of movement it offered during operations.

These particular low hills had been chosen for the OP because of the

---

86 Set up by Superintendant Peterson of Special Branch in Salisbury in January 1973. The first few, largely unsuccessful, deployments with the team were in Bushu and Madziwa Tribal Trust Lands.

very clear view of the surrounding cultivated fields, roads and villages. The hills did not have very steep sides, mainly large granitite rocks with thick thorn 'jesse' bush. The Bubi River, a tributary of the Gwai, wound its way through the hills.

The three troopers in Ngwenya's team were all black, two were ex-RAR the other was an ex-ZIPRA terrorist who had been 'turned'. The other Selous Scout team had two black soldiers and two white territorials, doing their 'six-weeks-in' continuous call-up[87]. The white soldiers sported thick bushy beards; as was the unofficial 'badge' of the unit. There was a practical side of growing a beard; it broke up the shape of the face making camouflage easier and more effective. The whole group wore a combination of various Soviet and East German uniforms, all carried AK-47 rifles, chest webbing, two RPG-7 launchers and projectiles, rifle grenades as well as other assorted Soviet equipment. They would pass as ZIPRA terrorists even under the closest scrutiny.

Ngwenya preferred working with his black colleagues on this sort of job, mainly because the white troopers struggled to keep 'black'. They had to be constantly aware of the camo-cream wearing off, needing to touch-up all the time. Some white soldiers even resorted to bathing in Condy's Crystals, potassium permanganate, to literally die their skin black. While the Condy's Crystals worked, the nose and ears still needed touching up from time to time. Ngwenya had a close shave when a CT in a group they were infiltrating had recognised one of their would-be comrades as a *mukiwa!* The ensuing firefight had resulted in the deaths of all the CTs in the band which had defeated the whole purpose of the infiltration, undoing months of work.

The insertion of the two Selous Scout teams had been a very careful and methodical process. Experience had shown that infiltrating ZIPRA held areas was very difficult. This was because ZIPRA were highly disciplined with a structured command and control system. Furthermore, the ZIPRA High Command were well aware of the Selous Scout pseudo operations so they had set up a system of codes, including pieces of clothing, bangles and passwords, to provide a means of positive proof of identification for their cadres. For all these reasons, the current mission was a 'hunter-killer' operation not intended to attempt to infiltrate the local ZIPRA band. To infiltrate successfully would have taken several months, instead the plan was to locate the terrorists and kill them with a Fireforce strike.

Despite the fact that they were dressed as pseudos, the Scouts still needed to get into the hills without leaving any tell-tale spoor. It was

---

87 The call to active service for territorial and national service personnel. The continuous call-up system in the latter stages of the war was 'six weeks in and six weeks out' and affected most territorial soldiers in the age group 18 to 35.

vital that they entered the OP position without being detected. This required careful anti-tracking techniques with each man climbing into the hill from a different angle. To ensure a perfectly clandestine entry into the area, the team had arrived on a bus that they had stopped on one of the entry roads. Riding on bus transport was normal CT practice so it worked perfectly. The bus took them to within a few kilometres of their respective OP positions. Once they were in position, Ngwenya sent the coded message to their handlers in Wankie, the message to 'freeze' the area. Once an area was 'frozen' no other security force, Intaf or police units were allowed to enter to ensure that the chance of clashing with a Selous Scout pseudo team was eliminated.

The Selous Scouts had turned observation into an art form. One person manned the OP at a time, concealed in a heavily camouflaged lookout. Each man kept a careful log of all that he saw, noting vehicles arriving and leaving, people living in the villages, each got a name based on their clothing and routine. At times, depending on the wind, it was possible to hear the villagers talking to each other, as they called across fields or roads. To the trained eye, village life has a very defined routine, early rise in the morning, cooking of food, working in the fields, fetching water, herding cattle, visiting neighbours, cleaning and preparing for the evening meal. They particularly noted the movement of young kids, especially boys in the age group seven to sixteen, as they were the eyes and ears of the CTs, the *mujibas*. It was not uncommon for the CTs to insist that the *mujibas* herd cattle, or if that was not possible, climb over the surrounding hills to look for SF OPs. This was most often the way OPs became 'compromised'.

Each OP had a 'base' where the off-duty team members could sleep or eat. This was also where they kept their radios and other equipment. There was no cooking of meals or boiling of water for tea, cooking smells and gas can be smelt a long way off. CTs didn't use gas for cooking. All possible sources of sound were also carefully considered, opening food cans, scraping of spoons, checking of weapons, cleaning weapons and the like. Talking was in hushed tones and only when absolutely necessary. Most communication was done with hand signals. These were very serious soldiers, handpicked, brutally trained; the Selous Scouts was definitely not a unit for the faint-hearted.

The Sun was beginning to set as Ngwenya, manning the OP, noticed a group of women walking along a path away from the village immediately in front of his position, baskets on their heads, chatting to each other happily. He could see from the movements of their heads, from their careful gait, that the baskets were heavily loaded. He noted the time, carefully described each woman, her approximate age, her clothing, the basket she was carrying, any adornments like necklaces or wristbands. As he watched them he thought - *where could you all be off to at this time of night ... with loaded baskets?*

*

ZIPRA Base Camp, Lupane TTL, north Matabeleland

Comrade Vladimir Benkov was also getting ready for the evening. He could not get used to the local diet, suffering from alternate bouts of constipation and diarrhoea. He had exhausted all the food he had brought with him, now having to rely on the food prepared by the local villagers. The effect of the local food on his constitution had not really been a consideration when he had planned the infiltration but it was now proving to be a serious problem. The medical kit he had with him was mainly for trauma, gunshot wounds, infection and injury. He had already exhausted the few tablets for diarrhoea he had brought with him.

The most recent flash radio communication had been very explicit. Lusaka needed a further escalation in the ZIPRA freedom fighter's activities in Northern Front Region 1. They were delighted with the attack on the heavy vehicle convoy, which had been extensively reported in the international press, 'regrettable ... the death of two police reservists in their sixties, two black truck drivers ... Deeply regrettable'. There was talk of a meeting between the Rhodesian Prime Minister Ian Smith and Joshua Nkomo the leader of ZAPU-PF. Comrade Nkomo was under pressure to meet Smith, pressure being exerted by Britain and the USA. Any attempt at an alliance or settlement needed to be derailed. Lusaka had mentioned a few further options that Benkov found interesting; in addition to the plans he had already put in train.

Benkov needed some decent food and medical supplies. As luck would have it, his most recent plan could deal with both, killing two birds with one stone. The problem was how to get the message across to Comrade Chabanga who was not supportive of any form of military escalation.

The Russian's painful stomach did not seem to affect his libido. He had a deal with his trusted band of cadres that if they supplied him with young girls then he would ensure that they would have first choice of any plunder resulting from their activities. Whenever he felt so inclined he would mention this to his band and at the appointed time a young girl aged between thirteen and sixteen would be presented. There seemed to be an endless supply. The girls were generally compliant with very little to say, seemingly resigned to their fate. He suspected that they had all been raped by various freedom fighters already.

Benkov had his own hut in an abandoned village close to the ZIPRA base camp. The Bubi River bisected the camp, in a thickly wooded valley, under a virtually uninterrupted Mopani forest canopy. The riverbed was dry with thick drifts of sand, providing comfortable sleeping positions for the cadres during the dry season. Above the steep riverbank the cadres had built shelters, heavily camouflaged with thick thorn scrub, making the camp virtually invisible from the air. An open field nearby was used for soccer matches, a common pastime for the locals and freedom fighters alike. At night Benkov preferred to sleep in the hut which provided privacy for his evening pursuits. His band kept guard outside the hut.

A young girl, about fourteen years old, was duly presented. In contrast to the others she was resistant and very agitated, needing to be held between two cadres. Despite her small size she showed considerable strength. The men had to literally toss her into the hut where she sank to the floor crying uncontrollably. As Benkov turned to remove his pants, she bolted for the door. He blocked her path, slapping her hard on the side of the head. He put his hand over her mouth, lifting her up under his arm. This just made her more determined; kicking out wildly she bit him hard on the hand, drawing blood. Yelping in pain Benkov was forced to drop her. She ran to the side of the hut shouting at him, pointing to the door that he was blocking. He could feel his anger rising, *a bit of resistance made the experience more enjoyable, but there was a limit*. His agility was not compromised by his size, he sprang at the girl, grabbed her, trying to hold her down while he loosened his pants. She screamed out, squirming beneath him wildly. He hit her again; she shrieked in distress, her nose began to bleed and blood dribbled from the corner of her mouth. He again put his hand over her mouth to try to stop the sound; it didn't stop her writhing desperately trying to get away from him. He slapped her again, this time on the top of the head. His anger and indignation grew as he fought to hold her down; he punched her, hard, full in the face. That finally stopped her squealing. Knocked senseless she crumpled to the mud floor. Benkov was a powerful man; a punch that hard would have felled an ox. The girl's face had become a gooey, bloody mess, both her eyes were swollen shut, she coughed up a tooth, spitting blood out onto the floor. Benkov looked at her smashed face, instantly losing interest; he stood up and walked over to his pack. He took out his spetsnaz knife, walked back over to the insensible heap on the floor, grabbing her by the hair he twisting her head to the side. As he did so, he neatly slit her throat from ear to ear. He then took hold of the body by the leg and dragged it out of the hut into the open.

Benkov called to his interpreter who was sitting nearby, talking quietly to two young *mujibas.*

'Comrade Mlungisi, get rid of this filth ... don't ever bring me rubbish like this again!' called Benkov in Russian.

Mlungisi, the interpreter, came over and looked at the mangled girl; he was completely immune to Benkov's brutality, seeing it so many times before.

'... Was she of no use at all Comrade?' said Mlungisi submissively.

' ... No use at all Mlungisi. You may have to find something slightly older next time. My requirements for a virgin may have to be relaxed.'

'No problem Comrade, I will send a message. There are plenty of other girls with a bit more experience ...' replied Mlungisi, winking at his leader.

Benkov merely grunted, turned to go back into his hut, the cramp in his stomach starting again.

Mlungisi called to the young *mujibas*, telling them to take the body away and bury it. The two young boys looked down in horror at what they saw, the head was almost severed completely from the body, the younger one started to cry. Mlungisi slapped him hard.

'Don't be a woman, this is what happens in our struggle ... this is what happens to traitors!'

After Benkov and Mlungisi had left, the young boys half dragged, half carried the body to a disused well in the abandoned village. They had not seen a dead body before but knew enough to know that the spirit of the dead was a potentially very dangerous thing, something to be feared and respected. They carefully lifted the girl over the low parapet and dropped the body down. They heard the thump as it hit the bottom. The two then ran home is if the very devil himself, the *Tokoloshe*[88], was chasing them.

In the hills above, Cephas Ngwenya lay awake in his sleeping bag; he had heard a scream drifting up from the valley below.

*

Kosami Mission – south of the Lupane District

The next evening found Comrade Benkov and his loyal cadres <u>sitting on a lo</u>w hill overlooking Kosami Mission. The mission was

88 In Southern African mythology, Tokoloshe is a dwarf-like water sprite or zombie. They are considered a mischievous and evil spirit. They can become invisible by swallowing a pebble. Tokoloshes are created from dead bodies by witch doctors ... if the witch doctor has been offended by someone. Many African people place their beds on gallon paint tins or bricks (some tales state that they are wrapped in paper) in order to lift them higher off the ground so that the Tokoloshe cannot hide underneath and attack them.

well to the south of the Lupane base camp. The mission complex was made up of a clinic, which looked like it accommodated about seventy patients, a small chapel, a communal kitchen and a number of residences and administration buildings. There was no fence or security of any description. An aged white, dust-caked, Land Rover was parked in the middle of the complex with the sign of the Cross of Jesus marked on the door. The mission was operated by the Roman Catholic Church and had a staff of about twenty people including two priests supported by black and white nuns from the Missionary Sisters of the Precious Blood.

Comrade Chabanga had agreed to Benkov's plan to attack the mission simply because the Soviet had promised that it was primarily to steal food and medical supplies. Benkov had been deliberately vague as to exactly how this was to be achieved. He had promised Chabanga faithfully that nobody would be harmed.

Benkov had no real understanding of religion; it was discouraged in the USSR, although his mother had prayed together with a few other people in his home from time to time. He had no concept of religious faith. His spetsnaz training had drummed into him that religion was irrelevant and that the interests of the State were most important. Benkov, therefore, saw the Catholic Mission below him as just another opportunity, a target like any other.

He signalled his band and they walked down into the mission complex. Benkov was wearing a woollen balaclava and thick sunglasses to hide his eyes. His face and hands were covered in thick camo-cream.

Father Gustav Schultz from Salzburg in Austria had worked for the Catholic Church in Rhodesia for twenty-three years, virtually building Kosami Mission 'with his bare hands'. He was a profoundly gentle person, completely dedicated to his task of ministering to the poor and the sick. Father Schultz saw the band of freedom fighters enter the mission compound from his office window. It was common knowledge that there were many freedom fighters living in the surrounding TTLs. He had provided medical attention to a few who had presented themselves for treatment.

The priest, dressed in his black vestments, hurried out to meet the approaching men, waving his hands, speaking to them in English but with his broad German accent. Without any hesitation, Benkov shot the man twice in the chest, the priest's forward momentum suddenly stopped, his upper body thrown back, legs and arms flying forward. The priest died before he hit the ground. He lay in the dust, his robes spread out beside him, like the wings of a bird.

The shots brought the rest of the mission staff to doors and windows. Sister Johanna Maria Steigler from Wiesbaden in Germany had been supervising the preparations for dinner when she heard the gunshots.

She knew instantly that all was not well. Running to the door of the kitchen she saw Father Schultz lying in the dust surrounded by men with guns. A scream caught in her throat, she sunk her face into her hands and felt her knees collapse from under her.

Comrade Mlungisi called out to the staff and patients to come outside; the people were quickly herded into the centre of the compound. Many of the patients in the clinic were pregnant; others clutched newborn children wrapped in sheets. The workers called out in siNdebele, crying out their shock and dismay, wringing their hands, holding onto one another. The nuns, all dressed in white habits, seeing the body of the priest, cried out, genuflecting, their hands held out in prayer. Sister Winifred Plommer, also from Austria, fell to the ground next to the dead priest, lifted his hand to her face, her body shaking with grief.

'Why are you here? We can do you no harm, take what you want and leave us,' Sister Plommer called out. 'There is no need to hurt us ... we are servants of the Lord. We can do you no harm.'

Benkov shot her too, in the forehead. She toppled backwards, the crisp white habit suddenly soiled with dirt and blood.

Pandemonium broke out as it became clear that the freedom fighters intended to kill them all. The missionaries and their workers broke in all directions in a hopeless attempt to get away. The freedom fighters randomly shot at the panicking mass of people, a few fell; others escaped through gaps in the buildings. Children were left standing alone, terrified by the bedlam around them, wailing loudly, shocked and confused.

The nuns grabbed at each other, huddled together, calling out to their God, '... have mercy on our souls.'

Mlungisi called out twice as he shot at the stricken nuns, 'Missionaries are enemies of the people!'

Killing absolutely everyone was not part of Benkov's plan. He pointed to Sister Steigler lying in the doorway to the kitchen. Mlungisi ran forward and grabbed her by the arm, dragging the senseless woman to the side of one the buildings. He spoke into her ear in his broken English, his words carefully rehearsed.

'You must tell the people that come that this was the work of ZIPRA, we have done this to draw the World's attention to our struggle. The Church must collect its people and take them home. We do not need them here.'

Mlungisi then thrust a carefully prepared, scribbled, hand-written note into her hand. It relayed the same sentiments, the Church was to close its schools and clinics and leave the people alone.

In what seemed like a few seconds the mission compound was

completely deserted. The cadres then set about ransacking the buildings, looking for money and valuables. Benkov went into the kitchen and collected all the food he could lay his hands on; two of the male mission workers were captured as porters for the food and provisions to be carried away. Fresh bread had been baked, Benkov stuffed as much in his mouth as he could. Benkov also found the very well stocked dispensary which had all the medication he was looking for. All the medicines were carefully labelled for various ailments to assist the untrained mission staff.

The jubilant group, with their stolen food, medicines and money, then left the mission moving to the south. One of the young cadres dragged one of the black nuns behind him. They had the whole night to make their escape. Benkov looked forward to sending his message to Lusaka. *This should make Comrade Nkomo's settlement talks more interesting!*

11

4 Independent Company (RAR) base camp, Sprayview airfield, Victoria Falls

Mike Smith sat on his bed in the tiny room he shared with 2nd Lt Gibbs. The mail had arrived; he had two letters from his mother, one from his sister, and one with writing he didn't recognise. He put it gently to one side and read the family letters first. His mother's letters normally covered every aspect of family life in detail, with his dad writing a paragraph or two at the end. The roses were now in bloom; locusts were bad this year; rain was desperately needed; the dog, a Labrador retriever named Judge, missed him terribly; Granny was feeling unwell, still recovering from her hip operation; the school had won its last two rugby matches; would he be home for Christmas? The letter contained two full pages of the latest information; *had he heard from Cheryl?* ... referring to his ex-girlfriend at university; his mother had always liked Cheryl ... *you should think about getting back together*. Helpful advice from his mother was always freely given. Smith knew his dad's work at the RIC meant that he knew where he was positioned every night, ' ... you have been busy ... keep your head down ... stay safe' were amongst his father's comments.

His sister's letters gave the same information just with a completely different spin. Dee was fighting with her mother over having a boyfriend. She was only fifteen; her parents had decided that she was too young for a boyfriend. She pleaded for his support in his next letter home, ' ... is it true that you are going out with Jane Williams? ... It's all over school!' she enquired.

The new letter had a pale lavender envelope, when he slit the enveloped open a faint smell of perfume wafted out. There were four pages of neatly written script, he quickly flicked to the bottom of the last page ... Jane Williams!

Mike Smith had a girlfriend at school but they had broken up when she had gone off to Rhodes University in Grahamstown South Africa. Cheryl had written a few times but her letters made him feel depressed. They were full of stories of parties, residence balls, picnics, parties and more parties. She sounded like she was having a wonderful time. Smith imagined how good it was going to be when his chance came. He had written to Cheryl to try to give her some idea of what was going on in his life. She was sympathetic but not really interested. Her replies were very matter-of-fact, posed only a few questions on his experiences in the army, focusing her letters more on her own experiences. That, he thought, was completely understandable in the circumstances, he didn't begrudge her the great time she was having.

Jane Williams was good to her word, she had written to him. Smith rapidly scanned through the letter, devouring the pages. She was eighteen, only one year younger than he was. Jane explained how things were going at school, writing A-Levels, 1st Team Hockey, trying to find a partner for the school dance, '... when will you be home on R&R next?' The situation at home after the death of Charlie sounded really difficult, clearly her parents were in bad shape. She explained how she was coping, by working hard, training as much as possible; she felt she had a crack at the Matabeleland School's team. She described the funeral in detail, how pleased she was that he had led the funeral detachment and the singing of the RAR song.

Smith found reading her letter strangely relieving. He couldn't quite explain the feeling that came over him. It was like a floating feeling. He held the paper up to his nose, it was definitely scented. Smith grabbed his writing pad from the trunk under his bed and began to compose a reply. He could not remember feeling this excited about anything; there was suddenly something different to think about. He tried to picture Jane in his mind, the colour of her hair, her eyes, *I must ask her to send me a photograph.*

*

2 and 3 Platoons finally rolled back into camp after their deployment on the River. Lt Gibbs looked tired and jaded with very little to say about the eight day bush trip. He had the shits literally and figuratively. He was, of course, oblivious to Smith's activities over the past week; that explanation would have to come later. As always, when a deployment ends the troops were exhausted, just wanting a shower and a coke. Beer would follow. Their kit was filthy and had to be unpacked, broken and missing kit replaced, sick or injured soldiers sent to the medic. Patrol reports had to be completed. Gibbs took himself off to report to Major Peacock, never a happy experience for him. The dilemma as to who was to run 3 Platoon continued; the Platoon had no commander or 2IC. As Smith had been absent, Gibbs had to run both platoons himself which was a very difficult job, particularly since he did not know the members of 3 Platoon well.

Smith hadn't got around to assigning a replacement for Fauguneze to his stick. This was important because, despite the fact that they normally patrolled as a full section, if they needed to operate from helicopters the allocation of sticks and stick leaders was important. He called Dube and Moyo together and asked their opinion. While it would appear to the casual observer that the appointment of a replacement was a formality, this was not the case. There was a hierarchy. The soldiers in the platoon commander's stick held the highest status, then the platoon 2IC, platoon corporals, lance corporals and so on. In the case of the most junior sticks, the more senior riflemen led these. 2 Platoon had two full corporals and three lance corporals, so all in all there were seven ranked stick leaders, including Smith and Gibbs, with only one stick commanded by a rifleman. In the very rare instance of the whole platoon being deployed by helicopter each stick would be numbered from Stop 1, Gibbs, Stop 2, Smith, and so on to Stop 8. With the death of Fauguneze, the soldiers on long-leave, the increasing list of soldiers on light duty with VD, malaria and tick-bite fever, the platoon could now only muster five full sticks.

Soldiers with VD were placed on a charge that often meant a reduction in rank and a docking of pay, the charge being, 'Damage to Government Property'. As the CSM would often scream at them, 'You don't own your dick, the Government does, look after it!' The worst punishment for the recalcitrant VD sufferer was joining a work detail under the CSM who had them all washing latrines, cleaning barrack rooms, the kitchen and other buildings. They could also be seen collecting and painting stones white, which were then used to demarcate parking places, boundaries and pathways. Running up and down with the heavy white stones was also part of the punishment, agonising when the penis is discharging thick, copious, urethral pus, making urination excruciatingly painful. The swollen testicles made wearing underpants also horribly uncomfortable.

Smith sat on a table in the mess while the two soldiers debated the decision of the replacement. The conversation was in animated siNdebele; eventually a person was decided upon. Smith didn't have the energy to enquire as to how the decision was made; in any event, it was irrelevant to him provided the other two were happy. As they relied on each other in a contact, this decision literally had life and death consequences. Moyo and Dube had kept him alive thus far so there was no way that Smith was going to countermand their decision.

Dube went over to the 2 Platoon barrack room to call the candidate. Consent on the part of the candidate was also very important for teamwork and protocol reasons. Rifleman Vukhani Sibanda presented himself, smartly dressed in beret and stable belt. He was about twenty-two years old, both his father and grandfather had served in the RAR, and he too came from a neighbouring village to that of Dube and Moyo.

'Sibanda we have decided to invite you to join our stick. This matter has been discussed by us and we believe that you are the right man to take on this job,' stated Smith importantly. Then, not waiting for a reply continued, 'You are free to decide for yourself and we will understand if you want to stay in Lance Corporal Nkai's stick.'

'*Siyabonga kakhulu Ishe*, thank you very much Sir!' answered Sibanda in siNdebele, a broad smile spreading on his face, 'I will be happy to join your stick.'

That was all he had to say, he braced up, the three stood, they all shook hands, Sibanda executed a neat about turn and marched off back to the barrack room, a delighted smile still on his face, a spring in his step. The unofficial reshuffling of sticks now began in earnest in the barrack room. The debate raged into the night as arguments were raised, cases put, issues discussed. Smith suspected that when a decision had to be made, Dube, despite his rank of rifleman, held considerable weight.

Smith was lying on his bed re-reading Jane's letter when the duty NCO knocked on the door, 'You are to report to *Ingwe* immediately' the man said.

Smith put on his boots and went off to see what was up, a sinking feeling in his stomach. He found Fullerton sitting in his office, his feet resting on his desk, as was his custom.

'Sergeant Smith, you did Afrikaans at school, did you not?'

Smith nodded.

'I have a very interesting job for you and your stick,' announced Fullerton, with a smug expression on his face. 'You have been carefully selected for this mission ...' he smiled, now obviously having difficulty believing his own bullshit. He sat forward conspiratorially, '... you are to assist our South African friends with a small problem they have.'

Smith did not volunteer a comment, standing rigidly in front of the Captain.

'You and your stick will be collected from the airfield tomorrow at 07:30 and flown to Katima Mulilo on the Caprivi Strip[89].'

Fullerton paused momentarily to gauge a reaction from Smith that was not forthcoming.

'From Katima you will be flown to a hill ... I know not where, whereupon you will protect a radio relay station. This radio relay is to assist with an attack on a place unknown to me ... by both South African and Rhodesian forces, ... I know not which. You should expect to be away for a minimum of three days. I will be accompanying you to Katima Mulilo on a separate mission ... that I cannot divulge,' smiled

---

89 The Caprivi Strip was the strip of South West Africa that stretches across the north of Botswana, where the eastern most point meets Zambia and Rhodesia at Kazungula (see Map 3).

Fullerton, more broadly this time, amused by his own ridiculously unhelpful explanation.

'Do you have any questions?' he enquired with feigned seriousness, sitting back in his chair, replaced his boots on the desk and gazed out the window disinterestedly.

'Sir, I have not manned a radio relay before. Will I be given some instructions?' ventured Smith. A million other questions now presented themselves. *Are we the only stick in this fucking Army?*

'You will be given signallers to operate the equipment. Your relay services will probably not be needed … this is just a back-up in case other radio comms go down. Piece-of-Cake. … By the way do not discuss this with anyone, nobody, not even Lt Gibbs.'

Not providing any further opportunity for questions, Fullerton stood up and left his office, his mind clearly on other things.

Smith dumbstruck watched his departure. *Fuck me, what did I do to deserve this! An External! The Caprivi Strip! A radio relay? Speak Afrikaans? I got a 'C' at O-Level!* Smith shook his head in disbelief, then resigned to his fate, he trudged off to organise his men, muttering unhappily all the way. The familiar sick feeling crept back in Smith's stomach. This was way beyond his level of training and experience.

Smith briefed his men on what kit they needed for the mission, unable to give any detail when questioned. The fact that *Ingwe* Fullerton was coming along was enough for them.

Feeling horribly worried and confused, Smith wandered down to the horse lines to find O'Connell for a chat. The sound of singing could be heard around the camp. O'Connell had a very small record collection, dating back to his days in Vietnam. Albums included the Beach Boys, Creedence Clearwater Revival, Bob Dylan and Neil Young amongst others, all in worn out covers, many showing signs of being soaked in beer. O'Connell's favourite song, *Sloop John B*[90] by the Beach Boys was almost an anthem for 3 Troop. He had rigged up a set of speakers in the trees above the horse-lines with the cables running back to the dilapidated turntable in his room. The Grey Scouts always played music when working in the horse-lines; it helped to pass the time. They were presently belting out their troop song.

So hoist up the John B's sail
See how the mainsail sets
Call for the captain ashore
Let me go home, let me go home
I wanna go home, yeah yeah

90 *Sloop John B*, traditional song, arranged by Brian Wilson, 1966

Well I feel so broke up
I wanna go home

The sentiment, *I wanna go home,* so real for a soldier, particularly a national serviceman.

Let me go home
Why don't they let me go home
This is the worst trip I've ever been on…

Smith stood watching the Grey Scouts going about their business. The happy and relaxed camaraderie amongst the men contrasted so markedly with his own experience. The feeling of separation and isolation returned. *I'm going to the Caprivi Strip and I can't tell anyone … for Fuck Sakes!*

*

Smith had his men standing next to the airfield at Sprayview at 7am sharp the next morning. Gibbs had been horrified to hear that his platoon sergeant was about to disappear on another jaunt. He had complained bitterly to Major Peacock and Captain Fullerton. Smith secretly praying that he would win the day. It was not to be.

Fullerton came striding across in full combat order, rifle and camo-cream; he had a HQ signaller, a rifleman and a MAG gunner with him. *This must be a big plane,* Smith thought to himself. They were all heavily loaded; he had made his stick pack six days of rations, extra ammunition, extra radio batteries for the A76 and extra smoke, white phosphorus and M962 shrapnel grenades.

The small contingent stood around waiting, some sat in the dirt leaning on their packs. Smith couldn't bring himself to speak to Fullerton in case he showed his nervousness. Fullerton spoke happily with the soldiers in seShona, laughing loudly at some private joke. The soldiers were totally comfortable in Fullerton's company, laughing and joking with him, enjoying his company. Smith looked on, his inability to participate in the conversation added to the feeling of being an outsider, a transient interloper. He stood to one side, ignored by the others.

In the distance, a loud clattering drifted in on the breeze. The noise grew steadily louder until across the end of the runway came a massive helicopter. Smith had only seen them in pictures, the SAAF Puma SA330. The pilot banked sharply and brought the aircraft into land exactly in front of where the troops were standing. The soldiers were absolutely amazed at this massive machine; they pointed and laughed, mostly to hide their surprise and apprehension. The engines were shut down and a SADF Major jumped out onto the tarmac. He strode across purposefully to where the group was standing.

Without any pleasantries the Major shouted abruptly, 'Who is in charge?' His strong Afrikaans accent in evidence.

'I am,' said Fullerton stepping forward offering his hand. The Major ignored it, instead looking past him at the men collected behind. He was about the same height as Fullerton, wearing the standard brown SADF uniform, with a beret and stable belt. The pilot and co-pilot of the Puma stepped down onto the tarmac behind the Major.

'Where are the troops to take with us?' the Major asked, looking about. Fullerton somewhat perplexed waved behind him, indicating the men, obvious in their combat order.

'Here they are!' he said, waving behind him, starting to get agitated at the Major's rudeness.

'I am not taking *Kaffirs* in my helikopter,' stated the Major indignantly, at the top of his voice.

In a flash, in one fluid motion, Fullerton planted his fist, using his full force, straight onto the end of the Major's nose. It exploded in blood and snot. A follow-up punch landed in the Major's solar plexus. He doubled over gasping for air, falling to his knees holding his nose and yelping in pain.

Unperturbed, Fullerton stepped past the broken Major towards the pilots.

'Good morning gentlemen, welcome to 4 Independent Company RAR, I am Captain Ian Fullerton and this is the contingent to be delivered to Katima Mulilo.'

The pilots looked closely at him with a quizzical look on their faces not sure whether he was in fact black or white; he had done such a good job on the camo-cream.

'It would appear that your Major has bumped his nose,' said Fullerton offhandedly, waving expansively at the Major still writhing in pain.

'Ja it looks like it' replied one of the pilots. They shook their heads obviously embarrassed by the Major's outburst; *there are arseholes in every army*.

'Well let's be off then … there's a war on … don't want to be late,' added Fullerton flippantly, walked up to the door of the helicopter, he threw his pack onto one of the seats.

The men, including Smith, hesitated, looking at the pilots to give them the order to load.

'For fuck sakes Sergeant Smith get your men onto the helicopter. We haven't got all day,' demanded Fullerton. With that they all climbed aboard. Nobody spoke.

Smith saw, out of the corner of his eye, Dube smack the doubled-up Major on the back of his head with the butt of the MAG. They had all heard the insult, the ultimate insult for a black man in Africa. *That Major better not find himself in a dark alley with Dube,* Smith thought to himself. The pilots assisted the bloodied Major who could not bring himself to speak; the pain and shock were just too much; a lump appeared on the back of his head, *a helikopter full of Blacks! My Lewe!*

The Puma skimmed across the trees on its way to Katima Mulilo, about 190kms to the west. The speed was amazing compared with the Alouette, 134 knots. The doors on either side were left open and the troops sat back to back in the centre seats, all strapped in.

The extreme western border of Rhodesia tapers to a point. That point borders Zambia, South West Africa's Caprivi Strip, and Botswana. The border with Angola is only 200kms due west. South West Africa had been under South African protection since a mandate provided by the League of Nations after the First World War. That mandate had been revoked by the United Nations, and South Africa was locked in negotiations with the UN Security Council on a transition to 'Namibian' independence. The liberation movement in South West Africa, which had also begun in the 1960s, was the South West African Peoples Organisation (SWAPO) led by Sam Nujoma. SWAPO were conducting raids into the Caprivi Strip from bases in Zambia.

The Zambian leader, Kenneth Kaunda, was naturally very supportive of the liberation struggles taking place along his borders and he was very much encouraged by the leaders of the other 'Front Line States' as they were called (Tanzania, Zaire[91] and the newly liberated, Mozambique and Angola). The result was the creation of a network of training camps and bases on Zambian soil to provide logistical support for the various liberation movements. In many cases the same Soviet, Cuban and East German instructors trained these armies in the same camps. The Cubans had intervened heavily in Angola, locking horns with the South Africans in major conventional battles. President Kaunda had made an error in his fervent support for the nationalist movements; he harboured *Umkomto we Zizwe,* the military wing of the ANC[92], the liberation movement for South Africa itself.

---

91 Congo, previously Belgium Congo.
92 African Nation Congress (South Africa), the leading black nationalist movement in South Africa together with the Pan-Africanist Congress and the South African Communist Party.

If there was one enemy in Africa that the South Africans feared above all else, it was the rise of the ANC. The fact that they knew that *Umkomto we Zizwe* was being trained in Zambia now meant that the Zambian bases became a target. The small Zambian logging village of Mulobezi lies about 120kms northeast of Katima Mulilo, as the crow flies. Just outside of the village was a large training camp that housed ANC, SWAPO and ZIPRA freedom fighters. The Zambians had cleverly registered the base with the UNHCR[93] as a Refugee Camp for which they received funding and food deliveries. Mulobezi was, nevertheless, now to become the focus for some other, unwanted 'attention'.

*

Katima Mulilo, AFB Mpacha[94], Caprivi Strip, South West Africa

The Puma followed the Zambezi River, keeping the river about a kilometre or two on the right as it flew. As they approached Katima Mulilo the aircraft banked to the left and approached the large airstrip from the east. The helicopter banked again and below Smith could see row upon row of vehicles, hundreds of them, armoured personnel carriers, tanks, armoured cars, heavy trucks and a myriad of other smaller vehicles. The RAR soldiers in the helicopter began to point and chatter excitedly, *this was truly amazing*. As the Puma touched down gently Smith could see three Dakotas, a DC-4, a huge C-130 Hercules, other Pumas and Alouette IIIs. There were South African soldiers and airmen encamped in tents along the full length of the airstrip. The small group of Rhodesians climbed out of the helicopter, very self-conscious in their full combat gear, their camouflage uniforms very conspicuous amongst the South African 'browns'. *What could they possible need us for?* Smith thought as he looked around him.

The South African Major had recovered a little from his bump on the nose and in a very surly fashion, led Fullerton and his group across the hard-standing to a line of single-storey buildings set back under some trees. Still holding his nose, he pointed to a tree and giving an unintelligible grunt, indicated for them to wait. He then disappeared into the largest of the buildings.

'Well Sergeant Smith, we haven't got off on the right foot with the South Africans. Not to worry, we will be out of here shortly I would suspect,' declared Fullerton confidently.

Smith studied Fullerton, resplendent in full combat order, blackened

93 United Nations High Commissioner for Refugees.
94 South African Air Force Base Mpacha was located a few kilometres south of the village of Katima Mulilo on the Caprivi Strip.

face, rifle slung over his shoulder, *nothing fazes this bloke*. He then glanced across at the rest of the RAR contingent standing talking animatedly to each other. They all looked impressive in their full combat kit. A wave of pride washed over him, these were 'his' men, *who better to go to war with*?

The size of the base and the vast number of men was truly amazing. The longer they sat and waited the more South African soldiers came over for a look at the visitors. Few of them would have been in combat before, plus none of them would have ever seen black soldiers.

A young corporal ventured forward, *'Wie is je?'* he asked. *'Van waar af kom je?'*

Smith replied in broken Afrikaans, *'Ons is van Rhodesië af, ons is RAR, almal in die RAR is swart.'*

'Vragtag!' the corporal exclaimed, and turned to his mates and said in Afrikaans, 'He says they are from Rhodesia, their unit is RAR and they are all black!'

The other soldiers shook their heads in amazement. The questions then came thick and fast, as the audience grew more inquisitive. Smith did his best to answer the questions to the obvious amusement of Fullerton. Dube in mock intimidation walked amongst the gathered men, his MAG belts shining in the bright sunlight. He made a point of standing in front of a few of the smaller men glaring into their faces inches away, to the obvious hilarity of the 4 Indep men. This gave the others the same idea and before long they were all mixing freely with the South Africans, completely oblivious to the many questions thrust at them in Afrikaans.

The discussion was broken up when the SADF Major came hurrying back. Fullerton and Smith were ushered into a briefing room that was full of SADF officers. They all turned to look at the two blackened camouflaged apparitions that had entered their midst. What followed was a mind-boggling briefing, at least half of which was conducted in Afrikaans; Smith could not follow all the content but the word 'Mulobezi' came up very often.

Finally, the officer conducting the briefing pointed to where the two Rhodesians were sitting.

'Here are the men that will man the relay, call sign six five. They will conduct the relay if the DC-4 Command Ship should be disabled. The reason they are here is because they have men who can understand both seShona and siNdebele. They can also speak English and Afrikaans and, therefore, they will be able to tell us if the camp we are attacking is calling in assistance using their own native languages. You should all contact call-sign six five one hour before H-Hour to check frequencies and equipment.'

The briefing officer then listed a set of frequencies to be used by the various contingents and units conducting the attack, including air force c/signs. There had been a change of plan in that Fullerton's original job had been cancelled. Fullerton was now to lead c/sign 65; Smith's relief was indescribable. Suddenly this mission sounded vaguely exciting.

By the time the briefing was complete, the sun was low on the horizon. The two men walked back to the airfield, Smith now deep in thought. The two things that Smith took from the briefing was that the DC-4 Command Ship's c/sign was *Spook*, Ghost, the second thing was that they would be on their own, with no support if they got into trouble. Fullerton did not ask any questions in the briefing, Smith would seriously have liked to have known what the back-up plan was if they were attacked. What confused Smith was, *if this is a joint operation why were there no other Rhodesian forces in this briefing?*

He plucked up the courage to ask a question, 'Why are none of the Scouts, SAS or RLI call signs here for the briefing Sir?'

'Our boys are conducting the attack with a limited involvement from South African Recces[95]. The majority of the enemy in the camp are ZIPRA but the South Africans are anxious to capture a few *Umkomto we Sizwe* and SWAPO terrorists.'

'Surely our air force should be here if we are conducting the attack Sir?'

'Our air force will deploy our troops from Wankie … The Slopes are just providing air support and top-cover in case the Zambians intervene with their Migs.' Fullerton abruptly stopped his explanation when he realised he was only speaking to a sergeant.

'But Sir, what will happen if our call sign gets into trouble?' persisted Smith.

'What trouble could we possibly get into? We are sitting on top of a hill in the middle of nowhere, there is no resident population anywhere near the relay site,' concluded Fullerton in a condescending fashion.

'Yes Sir … but what happens if we get into trouble, what happens if the Zambians find us?'

'For fuck sakes Smith, you are a bloody platoon sergeant, not Field Marshall Fucking Montgomery. We just go and do our job, a few hours on top of a hill, have a good bullshit session, then we go home … piece-a-cake,' declared Fullerton waving his arms dismissively, thrusting his head forward, glaring at Smith, daring him to ask another question.

Smith looked at his Captain, blushing brightly beneath the camo-cream. He considered whether he should press Fullerton further, his mind suddenly full of other questions.

---

95 1 Reconnaissance Commando, popularly known as 'Recces' was the main Special Forces unit of the South African Defense Force (SADF) in the mid-1970's.

Fullerton continued to stare at him petulantly.

'Smith … fuck off and check on the men, make sure they drink a lot of water and refill their water bottles.'

'Yes Sir.' Smith turned to look for where the men had disappeared.

Fullerton called after him, '… and you best get them to cook up a meal, they will not do any cooking in the relay site.'

In the darkness of early evening, c/sign 65, comprising Smith, Fullerton and their six troops, were loaded into a Puma together with three South African signallers and their radio equipment. High cloud with no moon meant the helicopter took off into pitch-blackness, heading north at treetop level.

The site for the 65 relay was a set of low hills about 50kms to the west of the Zambian village of Mulobezi. The southwestern corner of Zambia is very flat with very few hills; the area is mostly swamp, with thickly wooded river lines. The flight path had been designed to ensure that populated areas were not flown over, the nearest inhabited village was miles away. An advance party had cut a pre-arranged LZ; the helicopter flew directly over the LZ before executing a tight banking turn that made Smith's stomach turn. As Smith peered down into the blackness, a tiny flicker of light appeared through the trees. The helicopter seemed to hover for a few seconds as the pilots satisfied themselves that they were in the correct place, the helicopter then dropped rapidly onto the ground, bouncing gently on its undercarriage.

The RAR contingent exited the helicopter as quickly as possible, helping the signallers with their equipment. In seconds the Puma lifted back into the night, disappearing rapidly into the darkness, its engine noise quickly fading. Smith reflected momentarily on the feeling of being left behind by a departing helicopter, one of emptiness, of being cut off, abandoned by the 'safe' world. He stole a glance in the direction of the now distant helicopter; *I hope they are correct with their intelligence … that there are no Zambians or Gooks anywhere nearby.*

Two very rough sounding South African soldiers, almost invisible in the pitch-black night, met c/sign 65 on the ground. They hissed a few instructions in broken English then, without waiting for a response, moved off into the hills. The darkness was totally disorientating. Soldiers bumped into each other in the dark and unseen obstructions on the ground tripped people up. They moved as silently as they could in the circumstances but the noise of moving through the undergrowth was impossible to control in the dark. Matters were made worse as the signallers struggled under the unwieldy weight of their equipment. Numerous halts were called as the group attempted to reallocate the load of equipment. The two guides were not interested in helping, instead standing by impatiently, beckoning the signallers to hurry up. The three signallers were young South African national servicemen, quite obviously completely unprepared for humping heavy equipment through the bush at night. Dube, in frustration at the delay, grabbed the largest of the three radios and hoisted it onto his back behind his head. He then grunted loudly that he was ready to continue and the trip then progressed more smoothly.

After an hour the small contingent climbed up a low hill. It was no more than fifteen or twenty metres above the surrounding countryside. Thankfully it had good tree cover, but there were no rocks of any size to use to build protection. The hill was virtually conical while a low ridge or saddle connected it to another hill of about the same shape and size. The two guides made a few unintelligible comments then disappeared into the dark. Smith never saw them again.

Smith set about organising the scraping of slit trenches into the hard ground and dragging as much dead plant material as they could to provide camouflage protection should anyone be walking past the bottom of the hill. The signallers put up their dipole aerials by stretching them across from tree to tree. Then there was a lengthy period of checking of the radios and calling the various command groups elsewhere. By midnight c/sign 65 was on the air. Smith had the RAR group in all-round defensive positions. When the moon came up it was relatively easy to set up and instruct on fields of fire. Fullerton then ordered everybody to get three hours of sleep. H-Hour was at first light, 05:30. Smith lay down in the scrape he had dug, looking over at Fullerton who sat propped up against a tree, just below the crest of the hill, so as not to provide a silhouette. *Ingwe will not sleep tonight*. The metaphor comparing Fullerton with a leopard never seemed more appropriate, *Leopards silently hunt at night. The darkness is their natural element*. The sight of Fullerton sitting next to the tree, his rifle cradled in his arms, his eyes flicking left and right, somehow made Smith feel secure. The man radiated confidence; it seemed to rub off just being in his presence.

Smith lay in his sleeping position, choosing to lie on top of his sleeping bag instead of inside it. Lying on a lonely hill in Zambia gave him pause for thought. National Service had seemed a formality for Mike Smith, almost part of the natural scheme of things. *Everybody had to do it, so make the best of it*. The question of 'why' this war was being fought had not crossed Mike Smith's mind before. As he lay in his shell scrape, on Zambian soil far from home, for the first time the question crossed his mind. As a young, self-righteous teenager he was disturbed by the fact that people were *attacking our country. We must defend ourselves against the communist onslaught*. He had heard his parents talk about the Government's propaganda. They had voiced their concern at the direction that Ian Smith was taking the country. Smith had listened to Ian Smith's speeches on television, talking about 'those countries to the north of us', their corrupt, one-party states, the fact that black people were not equipped to run a country, they needed the white man. *It all seemed to make perfect sense the way he said it, in any event we are winning the war aren't we?* Ian Smith, affectionately known as 'Our Smithy', had ruled out the question of 'black majority rule'. He had said majority rule would never happen, 'never in a thousand years' he had said. More recently he had slightly amended his position to 'never in my lifetime', the implication of this not-so-subtle change in perspective lost on most people. *Everybody trusts Ian Smith, don't they? He will do the right thing, to get a political settlement on favourable terms ... in the meantime we need to 'fight through thick and thin, to keep our land a free land, stop the enemy coming in[96]'.*

The whole question of the 'futility of war', so often trotted out in novels and poetry, had not been something Smith had contemplated thus far. He had read Wilfred Owen and Siegfried Sassoon at school, reciting Owen's *Anthem for Doomed Youth* in class.

> *What passing-bells for these who die as cattle?*
> *Only the monstrous anger of the guns.*
> *Only the stuttering rifles' rapid rattle*
> *Can patter out their hasty orisons[97].*

That poem was written for a different war, very different to this. This bush war had been more of an exciting adventure for Smith thus far, but now, *People are dying, Fauguneze, Williams, terrorists, policemen, farmers and villagers. There seem to be terrorists everywhere. Where were they all coming from? I thought the black people were happy with their lot in life. Why would they want to support communist insurgents? Why don't they understand?* These were the questions that now occupied Smith's mind, *is there a possibility that we may be wrong? The whole world seems to be against us.* He took out Jane's letter that he carried in the pocket of his combat shirt, holding the pages to his nose to smell her scent. Eventually he dropped off into a fitful sleep.

Smith was shaken awake by Fullerton an hour before H-Hour. He carefully crawled to the next man in line instructing him to wake the rest. Each man duly did this in turn. It was perfectly silent ... then a Grey Lourie, *Pfunye*, called in the distance as if announcing the oncoming

---

96 A line from Clem Tholet's folk song, *Rhodesians Never Die*.
97 Wilfred Owen, *Anthem for Doomed Youth*, October 1917. Orisons - prayers, here funeral prayers

dawn, *oh waaa ... oh waaaa*. The signallers were wearing headphones, speaking in hushed tones, mostly in English.

The early morning sunlight had only just touched the top of the trees when a crash of sound like rolling thunder broke overhead. Three Canberra[98] bombers in a tight V-formation flew over at treetop level. No sooner had they passed ... then another group ... and then another. The sound was incredible, resounding in the chest as they passed. *Somebody was in for some serious shit*, Smith thought to himself. The Signallers turned up the volume on the external mike so that Smith and Fullerton could hear. The Canberra pilots could be heard clearly as they approached the target, their excited chatter as they successfully released their bombs onto the camp. There followed a cacophony of radio calls from helicopters and ground troops as they moved onto the target.

Spook, the Command DC4, came onto the air to check on intercepted radio traffic; the radios tuned to known terrorist frequencies remained silent. The battle raged on for at least three hours. On occasions they heard additional airstrikes being called in. A few jets passed over the relay at very high altitude. Smith tried to see what they were but all he could see was the puffy vapour trail in the clear blue sky.

'*Ishe* look,' whispered Sibanda, pointing off into the distance.

Smith followed the direction Sibanda was pointing, squinting through the bush. A line of troops could be seen in the distance approaching the hill; they could not have been more than a kilometre away.

Fullerton had already seen the men looming through the bush. He grabbed the radio transmitter. 'Break, Break, Break ... *Spook* ... this is 65 do you read?' His voice, in a hushed whisper, belied the sense of urgency.

'65 go' came the immediate response.

'*Spook* we have approximately fifty unknown soldiers approaching from our east ... over.'

Fullerton was looking at the soldiers through his binoculars.

'65 we have no friendly forces in your area ... standby.'

That's right, but there is not supposed to be anyone else either! Smith thought.

They all lay in their positions ... waiting for the reply, it seemed to take forever, in reality only a few seconds.

'65 ... *Spook*, we believe that those troops can only be Zambian

---

98 The English Electric Canberra B2, twin-engined, light bomber, supplied to the Rhodesian Air Force in 1959. The South Africans also operated Canberras but the more advanced version, BI MK12 Interdictors. The South African Canberras joined in on Rhodesian Canberra strikes on many external raids.

army. You must exit your position to the LZ … immediately … over.'

'*Spook* … 65, negative, they are not wearing Zambian uniforms. We cannot safely exit our position. They are too close. Can you provide air support? … Over.'

The Zambian Army wore a camouflage similar to the British pattern; these men were wearing khaki fatigues.

'65 … *Spook* … standby.' There was silence again as the Mission Commander in the DC-4 worked out the options. Another agonising wait ensued.

The approaching sweep line continued their advance, fortunately quite slowly. Fullerton whispered the word to all of the c/sign not to open fire until he did. The sweepline reached the bottom of the hill and stopped. They clearly did not know of the Rhodesian's presence on the hill. They stood around, one lit up a cigarette.

Smith lay next to Fullerton; it was too dangerous to try to crawl to his position further to the left.

'They do not look like Zambians; my guess is that they are either SWAPO or ZIPRA Gooks,' whispered Fullerton into Smith's ear.

Smith felt panic rise in his chest. *We are in a foreign country, miles from home. We have no real support. How the hell are we going to get out of this?* The temptation to get up and run was overwhelming.

The radio buzzed again, turned right down, '65 … this is *Spook*, do not engage the enemy unless it is absolutely necessary. We are sending air support, call-sign Orange 45, ETA fourteen minutes, you must retire to your LZ … Your extraction call-sign Orange 35, ETA twenty minutes.'

They had originally only expected to be extracted at about three that afternoon; this was a lot earlier than planned.

'Roger *Spook* … copied … 65 out,' Fullerton whispered. He looked across at the three signallers who sat ashen-faced, he cut across his throat with his hand then pointed at the radios, *turn them off!*

One of the cadres at the bottom of the hill started pointing up the hill, waving his arms; clearly his instructions to the others had not met with much enthusiasm. The voices drifted up the hill but it was impossible to hear what language they were speaking. Armies are the same the world over, ask a soldier to climb a hill for no apparent reason and expect whinging and whining. Eventually the man, who must have been the leader, won the day and the band began to climb the hill in a loose line, dragging their feet, making no attempt to disguise their presence. This was a classic example of raw, untrained, troops going through the motions.

The hill had a gentle gradient, not very demanding. The Leader was positioned roughly in the middle of the line, waving his arms to keep everyone moving.

As he got halfway to the top he shouted out in clear siNdebele, 'Move up, Move up on the left'… they were ZIPRA!

Fullerton waited as the band came closer and closer, Smith tried to keep his breathing as steady as possible, lining up a CT in his sights. The CTs stopped again, so close that their voices were clearly audible. The Leader harangued one of the cadres closer to him, shouting on the top of his voice. *Man these guys don't realise just how real this training exercise is about to become,* Smith thought to himself, his heart beating hard in his chest.

The Leader of the CTs called for the sweep line to start again, waving his arms once again. Smith could see their eyes clearly. He could even hear their heavy breathing with the exertion of climbing the hill. Fullerton waited for the absolute last minute, the sound of his first double-tap, released a wave of lead down the hill. The CTs in the centre fell where they stood. Dube corrected his MAG to the left, a long burst, dust flying into the air. The CT's did not fire one round in reply; they took off down the hill, yelling as they went.

Fullerton leapt to his feet, 'Throw all the extra weight out of your packs, destroy the radios, we are getting out of here … NOW!'

Everyone scrambled to their feet; Smith unstapled his pack throwing out the spare rat packs and radio batteries. Fullerton ordered the signallers to shoot up their radios. C/sign 65 then retreated down the hill towards the LZ, a full twenty-minute jog away. Fullerton threw a red smoke grenade onto the top of the hill as they left. As the smoke canister ignited, a few isolated shots from the bottom of the hill rang out.

The RAR men dashed off down the hill, weapons at the high-port. Dube always ran with the gun lying across his shoulder, upside down, barrel pointing backwards his hand on the butt to hold it in position, the belts of 7.62 bouncing and jangling as he ran. Fullerton took up the lead in single file, followed by his gunner with Smith at the rear with Dube immediately in front of him. At the bottom of the hill Fullerton stopped momentarily to check his bearings. As he did so a CT appeared in front of him only a few metres away. Fullerton had his map and compass in his hands, he looked up, 'FUCK OOFFF' he blared at the startled man. The CT stood in shocked amazement gaping at Fullerton before spinning on his heel and dashing off back into the bush. The gunner behind Fullerton was unsighted so it was the first rifleman that managed to get a few rounds off in the direction of the departing man.

More CTs appeared in the bush to the right. It occurred to Smith instantly that the ZIPRA group on the top the hill were only part of a much larger group that had walked around the side of the low hill used for the 65 relay.

Fullerton turned and hissed, 'we must get into a sweep line … Smith … go to the extreme right. Everybody, run, no stopping, shoot what you see.'

Fullerton then threw another smoke grenade before setting off at a steady trot. The thick forest canopy meant that the undergrowth was relatively light, easy to walk through, but running was much more difficult. The loose line of eight RAR soldiers headed off into the bush, running as fast as they could, the three South African signallers stumbling on immediately behind Fullerton, frightened out of their wits.

Not having had enough time to plot an accurate course to the LZ, Fullerton had simply glanced at his compass, taken a fleeting bearing, hoping the sound of the helicopter would guide him to the LZ.

The ZIPRA commander quickly summed up the situation, realising that he was only dealing with a small SF detachment. He and his men gave chase, firing wildly at the departing invaders. Hearing the crack and thump overhead, Smith glanced back but could not see anything. As the bush was fairly open, keeping in line was not too difficult, but the men were starting to bunch up, fatigue setting in. Smith looked up into the trees, *they would have needed bulldozers to cut an LZ here!*

A jet screamed low overhead, in the direction of the hill.

'65 … 65 this is Orange 45 do you read.' Smith heard the call from the pilot.

'45, I have you visual … dropped two smoke grenades marking our direction, I am throwing another … NOW … Green … Over,' replied Fullerton, his voice strained from the effort of running.

They ran on in silence, each man alone with his thoughts just the sound of crushing undergrowth as they passed.

'45 … I have Charlie Tangos to my rear, they are chasing us, can you slow them down? … Over,' asked Fullerton to the pilot flying overhead.

The jet roared back, the pilot assessing the situation by looking at the position of the three wispy smoke clouds drifting through the tree canopy. Another jet arrived overhead. The pilots could be heard talking to each other over the radio.

'45, 46 … Can you see anything?' one of the pilots asked the other, the pilots always sounded so calm and controlled.

'46 Negative, I can only see the smoke.'

One of the CTs made the error of shooting up at the aircraft through the trees.

'Roger I have tracer visual fifty west of the green smoke … I am rolling in.'

'45 … I will follow you.'

The jets burst overhead again.

'Smith … throw smoke,' Fullerton called out, he had used all of his canisters.

'Orange 45 … 65, I am throwing red smoke,' Smith stuttered into the radio, his breathing laboured.

The pilots clearly seeing the direction that 65 were heading in began to rake the bush behind them with rockets. They flew directly along the line of smoke grenades in the direction of the hill. Smith glanced up, an aircraft flashed through the trees above; he saw the SNEB[99] rockets leaving their pods. The sound of high-energy explosions was shattering, they seemed so close, the explosive heads shredding trees, cutting them down like a scythe.

Fullerton tried to call the extraction helicopter, 'Orange 35 … 35 … this is 65, do you read?'

He was completely out of breath, trying desperately to speak as he ran. Rounds were still passing overhead from the CTs behind. They may have been inexperienced but they were determined, they knew that the soldiers were heading for an LZ.

'65 … 35, I am five minutes out, I will orbit until you arrive,' replied the extraction helicopter.

They ran on, their exhaustion starting to take its toll. Dube was slowing badly with the gun bouncing wildly on his shoulder.

Smith got up next to him, 'Give me some of your belts,' he shouted. Dube just looked ahead stoically. *A gunner does not give away his belts.*

The helicopter could be heard in the distance, the pilot cavitated the blades as he pulled into an orbit around the LZ, *the sweetest sound*. They were too far to the east of the LZ. Fullerton stopped the men. All stood sucking for air, chests heaving with exertion.

'Okay … we are too far to the east, we need to move in that direction,' puffed Fullerton, pointing off into the bush. A CT appeared behind them, only a few yards away, he started to raise his rifle. Fullerton shot him in the chest.

'35 … 65 … I am to your east, maybe one click … over.'

'65 … standby.'

The helicopter could be heard coming towards them.

'Let's go … come on, a final push.' Fullerton took off again in the direction of the clattering helicopter with the men following closely behind.

---

99 The Lynx carried Matra 37mm SNEB rockets; Hawker Hunters carried Matra 68mm SNEB rockets. The aircraft in this contact were in fact 24 Squadron, SAAF, Blackburn Buccaneers S.50s, specialised ground-attack strike aircraft; they also carried 68mm SNEB rockets in four wing-mounted pods. The Buccaneer also had an internal bomb bay for carrying bombs and frantan.

'Smith … drop another smoke,' he yelled over his shoulder.

The CT sweepline had heard the shot Fullerton had fired and were now charging towards the sound. The smoke grenade fizzed red smoke, acting like a beacon. The fugitives were now crossing in front of the CT sweep line at right angles, shots rang out from Smith's right as he ran but he still could not see anything, not daring to look for fear of falling.

'65 I have you visual,' called the helicopter pilot. 'You have plenty Charlie Tangos to your north.'

The Puma was powerless to be of assistance, as it did not have door guns mounted or any offensive armament for that matter. The helicopter pilot flew low over the trees drawing the CT fire away from the Rhodesians, their tracer rounds lifting through the trees.

After what seemed an eternity, the exhausted group broke into the LZ clearing, the helicopter orbiting close in overhead.

Smith slowed, Dube just behind him, his face racked with exhaustion.

'Down, covering fire,' Smith called out, the two men slid to the ground. Dube dropped the gun onto its bipod, instantly firing into the bush from whence they had come. Moyo dived to the ground on the other side of Dube, also shooting deliberately into the bush. Smith stretched back for the spare MAG belt in his hip pouch. The gun chattered as Dube began slow deliberate fire, crack, crack … crack, crack, strangely comforting. Smith lifted his own rifle, firing into the bush; he still could not see anything to shoot at.

The two jets came back overhead. *What are they*? Smith couldn't tell, *Not Hunters*[100].

The Puma began to drop into the LZ. CTs appeared, shooting at the helicopter. The Puma had no armed protection. A crewman stood at the door firing an R1[101], over the heads of the 65 c/sign all lying on the edge of the clearing. The jets passed over again, releasing 450kg bombs, the bush disappearing in dust and foliage as they passed.

The Puma lined up on the LZ, the pilot rapidly descending … then touching down, bouncing on its undercarriage.

'GO…GO…GO' screamed Fullerton. 'Smith take the men, GO.'

The men got up and dashed for the open door. The dust thrown up by the blades stung, filling the lungs, choking, cramming eyes with grit. It was virtually impossible to see, Smith squinted, desperately seeking the door. He turned. As he did so one of signallers went down in the dust behind him. A rifleman from Fullerton's stick hobbled, he had dropped his pack dragging his rifle behind him. Fullerton, Moyo and the two MAG gunners were now up, backing towards the helicopter and

100 Hawker Hunter FGA9 Mk IX, ground attack fighter, delivered to Rhodesia in 1963.
101 South African manufactured version of the Belgian FN.

firing into the bush as they came. The dust was blinding, a red blizzard, destroying all visibility. The crewman at the door frantically grabbed at kit, rifles, men, hauling them bodily into the helicopter.

CTs appeared on the edge of the LZ, firing wildly, a bullet struck the helicopter door right in front of Smith's face. Smith threw his pack into the doorway, dashing back, grabbing the stricken signaller by his webbing. One of the straps gave way and they both fell over, bullet strikes appeared in the dust all around. Fullerton had the wounded rifleman under his arm, carrying him as he would a sack of potatoes. Dube threw his gun into the helicopter, running back to help Smith with the wounded signaller. The helicopter was now taking heavy fire; the crewman was screaming, urging them to get in. The jets came back over, this time releasing frantan. The bush disappeared into fire and smoke, so close that the heat forced Smith to close his eyes. The helicopter's blades started biting at the air as the pilot applied full take-off power, starting to inch forward. Fullerton was the last into the helicopter, having to jump for the step as it lifted into the air, the twin turbines ear-splitting on full power. The pilot banked into a tight turn, green tracer clearly visible, following them as they went. The two jets strafed the now empty LZ, a huge pall of smoke lifted into the air from the burning fran strike.

The signaller was hurt badly; the bullet had passed through his back and exited through his chest. The frothy blood was coming out of his mouth. He coughed, blood splattered all over the front of Smith's shirt. Smith plunged morphine into him, snatching at the field dressings in his medic pouch, pushing them into the chest wound, the blood pulsing through his fingers.

'Dube … hold these in place' shouted Smith above the engine noise.

'Am I going to die Sarge?' the signaller asked, with a clear English accent.

'Where are you from soldier?' Smith replied, concentrating on unpacking a drip.

'Durban … Westville,' the man's voice was now softer, his strength ebbing away.

'You will be fine, hang in there … not far to go,' Smith bit open the pack holding the saline drip, forcing the catheter into the rubber stopper, tourniquet in place, trying to find a vein …

'It's Okay Sarge … can you tell my mum … I love her?'

'You can tell her yourself.' Smith spoke as calmly as he could to the stricken soldier. 'Its not far to go … I am just putting in a drip …'

The man died then, his muffled voice trailing off, blood flowing freely from his mouth, his face strangely serene despite the fright and horror of his death.

Smith looked up blankly at Dube whose hands were still pressing down on the wound, blood now running back and forth across the floor of the helicopter as it banked and turned.

> *No mockeries now for them; no prayers nor bells;*
> *Nor any voice of mourning save the choirs,* [102]

Fullerton looked across from where he was sitting, the wounded rifleman passed out in his arms. He lifted his fist, thumbs up. Smith stared at him blankly too shocked to make any response. The deafening roar of the helicopter drowned out Smith's thoughts, *A piece-a-cake!*

---

102 Wilfred Owen, *Anthem for Doomed Youth*, October 1917.

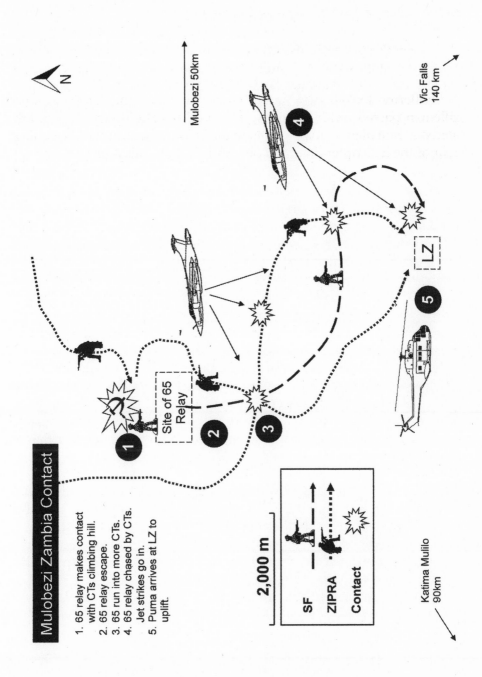

Mulobezi 50km

Vic Falls 140 km

Mulobezi Zambia Contact

1. 65 relay makes contact with CTs climbing hill.
2. 65 relay escape.
3. 65 run into more CTs.
4. 65 relay chased by CTs. Jet strikes go in.
5. Puma arrives at LZ to uplift.

Site of 65 Relay

LZ

2,000 m

SF
ZIPRA
Contact

Katima Mulilo 90km

12

Police forensic laboratory, Bulawayo

The massacre at Kosami Mission had resulted in an unprecedented follow-up operation. D Company, 1RAR were sent together with a large police Special Branch and Ground Coverage contingent. They sifted through every part of the Mission, they marked and collected all the shell casings and bullets they could find embedded in the walls. The forensic teams would attempt to identify each weapon used in the massacre. The surviving nun and the few workers that had escaped all gave their bitter accounts of what had happened. The nun remembered that one of the terrorists wore a balaclava and sunglasses - *He seemed to be in charge … No, he did not say anything … No, he had not made any demands … No, I don't know what he looks like – he seemed to be very tall.* At the time it did not occur to anybody that it was virtually dark when the attack took place yet the terrorist was wearing sunglasses. The CTs often wore balaclavas - but in 38° heat?

D Company created a search area and began a methodical sweep, slowly moving out, 5kms, 10kms, 20kms. The terrorists appeared to have disappeared off the face of the Earth. D Company did find the kidnapped nun after three days, her throat had been slit.

In a police forensic laboratory in Bulawayo, a technician in a white lab-coat walked across to his supervisor. He held up a chart. There was a match between the bullet taken out of the dead rifleman Fauguneze and one found in a victim at Kosami Mission. There was also a match with a bullet found at Kosami Mission with one taken out of a Police Reservist killed in the ambush of the heavy vehicle convoy on the Bulawayo-Wankie road.

The supervisor picked up the phone and dialled, the line was picked up almost instantly, 'We have a link between Kosami and the convoy, it's definitely the same group that 4 Indep hit at Kamativi.' He got up and walked to a large-scale map on the wall, took a piece of red string and connected the three points on the map. The centre of the triangle made with the string was Lupane TTL.

'Got you swines,' he said under his breath.

*

ZIPRA Base Camp, Lupane TTL, north Matabeleland

Comrade Tongerai Chabanga was in a state of extreme agitation.

The massacre at Kosami Mission had shaken him to the core. Chabanga had himself been educated at a Catholic Mission. His own leader, Joshua Nkomo, also had deep roots in Christian religion. His father had been a lay preacher for the London Missionary Society. Chabanga had spent his early childhood playing in the mission grounds and the Church had arranged for his high school education. The priests and nuns were as close to him as his own family. He had listened to the communist teachings about religion and how it interfered with matters of State, but he did not believe it. The liberation struggle could not be a war against the Church as well. Attacks against the Church would turn the People against the freedom movement and discredit the movement's international supporters. The World Council of Churches[103] was a great supporter of the freedom struggle, providing financial and humanitarian aid but most importantly, strong political support.

Chabanga did not see himself as a terrorist. He was a freedom fighter in a legitimate struggle against an oppressive and illegal regime. Chabanga knew that he would take the blame for this massacre as it was in his region of control. The SF were now bound to come looking. This was the last straw. It was now time for Comrade Benkov to leave or to die and Chabanga did not care which. He sent out his most trusted cadres to look for Benkov and his band. They were to bring Benkov to him. Chabanga looked up into the surrounding hills, his mind lost in confusion and shock, not realising the whispering death that crouched there amongst the rocks.

In the hills above Chabanga's network of bases, Sgt Cephas Ngwenya and his fellow Selous Scouts had made some very interesting observations. There was definitely a picture unfolding. The morning and evening trips by women and young children into the deep river line was a clear pattern. This was the case all the way up and down the valley, in all of the villages. The question that needed to be answered was just how many terrorists were living in that river line. The only way to answer that question was to get down into the valley and look around. The Selous Scouts discussed their options and talked to the other c/sign on the radio. It was agreed that Ngwenya and one other would go into the valley that night to find out just how big this camp was. Dressed as they were like ZIPRA terrorists, the risk was very low; they had done this many times before.

The sun set in its normal spectacular way as it does in the African bush. The last of the suns rays bounced off the rocks at the top of the hill on which Ngwenya sat. The rocks shone in bright golden colour, then faded rapidly to darkness. The horizon changed from yellow to orange, purple, then just a thin film of light before darkness fell, like

103 The Catholic Church was never a member of the WCC.

closing a curtain on the day. The familiar night sounds began, crickets and cicadas buzzing and the last birdcalls. A baboon barked in the distance, warning his troop against the dangers of the night.

Ngwenya had always feared the night as a child. The stories of evil spirits and wild animals had frightened him. The Police Special Branch had finally cured any of those deep-seated fears. He saw the night now as a sanctuary, a place to hide unseen, to move freely with low risk of discovery. The night was like a friend, providing protection and concealment. The night, his refuge.

The two Selous Scouts crept to the bottom of the *kopie.* It took a long time getting through the thick thorn bushes. Once on level ground it made no sense to creep around in the dark. Trying to remain concealed, while dressed as terrorists, would have created suspicion if they were seen. They took a circuitous approach to the river-line. They first headed away from their hill, in the opposite direction to their target, and then steadily corrected the angle of their approach to enter the riverbed well downstream to the west. They carried only their AKs with ammunition pouches and a small pack with empty water bottles that they hoped to refill if they could. Water was always the limiting factor in long-term OPs. They wore the same boots as the terrorists, so there was little risk of being discovered.

The two men climbed into the dry riverbed; walking along the bank it was quite wide in places. The trickle of water could be heard from the tiny stream that ran down the centre. The river had cut a wide path through the hills, its meanders cutting deeply into the surrounding countryside. Tall trees grew along the bank; the riverbed had clumps of tightly bound papyrus-like reeds, impenetrable to all but the most fiercely determined. The riverbed was thick sand with a few smooth boulders; driftwood had collected around the largest rocks. There were a few thickly wooded islands in the riverbed and in places the trees leaned over from both sides, almost touching.

Moving steadily, cautiously, within a few minutes they came across the first CT outpost. They crouched down to listen. Six or seven different voices could be heard including the giggles of a few women. The sound of singing drifted down from up ahead. Carefully skirting the first group, Ngwenya moved in the direction of the singing. They counted eight other small CT groups in the riverbed along the way. The singing became increasingly louder as they moved closer then, turning a bend in the river; the sight that confronted them took their breath away. The river had cut a natural amphitheatre. Sitting in a large group were well over a hundred and fifty people, men and women and a few young children. They were singing *Chimurenga*[104], revolutionary,

---

104 The liberation war for Zimbabwe. The ZIPRA called the First Chimurenga the

songs. Standing around the edge of the crowd of villagers was at least the same number of CTs, all holding their weapons. The song came to an end and a man made his way to the front of the crowd, an AK strapped over his shoulder. He seemed very short, but his voice was vibrant, authoritative, as he launched into a long diatribe exalting the importance of their co-operation in the freedom struggle. Ngwenya could hear every word as clearly as if the man was standing next to him. The main focus of the speech appeared to be the provision of food. It seemed that the local villagers were not providing enough food and this was presenting problems. The man urged them to go further afield, to steal white farmers' cattle and bring them to eat. The songs then recommenced and went on for another half hour.

Ngwenya and his companion then continued up the river valley, mixing easily with the departing crowd. The villagers were talking to each other in hushed tones, trying to avoid the freedom fighters, including the two imposters. The people clearly did not want to be overheard. It was obvious that the demands for more food had not gone down too well.

The two Selous Scouts came to the end of what they thought was the main CT base camp. The whole complex stretched over more than two kilometres. Ngwenya signalled that it was time to return. They dropped down into the riverbed to fill the water bottles, then the two of them started off on the convoluted trip back to the OP.

They walked out of the thick undergrowth along the river-line onto a path between two villages. As they passed the first hut a man stepped out, he saw them and said in siNdebele, 'Litshone njani, good evening, Comrade.'

'Salibonani, hello' Ngwenya said in reply. The CT looked very young, no more than twenty years old.

'Where are you going?' the CT asked.

'We are going to look for women,' Ngwenya responded.

'Good, I will come with you,' the CT replied.

Ngwenya reacted in an instant, his training kicking in like a shot of adrenaline. He chopped down on the back of the CTs neck with vicious force, at the same time grabbing his mouth to avoid any sound. The young man collapsed in his arms. Ngwenya's companion took the man's legs and they carried the comatose man off towards the surrounding hills. This was an opportunity Ngwenya had not yet considered. *If you want to know something, why not ask the person directly?*

Matabele Rebellion of 1890. ZANLA referred to the First Chimurenga as the Shona Rebellion of 1893, while the Second Chimurenga is believed to have started, by both ZIPRA and ZANLA, with the battle of Sinoia on 28 April 1966 in which 21 freedom fighters were intercepted by Rhodesian forces and killed.

Once well away from the villages they took time to tie up the young terrorist, binding his mouth tightly. The man awoke, disorientated, then seeing the two men, instantly urinating and defecated into his trousers. He was terrified out of his wits, his head shaking wildly from side to side. Ignoring the mess Ngwenya hoisted the CT onto his shoulders in a fireman's lift, moving off as fast they could, taking about three hours of hard work to get back to the OP position. Once back they dropped the young CT on the ground, both completely exhausted immediately lay down and went to sleep. *The next day held some promise. My SB training is about to be brought into some use,* Ngwenya thought as he closed his eyes.

*

4 Independent Company (RAR) base camp, Sprayview airfield, Victoria Falls

Sgt Mike Smith returned to 4 Indep a very tired and troubled soul. The wounded rifleman would not have permanent injuries, he had been sent off to hospital in Wankie. The run to the LZ in Zambia had severely shaken him and the death of the South African signaller was traumatic. The chaotic chase through the bush had taken his understanding of what it was to be frightened to a whole new level. He was feeling mental strain that seemed to manifest itself in a profound tiredness. He still had over two weeks to wait for R&R. It couldn't come quick enough.

Despite the feeling of exhaustion, the whole experience of the mission with Fullerton was again strangely uplifting. The nagging doubts seemed to have lifted slightly. Fullerton had not spoken to him directly about the mission, all he had said when they were dropped back at Sprayview was, 'Smithy, arrange passes for your stick, they deserve it. You and I should go for a beer.' It was the best possible indication of a level of acceptance that Mike Smith had not experienced before. It seemed that he may have graduated from driver and general dog's-body to fellow soldier.

'Heeee ya Goin Mate?' came the familiar cry from across the camp, 'Good on ya, for killing some more Gooks. You need to leave a few for us you bastard!'

Colour-Sergeant O'Connell strode across from the horse lines, slapping Smith hard on the back. Sheila's punishment seemed to be over as she was following on behind. Smith detected a friendlier demeanour in her. She looked over O'Connell's shoulder, lifting her lip almost to say, *You've got some potential son*!

Captain Fullerton was delighted with their 'external' as he called it. He was on a real high, insisting on a major piss-up to celebrate. Unfortunately, 2 Platoon had once again been deployed onto the River and 3 Platoon waited in camp for the arrival of their new leaders.

Lt Dawson, O'Connell and his other Troop NCOs enthusiastically received the prospect of a piss-up. They all sat on the patio under the trees at the Victoria Falls Hotel and got wasted. Smith felt a lot better after letting off a bit of steam. Fullerton led a rousing rendition of Clem Tholet's, *Rhodesians Never Die*[105],

> *'cause we're all Rhodesians*
> *And we'll fight through thick and thin*
> *We'll keep our land a free land*
> *Stop the enemy coming in*
> *We'll keep them north of the Zambezi*
> *Till that river's running dry*
> *And this mighty land will prosper*
> *For Rhodesians never die.*

… Enthusiastically received by the onlookers who clapped and shouted for more. Fullerton bowed expansively as if on the stage at the Last Night of the Proms.

The evening ended with a bit of 'Boat Racing', a drinking competition, also called down-downs, a team was required to down beers in quick succession, each placing the empty glass inverted on the head, the fastest team wins. This was Fullerton's favourite game; he eagerly picked out the two best-looking ladies in the crowd to be the judges of 'spillage'. It was 'on for young and old', the first race was RAR v Grey Scouts, the teams lined up opposite each other kneeling on tables pushed together. The 'off' was called, Smith second last in line gave a good account of himself with minimal spillage, onto Fullerton at anchor against Dawson. They raced neck and neck, glasses lifted; a dribble of beer down Dawson's chin, a loud objection was called … SPILLAGE! The two petite judges conferred, they pointed to the RAR, the winners were declared to howls of delight. The RAR team embraced, leaping up and down. O'Connell stepped forward, a Test Match was called; Australia v Rhodesia, the idea was met with enthusiastic applause by the surrounding holidaymakers. O'Connell did some hasty recruitment from amongst the crowd, he provided Australian citizenship to two Poms and one German, '… don't mention the War!' he admonished his team to raucous laughter. He then pulled rank on one of his troopers who objected vainly at becoming an Australian;

105 *Rhodesians Never Die*, Clem Tholet and Andy Dillon, 1973, Blackberry.

threats of all-night radio watch were issued. Before the Test Match could kick-off O'Connell insisted on his team singing *Waltzing Matilda*,

> *Once a jolly swagman camped by a billabong*
> *Under the shade of a Coolabah tree.*

Tension mounted as the two teams lined up. Smith gained Rhodesian selection as the third man, followed by Dawson and Fullerton. The race was desperately close, the judges again called upon for a decision … Yes Rhodesia! The crowd erupted, clapping from the hotel veranda; the winners did a victory lap around the patio. O'Connell, standing on a table shouted his objection; his bitter protest drowned out by the spectators.

The delighted soldiers make their way out of the hotel, the holidaymakers clapped and shouted, lining the route of departure. On the way out, Fullerton, still in enormously high spirits, hesitated, and then challenged the Grey Scouts to a swimming gala, pointing to the reflecting pools in the hotel courtyard. The pools weren't more than two feet deep so it would be more of a crawling race through the water lilies so lovingly nurtured by the hotel grounds-man. Once again the teams were selected, lining up at the edge of the pool. Nyika stood on the steps leading to the foyer pleading with Fullerton that this was not a good idea. The race was a blur in Smith's mind, crawling through the thick slime. He took in too much water resulting in a severe bout of coughing and 'hurling', which was a blessing as it purged an otherwise humdinger of a hangover. A winner could not be determined; one of the Grey Scouts needed rescuing, helplessly stuck in the mire. He was dragged out, draped in waterlily, covered in horribly stinking slime.

*

The next morning Smith, nursing a not too serious hangover, sat eating a huge helping of eggs and bacon. Another letter had arrived from Jane and he devoured the pages, open on the table in front of him, with the same relish that he attacked his breakfast. The mess was full of laughter and discussion about the night before. Smith really enjoyed the company of the Grey Scouts, as a party with his own men was impossible, the cultural divide just too great. The Scouts could see him reading his letter.

'Can I read the sports page when you have finished Smithy?' one of them asked. The so-called 'sports' page was the part of the letter where girlfriends got into the passionate stuff. These pages were often swopped by the men, to be read out loud to everyone's great amusement.

'Bugger off!' replied Smith with a grin.

As he sat eating, a sight across at the Ops Room, attracted his attention. A soldier stood on the veranda, 6ft 6" if he was an inch. He wore an RAR beret and stable-belt, chest webbing, including grenades, with his rifle at shoulder-arms. Emerging from the Ops Room into the bright sunlight, Fullerton looked across at the mess. Smith averted his eyes, concentrating hard on his letter and his meal, trying desperately not to be noticed.

To no avail, Fullerton called him over.

'Sergeant Smith, let me introduce you to Lieutenant Light, newly arrived from the School of Infantry, late of the 2nd Green Jackets, The King's Royal Rifle Corps, declared Fullerton expansively, full of his own importance. This was Lt George Light, the new CO of 3 Platoon. Smith threw a smart salute which was returned equally smartly.

'Gdaay to yew Sarnt Smith, Capt'n Walker sends his best regards,' said Lt Light in a broad Yorkshire accent.

Smith groaned inside, *Oh Please, not another Pom,* replied politely, 'Welcome to the Company Sir, I hope that Captain Walker is well?'

'Aye he is quite well, lookin forw'rd to returnin to the RLI when t'current course finishes. He is to take oer a Commando, I believe.'

As it transpired Lt Light had attended Sandhurst, thereafter, posted to the Royal Green Jackets. The remote possibility of war and the boredom of peacetime army life had caused Lt Light to resign his commission to come out to Rhodesia 'lookin for a spot of action' as he described it. He was truly a massive man, twenty-four years old with a barrel-shaped chest. His posture was perfectly upright and he held his shoulders back in ramrod fashion. His hair was a sandy colour; his fair skin had turned a disturbingly red colour from the hot Rhodesian sun. His eyes were deep brown surrounded with deep laugh-lines that crinkled up whenever he laughed, which was a booming, hearty affair. Smith's first impression was that Lt Light's eyes bore a scary resemblance to Sheila's; they had a wild, almost demented, look about them. As it would later transpire, there were other similarities as well.

Lt Light beamed at Smith. 'Sarn't Smith, I am expectin my Platoon 2IC to arrive at any mom'nt ... he is WO2 Nduku on transfer from A Company, 1RAR. Please show him round as soon as he arrives,' instructed Light in a way that left little doubt that he expected his orders to be carried out to the letter.

This is going to be bloody interesting, Smith thought as he walked back to his now cold breakfast.

WO2 Nduku arrived within an hour of the instructions issued by Lt Light. He was another impressive man. Not anywhere the same size as Light, he radiated a deep sense of strength. Nduku was an 'old soldier' in his late thirties, brought up through the ranks of A Company, 1RAR. Others had blocked his progress and promotion, so he had taken the transfer to 4 Indep as a warrant officer when it was offered. Smith introduced himself, braced up, with the respectful 'Sir' as demanded when addressing warrant officers. Nduku was quietly spoken, saying little while Smith showed him around the camp, the 3 Platoon armoury and their barrack room. Nduku said nothing to the few 3 Platoon riflemen in the barrack room at the time, but the look in his eyes said everything. Sergeant Iz Kennedy had not been the most boned[106] soldier in the world and his platoon had formed a few bad habits, made worse since he had left. Smith reflected on what he saw, *3 Platoon is in for the fright of their lives.* That message would be around the Company in a flash. Sergeant-Major Nduku came with a reputation.

The next morning at 5am Smith heard the beginning of the 3 Platoon nightmare unfolding. He looked out of the door of his room to see WO2 Nduku in full combat dress standing next to Lt Light who was dressed exactly as he had been the previous day, rifle once again at shoulder-arms. The rank and file were lined up in various stages of undress, being issued a few clear instructions. What transpired in the next four hours was something to behold. Change parades were first, making the soldiers change into alternative dress, best dress, combat, PT, over and over again. Nduku then decided on a bit of rifle drill, up and down in three ranks, 'Quick March … Squad will advance … Squad will retire … Attention, Squad, at ease, Present arms.' Then combat dress, webbing, packs and rifles with a run to the rifle range, a good 6kms away. Both Light and Nduku accompanied them, running out in front, leading the way. Lt Light came from a proud rifle regiment, and he intended that his platoon would be the best shots in the Company … correction, the Army! He had a lot of work to do.

---

106 Rhodesian slang, boned was used to describe a soldier who did things correctly, well organized and efficient. It was derived from the process of boning boots, using heated spoons and boot polish gives boots a high sheen.

13

Lupane TTL, northeast Matabeleland

There were two very disturbed little boys in Lupane. Since they had disposed of the young girl's body down the well, they had been unable to sleep with the younger one refusing to leave his mother's hut. This was very disturbing for their mother, as she could not get the boys to explain what had upset them. She was concerned that evil spirits may have possessed her boys, which was not a matter to be taken lightly. The only way for her to get some piece of mind was to visit the local spirit medium, a *Sangoma*.

She arrived outside the *Ndumba*, the sacred hut, and the place that the ancestors gather, at the appointed time. The three of them sat huddled together, the boys shivering in fright. The younger boy began to cry as he had been doing on and off for a week. The situation was very distressing; the mother pulled the boy close to her, hugging him tightly. The Sangoma came out of the hut and stood imposingly in front of them. He was a formidable sight, with natural ochre streaks on his face. He wore a straw headdress covered in Guinea Fowl feathers with leather tassels that hung across his face making him appear even more sinister. His shoulders were draped with a leopard skin while strings of beads and bones were hanging from his wrists. An Impala skin skirt hung from his waist, and large wooden beads were strung around his ankles, which rattled together when he walked. He silently beckoned the three into the hut; they removed their shoes at the entrance. Upon entering the dark interior they knelt down, each clapped twice to greet the spirits. The mother leaned forward, placing the payment for the meeting under a small straw mat in front of her.

The Sangoma spoke soothingly to the sobbing child telling him that all would be well. *The spirits had the power to cure all ailments.* They all sat in silence for a few minutes, the young child continuing to whimper quietly. The Sangoma, to summon the spirits to the meeting, then shook a rattle made from a small calabash. He then lit a tuft of dried elephant dung which smoked gently in the centre of the hut, a sweet, comforting smell.

The space had now been made clear for the arrival of the spirits. The Sangoma untied a leather pouch from his belt and poured the contents onto the earth floor in front of the young boy. The boy looked down at the animal bones in front of him. He did not know their names but they included bones from lions, hyenas, anteaters, baboons, hares, lizards, owls, crocodiles, wild pigs, goats, antelopes and other birds and animals. The primal energies and attributes the animals represent hold awesome power. The hyena represents the thief that comes in the night; a hyena bone is often used to locate a stolen object. The anteater or aardvark is the animal that 'digs the grave'; it may be used where death is concerned, or it could represent a deceased person or their spirit. The antelope is swift of foot, when it appears in a reading it warns against ignoring an important relationship with someone in power or importance.

The Sangoma gestured for the boy to put the bones back into the pouch. He then started a slow chant, shaking the rattle vigorously at the same time. *The spirits were with them.* The boy was then instructed to blow into the pouch, to say his name out loud, then to empty the bag once again onto the floor. The Sangoma repeated this process three times, with a considerable period of contemplation in between each throw. As he studied how the bones had fallen he mumbled to himself incoherently. At one point he leaned forward and placed his hand on the young boy's forehead as if testing his temperature.

'There is an unhappy spirit, she is crying and cannot find her place, she is lost and seeks help,' said the Sangoma to the young boy.

He continued in a voice so soft they had to lean forward to hear him, 'The bone of the hare is next to that of the baboon, the spirits have said the hare tricked the baboons into chanting that they had killed the cubs of the lioness, not realising that they were innocent, the lioness then killed them.'

The Sangoma paused for a few seconds then spoke quietly to the boy.

'… You try to imitate and follow the opinions of others?'

The young boy was stricken by the words and began to shake uncontrollably as if he was having a fit.

'It is the girl we threw into the well,' he shrieked, 'Please save me from her spirit.'

The older boy tried to make his brother stop but the youngster could not hold it in any longer. The story came gushing out, the words tumbling as he fought back his tears, sucking in his sobs. In the end he begged the Sangoma to ask for forgiveness. The Sangoma stood up gesturing for the mother to follow him out of the hut. He then spoke earnestly to the mother explaining the outcome of the reading. The Matabele believed that death brought a bad omen to the nearest living relatives of the deceased and such an omen could be passed on to neighbors. The matter was made worse for the participants in a murder. It was necessary for the boys to be cleansed by making sure the girl's body was found and put to rest. If this was not done, vengeful spirits would attack the boys for the remainder of their lives. The mother began to cry, dissolving into uncontrolled wailing, holding her hands over her face. Her grief was so heartfelt that the dead spirits, the *Idlozi*, would surely have heard. The dead child's body must be *recovered and properly buried*.

The Sangoma had been told of the missing girl from the south, her family had been looking for her.

The next day the Sangoma assembled some men from the village, having already sent word to the family of the missing girl. The silent procession followed the Sangoma and the two boys to the place that the girl had been killed. A man was sent down the well on a rope; eventually the small broken body was brought to the surface. The Sangoma chanted, pleading with the girl's departed soul; he promised that she would be returned to her family. The Sangoma was not a violent man he was disgusted by what he saw, this was the work of the most evil of men, the injuries were such that they could only have been made by a person possessed of the devil. He vowed that justice was to be done. His arms held skywards; he calling up into the heavens, appealing to the spirits, *the men who have perpetrated this crime must die*.

This man of the spirits was sympathetic to the liberation struggle, he had read the bones for many of the freedom fighters, but this act of violence was reprehensible.

*

Hills above ZIPRA Base Camp, Lupane TTL, north Matabeleland

In the hills above, Cephas Ngwenya was speaking quietly to the bound-up terrorist he had captured. The gag in the CT's mouth was still in place as Ngwenya carefully listed the information he required and the order the information must be given in. The first task in pseudo-operations was to try and 'turn' the terrorist. Ngwenya had seen this happen remarkably quickly, on one occasion in less than an hour of conversation. Many of the CTs were unhappy at the brutal treatment by the Political Commissars together with the constant hunger and fear of attack. The problem for Ngwenya was that time was of the essence; he needed accurate information now!

The young CT's eyes were wide as he looked up in terror at the face of his captor. Ngwenya carefully explained the pain he would inflict on the young terrorist if the information he asked for was incorrect. This was all repeated in a slow methodical way so that the CT clearly understood what was expected. Ngwenya then leant forward to untie the gag, holding his hand over the man's mouth to ensure that he did not call out. The gag came free, and the young terrorist immediately blurted out the information that was requested. He spoke fast, anxious to please. The questions were structured in such a way that the information that the Selous Scouts already had could be corroborated. The CT started off well, but as his confidence grew he started to slip in a few lies. This was particularly on the subject of the exact position of the cadres in the CT base camp. Ngwenya asked if he was sure of the information he had given. The CT nodded enthusiastically.

Without making any fuss Ngwenya once again carefully replaced the gag on the young terrorist. Ngwenya then spoke again in the same deliberate, hushed tones. He explained that the information given was not correct; the consequences he had promised would now follow. In slow methodical movements, he removed his hunting knife, placing a hand over the man's gagged mouth. Then, leaning across, he neatly slicing a small chunk out of the terrorist's ear. The terrorist looked up in disbelief, his scream only too clear to see, his head twisting violently from side to side as Ngwenya pushed down hard on the gag. No sound escaped. Ngwenya lifted up the small piece of ear he had cut off, waved it in front of the CTs face, then placed it gently onto his heaving chest. He lifted his finger to his lips indicating that the terrorist should now be quiet again. The young man was distraught, crying, tears rolling down the side of his face, dripping onto the rock behind him, mixing with the blood from his cut ear running down into a neat pool in the earth below.

The interrogation went very smoothly from that point onwards. The terrorist was careful not to make any more mistakes. He divulged the number of CTs in the camp, their locations in the valley below, the names of the camp commanders including the Brigade Commander Comrade Tongerai Chabanga, giving a detailed description of the man. He confirmed that the attack on the heavy vehicle convoy had been made from this camp but that the band that did it had left. He did not know the leader's name; he had only seen a glimpse of him. This band did not mix at all with the rest of the cadres; they had only recently arrived from Zambia. He confirmed that this leader stayed in an abandoned village, guarded there by the men that he had arrived with. Comrade Chabanga would go there for meetings. The terrorist did not know anything about the attack on Kosami Mission.

Ngwenya finished the interrogation, and then carefully dressed the bleeding ear with antiseptic powder and a field dressing, administered a phial of morphine, and then replaced the gag. The drug sent the young terrorist into a relaxed sleep. The four Selous Scouts began to compile their lengthy sitrep using button and shackle codes, *this camp needed to get hit ASAP!*

*

Southern Boundary of Lupane TTL

Comrade Vladimir Benkov knew that he could not return to meet with Comrade Chabanga again. He did not trust Chabanga's reaction and he certainly did not trust Chabanga himself. The first part of Benkov's mission had been completed. He now had a second major task to complete and that meant that he had to move his band further north. He was sorely tempted to steal the Land Rover from the mission but that would have alerted the Rhodesians to a different type of freedom fighter. Imparting that information was premature. The fact that he had to walk resulted in slow progress. He had sent his report through to Lusaka and they had congratulated him on an excellent result. The international press was full of the details of the massacre. Serious questions were being asked of Joshua Nkomo's leadership; *Comrade Nkomo was now in a difficult position … a perfect result!*

The attack on the mission with the premeditated murder of the missionaries left Benkov completely unmoved. He had no difficulty whatsoever with the label 'terrorist'. That was exactly what he was, that was what he had been trained to be. The main terrorist training base Benkov attended was at Zheltyye Vady, in the Ukraine. This was adjacent to a concentration camp for political prisoners. The camp inmates provided 'living training aids' for martial arts. Benkov enjoyed punching, gouging, and maiming to his heart's content. The 'practice' provided him and his fellow trainees with a taste for blood, much more realistic than punching a sandbag. Benkov's spetsnaz training was brutal, uncompromising, in order that he, in turn, could produce violent terrorists who would not hesitate to carry out any order, no matter how depraved. The terrorist organisations he had worked with around the world, the PLO, IRA, ETA and the Red Army Faction, were trained to perform atrocities. Atrocities were the lifeblood of these organisations as they created legitimacy amongst their respective constituencies. Legitimacy, in turn, attracted a larger following, which in turn provided greater power. Power and domination was the ultimate goal.

Benkov needed to get into position for his next attack, and that was going to take at least another week to achieve. His band of freedom fighters numbered fifteen, but he knew he needed at least another twenty. The truth was that he was not going to be able to get these men from Chabanga's group. Lusaka had told him of the imminent arrival of another large group of freedom fighters. They were due to cross the Zambezi above Victoria Falls, travel south through the Zambezi National Park, the Matetsi Controlled Hunting Area, and then cross into Botswana near a village called Panda-ma-Tenga. He was to collect his reinforcements from this group near the village of Dett; they too would have a radio.

*

4 Independent Company (RAR) base camp, Sprayview airfield, Victoria Falls

Back at 4 Indep the 'introduction' of 3 Platoon to their new leadership team continued unabated. The poor sods were seen marching, preparing for inspections, marching some more, running to the rifle range, then further inspections. It was exactly like 1st Phase training for them all over again. The energy and enthusiasm that Light brought to the retraining tasks was as impressive as it was exhausting for the 3 Platoon *squaddies*, as Light called them. Light had also started teaching his men the words to the Yorkshire folk song *Ilkley Moor Bar T'at*. His hometown of Cullingworth was only a few miles south of Ilkley Moor, he said the song reminded him of home. It was absolutely hilarious listening to the black soldiers struggling to get the words;

> *Where 'as tha bin since ah saw thee, ah saw thee*
> *On Ilkley Moor b'ah t'at*
> *Where 'as tha bin sin ah saw thee*
> *Where 'as tha bin sin ah saw thee without thy trousers on*

Light had them practising first thing in the morning on muster parade and last thing before calling 'Dismiss' in the evening. The evening rendition inevitably attracted a crowd who yelled encouragement, some joining in with the chorus, Light leading the way at the top of his booming voice;

> *On Ilkley Moor b'ah t'at owzat?*

An obvious rapport had built up between Nduku and Light, despite the fact that they came from such different backgrounds and cultures. Smith found it incredible to see such a vivid example of soldiering being the ultimate leveller. They had a common bond being their love of the military life. He suspected that a degree of competition was emerging between them, quite evident when they were running and shooting, *The Pom v The Matabele, the colonial invader verses the tribal warrior, what irony!* Smith thought.

Smith's stick kept their heads down big time, in mortal fear of Sergeant Major Nduku adding them to his merry band. Smith mentioned to them that keeping their barrack room tidy, cleaning their kit and making sure they were dressed smartly at all times might be a good idea. The young NS Sergeant also tidied himself up a bit in case Fullerton decided that he and his stick could do with a bit of 'retraining'.

While doing an informal kit inspection, Smith was called to the Ops room, where the Duty NCO asked him to deliver a suitcase to the AZambezi River Lodge hotel. Apparently the Major's wife had come up to Victoria Falls from Wankie for the weekend and had left the suitcase in the car. Smith drew a Two-Five from the MT and drove down to the hotel. He always enjoyed driving around the Falls in the military vehicle. The place was a busy holiday destination for locals and overseas visitors; it was good to see the 'normality' of it all. Many visitors would wave at him in the vehicle, some would shout out, 'good luck soldier', or 'keep your chin up soldier'. Smith took the long way around to the hotel by driving down to the main carpark at the Falls, then along the river road past the 'Big Tree', then the Elephant Hills Hotel, the golf course, on to the AZambezi River Lodge. He found parking in the hotel carpark, as far away from other vehicles as possible, jumped down from the vehicle and carried the suitcase into the reception area.

The AZambezi reception was cavernous, with a high thatched roof and concrete floor polished to a high gloss. A large round, woven, sisal mat dominated the centre of the floor. It was cool inside, with the wonderful smell of floor polish and thatching grass. He stood for a moment, soaking up the feeling of being on holiday. Prints of Thomas Baines' paintings of Africa and the Victoria Falls were mounted on the walls and Smith looked carefully at each one in turn. The receptionist, *really cute*, smiled broadly at him and asked if she could help. He asked for Mrs Peacock to be called, the girl made a call to the room, offering to get one of the porters to take the suitcase up. Smith declined, preferring to deliver it personally, *no risk of screw-ups*. Three Dog Night's *Joy to the World* [107]played softly over the piped music system and he found himself tapping in time on the reception desk,

> *Jeremiah was a bull frog*
> *Was a good friend of mine*

107 *Joy to The World*, Hoyt Axton, 1971

I never understood a single word he said
But I helped him a-drink his wine
And he always had some mighty fine wine

Singin'
Joy to the world

Smith did not know quite what to expect. He was intrigued to see what Mrs Peacock might look like. If anything like her husband, she would be singularly unpleasant. He chatted easily to the receptionist, 'Elizabeth' on her name tag, waiting for either the Major or his wife to appear …

'So you went to the Convent in Bulawayo; Oh you are from Wankie; do you know the Hogans?' *Elizabeth seems really cool, worth a crack some time*, Smith contemplated.

A straight shootin' son-of-a-gun
I said a straight shootin' son-of-a-gun

Joy to the world

Mrs Peacock's arrival dispelled any fear of a frumpy, overweight, middle-aged housewife. She came floating into reception wearing a pale blue bikini top that was amply filled, a white wrap or sarong around a very tight waist, a wide straw hat and light leather sandals. Her eyes were covered with large, round sunglasses and she wore light pink lipstick. Her hair, almost black, hung down her back, pulled off her face with a low ponytail. As she turned, the outside light silhouetted a pair of perfectly formed legs, suggesting a sporting interest. Her skin was lightly tanned, clearly responding well to the hot Rhodesian sun. It was impossible to tell her age. She was only fractionally shorter than Smith. She saw him waiting, and drifted over to where he was standing, awkwardly holding the suitcase. She removed her sunglasses, looking him straight in the eyes. He caught a whiff of perfume mixed with suntan lotion.

'That must be my suitcase Sergeant,' she said in a deep lustrous, almost purring, Irish accent. Smith blushed brightly, trying to avert his eyes; having stolen a glance at the blue bikini top, just inches away. Smith's mind went completely blank as Mrs Peacock's green eyes studied his.

'Would you arrange for my suitcase to be taken to my room please,' she said to the receptionist, her eyes still fixed on Smith's face.

'Have you time for a cup of tea Sergeant?' she enquired, tilting her head fractionally with the question. '… You needn't worry, the Major has had to return to Wankie for some military thing, he won't be back until tonight.' Her Irish accent lilted. She was truly captivating.

Smith was completely uncertain of what to do, unsure of whether saying 'No' would be rude, or whether tea with a senior officer's wife was in any way acceptable.

'Thank you Maam that would be very nice,' he said, deciding against rudeness.

She flashed a stunning smile at him in a way that melted his insides.

'Great!' she said replacing the sunglasses, leading him out onto the wide covered patio packed with other hotel guests. A large pool nearby was full of kids splashing and screaming delightedly. Smith was the only person in uniform so that attracted the inevitable glances. He removed his beret and slipped it into an epaulette.

Mrs Peacock wound her way through the tables, choosing one well away from the other guests. She then signalled to one of the waiters for tea and scones.

Scones! Smith thought, his mind racing back to his childhood visits with his mother to the cafeteria in Haddon & Sly in Bulawayo. The department store had made the best jam scones in the world. The treat of going there for tea was a highlight growing up.

They sat down on comfortable cane lounge chairs, the sort that obliges the occupant to sink into them.

'What's your name Sergeant?' Mrs Peacock enquired in her direct style, leaning forward as she did so, the bikini top straining at its thin straps.

'Smith … Maam,' he replied hesitantly, still not sure where to put his eyes, sitting rigidly upright, as if in front of a senior officer.

'No, your first name silly, we are not in the army here. My name's Sandra, you can call me that.' She smiled once again which made him feel a little more at ease. He looked at her trying to figure out how old she was, he guessed late twenties.

'Michael Maam … I mean Sandra. My friends call me Mike,' he stammered, trying desperately not to appear like a schoolboy talking to the headmaster's wife.

'You seem rather young to be a Sergeant?' she enquired gently, slowly removing her sunglasses again to reveal her emerald green eyes. They again fixed him with their gaze, a glint of a smile; she had tiny laugh lines around her eyes.

'Yes, it is unusual,' he started, not willing to get into a whole explanation of the School of Infantry thing; he copped out, '… I guess they are short of people.'

Sensing his discomfort, she leaned back in her chair.

'Well Mike, tell me all about yourself. Where are you from, where did you go to school, you may leave out everything to do with the army...' she enquired, lifting her tone, her sincerity completely disarming.

Mike told her of his hometown, school, his parents and sister. She seemed genuinely interested, prodding with questions that made him feel more relaxed. He found himself talking about his plans for university and his ideas for a career in engineering. The relationship with Cheryl came up as Sandra asked him pointedly about his 'girlfriend'. He explained that Cheryl was at Rhodes University in Grahamstown, how they had broken-up as she had needed her freedom.

The tea was served; he continued to chat away, really beginning to enjoy himself and her company. He polished off all the scones. Sandra could see his enjoyment and insisted that he eat hers as well. Smith was unsure whether he should be asking her questions about herself and decided that if she wanted to she would volunteer the information.

She listened intently to his discussion, smiling receptively at the same time.

Then suddenly she interjected, 'So Mike what do you think about my husband?' The question was pointed.

Smith's train of thought was completely derailed. He searched for an answer, desperate not to give the wrong impression.

'He is a good soldier Maam ... I mean...' The reference to the Major had clicked his brain straight back into the army. 'I don't know him very well at all, we NCOs don't really mix with the senior officers much.'

'Is he well liked Mike?' Her directness was like trying to dodge a bullet; her eyes searched his face, which easily marked his indecision.

'Maam ... sorry Sandra ... you have to understand that the army is not really about liking people it's more about following orders, respect for those in charge. It's not a popularity competition.'

Smith felt his face burning as he tried to give the official line. *Surely she can see through my bullshit*, Smith thought, embarrassed that he could not give a straight answer.

'Well do you respect him then?' questioned Sandra more demandingly, refusing to let him off the hook,

'Yes, I do,' he lied, blushing again horribly. He looked away, disgusted with himself for not telling her his true feelings, suppressing the urge to get up and run.

'Mike, it's okay. My husband is a prick.' The word 'prick' all the more emphatic when said with an Irish accent.

She smiled again. 'I shouldn't put you on the spot like this. I'm sorry,' she said, leaning forward again touching him reassuringly on the arm, squeezing it every so slightly.

Her touch was like an electrical shock running through his system, his arm jumped involuntarily. He blushed brightly again, feeling that his head was about to explode.

Sandra fell back into the chair and laughed, her head tilted, her shoulders shaking at the combination of his embarrassment and the obvious effect of touching his arm.

'Mike,' she laughed, 'the Major is an idiot … It's okay.' She laughed so loudly people turned to look …

'… You blush so beautifully,' she said, pointing at him. Her laugh was infectious; Mike too began to laugh with her, the pair of them sat opposite each other, laughing until the tears ran down their cheeks. Those nearby smiled at the couple having a good laugh together.

The Sergeant and the Major's wife finished their tea. He reluctantly explained that he had to get back. She walked him to reception, then out to the Two-Five in the carpark. The young receptionist watched incredulously as the couple walked past, *are they an item?* written all over her face.

'Thank you for having tea with me Mike, I really enjoyed it,' said Sandra happily.

'Thank you too … Sandra I haven't had this much fun in ages, I appreciate your listening to all my rubbish.'

'It's not rubbish Mike. I'm really glad you spoke so openly. We should do this again sometime, maybe a beer or something.' With that she pecked him neatly on the lips, dissolving again into laughter as he blushed again, even his ears were burning.

He turned and jumped up into the driver's seat then looking down at her, smiling at him, shaking his head at her obvious joy at his discomfort.

'A beer would be great!' he replied, no matter how impossible that seemed.

She watched as he reversed the Two-Five, waving as he headed off back to camp. Mike Smith was in a state of emotional upheaval, his drive back to camp lost in confused and complicated thoughts. Not quite nineteen, he had met his first real live, earthy, sultry woman, a 'real' woman who found him interesting. *No, that's impossible she was just having fun with me, pulling my leg.* He asked himself repeatedly, *What happened there? 'Maybe a beer or something', what does that mean? She is the Major's wife for Christ's sake!*

14

4 Independent Company (RAR) base camp, Sprayview airfield, Victoria Falls

Sergeant Smith spoke to Captain Fullerton and explained that he would like to rejoin his platoon on the River as it was still the best part of a week before they were due to return. Frankly, Smith wanted to get out of camp while Light and Nduku 'retrained' their platoon. He did not want anybody to get the idea that he needed to do a bit of retraining of 2 Platoon or, worse still, place him and his stick into the same retraining regime. Fullerton had no problem with his idea, 'carry on' he told Smith dismissively.

Smith negotiated a lift with the sergeant in charge of the 4 Indep Tracker Section. The Company had the requirement for a group of trained trackers whose job it was to maintain the drag[108] along both sides of the main tar road between Vic Falls and Kazangula in the west, a distance of about 65kms. The 'drag' was a pile of old car tyres, chained together in a web shape, towed behind a Two-Five along the reserve next to the tar road. The soil in that part of the world is primarily a fine, creamy sand, so when the Two-Five passed over it, dragging the tyres behind, the result was a smooth surface, so smooth that it was possible to detect a beetle scurrying across it. The trackers sat on the bonnet of the Two-Five, as it slowly progressed along the road; they studied the smooth, sandy surface for signs of a terrorist 'crossing'.

The CTs were perfectly aware of the consequence of being detected crossing the drag. No matter how the CTs sought to cover their tracks the smooth continuous surface was like an open book for the trackers. The CTs tried all sorts of anti-tracking techniques; the most common was to follow a herd of elephants or buffalo across the drag, in a vain attempt to hide their tracks amongst the animal spoor. This of course was not always possible, often they would cross while trying to imitate animal spoor, a complete waste of time. The CT plan was to cross the Zambezi at night as early as possible, avoiding the SF ambushes set at various places along the river and then walk to the drag. The distance from the River to the drag varied but it averaged about 15kms. They would cross the drag, then move as fast as possible down to the Botswana border to cross into safety. Sometimes they would loop around to the east,

---

108 Road, dirt roads were sometimes 'dragged' by a vehicle towing chained together tyres. This helped to detect the tracks of insurgents crossing the road. The road from Victoria Falls to Kazangula had a 'drag' on each side of the main road for this purpose. Colloquially 'drag' was used to describe virtually any road, for example the man road to Bulawayo would be referred to as the 'main drag' to Bulawayo.

crossing into the Wankie TTL, from there further east into the other tribal trust lands towards Lupane and Nkai and then south into the very centre of the country.

Smith loaded his much relieved stick onto the back of the Two-Five then at first light they drove out of camp. Behind them followed a Four-Five and two armoured, mine-protected horseboxes, carrying the Grey Scouts. The idea was that if a crossing was detected the Grey Scouts would immediately deploy on follow-up. The Grey Scouts had their own mounted trackers for this purpose. On this particular day the Grey Scouts were led by Colour Sergeant O'Connell, *Bhiza*, mounted on *Murwisi*. He stood in the cab of the Four-Five with the hatch open, reminiscent of his days in Vietnam in armoured personnel carriers. *Just like bloody General Patton,* Smith thought to himself, smiling at the antics of his Ozzie mate.

The small convoy passed out of town to the south, then turned right onto the Kazungula road. The Police and National Park Rangers manned a roadblock about 5kms along the tar road to check for 'travelling' terrorists and poachers. It was from this point onwards that the trackers hitched up the tyres and drove out onto the drag. The Grey Scouts followed on behind, staying on the tar road. The speed was no more than 15km/h so this allowed O'Connell to maintain a conversation with both Smith and the trackers as they progressed along their way. The normal O'Connell bullshit was in evidence as he continued a running commentary, to no one in particular, on the goings-on at Vic Falls. This included discussion on the two new croupiers at the Casino, the new primary school teacher, which one of the UTC 'birds' he liked and his latest run of good luck at roulette. Sheila could be heard kicking the hell out of the horsebox, another one of her dislikes. Fortunately it was made out of half-inch armoured steel so she was unlikely to cause any damage.

Unbeknown to the troops out on the drag, the CSM had chosen this day for a spot of poaching. He, too, left the camp in a Two-Five with his favourite tracker, passed through the roadblock where he explained to the occupants that he was part of the 4 Indep drag-tracking team. The CSM drove about 10kms further and then turned left off the road into the trees, out of sight of the main road. There were plenty of impala and kudu in the area; they made excellent *biltong*[109]. The CSM took a radio with him on his poaching trips but kept it turned off in case someone tried to get hold of him. Poaching was a serious business; he did not need any distractions. He would use a bush track that he had found some time before, to bypass the roadblock on the way back into town. His hunting style required his tracker to go out on foot on the spoor

109 Afrikaans, dried meat, jerky.

while the CSM followed in the Two-Five until an animal was found. Only then did he go on foot himself, poaching in the Zambezi valley was a hot business.

Out on the drag, at the 18km peg, one of the trackers on the front of the Two-Five held up his hand. As the vehicle stopped he jumped off into the soft sand.

'CTs *Bhiza*!' He pointed at the ground where there was a clear sign of disturbance across the drag. The other trackers, including the Grey Scout tracker got off the vehicles, quickly analysing what they saw on the ground. They then entered the bush on either side of the road, starting to 'cut' by walking left and right, parallel with the road, to see whether the CTs had crossed in other groups. Smith sat on the back of the truck to await the outcome. O'Connell and his Troop climbed off of their vehicles and waited in the middle of the tar road. They smoked and chatted excitedly about the prospects for the day. There was no point in unloading the horses until absolutely sure what they had on their hands.

The surrounding bush was perfect horse territory, pretty much flat, with open dry bush-land studded with trees but very easy to ride or walk through. The bush was criss-crossed by game trails, there were also a few dirt tracks used by National Parks rangers. The area was very dry at that time of the year so the *vlei* lines were all dry and hard with very little vegetation. There were a few small waterholes, fed by boreholes with wind-pumps allowing the game to stay in the area pretty much all year round.

After about half an hour the small group of trackers, together with Smith and O'Connell, congregated in the middle of the road.

The tracker NCO then gave an account of what they thought had happened.

'The CT's came up from the River in three groups of ten, they tried to clean their spoor away with bushes. They then walked down the road for five hundred metres and crossed walking one behind another.' He pointed in the direction that he was talking about.

Pausing while everyone absorbed the information, he continued, 'They were careful to tread in each other's footprints, but of course we can see that ten men, walking one behind each other, make too much of a deep impression in the sand. They then walked off into the bush over there and re-assembled in a group about fifty metres in.'

The Tracker NCO paused again to make sure his audience was still paying attention.

'Once they RV'ed across the road they then walked off to the south in single file. The spoor is at least ten hours old. They look like they are heavily loaded - I would estimate that they are each carrying about thirty-five to forty kilos of weight.'

Listening intently, O'Connell then did some quick sums in his head.

'Okay that means that at about three Ks an hour plus rest stops, they are about twenty to twenty-five Ks in,' stated O'Connell, pleased with his estimate.

He turned to his troop who had now gathered behind him.

'Unload the horses, the Gooks are about three or four hours, max five, ahead of us at our tracking pace. Right, get cracking!' ordered O'Connell, obviously excited at a chance for some action.

He then turned to Smith who was standing behind him, 'Smithy, can you call 4 Indep and speak to Captain Fullerton. We are going to need support for a contact at about one o'clock this afternoon ... if all goes well.'

If all goes well, for fuck sakes! Smith thought.

'Okay Colour, good luck ... Mate,' replied Smith as confidently as he could, trying to hide his feelings, knowing that O'Connell would appreciate him adding the word 'Mate'.

Sheila came out of the horsebox like a bat out of hell, eyes wide, itching for a fight. She loved the adventure of being out in the bush. She jumped and squealed in excitement. O'Connell had to shout at her to calm down and belted her with his open hand so that he could throw the saddle on.

Smith clicked his radio, calling 4 Indep, 'Hello 4 ... Hello 4 ... this is 42Alpha do you read ... over'

'42Alpha, we read you fives.'[110]

'Roger 4, get 44 ... over.'

There followed a long delay while the Duty NCO would be looking around the camp for '44', Fullerton. The eight Grey Scouts were mounted in no time, moving off onto the spoor. Sheila only had one pace, which was break-neck. She threw her head up from side to side, straining at the bit to get going.

After the Grey Scouts had disappeared into the bush, Smith overheard Dube commenting to Moyo and Sibanda, 'Murwisi wants to kill some Gooks today.'

Eventually Fullerton came up on the radio. Smith gave an account of their status and the initiation of the follow-up. Fullerton summed up the position quickly and then issued Smith his instructions. He was ordered to return immediately to the main Vic Falls International Airport and wait for him there. He was going to call helicopters up from sub-JOC at Wankie. The trackers were to continue with the drag

---

110 Radio voice procedure requires the parties to understand how good the reception is on the other side. A system of numbers 1 to 5 was used to tell the other party how clearly they were being heard - with 1 being almost impossible to hear and 5 being perfectly clear.

to see if there had been any other crossings. O'Connell was listening to the communication on his radio; his c/sign was 25Bravo.

While all this was going on the CSM had found some fresh kudu spoor. He was now following a parallel course to the Grey Scout follow-up team, looking forward to the prospect of a good hunt, quite oblivious to the drama unfolding around him.

*

Victoria Falls International Airport, south of the town of Victoria Falls

Smith's stick loaded their kit onto the Grey Scout's Four-Five, and he instructed the driver to take them to the airport. The Victoria Falls International Airport is about 19kms due south of the town. The airport was not very busy; it had a daily South African Airways 737 service from Johannesburg with two or three Air Rhodesia Viscount flights from Salisbury, Bulawayo and Kariba. The airport was protected by a troop of Eland 90[111] armoured-cars, plus the Police and Guard Force. Once all the passengers from the various flights had cleared customs and immigration they were all loaded on luxury buses, then escorted by the armoured cars into the town to the various hotels. All this was very impressive and exciting for the holidaymakers.

On the drive to the airport, Smith had the same feeling of foreboding he had when he was sent to Katima Mulilo. The reality of a Grey Scout follow-up was that contact with the enemy in these circumstances was almost a certainty, particularly with such a large group. It was impossible to lose the spoor in the dry, baked sand, plus the Grey Scouts moved so fast. In the rainy season it would have been more difficult because the grass was longer, the bush thicker, plus the *vlei*-lines were muddy and churned up by the wild animals, making riding slow and difficult.

Smith knew that when O'Connell said a contact was likely sometime between 1 and 2pm, that probability was very high. The Grey Scouts did not trot or canter their horses because that dislodged the equipment they carried and the exertion compromised the horse's stamina. Instead, they walked the horses at a very fast pace, made easier when the spoor was so clear. The fast walking pace meant that the horses could carry on all day, with little need for rest, despite the heavy load of rider and equipment.

111 South African built, Eland Mk9 - Also known as the Eland 90 - Modified version of the French AML H 90 armored car, keeping the Panhard chassis but having a Hispano-Suiza designed turret with a 90 mm GIAT F1 gun.

By the time Smith arrived at the airport he found most of 3 Platoon already lounging about on the grassed apron next to the hard-standing. Lt Light and Sgt-Maj Nduku had their men divided into sticks and both wore full combat kit. Lt Light was still walking around with his rifle at shoulder-arms.

Captain Fullerton saw Smith arrive and called him over to where they were standing.

'Right ... everyone listen up ... we have three helicopters coming up from Wankie, a K-car and two G-cars. Lucky us! ... We are hoping for a Lynx as well, but it appears to have some sort of mechanical problem.'

Fullerton paused to make sure he had everybody's undivided attention. He was quite obviously in his element.

Ingwe then began his briefing, 'Smithy, I want you to take Stop 1, this is Lt Light's first scene, he needs to get a feel for how this all works.'

Smith blushed brightly under his camo-cream as Light glanced across at him. His sudden elevation as the 'experienced' soldier was obvious to all the others.

Fullerton continued, 'Sergeant-Major Nduku will be Stop 2. Lt Light, Stop 3, and one other c/sign, Stop 4, will come in on the second wave. If necessary we will bring in a third wave, Stops 5 and 6. I will fly in K-car, call-sign 'Sunray'[112], giving you all your instructions once we get on the ground.'

Fullerton then spread a 1:50,000 map of the area on the grass and they knelt down to study it. He pointed to an arc that he had drawn on the map giving an approximation of where the CTs would likely be when contact was initiated. The idea was to narrow down the likely contact area once O'Connell, c/sign 25Bravo, started to call in with sitreps. It all depended on whether the CTs headed for the Botswana border or looped around into the Wankie TTL.

'Okay ... all of you get a bit of rest and maybe something to eat. We are in for a busy afternoon,' concluded Fullerton, excitement in his voice, delighted at the opportunity to fly as K-car Commander. A *steely-eyed killer from the sky*; is how he would describe himself.

Soon after the briefing had been completed the daily SAA[113] flight from Johannesburg turned onto its final approach, gently setting down onto the runway. The 737 then taxied onto the hard-standing where one of the ground crew directed it to park using large red paddles. As the 737 engines shut down, the three helicopters came skimming in over the treetops, the pilots banked hard then landed one behind each other, taxiing into position on the opposite side of the hard-standing to where the 737 was parked. The 85km flight from Wankie meant that

112 Rhodesian voice procedure, Commander, or senior officer.
113 South African Airways

they would need to top up their fuel tanks. A Two-Five with drums of Avtur[114] on the back stood on the side of the runway, but the pilots signalled the BP refuelling truck, it was quicker.

The stairs had been pushed up against the 737 and the passengers started to disembark. Smith, Fullerton and Light all observed the passengers through their binoculars.

'Shit that blonde looks bloody fantastic' observed Fullerton. The others all murmured their agreement. At least three other likely prospects were identified. Fullerton called up the armoured-car commander on his radio.

'Hello Golf 5 … 44 do you read.' There was a short delay while Fullerton repeated his call.

'Roger 44, Golf 5, go.'

'We have four good prospects visual; please confirm which hotel they get off at, the blonde in particular.'

Knowing which hotel the girls were staying at saved a great deal of time and improved the prospects of a successful 'contact' significantly.

'44, copied, we will let you know … Golf 5 out.'

O'Connell, on follow-up, heard the discussion on his radio and came up, '44, this is 25Bravo, a little Aussie charm will do the trick, you'll see.'

The frustrating wait now began. The sun passed through its zenith, beating down on the concrete of the hard-standing. A heat haze shimmered across the airfield, the air perfectly still, at 37°C. The men retired to the shade of the control tower, most taking the opportunity for a sleep, a 'gonk' in army slang.

The CSM, meanwhile, was having a rest under a tree while his tracker figured out which of the Kudu he was following was the best prospect. The day had grown hot and the CSM was out of condition, sweat saturating his uniform, dripping down his face in rivulets. He did not have the energy to run around on a wild goose chase. He needed to be taken directly to the chosen animal; driving the open Two-Five in blistering heat was a tiring business.

'44, 44 … 25Bravo do you read?'

'25Bravo go.'

'Roger 44, the Charlie Tangos are not heading towards the border. They are tracking due south approximately fourteen clicks west of your loc … Over.'

'25Bravo confirm estimated time to contact?'

114 Aviation fuel turbine, fuel for piston engines was called Avgas, aviation fuel gasoline.

'44 … two hours over.'

The radios hissed faintly. Smith felt the knot in his stomach tighten.

'Does anyone feel like a Coke?' asked Smith, walking to the airport terminal. Three takers put their hands up. The waiting in the heat was making him feel nauseous, *Two more hours, for Fuck Sakes!*

Smith looked across at Lt Light who was talking in an animated fashion with Fullerton, his arms swinging about in excitement. Light paced up and down, full of nervous energy. Being singled out by Fullerton had lifted Smith's spirits, but the Captain's expectation of his performance weighed heavily on his shoulders. The tension caused by the waiting and his nervousness seemed to drain him of his strength. Many of the others sat smoking, cigarette after cigarette. Smith had tried smoking, but it had made him violently ill. He tried to close his eyes, but all he could think about was a bucking helicopter on the way to the contact.

The CTs have taken a longish rest, they must be really heavily loaded, Smith thought.

'44 this is 25Bravo, spoor is now thirty minutes … standby … Over.'

'25Bravo, 44 copied, confirm your loc,' replied Fullerton.

'44, I confirm spoor is thirty minutes. I can see wet piss … Over.' O'Connell then gave his position by calling in the map reference.

Fullerton called the Stop groups, including the helicopter pilots, together again. They all crowded around the map which he stabbed with his finger.

'Looks like the Gooks are here,' he said emphatically, pointing to the edge of a large *vlei*. The ground was so flat that the thin brown contour lines were spaced very far apart. The *vlei* was marked on the map by a dotted blue line showing the centre of the stream, little green tufts showing the surrounding 'swampy' area.

'My guess is that they are on the other side of this *vlei* and moving through this area here,' he said, circling a spot with his pencil.

Nobody replied or made any comment, all in deep contemplation of what was about to unfold.

'If I'm right, then the Stops should be dropped here … and here, then the second wave … here and…. here,' stated Fullerton, marking four spots on the map in a fan shape to the south of the follow-up group. He was anticipating that the Grey Scouts sweepline would drive them in that direction into the Stop groups.

The Grey Scouts were at that very moment spread out in line abreast crossing the *vlei* line. There was no cover at all with the base of the shallow depression virtually devoid of vegetation. They crossed as quickly as possible so as not to get caught in the open. On the other side they regrouped. O'Connell got them to fan out again but not quite so far apart. Sheila's head twitched, lifting up, she had the scent of the terrorists ahead. O'Connell held the reins tightly; he could feel the energy building in Sheila's body as she shook with anticipation. The other horses seemed to respond to her, they too seemed to tension up.

Less than a kilometre to the east of O'Connell, the CSM had finally tracked down his Kudu. There were three of them, a large mature bull and two cows. He signalled to his tracker, climbing down off the Two-Five to get into position for the shot. The bull had a magnificent set of horns. The CSM had visions of them mounted on his veranda at home. He crept forward as the bull gently pulled at the leaves of a tree. The two Kudu cows had moved off ahead. It was absolutely perfectly quiet, not even a birdcall. The heat was intense the CSM shook his head to try and get the sweat out of his eyes. The cover was very limited so he knew that he was not going to get very close, the shot would be at least a hundred metres or more. There was no breeze, just stifling heat. The CSM was an excellent shot. He did not use a telescopic-sight, just the standard peep-sight on the FN.

Eventually getting into a position for the shot, the CSM slowly moved behind a tree with a low-hanging branch to use as a rest. His experience dictated very careful breathing, in and slowly out, his movements very slow and deliberate. The weapon was cocked and ready, safety off. The Kudu continued to nibble at the leaves, magnificent in the bright sunlight, its shining grey coat with faint white stripes, a thick mane running from the base of his throat to his chest. At that distance the CSM knew his best shot was at the base of the neck. Leaning on the tree, he inched the rifle over into position then pulled the butt firmly into his shoulder. His finger moved to the trigger caressing it gently to feel for the correct position. He looked through the sight, moving it fractionally, finding the correct spot on the neck. The animal was browsing so its neck was fully extended, in constant motion. He fired … CRACK!

O'Connell's head shot round in the direction of the shot. *What the Fuck was that?* The group of terrorists, no more than 500metres in front of O'Connell, turned around with precisely the same thought on their minds.

The Kudu bull jumped from the sound of the gunshot, instantly running, bounding, darting from side to side, in an instant, disappeared into the bush. The CSM swore in frustration.

The terrorists were not sure what to do, it had definitely been a shot but not at them - *Maybe they were being followed by SF and one of them had an AD*[115]. *That could be the only explanation.* The leader got his band together in a huddle, instructing them to bombshell[116] in groups of five but to make their way to the prearranged RV point in the south. He was an experienced man; this was his third infiltration into the country. His instructions were delivered rapidly but succinctly. Each group ran off into the bush as fast as they could.

'44 … 25Bravo, we have just heard a single shot somewhere off to our east. Is anybody else out here?' O'Connell's voice was tinged with his sudden shock and anxiety.

'25Bravo … negative, negative … no other Sierra Foxtrot in this area.'

O'Connell sat in his saddle trying to comprehend what was going on. He had terrorists to his front, probably very close, but now some strange shot out in the east. *Could be National Parks! Could be a different group of Gooks shooting for the pot!* He made his decision, signalling to the troop by pointing forward. He urged Sheila to increase the pace; shivering with expectation, she did not need much encouragement.

The CSM was disgusted with himself. He would have made that shot nine times out of ten. He walked back to the Two-Five bitching and moaning and climbed back up into the driver's seat. He sat in the vehicle contemplating the possibility of continuing the hunt; the Kudu would have run a long distance before stopping. He decided to turn back to cut along one of the bush tracks to look for other opportunities. He was stretching down to start the truck when a CT appeared in the bush ahead, trotting along, followed by another, then another. While the CSM was a complete misfit, one thing he could not be accused of was shying away from a fight. He leant forward to get his rifle that was clipped to the dashboard. The tracker, standing on the ground next to the vehicle, swung around when he saw the terrorists, letting loose with a few rounds. The CTs, not sure who was firing at them, fired back over their shoulders, increasing their pace. The CSM banged at the starter button, jammed the Two-Five into gear, let go of the clutch and the vehicle lurched forward. The tracker leapt onto the back as the CSM accelerated away, tires spinning in the sand.

O'Connell reached the spot where the terrorists had bombshelled as the war broke out to his east. Sheila bucked at the sound of gunfire,

---

115 Accidental discharge.
116 An insurgent tactic when attacked or compromised, breaking off in all directions so as to make tracking/follow-up more difficult

come on Bruce we are missing out on the action! The Grey Scout tracker was on the ground looking at the spoor, trying to figure out what was going on. The shooting was a fair distance off. The troop began to mill about, confusion building, everyone giving unsolicited advice.

The sound of the CSM's contact had carried to the airfield where Fullerton and his Fireforce were waiting. Fullerton naturally assumed that 25Bravo had made contact.

'44, 25Bravo there is a firefight to my east, you best get airborne. I have no idea who it is,' called O'Connell, urgency in his voice.

Fullerton did not hear O'Connell's message as he was already running to the helicopter, his headset not yet plugged into the K-car radio. The helicopters started to warm-up, blades turning slowly. Stops 1 and 2 were loaded.

O'Connell was now in a serious quandary. He resolved to keep chasing one of the groups his tracker had identified. They were still very close. Out ahead of him the CTs were rapidly making good their escape.

The flying time to the contact was no more than a few minutes; K-car, flying at treetop level, led the two G-cars in line astern. Smith slipped the headset on to listen to the banter between the pilots and Fullerton's instructions. The G-car lurched left and right as the pilot kept the aircraft in its tight formation.

The CSM slid to a halt on the edge of a *vlei*, the terrorists could be seen running out in front of him, as if in Olympic trials. In one fluid motion the CSM lifted his rifle and dropped the rear-most terrorist with a single shot, the man sprawled in the dust. He then corrected his aim onto the next terrorist; he too was sent flying to the ground. Two down, three to go, the CSM was starting to enjoy himself. The K-car flew right over the top of the CSM. He ducked instinctively.

Fullerton, not seeing the Two-Five on the ground, focused on the CTs running through the middle of the *vlei*. 'Go left ... Go left' he called to the pilot.

The K-car banked into its orbit, rapidly turning onto the target with the two G-cars following behind. The tech in the K-car lined up the 20mm cannon mounted in the door.

'K-car is firing,' the tech called as he brought the gun to bear, popping the large shells at the panic stricken men running through the bush below. The 20mm cannon had an explosive head making the kill-zone a good 10m or more. The experienced tech very quickly despatched the three surviving CTs in a cloud of dust and blood.

'Is that a vehicle down there?' one of the G-car pilots was heard to say over the radio. His call was instantly drowned out.

'CONTACT … CONTACT… CONTACT, Sunray this is 25Bravo.' O'Connell had caught up with the group of CTs he was following.

'Roger 25Bravo … can you see or hear me … over,' replied Fullerton anxiously.

The whine of the three helicopters and the loud thudding impact of the 20mm cannon could be easily heard by the Grey Scouts.

'Sunray you are to my east,' answered O'Connell, then rapidly directed the Fireforce onto his position. He had thrown a green smoke grenade that was clearly visible in the sparse bush below. The Grey Scouts were not cavalry; they were mounted infantry, which meant that they were trained to dismount to go into battle. It was virtually impossible to shoot accurately from horseback. In this case the CTs were not in any way interested in standing to fight they were running for their lives. All they had seen were eight large monsters looming out of the bush, terrifying them out of their wits.

A few of the Grey Scout troopers dismounted, firing shots at the escaping CTs. O'Connell made another decision, ordering them to re-mount to sweep the CTs towards the Stop groups. The bush was so sparse and dry that visibility was excellent. They set off at a steady pace, in extended line.

The K-car gained a bit more altitude in order to give Fullerton a better picture of the ground below. He could see at least two of the bombshelling CT bands, one being the group being chased by O'Connell. He decided that the O'Connell group was the higher priority.

'Blue 1, drop Stop 1 in the next *vlei* line to the south,' Fullerton instructed Smith's pilot.

'Blue 1 copied,' the pilot replied. Smith felt the helicopter heel over as the pilot corrected his orbit, diving rapidly at the point Fullerton had indicated. The bush was so open that the people moving on the ground were clearly visible.

'Blue 2, drop Stop 2 one hundred metres to the west of Stop 1.'

'Blue 2, copied,' Nduku's pilot replied.

'Blue 1 and 2 … fetch the second wave … Over.'

Fullerton issued clipped, clear instructions, rattling them off confidently.

Smith and Nduku, Stops 1 and 2, were duly dropped about a kilometre ahead of the fast-moving CTs. Once they were on the ground, Fullerton started to direct traffic.

'25Bravo, the Charlie Tangos are now one hundred and fifty metres due south of your position, sweep ahead,' Fullerton instructed O'Connell; he then paused momentarily, watching the CTs sprinting below him.

'Stop 1, go forward fifty metres to the tree line in front of you … take cover there.'

'Stop 2 … move to your left to the large anthill … wait there.'

He was setting up the perfect ambush, on both flanks; the CTs were closing on the trap fast.

Smith, lying prone, had Dube next to him, they all waited expectantly, Dube cocked the MAG loudly. Smith signalled to his men, pointing in the direction for them to look. He lifted his rifle onto his elbows and took aim into the bush in front of him. *Stay cool, any second now.*

'Stop 1 … Charlie Tangos to your front … forty meters … thirty meters,' Fullerton called steadily.

The CTs suddenly appeared, running fast, trying to dodge obstructions in front of them, glancing up at the K-car high above. Dube fired, the gun emptying a stream of lead, the belt leaping up as the gun dragged rounds through its mechanism. They all fired, two CTs fell, while the other three jumped to their right, away from their attackers, running forward again directly into the waiting Stop 2. A short burst from Nduku on Smith's left and it was all over.

'Good shooting boys!' yelled Fullerton from K-car.

Scrambling to his feet, Smith called his stick forward to check on the two CTs they had shot. They were both dead, one had been hit in the head, bits of skull and brains were splattered on the tree behind him.

The Grey Scouts appeared in the bush ahead. Smith waved at them to ensure they had seen him as the risk of being shot at by friendly forces always present.

'25Bravo clear the contact area, collect the bodies … standby.'

'Stop 1 and 2 retire back to your LZ … standby,' came Fullerton's quick-fire instructions, now moving his attention to the other group of CTs he had seen.

The leader of the freedom fighters rapidly assessed the degree of trouble he was in, realising that he had to try to get rid of the K-car, somehow. He brought his band together as continuing to move with helicopters overhead, with such little cover, was suicide. The group had grown to seven, as the bombshell process, in such open ground, had not been effective. They took what cover they could and he began to issue a new set of instructions. The younger members shivered in terror, this was way beyond their expectations. They were totally unprepared for the violence they were experiencing.

The K-car had now entered a wider orbit to try and pick up the other CTs as they departed. The two G-cars returned from the airport with Stop 3, Light, and Stop 4. Fullerton gave instructions to widen the search. All three helicopters now scoured the ground below but nothing was moving.

'The Charlie Tangos have gone to ground … look under the trees,' called Fullerton, frustration building in his voice.

The G-car carrying Stop 4 passed right over the CT leader, no more than 200ft above him. All seven of the freedom fighters leapt to their feet firing their AKs on fully automatic at the helicopter. The helicopter took hits in the engine bay; bullets also hit the perspex canopy. The enemy's green tracer passed on either side of the helicopter as the pilot pulled the machine into a tighter turn; he felt a hard thud as a round hit the back of his armoured seat. One of the riflemen in Stop 4 slumped over with a bullet in the back. The pilot fought to keep control, the engine beginning to lose power. The aircraft spun around violently as power was cut to the tail rotor.

'Sunray, Blue 2 … I am hit. I am going to have to put down,' called the pilot urgently.

The helicopter, spinning violently, plummeted out of the sky, the pilot trying to auto-rotate to soften the impact. It hit the ground, rotors disappearing into twisted metal as they struck the surrounding trees, the tail rotor digging into the hard ground, disintegrating into pieces. The impact threw the tech and one of the riflemen out onto the ground; they tumbled in the dust. The tech's head hit a stump knocking him unconscious. The dying soldier lay sprawled on the floor of the helicopter his back covered in blood. The bullet that killed him had travelled through the skin of the aircraft, turning into a tumbling, spinning, hacking, missile, the damage catastrophic.

'Blue 1, drop Stop 3 next to the crash … get them down … NOW.'

Fullerton looked down in horror at the smashed up helicopter. Blue 1 carrying Lt Light flared into a nearby clearing.

The freedom fighter leader, seeing that he had been able to bring down the helicopter, took his opportunity; he ordered three of his men to run forward to kill any survivors from the downed helicopter. He then concentrated his band's fire onto the other helicopter trying to land.

'Sunray … Blue 1 … I am taking heavy fire.'

Holes appeared in the perspex in front of the pilot.

'I need to abort … pulling out.' The pilot gunned the engine, tilting the aircraft forward to regain altitude, bullets striking the rotor blades as the helicopter passed over the CT position.

'Blue 1 … get that Stop down, Charlie Tangos are approaching the crash site,' called Fullerton, watching in horror as the CTs dashed forward towards the downed helicopter.

K-car pulled closer, the tech desperately firing 20mm rounds at the approaching CT's.

The freedom fighter leader, turning his attention to the K-car, fired up at it, muzzle flashes followed by green tracer, arching upwards. The K-car pilot, seeing the danger, jinked and turned to avoid the flack rising from below. The 20mm gunner's aim was thrown off and the rounds flew wide. The CTs, suddenly free from attack pressed their charge towards the crash site.

Blue 1, carrying Lt Light, climbed out still being chased by bullets as they went. The pilot scanned the ground for a safer LZ, pinpointed another landing spot he immediately dropped into it. Light, not waiting for the aircraft to hit the ground, leapt into space, crunching onto the ground, performing a neat para-roll, instantly covering his massive bulk in dust. Light's stick followed him onto the ground but he had already disappeared into the bush ahead, running at full tilt.

'Stop 3, Charlie Tangos one hundred on your left,' called Fullerton urgently. The CTs were fast approaching the smouldering wreck.

' … faster man!' Fullerton called again, desperation now in his voice.

Light sprinted forward, seeing the crashed aircraft ahead. A CT appeared to his left, Light fired but missed. The Englishman charged onwards, firing from the hip, he gave out a blood-curdling scream. The CT glanced up to see the approaching giant bearing down on him, he tried to turn but it was too late. Light hit him full force in a body check, bowling the man over. Fullerton watched from the air as Light smashed down on the CT with his rifle butt crushing his skull in a single killer blow. The other two CTs turned to run, disappearing in dust and blood as the K-car 20mm cannon finally found its mark, destroying them instantly.

The freedom fighter leader broke cover when he saw the K-car re-engage, hoping that the downed helicopter would divert attention away from him. The three men he had sent forward had been sacrificed. His remaining band dropped their backpacks and sprinted after their leader making their final bid for safety.

As the CTs broke cover Fullerton saw them. 'Blue 1 … pick-up Stop1,' he called, needing to get some people on the ground out in front of the escaping CTs.

The K-car pilot pulled his orbit directly above the fugitives.

'George can you get a bead on those bastards?' the pilot called to his tech on the 20mm cannon.

'Negative … too tight an angle of bank … roll-out slightly.'

The tech pulled the cannon around trying to get onto the target. The helicopter jinked as the pilot corrected his bank to bring the gun platform to a more level position. There was no need for further corrections; the gunner started pumping rounds into the bush below.

He 'walked' the exploding rounds up behind the CTs who were now running in a wide arc. One of them disappeared in blood and gore with a direct hit.

Hearing the instruction to be picked up, Smith had his men trotted back to the LZ; he threw a smoke grenade to help the pilot orientate himself.

'Blue 1 … Stop 1, red smoke.' He was learning fast.

The wait for the helicopter's return was short-lived. As it touched down Smith's stick dashed for the doors and they were back in the air in moments. Smith could see the K-car out ahead, the 20mm cannon firing, puffs of cordite smoke washing back as the gun fired. Blue 1 turned in behind the K-car, the G-car gunner at the door joining the cacophony with the twin .303s. Both helicopter crews were desperate to kill the CTs that had downed their colleague. The helicopters weaved, turned, banking hard left and right, opening and closing the gap between them. The pilots handled the helicopters as if an extension of themselves, gunners firing continuously. Smith saw CTs going down, one after the other, as the howling, avenging, helicopters chased them to their death.

The .303 in Smith's helicopter suddenly stopped. The tech shouted out in frustration, yanking at the .303-belt jammed in the breech, desperately trying to clear it, smashing at the gun frantically with his fist.

The pilot looked over his shoulder at his tech who threw his hands up in resignation. 'Sunray, Blue 1 … Stoppage.'

'Copied Blue 1, drop Stop 1 in the *vlei* two kilometres to your north-west, these Gooks will have to cross there at some point.'

'Blue 1 copied,' Smith's pilot replied instantly.

'Blue 1 … pick up Stop 2. …' Fullerton continued.

A now more dangerous situation was in play with only one airborne gun still in operation. Smith's helicopter broke off, heading to the wide expanse of *vlei* ahead. The *vlei* was dry littered with chunks of cracked mud totally devoid of vegetation. Smith's stick was completely exposed as they de-planed, not needing any encouragement to sprint forward into the cover of the low trees on the edge of the *vlei*. The helicopter was instantly back in the air to fetch Nduku, Stop 2.

Looking around him, Smith quickly established that there was no cover at all beyond the few desiccated thorn trees. The ground was parched; the few trees were small and scraggly, with very little foliage. A few were pushed over, testament to a resident herd of elephants. Smith arranged the four of them in all-round defence in the shade of a tree facing outwards their feet almost touching in the middle as they lay down. Smith figured that if the CTs tried to cross the *vlei* anywhere within half a kilometre he would see them. They lay and waited. Smith felt remarkably relaxed despite the shock of seeing the helicopter go down. He took a long drink of water not realising how parched his throat was; *Maybe I'm getting used to this?* he thought.

Nduku was dropped with Stop 2, further to Smith's west. He called Nduku on the radio to confirm his own position; he had Nduku's stick 'visual'. Nduku was no sooner on the ground than one of the terrorists took his chance to cross the *vlei*, at a point midway between the two waiting stops. The man was sprinting so fast that he was already thirty or so metres into the *vlei* before he was spotted. Both Stop 1 and Stop 2 opened fire. Dube pulled the gun around, chasing the terrorist with bullet strikes as he ran. Out of the corner of his eye Smith saw Nduku get to his feet, then take off after the CT. The fleeing man was rapidly approaching the tree line on the opposite side. Everyone watched in awe as Nduku crossed the *vlei*, his legs pumping, swiftly catching the now exhausted CT. The terrorist glanced back, realising that it was futile to continue he stopped and turned, dropping his weapon as he did so. Nduku pumped half a magazine into him.

The contact was over.

Way in the distance, out of earshot, a Two-Five started up, departing rapidly towards the north, the CSM prayed that he had not been seen. The mystery of the isolated shooting that had initiated the contact would remain. Nobody really gave it a second thought, lost in the drama and excitement.

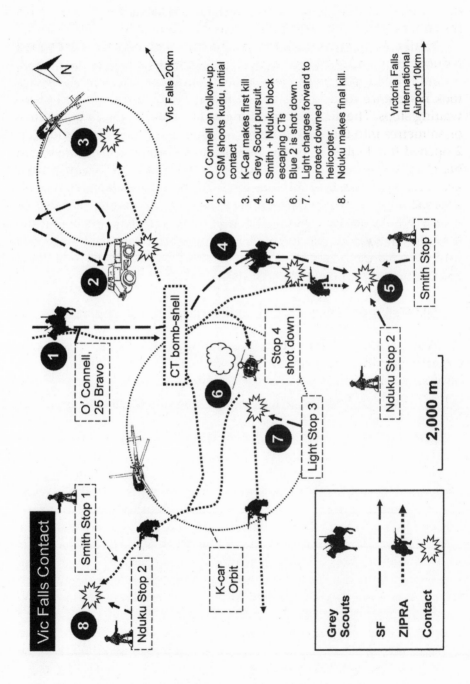

N

Vic Falls 20km

1. O'Connell on follow-up.
2. CSM shoots kudu, initial contact
3. K-Car makes first kill
4. Grey Scout pursuit.
5. Smith + Nduku block escaping CTs
6. Blue 2 is shot down.
7. Light charges forward to protect downed helicopter.
8. Nduku makes final kill.

Victoria Falls International Airport 10km

1

O'Connell, 25 Bravo

2

3

4

CT bomb-shell

5

Smith Stop 1

Nduku Stop 2

Stop 4 shot down

6

2,000 m

7

Light Stop 3

Smith Stop 1

Nduku Stop 2

K-car Orbit

8

Nduku Stop 2

Vic Falls Contact

Grey Scouts

SF

ZIPRA

Contact

15

Police Camp, Wankie, northwest Matabeleland

The intelligence picture of Lupane TTL initiated by Sgt Cephas Ngwenya and the Selous Scout c/signs had now been fully developed. The Police Special Branch and Army commanders met at the Police HQ in Wankie to discuss their options. One of the attendees was Major Peacock from 4 Indep. The Selous Scouts had been on the ground in the Lupane TTL for nearly a week. It was agreed that they should remain in place so as not to risk the possibility of their exit being detected. The forensic information had all been accumulated and studied with conclusions drawn. One of the policemen gave the assembled group a detailed briefing on the connections they had found between the large group intercepted by 4 Indep at Kamativi, the convoy attack and the massacre at Kosami Mission. The Selous Scouts had also confirmed through interrogation of their captured terr that the convoy attack had been initiated from the camp in Lupane.

A detailed plan for an attack and sweep through Lupane was put into effect.

*

ZIPRA Base Camp, Lupane TTL, north Matabeleland

Comrade Tongerai Chabanga had not received any word of the whereabouts of the Soviet Advisor, Benkov. He had cursed the Russian's disappearance fearing the now very real possibility of a Rhodesian sweep in his area. The interview with the local Sangoma about the murder of the young girl had also disturbed him. Chabanga realised that the local villagers were deeply traumatized by the murder and they were demanding vengeance. The death of the girl at the hands of a freedom fighter and the fact that his large group were making increasing demands for food made the situation worse. He had no way of giving the people retribution, as he did not know for sure who had killed her. All he knew was that Comrade Mlungisi in Benkov's band had instructed for her body to be disposed of. This indicated strongly that either Benkov or someone in his band had killed her. The problem he had was that there was no one to deliver to the villagers for punishment. Punishment in the form of death was what the Sangoma had demanded. The Sangoma had reminded Chabanga of the possible consequences of the girl's spirit being left without any retribution. Her spirit had to be put to rest or dire consequences would result. Chabanga was a sophisticated man, not believing in all this tribal hocus-pocus, but his people did. That was what worried him.

Chabanga's options were now few in number. He could divide his brigade up into smaller groups and disperse them to try and alleviate the food shortage, or he could move the whole group to another part of the TTL. It was also possible that he could move to another region all together, probably further south where food was more plentiful. Other possibilities included much more aggressive raids on white farmers and trading stores to collect food. All of these options were fraught with risk and danger.

The food shortage was probably the worst problem as that was more likely to result in a mutiny, with cadres deserting of their own accord. The Lupane TTL bordered a large, expansive, white-owned, cattle-ranching area. There was a possibility of raiding these ranches to drive cattle back into the TTL, to be slaughtered for food. His experience with stealing cattle was that the police would likely send out teams to look for the stolen cattle. The police had a very enthusiastic Stock-theft Unit in the area. Comrade Chabanga's world was in disarray. He needed a plan, and he knew he needed it fast.

*

Cattle Ranching Area south of Dett, northwest Matabeleland

Comrade Vladimir Benkov, on the other hand, was well on his way to Dett in the north. Having exhausted their food supplies, his group needed to replenish. He was not keen to take food from the local villagers, as he was anxious to keep the presence of his band a secret. The only solution was to rob a trading store or farmhouse. Benkov had satellite photographs and maps of the country with him, so it was not difficult to navigate. He had picked out a few likely farmhouses as possibilities, but they were all very heavily protected with security fences and guard dogs. Some farmers had armed their workers as security guards together with the fact that the farmers and their families were all well armed themselves. Many of the larger farms maintained a trading store that was supported by the farm workers and the local villagers. In most cases the trading stores were located outside of the farmhouse compound.

Benkov sat on a hill overlooking a trading store that he had selected as a target. He had been observing the comings and goings of the occupants of the farm for two days and now felt he had an understanding of the routine. The plan he had formulated revolved around a diversionary attack on the farmhouse from the opposite side to the trading store. This would keep the farmer busy while he would break into the trading store and steal what he needed. His concern was that the trading store had thick steel bars on the windows while the front door was heavily reinforced with bars and steel mesh. It was also chained and padlocked. He figured that if he tied a few stick grenades together with a lump of plastic explosive that should blow the door open, or as a Plan B, he would have to use an RPG. Once again, a successful escape depended on an early evening attack so they had the rest of the night to get away.

As the sun descended onto the horizon, Benkov sent two of his cadres to lay a TM-46 landmine on the approach road to the farm compound. This was planned to slow down the police or army when they responded to the attack. They also laid three PMN-1 anti-personnel mines on the side of the road adjacent to the landmine.

The time came for the attack as soon as darkness closed in. Benkov sent his trusted lieutenant, Mlungisi, who had now assumed the role of 2IC in his band, to the south side of the farm compound. His orders were to open fire with at least one RPG round aimed at the house. Benkov made his way to the opposite end of the compound and waited for Mlungisi to initiate the attack.

As the freedom fighters moved carefully into position, a dog started barking in the security-fenced area surrounding the farmhouse. Benkov could see at least three large dogs running along the inside of the fence, *the dogs know we are here!* The farmer now alert, switched on a set of security lights which lit up the compound, other spotlights pointed into the surrounding bush, throwing deep shadows in the trees. An area of at least fifty metres had been cleared around the entire fenced perimeter meaning that anyone approaching the fence would be completely exposed. Benkov waited.

The early evening calm was disturbed as Mlungisi initiated the attack with a sustained burst from an RPD, sending a rocket grenade whooshing at the house. It detonated on the perimeter fence with an impressive explosion, leaving a wide hole, but no damage was caused to the house. Mlungisi quickly switched his firing position to a different angle to give the 'target' the impression of more attackers. The security guard, armed with an old World War II Lee-Enfield .303, ran to the side of the house where Mlungisi was attacking from, firing into the bush, rapidly working the bolt of the antiquated weapon.

Inside the house the farmer walked calmly to his Agric-Alert radio[117], calling up his neighbours to sound the alarm. The same signal was received at the local police camp. The farmer and his wife together with their eldest son began to return fire, aiming carefully at the muzzle flashes. This was not the first attack on their farm.

Benkov and three of his cadres sprinted across the cleared area to the door of the trading store. He quickly took out three stick grenades that he had already tied together, stuck a small lump of plastic explosive in between with a detonator attached, then wedged them next to the base of the door. He ducked around the protected side of the store and triggered the explosive with a small battery. The loud thumping explosion reverberated in the night air. Glancing through the smoke and dust at his handiwork, Benkov could not believe his eyes. The door was still largely intact, missing a few metal panels but there was no room to squeeze through. On the other side of the compound the firing had reduced to a few sporadic shots.

The explosion alerted the farmer to the fact that his store was being robbed. He started a steady rate of fire in the direction of the trading store, joined by his wife. One of Benkov's cadres shot another RPG at the house this one passed through the fence impacting the side of the house with a loud bang. The RPG can punch through two or three inches of armour-plated steel so a brick wall presents no obstacle. In this case, the rocket hit a steel reinforcing bar in the brickwork that caused it to explode, knocking a hole in the wall at least a metre in diameter, spreading pieces of brick and masonry into the house. The newly created hole provided the farmer with an improved shooting position and field of fire.

Fortunately for Benkov the door of the trading store faced away from the house providing cover. He now contemplated his next move. He tried shooting at the hinges of the door with his AKM, but that also didn't work. Increasingly desperate, he called for the RPG launcher and loaded a projectile. He knew he couldn't shoot from too close. There was no option, he ran out into the open in a crouched position, turned, firing as soon as he could. Bullet strikes appeared in the dirt around him, the farmer had seen him. The rocket ignited, bursting from the launcher, passing neatly through the steel door, as it was designed to do, exploding on the inside of the store. Benkov was not to know that most trading stores carried methylated spirits and kerosene used by the local people for filling their cooking stoves and lamps. The RPG set

117 The Agric-Alert system was a radio network set up between farmers and the police within agricultural districts. The radio communication helped neighbours to keep in touch without travelling on the dangerous farm roads. Every evening and every morning each farmer would call in with a sitrep. When a farm was attacked, the Agric-Alert system would allow the farmers to respond to their neighbour's plight as well as alerting the local police.

off secondary explosions as the drums and bottles of highly flammable liquid ignited.

The trading store quickly turned into an inferno. Benkov's plan was now in disarray. The farmer, gaining in confidence, jumped through the hole in the wall, beginning a professional skirmish towards the burning store – fire and movement. Benkov could not have known that the farmer was a retired member of Support Commando, 1 RLI, and in more recent years, despite his greying hair, spent much of his time as a Stick Leader in the local PATU[118] contingent. The other members of his PATU stick were making their way to the farm at that very moment.

Benkov realised that the attack had failed and it was time to get away. The attack had taken way too long and the fire made the mission impossible to accomplish. He signalled the cadres with him and they set off back across the brightly lit open space to the safety of the bush beyond. The farmer saw them break out from the side of the store, lifted his rifle, tap … tap. Two of the escaping cadres fell, one died instantly as the bullet passed through his back, turning his chest into mush while the other took a bullet in the right hamstring which passed through the thigh bone, leaving the leg virtually amputated. The wounded man screamed in agony, rolling in the dirt. Benkov and the surviving cadre made it to the protection of the bush, running to their pre-arranged RV point.

The wounded freedom fighter rolled in the dirt clutching at his leg, calling for help, pleading in siNdebele for someone to take away the pain.

'*Ngisize!* Help! *Ungangisiza* … - *cela*? Can you help me … please?' he pleaded.

The farmer stood at the security fence watching as the cadre tried to drag himself to the bush beyond, his half severed leg leaving a trail of blood and gore behind him, eventually he collapsed from shock and loss of blood.

'Suffer you bastard,' the farmer called out in siNdebele.

The farmer had turned his 7.62mm rounds into 'dum-dums' by carefully cross cutting groves into the bullet heads. The effect was to ensure that when the bullet struck it flattened or mushroomed, transferring maximum kinetic energy to the target instead of blasting a hole through it. The result was a wound so massive that survival was almost impossible.

Back down the approach road to the farm two police Land Rovers

118 Police Anti-Terrorist Unit. Many members of PATU were farmers and they specialised in conducting follow-ups on terrorist groups. As they knew their operational areas very well they often performed better than army units not permanently stationed in the district.

raced along as fast as they could, bouncing on the twisting and uneven road. The first one passed over the landmine safely, the second struck it with the passenger-side front wheel, turning the vehicle into a tumbling, somersaulting, disintegrating wreck, instantly killing the driver, his passenger and two constables in the back. The fuel tank burst into flames as the vehicle came to a rest, quickly setting the surrounding tinder-dry bush on fire. The lead vehicle stopped, the occupants jumped out and ran back down the road but could not approach the burning vehicle, the intense heat spread with the bushfire, forcing them back. The rounds in one of the rifles in the cab started to explode like firecrackers. There was nothing they could do. Not knowing what lay ahead, they drove to the farmhouse, expecting the worst.

Benkov looked back at the burning beacon of the trading store, for the first time in his military career he felt a slight shiver of uncertainty.

*

4 Independent Company (RAR) base camp, Sprayview airfield, Victoria Falls

At 4 Indep the participants in the day's follow-up and subsequent contact had all arrived back. Light had his 3 Platoon singing in the back of the trucks as they rolled into town, insisting on a spin down the main road past the shopping centre, everyone singing at the top of their voices and waving at the onlookers.

> *Then we shall ha' to bury thee*
> *On Ilkla Moor baht 'at*
> *Then we shall ha' to bury thee*
>
> *On Ilkla Moor baht 'at*

The pilot and tech of the downed helicopter were badly shaken but not seriously injured; the pilot had broken his wrist while the tech was concussed from his blow on the head. The K-car and remaining G-car had carried the injured airmen to the hospital at Vic Falls; the G-car returning to lift the four sticks back to the International Airport, only a few minutes flight away. The two helicopters were parked on the hard-standing at Sprayview airstrip, it being too late to fly back to Wankie. A truck had been sent into the contact area to collect the bodies and equipment. O'Connell and the Grey Scouts rode out to the airport for recovery by their vehicles. Fullerton arranged for the remaining members of 3 Platoon to guard the helicopter wreckage.

The CSM drove back into camp just after dark, deciding to keep a low profile for a few days.

Ingwe Fullerton, as always, was fired up after the contact and he needed a party. The K-car had no sooner shut down its engine than he was on the phone to his connection at UTC. He asked her whether there was any room on the evening 'Booze Cruise' on the River to Kalunda Island. The hotels and resorts were busy so the tour company had put on two boats that evening. She said if they could get down to the jetty in twenty minutes they would make the second boat, she also reminded them all to wear civies[119].

Orders were rapidly issued, participants changed, a rushed attempt was made to remove camo-cream, in most cases unsuccessful in the time allowed. The Two-Five, with Fullerton, O'Connell, Smith, Dawson, Light and the four airmen, raced to the jetty located close to the AZambezi River Lodge. The truck screeched to a halt at the ramp and the group excitedly made their way onto the boat that been asked to wait for them. The boat was packed with tourists who had already tucked into the liquor. The 'Booze Cruise' was marketed as the 'Sunset Cruise' providing all you could drink. *Just what the doctor ordered* Smith contemplated.

The soldiers and airmen, the latter in Fullerton's borrowed clothes, made their way to the top level of the double-decker riverboat. Fullerton loudly ordered a round of *jimboolies*. The party started in earnest with the lads giving a detailed account of the day's events to the awestruck tourists, hands used to imitate helicopters flying, the sound effects provided by the airmen. Beers were sunk in quick succession there was no standing on ceremony. Under the rapid onset of alcohol the 'war-stories' raged on, being embellished with each retelling until it sounded more like the D-Day invasion than an isolated skirmish. Smith was careful not to describe the circumstances of Nduku's lone charge across the *vlei*; some stories are better left untold.

O'Connell, of course, with a bit of liquor in him gave the impression that the Australians were really behind the victory. He described in minute detail the charge through the bush, *cannon to the right of them, cannon to the left, into the jaws of death*. The audience were reduced to tears of laughter as O'Connell, perched on Dawson's back, described the battle and the ensuing victory, the irony in the metaphor of Tennyson's *Charge of the Light Brigade* lost on the inebriated crowd. The pilots, balancing on chairs on the bench tables, gave a description of the air battle, their techs holding empty beer bottles, mimicking the sound

119 Civilian clothing, anything other than the army uniform, worn in civy-street.

170

of the twin 303s and the 20mm cannon.

The *Charge of the Light Brigade* metaphor was taken a step further when Fullerton described Lt Light's charge across the bush to save the occupants of the downed helicopter, *Theirs not to make reply, Theirs not to reason why, Theirs but to do and die.* Light was offered three cheers from the crowd, while Fullerton led a chorus of *For he's a Jolly Good Fellow.* Light stood beaming amongst the tightly packed onlookers, head and shoulders above them all, thanking everyone politely, 't'was nawt, honestly.'

The boat ploughed slowly up the river, the sunset magnificent, spellbinding, but lost in the entertainment provided by the exuberant soldiers. As the boat reached the southern edge of Kalunda Island the Captain began a slow turn back downriver. Lt Light, having sunk a good many beers, was indignant that the halfway point had been reached so quickly.

He stood in the bows of the upper deck shouting loudly for 'Anchors Awa! ... Anchors Awa!' with no effect on the crew whatsoever, but with delighted encouragement from the crowd. He went off very indignantly to enquire from the Captain of the boat why he was returning so soon. The Captain, quite used to this question, politely explained to the giant Pom in front of him that the tour had to end at a particular time for security reasons.

'BOLLOCKS!' Light shouted at the top of his voice, then, without so much as a second thought, dived headlong into the river.

'MAN OVERBOARD,' bellowed the accompanying soldiers.

The round life-preservers were duly thrown to the swimming Yorkshireman who grabbed onto them, happy with his evening swim. The Zambezi is notorious for its vigorous current, Light rapidly began to fade into the distance. A rope was then thrown to him that he managed to grab.

'Light ... you stupid Pommie bastard, get back onto the boat, the river is crawling with flat-dogs,' Fullerton shouted.

The Pom had no idea what that meant, continuing to use the two life-preservers as a giant set of water-wings. Attempting now to lead the assembled crowd from the murky depths with,

Row, row, row your boat,
gently down the stream,
Merrily, Merrily, Merrily, Merrily
Life is but a dream!

'Crocodiles, you blithering idiot, crocodiles,' Fullerton yelled.

The Captain was forced to shut down his engines, slowly drifted back down-stream as Light was fished out of the river. He arrived back on deck to tumultuous applause for his great personal sacrifice in extending the duration of the cruise, followed by another round of *For he's a Jolly Good Fellow*.

Song after song followed, including a stirring rendition of *Danny Boy* by Lt Light, in a booming bass voice, standing to attention on a table. O'Connell would not be outdone. He pushed his way through the crowd on the upper deck to get to the Captain's console, clicking through the collection of cassette tapes, then finding one he liked, he thrust it at the hostess.

'Play this,' he said, '… crank it up.' Creedence Clear Water Revival[120] boomed out.

> *I see the bad moon arising.*
> *I see trouble on the way.*

The soldiers on the deck immediately took up the chorus on the top of their voices.

> *Don't go around tonight,*
> *Well, it's bound to take your life,*
> *There's a bad moon on the rise.*

Now into it, the crowd on the boat joined in.

> *I fear rivers overflowing.*
> *I hear the voice of rage and ruin.*

With the stress of the previous weeks and the ten beers on an empty stomach, Mike Smith threw up overboard. He hung onto the ship's rail, hopelessly trying to regain his feet. Emotion borne of too much alcohol, and the relief of finally achieving a level of acceptance by Fullerton and the others, brought involuntarily tears to Smith's eyes. He sat in a heap next to the rail, tears dripping down his cheeks, his shoulders shaking with delayed reaction. Nobody noticed except Rob Dawson who knelt down beside him, 'It's okay Mike, it's okay … let it go man.'

Dawson took Smith by the arm and lifted him back to his feet and they both spontaneously burst into laughter, the manic, uninhibited laughter that only alcohol can engender.

The public address announced the end of the cruise. The crew moved as quickly as possible to get the passengers off the boat to avoid cleaning up the vomit that was bound to follow shortly. The soldiers

120 *Bad Moon Rising*, John Fogarty, 1969

and airmen staggered off the boat, still singing, arm in arm. Fullerton insisted that they adjourn to the nearby AZambezi River Lodge for something to eat and a few more beers. Smith threw up again on the side of the road.

The intoxicated bunch reeled into the pub at the AZambezi, Dawson supporting Smith who was far from steady on his feet. Fullerton was absolutely delighted to see the blonde he had seen getting off the SAA 737 that morning. He steered a course in her direction followed by the rest of the drinking party. As it transpired she was an SAA airhostess on leave with a few of her friends. Dealing with a bunch of drunks was all in a day's work for her.

A two-man band was set up in the corner of the pub, banging out drinking songs. The 'boys from the bush', were still in fine voice and joined in enthusiastically, Lt Light imposing a 'request' for Lindesfarne's *Fog on the Tyne*[121].

> *Sittin' in a sleazy snack-bar*
> *Snuckin' sickly sausage rolls*
> *Slippin' down slowly, slippin' down sideways*
> *Think I'll sign off the dole*

Light led the chorus enthusiastically,

> *'Cause the fog on the Tyne is all mine, all mine*
> *The fog on the Tyne is all mine ...*

The crowd loved it, clapping and shouting, 'encore, encore'; Light bowed deeply, returning the microphone to the singer who laughed and clapped at this giant Pom, covered in streaks of camo-cream.

Fullerton, never to be outdone, duly ordered a round of Peppermint Liqueur 'Depth Charges', challenging the 'Blue Jobs' to a boat race. This concoction is made by inverting a liqueur glass of the deep green *Crème de Menthé*, then carefully pouring in a beer over the glass, gently removing the liqueur glass to leave a beer with a thick layer of 'green-death' at the bottom of the glass. Fullerton lined up with Dawson and Light with O'Connell as the anchor because of his renowned expertise at this type of racing. The holidaying airhostesses were appointed the judges of speed and 'spillage'. The four airmen lined up across the table. The other revellers in the bar eagerly crowded around to cheer on the racing teams. All the participants put their hands on their heads, leaning over with their faces only inches from the glass, waiting eagerly for the start. Someone gave the off; Fullerton and his man opposite grabbed a

121 *Foy on the Tyne*, Alan Hull, 1971.

glass, down the beer went, both knowing what to expect when the thick green fluid hit their throat. Finished, the glass was inverted on the head to check for spillage; Dawson's turn next, still neck and neck, a bit of spillage from the airmen. Light, choked when the green muck hit his throat, spluttering green slime over his opposite number. It was all up to O'Connell to bring the team home; the two men gulped down, up the glasses went onto the respective heads while the crowd screamed their encouragement. The Judges needed to confer; the 'Brown Jobs' had it by a neck. The soldiers danced around in a circle, arms across their shoulders, whooping their victory. The airmen appealed to the judges for review, nothing else for it, a rematch was called. The crowd bayed for more.

Smith gently slid to the floor under the bar, his mind numb. Needing the toilet again he tried vainly to regain his feet. Then giving up trying to walk he crawled towards the door, eventually assisted to his feet by two holidaymakers. After three attempts he managed to follow the receptionist's instructions to the toilet but forced to make a short detour to the garden to throw-up. As he exited the toilet he heard, 'Hello soldier' from behind him in a very familiar Irish accent.

He turned, Sandra Peacock stood in front of him wearing a very tight, sleeveless, black pantsuit, with a high collar and a deep V-neck that plunged tantalisingly low. Her hair was tied back and she wore dark eye make-up that accentuated her deep green eyes. Smith was instantly struck by the same confused feeling he felt when last they had met, albeit severely impaired.

'Shandra … I mean … Maam, … Misshes Peacock,' he slurred, looking to see if the Major was behind her. He had great difficulty standing, so he leaned against the wall, trying for all he was worth to seem sober. The more sober he pretended the more obviously drunk he appeared.

'You're out for a few drinks Mike, what is the occasion?' her voice, soft and sultry.

'I had another contact … today … I am with Captain Fullerton … shum Grey Scouts and shum pilots,' he tried pronouncing each word in turn, to try to avoid slurring. His eyes were now fixed on the plunging neckline.

'I am shorry … but I feel shick …' the effort of speaking was becoming increasingly difficult; his stomach ached with bile, any attempt at averting his eyes from the pantsuit was lost.

'Mike … you better come with me' she said, taking him by the hand … leading him.

'I don't think, I should … the Major may …'

'Shhhh Mike, it's fine the Major isn't here, it's okay,' she put his arm over her shoulder supporting him to her room.

'We need to get you cleaned up, you stink to high heaven,' she said soothingly.

Mike Smith capitulated; his addled brain contemplated the prospect of furthering his education. *Who said the army didn't teach you anything?*

16

ZIPRA Base Camp, Lupane TTL, north Matabeleland

Comrade Tongerai Chabanga had made a plan. It was not his best option but it was better than not doing anything at all. He had decided to split his forces into two groups, one to stay where they were, the other to move more to the east. He had also been forced to send a raiding party into the neighbouring farming area to steal cattle. This was as much to appease the local villagers as it was to feed his men. Cattle were a very important determinant of wealth. The number of cattle he owned judged a man's status. The number of cattle also had an effect on how many wives a man could take. As the family of each wife demanded cattle in payment, *lobolo*, as a dowry, the more cattle a man owned, the better his prospects. Chabanga's force had severely impacted the collective wealth of the local villagers in the sense that they were eating cattle, goats and stored grain stock, while also defiling the young women that reduced their value to potential husbands. The adverse economic impact that the Chabanga Brigade's presence was having was just as debilitating to the locals as their brutality and violent intimidation.

Bringing his section leaders together, Chabanga explained his plan. There was a great deal of debate about the practical aspects and the advisability. The cadres had become comfortable in their surroundings; many of them had struck up meaningful relationships with the local women. Eventually Chabanga had to call a halt to the discussion and do what all army commanders do when they cannot find consensus, he gave an 'order'. The date for the departure of the split group was set for one week to give enough time for a reconnaissance party to scout out a new base camp with enough water and food supplies. This was planned to be further upstream on the Shangani River, closer to the district of Nkai.

Sitting on the hill above, Cephas Ngwenya Selous Scout, made a careful note of the departure of eight CTs to the east. This was Chabanga's reconnaissance party. A much larger group, probably double the size, departed to the west. This was the cattle 'rustling' party. Such obvious overt activity meant only one thing to Ngwenya ... something was up. He weighed the alternatives up in his mind, *this camp needed to get hit and quickly!* Ngwenya crawled back to his team to report what he had seen and prepare a message for their controllers.

*

Cattle Ranching Area south of Dett, northwest Matabeleland

The farm that had been attacked by Benkov was a hive of activity. The PATU stick that had arrived by Land Rover waited until first light, then immediately set off on follow-up. The landmine explosion had meant that the road was impassable until it could be cleared. The farmer had a grass airstrip on his property so the Police Reserve Air Wing (PRAW) managed to fly in a Special Branch investigation team and another PATU stick for follow-up. The surviving terrorist managed to live through to ten the next morning before he passed away. The farmer and the members of the PATU stick had tried to save him by putting drips and morphine into him and attaching a tourniquet on the dismembered leg but to no avail. They were disappointed, as they knew how important it was to keep him alive for questioning.

The two AKs from the dead terrorists were collected and their backpacks inspected. The policemen all marvelled at the photograph of the dead CT and his Russian girlfriend standing in front of the Kremlin in Red Square in Moscow. The farmer commented on the fact that the CT that fired the RPG at his store was wearing a balaclava and that he seemed very tall. He thought that the CT seemed to have lighter skin, maybe a *goffle*[122]. This description was consistent with the earlier intelligence reports.

The casualties from Benkov's raid were increased still further when a young, enthusiastic, NS Engineer stood on one of the AP mines laid on the side of the road. His leg was blown off below the knee, but fortunately the Engineer medic was very experienced and he managed to save the man's life. The PRAW flew the badly injured man directly to the Bulawayo General. Benkov, if nothing else, had succeeded in seriously pissing-off a bunch of policemen who were now after his blood.

On the other hand, Benkov was making a resolute attempt to put some distance between him and the farm he had attacked. His band, with nothing to show for the raid on the farm, were now forced to go into the villages they passed to collect food. Benkov always remained outside the village when this was necessary. He gave no time for rest; they travelled all the next day and night with only short stops for food and water. As they passed village after village, they instructed the villagers to brush their spoor away to slow down the follow-up team that they knew would be behind them.

---

122 Rhodesian slang, person of mixed race, a coloured person

The PATU follow-up team got further and further behind because they couldn't track at night. Benkov had succeeded in putting thirty kilometres between his band and the follow-up before he had another lucky break when they commandeered a truck near the main north-south railway line. The truck was halted when a freedom fighter stepped into the road with a RPG; the driver needed very little persuasion. This effectively put paid to any chance of being caught. Mlungisi got the driver to drop them off when they got close to the village of Dett, then disappearing once again into the bush going north.

*

AZambezi Rive Lodge Victoria Falls

Mike Smith awoke the next morning with the most frightening hangover of his life. The night before was a hazy, blurry picture, no matter how hard he tried, it would not come into focus.

'We better get you back to camp soldier,' said Sandra Peacock who stood above him dressed in a light cotton top and skirt. She had ordered breakfast from room service. Smith wolfed it down, leaving nothing, even scraping the remaining jam out of the jar with his finger. She watched him eat, sitting in a comfortable chair, relaxed in silence.

Mike looked at her sitting watching him in quiet contemplation. He felt embarrassed, not sure of what had transpired the night before, not sure how he ended up in Mrs Peacock's room.

Eventually plucking up courage, 'Did anything … happen … last night?' he asked sheepishly.

'Let's not worry about that now … we will get you back to camp and we can talk about this when next we meet,' she said softly.

'Did I … did we?' Smith pushed for an answer.

'A lady never tells … Sergeant!' she replied in mock indignation, her hands on her hips. She bundled him out of the room, still dressed in his civvies, and drove him back to camp. He lay down on the back seat so as not to be seen, his head throbbing as if to burst. Sandra dropped him at the bottom of the dirt road leading to the camp making sure that nobody was about.

Smith walked up the road into camp then ducked through the bush so that he could approach from a point closest to his room. He looked through the trees carefully, there were only a few people about, the Grey Scouts were feeding and grooming their horses. He made a run for it; his head feeling like it was about to explode.

'Sergeant bloody Smith, what the fuck happened to you last night?'

The all too familiar voice echoed across the camp. The sound resonated in Smith's head like a crashing cymbal. Stopping in his tracks, Smith looked around to see where Fullerton was calling from, squinting in the bright sunlight.

'Over here you little NS wanker,' called Fullerton from the canteen.

Fullerton, Dawson and the helicopter crews were having a late breakfast together. Smith shuffled over to where they were sitting, self conscious in his civvies, not knowing what he could expect in the form of punishment. *Extra guard duties, all night radio watch, who knows what?* The occupants of the canteen stopped talking and watched in silence as he slowly approached.

'Where have you been Smithy?' asked Fullerton quizzically.

The canteen was perfectly still, all watching expectantly to see what was to happen.

Then a sudden realisation struck Fullerton. 'Fuck me, but I think Sergeant Smith got his leg over last night,' he shouted triumphantly pointing his finger at Smith.

The breakfasting officers broke into spontaneous applause, quickly joined by the other diners. The canteen was in an uproar with the black soldiers banging their mess tins and slapping the tables with their hands. The noise made Smith's head pound mercilessly, the bright sunlight was hurting his eyes.

'Who was the lucky lady, Sergeant Smith?' asked Fullerton, stalking around him as if to smell the woman's perfume on him, stooping down, looking a bit like Riff Raff from the movie Rocky Horror Picture Show, '… or are we all victims of a giant hoax - Sergeant Smith?'

Smith looked around at the sea of faces all waiting eagerly for the answer. He gave the only response that any experienced eighteen-year old womaniser could give.

'Yes Sir … I got lucky Sir … an older woman … separated from her husband.'

That brought the house down, cheers and wolf-whistles. He tried to smile, in that knowing fashion that all successful ladies-men have perfected, just as James Bond would have done.

'Fuck me gently, but our Sergeant Smith is no longer just a steely-eyed-killer from the sky.' 'You better pray that the husband doesn't find out. Shit, he could be a Colonel or something!'

Smith gawked back at him trying to decipher whether Fullerton had put two-and-two together.

Fullerton shook Smith's hand extravagantly, slapping him hard on the shoulder with his free hand. 'Bloody good show!' he said loudly to continued applause, then leaning forward he shouted, 'Now fuck off and get into uniform you little shit.'

The sound was like someone had stuck a red-hot poker into Smith's brain.

Then, leaning even closer to Smith's ear, he hissed, ' … and don't you ever, I repeat ever, leave one of my piss-ups without permission again … shithead!'

Smith wandered off to his room, his head pounding like there was no tomorrow. *I think he likes me*, he reflected. *Shit, is it possible that I may be starting to enjoy this?*

*

Finally 2nd Lt Gibbs and 2 Platoon rolled back into camp. Gibbs had a lot of catching up to do, but was delighted to see the arrival of Lt Light which removed his responsibility for 3 Platoon. His deployment had been largely uneventful although he did tell a rather amusing story about being chased by elephants. The members of the platoon cleaned up and headed for the beerhalls, Dube, Moyo and Sibanda joining them. Smith made it very clear that any bad behaviour would result in a charge and a loss of their R&R that was in a week's time. Nobody wanted to lose R&R so Smith felt confident that he had little to fear. Sgt-Maj Nduku's arrival had created a definite air of expectation around the camp, nobody wanted any of his 'retraining', which could well have been the consequence of a transgression. While he was not the CSM, Nduku was certainly respected far more. *How different it is getting the job done through respect and teamwork, rather than through fear*, Smith reflected.

While Nduku was too professional to comment on, or discuss the CSM, his demeanour when the CSM was around could hardly be described as collegiate. Normally warrant officers are a very tight bunch partly because they are the 'meat in the sandwich' between the officers and the junior NCOs, but mostly because they were largely responsible for maintaining standards and discipline. Nduku was very courteous and civil, referring to the CSM by his title. They were of equal rank, so there was no need for 'Sir'. Nduku's physical presence and his record intimidated the CSM and he pretty much kept out of his way. The CSM was bigoted, a racist and he could not help but show it. He could get away with that sort of attitude in the RLI, which was exclusively white, but not in the RAR. He was clever enough not to say or do anything when officers were about but his dislike of the black people followed him around like a dirty smell. He did his 'job' in a reasonable fashion so the officers tolerated him. The black soldiers, on the other hand hated him with a vengeance, murmurs and mutterings in their language could be heard whenever he passed by.

The Major was completely oblivious to the CSM's attitude and behaviour. The CSM was always at great pains to keep the Major informed of even the slightest indiscretion by the young Subbies[123] and the junior NCOs. The CSM also resented the fact that Fullerton quite obviously favoured the NS officers and NCOs, never having invited him for a beer or celebration. Fullerton's dislike for the Major meant that anybody allied with the Major, like the CSM, could not be trusted. Fullerton, however, did not interfere with the CSM's duties, and was careful not to intervene if the CSM meted out punishment.

The next morning 1 Platoon arrived back from R&R. For the first time that Smith could remember, other than when he first arrived, the whole Company was together in camp. There was a festive atmosphere as friends from the Company got together, and Smith was kept busy ensuring that his platoon behaved themselves in the local township. The Major had returned from Wankie and he summoned the officers for a dinner in town. They needed to welcome Lt Light properly into the fold. This was not before the Major instructed the whole Company to be ready to move out the next morning at 07:00am. He wanted trucks and trailers with enough provisions for ten days. No other information was given. Even if Gibbs knew what was going on, he would not say anything to Smith when he enquired.

The afternoon was spent packing trailers and drawing enough dry rations for the ten days. Smith made his Platoon stand inspection at five o'clock that evening to make sure their kit and weapons were in order. They stood in their barrack room while Smith went through the inspection, relieved that they were not subject to the banging and crashing going on in the 3 Platoon barrack room next door. Nduku was unhappy with the turnout of his men and was looking for 'dust' under the metal lockers they kept their kit and private possessions in. The 3 Platoon 'inspection' was still going at 8:00pm that evening. Smith had a chat to Sgt Dave George, the 1 Platoon 2IC, suggesting that he be a little more diligent than he might normally be, just in case Nduku took an interest in his platoon as well.

Smith went into town for a few beers with Bruce O'Connell and Dave George. He invited Nduku who politely declined. He didn't say so, but Smith felt that Nduku probably did not feel like watching the other NS NCOs getting blasted and having to nurse them back to camp afterwards.

---

123 Regimental Subaltern, 2nd Lieutenant.

17

Hills above ZIPRA Base Camp, Lupane TTL, north Matabeleland

Sgt Ngwenya was on OP duty as he and his stick had been for nearly two weeks. The stress and tension were starting to tell on the four of them. The trips to get water were becoming more hazardous. The very large CT group in the valley meant that if the OP was compromised, they could easily be attacked and wiped out. There was no support anywhere close enough to make a difference. He was also concerned about the delay in mounting the attack on the base. The longer they waited, the more could go wrong. The CT movements in the valley were now much more overt, they seemed to be preparing for something. Ngwenya was concerned. No confirmation of the attack had been sent through to him from Wankie, and the feeling of being forgotten and out of touch, was unpleasant to say the least.

The Selous Scout sat watching the villagers in the valley below going through their daily routine, fetching water, cleaning and working in the fields in preparation for the first rains. A group of women had been working in the field below him for a week, their *badzas* or hoes smashing away at the hard dry ground to open the topsoil to allow the rain, when it eventually came, to soak in. They worked in lines next to each other so that it was easy to maintain a conversation, steadily progressing backwards down the field. The communal cooperation was planned so that everyone worked one field at a time, moving through each field on a rotation to ensure that all the fields were ready for planting at the same time. The lay of the land meant that they had been working in a direction towards his position, their backs to him. Ngwenya could clearly hear their conversation, not each word, but he could catch the general gist of what they were saying. The scene below reminded him of his own village, the sound of the hoes bashing at the ground, the singing in chorus and the animated discussions on domestic affairs in the village.

Gazing through the binoculars, Ngwenya adjusted the focus, changing his field of vision. It was late afternoon. The sun had lost its intensity and the shadows were beginning to lengthen. He passed his eyes casually over the workingwomen. Then one of them looked up at the hill, straight at him, her face filling the lens of the binoculars. He blinked, took the binoculars away and scanned the field with the naked eye. He could not believe what he saw. The blood drained from his head, he felt dizzy as a sick feeling rose in his gut. He looked again to make absolutely sure, there was no doubt; the women had changed the direction they were working. They had turned around. Instead of facing away from him they now faced him. As the enormity of what he saw sunk in, the same woman looked up at the hill again, as if she knew exactly where he was sitting. *Bhaudha! Fuck! We have been compromised!*

Ngwenya hastily ducked back to the base area to tell the others what he had seen. A man was sent back to the OP to make absolutely sure, one last time. He was back almost instantly. They had definitely been compromised the women were taking turns observing the hill. In an instant the hunters had become the hunted. The 'compromise' could have been caused by just about anything, the missing CT still lying tied up in their camp, a footprint in the valley below, a reflection off the lens of the binoculars. It didn't matter. The fact was they were in deep trouble. The CTs would now be studying all the surrounding hills including the one being used by the other Selous Scout c/sign. It was now only a matter of time before *mujibas* were sent up the hill to confirm the SF presence, or worse, the CTs would mortar the hill before sweeping over it.

Ngwenya got on the radio to the other c/sign to sound the alarm, then onto their controllers in Wankie. The attack, as planned, was still two days away. Fireforce had not been assembled; they were due to fly in from Bulawayo the next morning. 4 Indep were also due the following day but had at least a twenty kilometre march to get into their stop positions. The Selous Scouts were told to 'stand-by' as the sub-JOC Commander got his officers together for a meeting. A radio message was sent to 4 Indep to move out immediately. Another message was sent to 1 Brigade in Bulawayo to get the 1 RAR Fireforce in the air ASAP to reposition at Wankie. A message was also sent to Thornhill Airbase at Gwelo, the main fighter airbase for the country, the home of 1 Squadron, to send Hawker Hunters to Wankie. The Lynx pilot based at the JOC was hurried in for a briefing. He was the only source of immediate air support for the Scouts if the 'shit hit the fan'.

*

4 Independent Company (RAR) base camp, Sprayview airfield, Victoria Falls

The duty NCO at 4 Indep got the message off the telex marked URGENT, he raced out to a Land Rover and sped into town to where the Major was entertaining his officers. At first Peacock refused to see the NCO who was forced to stand outside the dining room. In frustration, the NCO pushed past the waiter at the door of the private room and handed over the message. The Major showed his irritation at being so rudely interrupted, but he read the message, flushing brightly as he did so.

The party broke up instantly as the gravity of the message sunk in. Maj Peacock had taken time to brief his officers before dinner started, but exact details of timing, drop-off points and routes to start-lines had not been finalised by sub-JOC.

The rounding up of the men in the Company began. The police were alerted. They started moving through the beerhalls, pubs and hotels looking for 4 Indep members, fortunately easy to spot in their berets and stable-belts.

By midnight the company was assembled and each platoon took roll-call. Smith had twenty 2 Platoon men answer their names, most in reasonably good shape. Each Platoon had two Four-five trucks and trailers plus the HQ group in another two Four-Fives including the Major, Fullerton, signallers and medics. The CSM had a Two-Five at the rear of the convoy towing a trailer carrying drums of Avtur helicopter fuel. The convoy rolled out on the road to Wankie in the south at 12:30am exactly. It was now a race against time.

The full moon hung in the night sky, its brightness illuminating the bush on either side of the road. Smith looked up at the stars, the evening cold biting through his combat jacket, he felt a sudden tremble of anticipation.

> *Don't go around tonight,*
> *Well, its bound to take your life,*
> *There's a bad moon on the rise.*

*

ZIPRA Base Camp, Lupane TTL, north Matabeleland

Comrade Tongerai Chabanga was shocked when he was told of the news. The villagers were convinced that SF were in the hills above. This information was in addition to the fact that one of the young cadres had been reported missing. No sign of him had been found despite an intensive search. In the fading light Chabanga gazed up at the rugged, granite kopies, trying to fathom what to do. *How long had they been there? Please may they not be Selous Scouts, the Skuz'apo[124]. If the Skuz'apo are here it is as a direct result of Benkov and his madness. If he were here I would kill*

---

124 Shona derivative nickname for the Selous Scouts. Broad meaning, 'excuse me for what I have just done'. This is a play on the fact that the Scouts stealthily infiltrated terrorist bands, pretending to be friends, killed mercilessly, and then vanished.

him with my bare hands!

Chabanga knew that if the Rhodesians were in the hills then it was only a matter of time before he was attacked, but he did not know for sure. The young man could have just run away, or he had gone looking for food, or he was shacked up with a woman. Chabanga felt like his brain was going to explode. He gave orders for *mujibas* to be sent into the hills that night to look for the Rhodesians. It was full moon, they would be able to find them if they were there. If the Rhodesians were present he would know by morning then he could plan accordingly. He was confident that they would not attack him at night[125]. In the meantime he sent out an alert to all his cadres to be ready to move at a moments notice.

*

Sub-JOC Wankie

Eventually sub-JOC Wankie got back to the two Selous Scout c/ signs who were anxiously waiting for instructions. They were given the freedom to make their own decision as to whether to wait for the morning or to make their escape that night. There was no way that the attack was going to go in at dawn as originally planned. The best H-hour they had was 10am, to give 4 Indep time to get into position. The location of the camp and its exact dimensions were well known, so the air force could plan their opening strike with great accuracy. *If the Gooks were still there that was!*

It became clear during the night that only two Dak loads of B Company, 1RAR were going to make it to the attack in time. These were all experienced, hard-core, parachute-trained troops; they would be part of the first wave. B Company arrived in Wankie in the dead of night. They slept in the aircraft and under the wings waiting for the morning.

As 4 Indep raced to the south, sub-JOC Wankie sent a signal that four sticks were to be dropped on the main road to be picked up by helicopters as part of the first and second waves. The CSM was to wait at the same spot to refuel the helicopters. The Major, after a short heated debate, agreed that Fullerton could take a stick plus Smith, Nduku and George, Stops 1 to 4. The Subbies were not happy at losing

---

125 Rhodesian forces seldom attacked terrorist bases inside the country at night. The fear of taking too many civilian casualties and the darkness made command and control of aircraft impossible. Fireforce relied on close air-support, on being able to see the enemy on the ground. At night the risk of contact with friendly forces was also exponentially higher.

their respective 2ICs but they had to lead their Platoons into the sweep positions.

*

Hills above ZIPRA Base Camp, Lupane TTL, north Matabeleland

In Lupane TTL, Ngwenya and his stick had agreed to wait in their OP. They had decided that it was better to stay in the hills where they remained concealed. Even if they were attacked they would be very difficult to dislodge. The CTs would need their whole 'brigade' to do so.

The moon rose, Ngwenya could hear the people at the base of the hill calling to each other. *The Makandangas*[126] *are sending mujibas over the kopie to look for us!* The four Selous Scouts sat in a huddle whispering their plan. Ngwenya regretted what had to be done but they were left with no choice. He went over to where the young terrorist lay sleeping, he knelt down, said a prayer under his breath, and slit the man's throat. There was no hesitation; the risk of the CT making a noise was too great. The young man died without knowing what had happened.

The undergrowth on the *kopie* was very thick and thorny, making it difficult for the *mujibas* to move up. Young and very nervous, they needing to chatter to each other to keep up their courage. They knew that leopards lived in these hills. Ngwenya counted five different voices. They were climbing very close to each other for mutual protection. The four Selous Scouts crept down the *kopie* to get in position behind the boys as they climbed. It took a good half hour to get around behind them. The moonlight reflected off the smooth rocks and it was easy to see the young *mujibas* silhouetted against the sky. They looked no more than eleven or twelve years old.

Ngwenya crept forward like a cat, seeking out the slowest of the five. The young *mujiba* paused, taking a short rest, Ngwenya stretched out and grabbed the boy around the head, his hand tightly clamped over the mouth, his free hand slitting the throat, making sure the vocal cords were cut through cleanly. The body slumped instantly, his young life gone. The other Selous Scouts attacked, deadly nocturnal killers. The young boys did not know what hit them; silent death came in an instant. A Wood Owl, *uMabhengwane*, hooted, *WHOO-hu, WHOO-hu-hu-hu, hu-hu*. Ngwenya, not an overly superstitious man, shuddered involuntarily, *owls can speak to the spirits*.

At the base of the hill the freedom fighters waited for the report of what had been found, happy to send children to do their work for

126 Terrorists, insurgents.

them. They called up the hill to give encouragement, laughing loudly.

Comrade Chabanga waited for the reports to come back to him. Slowly one by one the messengers returned, hill after hill was reported as clear. Two hills remained. Chabanga sent more men to look for the *mujibas* on the two hills … they could not be found … the darkness making the search doubly difficult after the moon had set. *Had they gone home? Had they been missed in the dark? Were they playing little-boy tricks? Had the Rhodesians killed them?*

Chabanga was by now beside himself. If he ordered his men to disperse he might never see them again. Eventually, he could wait no longer, he ordered his men to move out. He had divided his force into two groups, one was to move 10kms downstream; the other the same distance upstream, both then to wait for further orders. They were to move at first light.

*

Lupane TTL south of Wankie

Dawn found the 4 Indep platoons moving in a broad sweep line along the banks of the Bubi River. Major Peacock placed himself in the centre with 1 Platoon to his right, 2 Platoon to his left and 3 Platoon in reserve. The Company was moving fast, they carried the barest minimum in weight, with eight or nine kilometres still to go to get into position.

Fullerton and the other three sticks waited on the Bulawayo Road. Smith shivered in the early morning cold, his stomach in a knot. He cursed under his breath. They did not have long to wait; the helicopters arrived within minutes of first light. The K-car landed on the road first followed by the two G-cars all rapidly shutting down their engines. The CSM quickly positioned the trailer with the 44-gallon fuel drums, allowing the techs to start refuelling using hand pumps. It was estimated to be about fifteen to twenty minutes flying time to the target following an indirect route. The Paradaks, carrying sixteen men in each, were to fly in as soon as the 4 Indep stops got into position. They were already airborne in a holding pattern to the south.

The K-car commander, the OC of B Company, was pleased to see Fullerton. They shook hands laughing like old friends; *We are going to do a bit of culling*[127] *today!* The K-car commander called the stick leaders together to go over the plan one more time. They all listened intently. He then questioned each stick leader in turn to make sure that

127 Rhodesian slang, killing – derived from the term used for reducing the number of large game animals like elephants in national parks and game reserves.

each understood his role. This was a very big base camp; well over a hundred and fifty, maybe even as many as two hundred. They needed to be switched on.

On top of the OP, Ngwenya looked across at his bedraggled c/sign, now eager to get the job done. They had been in ambush since 4am waiting for the CT sweep of their *kopie* that they felt certain was coming. As the first of the sun's rays struck the valley below, it was clear the whole CT base camp was on the move. He had not yet seen such a high concentration of ZIPRA terrorists in-country, but had, of course, been involved in OPs watching training camps in Zambia and Mozambique, where the numbers were in the thousands. He watched as the CTs moved down-river below their position. In the distance he could see another group moving up-river.

On the Bulawayo road the K-car radio crackled, 'Sunray, this is Sierra 1 do you read?' Ngwenya from the Selous Scouts was calling.

'Sierra 1, Sunray go.'

'Sunray, the Charlie Tangos are moving … in two groups … to the east and to the west. What is your Echo Tango Alpha … Over.'

'Sierra 1, we still need two hours … over.'

'Sunray, they will have gapped it by then … what do you suggest?'

'Sierra 1, you need to follow them. I will call you when we are airborne … you will need to call us in.'

'Copied, Sierra 1 out.'

Ngwenya conducted a short conference with his stick after which he called the other Selous Scout c/sign to discuss options. It was decided that unless they followed the departing CTs nobody would be in a position to call in the airstrike or the paratroops when the time came. This decision was hazardous for many reasons, not the least of which was potentially being taken out by their own troops when the stops were dropped in position, plus the K-car would shoot at anything that moved. They had waited nearly two weeks for this and were now determined not to let their work come to nothing.

C/sign Sierra 1, led by Ngwenya, rapidly picked their way down to the bottom of the *kopie* moving off in pursuit of the departing CTs. The other Selous Scout c/sign, Sierra 2, went off downriver. Not trying to conceal their presence, Ngwenya's c/sign settled in behind the rear group of CTs. He watching closely to make sure that his stick was not drawing any undue attention. They were ignored completely as the escaping CTs were clearly focused on getting away as quickly as possible. Ngwenya'a radio was switched off and concealed in his pack. Their plan was to call the attacking Fireforce again after half an hour.

Back on the Bulawayo road the K-car Commander called all the sticks together again, 'Okay … this scene is going to get very difficult. We are going to have to improvise. We have nobody to the east of the Gooks but we have 4 Indep to the west. My guess is that we will attack the eastern group first and try and drive them back … hopefully into the 4 Indep sweep line.'

There was no point in waiting any longer. The airmen finished refuelling the helicopters. Once that was done, the K-car Commander called the Hunter pilots still waiting on the ground in Wankie. He then called the circling Paradaks[128], handing them both over to the Sierra 1 c/sign when they came back on the air. Ngwenya was going to have to call them in onto the target when the time came.

The Alouette pilots began to wind up the turbines. The unmistakable sound shook Smith once again into the reality of another contact, the certain knowledge that people were going to die. The laden helicopters taxied slowly down the tar road, then rose into the early morning light flying to the east at low level.

A Paradak carried sixteen fully equipped men, divided into four sticks. 4 Indep approaching from the west were using their normal operational c/signs, starting with the Major as 4, 1 Platoon, Rice, 41, 2 Platoon, Gibbs, 42 and 3 Platoon, Light, 43.

Smith, sitting in the back of his helicopter with the headset on, heard Sierra 1 come up on the radio giving the Dak pilot a line to drop on. Two Hunters, carrying 450kg Golf Bombs, frantan and 68mm SNEB rockets, were airborne from Wankie, Green 1 and 2, had positioned themselves about 10kms to the north at an altitude of 25,000ft, waiting for the call for the first strike. The Golf Bombs were high pressure bombs, filled with a diesel and ammonium nitrate fertilizer mix, in a steel casing including thousands of chopped 10mm steel rods. The killing area was over 90m wide by 130m long, pulverising everything in its path, clearing the bush completely. The Lynx, Green 3, took off from Wankie, carrying two fran canisters plus two pods of 37mm SNEB rockets.

*

Bubi River, Lupane TTL

Tongerai Chabanga had decided to accompany the eastbound group of freedom fighters. He made sure that he had two RPD gunners in his section and two other men carrying RPGs. He estimated that he had about eighty men with him, all walking along the riverbed spread

---

128 Douglas DC3 converted for delivery of parachute troops. One Rhodesian 'Dak' was rumoured to have taken part in the Arnhem drop in World War II.

over a distance of 400m. A large number of women and children accompanied the band, wives, girlfriends and *mujibas*. Chabanga sent a reconnaissance section off ahead with orders to look for any SF presence. The whole plan, if attacked by SF, was to bombshell to pre-arranged RV points unless the attacking force was small in which case they would take them on. They were moving at a fast walk, almost trotting. The riverbed was mostly open, easy to walk through. The bush on the riverbanks was dense with tall trees providing good cover from the air while low hills were visible to the north.

A sound of thunder was heard in the distance. Chabanga looked up into the clear blue sky there was not a cloud in sight. The sound was repeated. The cadres all stopped and looked into the sky. The sound was the sonic boom caused by the two Hunters entering their power dives for the strike, pushing through the sound barrier.

With no warning the riverbed in front of Chabanga turned into a maelstrom of flying steel, rocks and body parts as the Hunter strike went in, SNEB rockets and Golf Bombs together. The roar of the engines could only be heard after the jets had passed overhead, gone in a split second, leaving absolute destruction in their wake. At least a quarter of Chabanga's force was vaporised in the first second. The freedom fighters broke into horrified panic. Those close to the impact zone were bleeding from their noses and ears from the effect of the explosion's overpressure. Running in all directions, some tried to climb out of the riverbed, slipping and sliding on the steep sides. The civilian camp followers, milled around, dazed and confused, many bleeding from wounds. Women screamed in shock and despair, children cried.

Chabanga froze momentarily, trying to comprehend. In the distance a slow, ponderous Dakota flew across the line of his planned escape. As he watched he saw the first speck jump from the door, instantly followed by the white mushroom of the canopy, and then another … and another. Before he had time to think, the Hunters were back, this time with 30mm cannon, raking the riverbed. The sand lept in neat columns as the explosive shells burst in the soft sand. A young woman, not ten metres in front of him, disintegrated from a direct hit from a 30mm shell. He turned, trying to get his legs to move faster. Behind him a few cadres stood watching him, waiting for his decision. As he looked back down the riverbed, in the direction they had come from, he heard the crackle of rifle-fire, *there must be Rhodesians that way. I must get away! I must get out of this riverbed. I need to get into the hills!*

Chabanga's decision, taken in a split second, was suddenly made more urgent by the arrival overhead of the helicopters. He dived for the northern riverbank, clawing the soft soil, scrambling; shouting for his men to get out, to head for the hills. The noise was intense, the thundering jets overhead, the rattling helicopters, then the slow thud, thud … thud, thud … thud … of the K-car's 20mm cannon. The smell of burning flesh, the crying of the wounded and now the gunfire from behind him became more concentrated. Men came running back along the riverbed looking for ways to climb out.

To reach the top of the riverbank Chabanga had to crawl using tree roots to support his weight, finally scrambling over the edge. In front of him people streamed away, cadres and civilians mixed together. He saw a helicopter ahead, gliding out of the sky like a giant wasp, with a sting more deadly. Still lying prone, he lifted his AK directing his fire at the helicopter while other cadres followed his lead. The helicopter was shooting back at him, he saw bullet strikes in the dirt to his left. *I must keep moving!* He struggled to his feet, beginning to run, diverting to the left, away from where the helicopter had landed. Breaking into a sprint he ran for his life. The helicopter came back off the ground over the trees, the guns on the side spewing red hot tracer, hitting the ground just in front of him, *God save me. Please God, Nkosi. Save me!*

Blind terror gripped the ZIPRA Brigade Commander. He ran like he had never run before. Rhodesians appeared in the bush in front of him, to the right, *they are all black … how can this be?* The freedom fighters were running in all directions, too many for the Rhodesians to shoot, blinded by panic. Chabanga watched the four Rhodesians who were kneeling against trees and rocks, shooting, trying to kill the freedom fighters that, like frightened antelope, were jumping, running, darting left and right. There was no control, just panic and death. The entire training and planning meant nothing. Chabanga's only thought, *I must get away! I must live!*

As Chabanga reached the hills the noise of battle began to recede. He was alone, having run for half an hour without stopping, looking back constantly to see if he was being followed. The helicopters were still visible in the distance. The wind carried the constant thud … thud of cannon fire. Jets circling at high altitude leaving vapour trails in the clear blue sky, engines roaring like banshees, hungry for more blood. His legs felt like lead. Completely exhausted, he sucked for air, panting like a rabid dog, saliva running down his chin. Drinking from his water bottle, he gulped the cool liquid down trying to find relief. He had never felt more alone in all of his life, the feeling of utter desolation. Looking about for a place to hide, he decided to climb into a rocky outcrop where he sat down, his head in his hands. Suddenly overcome with emotion, he wept tears of despair and frustration. *How can I start again? Control of Lupane had taken years to achieve. This should not have happened. If I catch that Soviet I will cut off his balls and feed them to him!*

Hate and disgust filled Chabanga; he resolved to find the demented Captain, no matter how long it would take. *He must be made to pay for this disaster.*

*

Smith had watched the paratroopers exit the aircraft, gently floating to the ground. The terrain was broken and heavily wooded. Many paratroopers landed in trees, some landed in the riverbed where the soft sand cushioned their fall. Within seconds of their landing, the first CTs were running into the still disorganised sweepline. Heavy gunfire erupted as the paratroops tried to stop the CTs passing through their position. Smith watched the Hunter strike. The percussion from the golf-bomb shockwave buffeted the helicopter. The CTs on the ground were like scurrying ants, running in all directions.

The K-car commander called the G-cars with drop instructions, Smith felt the familiar tightening in his gut as the chopper flared for the landing, 'GO, GO, GO'. Smith, Stop 2, was dropped to the south of the river line while Fullerton, Stop 1, was dropped to the north. There was no time to get into position. Smith's stick was dropped in amongst the CTs who, bent on escape, ran past wildly, many not seeing the Stop in front of them. Completely surrounded by fleeing CTs, Smith and his stick shot as many as they could, staying tightly bunched in a small rocky outcrop. Aiming was almost impossible, shooting down open sights with both eyes open. Many of the CT's were shot at point blank. Dube emptied belt after belt, never short of targets. Dead and dying CTs lay all about, too many to count.

'Stop 2, Sunray, move forward onto the river line,' the K-car Commander was calling him.

'Stop 2 copied,' replied Smith, he moved his men forward in extended line, the bush got thicker as they approached the riverbank. BRRRRRT, Dube destroyed a CT hiding behind a tree. They could hear shots out to the right as the paratrooper sweepline cleared the river and surrounding bush, moving towards their position.

K-car called Fullerton. 'Stop 1, Sunray ... I can see three Charlie Tangos in rocks to your front ... one hundred metres.'

'Stop 1 copied.'

There was a short pause as Fullerton ran forward and hurled a white phos grenade into the rocks; then there were sounds of shooting as he took them out, their flesh burning from the deadly chemical.

As Smith approached the edge of the riverbank, heavy gunfire erupted again to his right, a few stray rounds passing high over his

192

head. He ordered his men to get on the ground and leopard-crawl forward. Smith reached the edge of the riverbank first then looked over the edge. A scene of utter devastation confronted him. The riverbed below seemed to have been charred black as if subjected to a blowtorch. Bodies lay everywhere, some still moving, the sounds of burnt and mortally wounded people begging for help filled the air. Women and children crying uncontrollably sat huddled together. A woman with loose skin hanging from her burnt arms was carrying a dead child along the base of the cliff below, hobbling on unsteady legs. She wailed in distress, her face turned to the heavens. Smith watched in morbid fascination as she eventually collapsed into the sand, overcome by her wounds.

Clumps of dry reeds and driftwood were still smouldering in the riverbed, adding thick black smoke to the gruesome scene below. The stench of burnt flesh was unbearable.

Soldiers appeared away to Smith's right wearing parachute helmets. They approached cautiously, shooting at bodies they came across, taking no chances of a CT 'playing dead'.

'Stop 5, Stop 2, I am two hundred metres to your front. I have thrown green smoke,' called Smith anxiously.

'Stop 2, Roger I have you visual … standby,' came the prompt reply.

Fullerton appeared on the far bank, waving at Smith expansively, quite obviously happy with his day's work.

The B Company paratroopers linked up with the two 4 Indep stop groups. *Ingwe* was welcomed like the long lost brother he was. The old soldiers crowded around to shake his hand. The paratroopers wore helmets and jumpsuits, chest webbing with small lightweight packs. The senior man was a Sergeant Major. He and Fullerton sat down to discuss their next move. The K-car and the two G-cars had left to refuel. The Lynx still orbited above, waiting for his turn.

The job now was to sweep back downriver towards the advancing 4 Indep. The sweepline spread out on each bank of the river, Fullerton and Smith remained in the riverbed. They passed body after body, most with sickening wounds. The few survivors were shot where they lay. Smith tried not to watch, allowing the others to finish the grisly business.

Ngwenya called on the radio, warning the sweeping RAR that his c/sign was in front of them. As the sweepline followed a turn in the river, Smith saw, sitting on a rock in the centre of the riverbed, the four meanest, most frightening looking men he had ever seen. Their eyes flashed left and right, like predators summing up the potential for a kill. They sat without moving, making no sound.

It was possible to smell the Scouts from twenty paces, their uniforms, if that was what they could be called, horribly soiled, torn and rotten. Their hair was long, their faces covered with scraggly beard. They looked emaciated, their cheeks sunken. Dead CTs lay all about them. A few wounded were moaning in agony. The four men seemed completely oblivious to the death around them. They had annihilated any CTs that had made the mistake of running back down the riverbed towards the base camp.

'*Kanjani*, hello,' Fullerton called from a good distance away.

'*Mangwanani*, good morning,' came the reply.

'You smell…. *shamwari*! Friend!'

'You are ugly' was the reply. They all laughed together, with the release of tension. Selous Scouts weren't big on respect for rank or authority.

Out in the distance, downstream, another firefight started. Radios crackled into life. The 4 Indep sweepline led by Major Peacock had run into the escaping CTs. The helicopters were back; K-car was calling instructions and the second Paradak lined up for its drop.

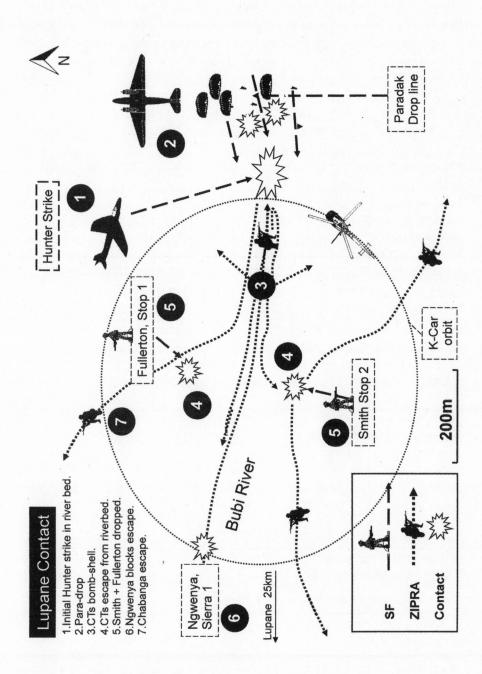

Hunter Strike

Paradak Drop line

Fullerton, Stop 1

Smith Stop 2

K-Car orbit

200m

Bubi River

Ngwenya, Sierra 1

Lupane 25km

Lupane Contact

1. Initial Hunter strike in river bed.
2. Para-drop
3. CTs bomb-shell.
4. CTs escape from riverbed.
5. Smith + Fullerton dropped.
6. Ngwenya blocks escape.
7. Chabanga escape.

SF
ZIPRA
Contact

18

Bulawayo

'RUN … RUN … KEEP MOVING… DON'T LOOK BACK.'

'Mike, it's okay, wake up … Mike its okay.'

Mike Smith awoke with a fright, someone was shaking him. The room was dark. *What was going on?*

'Mike it's me, its Mum … you're at home, its okay.'

Mike struggled to comprehend; the nightmare was so vivid, running through the bush, running and running, trying to get away. His mind was trying to come to grips with reality. The signaller was dying in front of him, the look of surprise on his face, the eyes staring.

'I'm sorry Mum … did I wake you? It's just a bad dream. I didn't know where I was.' He was sitting upright in bed, his mother sitting in front of him, his father standing at the door not knowing what to say.

'Can I make you a cup of tea?' That was the universal panacea. Mike's mother had the view that tea cured everything. That is, everything not cured by either Milk of Magnesia [129] or Friar's Balsam[130].

Mike Smith lay back in his bed feeling confused and disorientated, the familiar loose spring digging into his back. Slowly his mind cleared. He lay looking at the ceiling, at an Airfix model of a B-29 Superfortress, still suspended above him. Memories of childhood now seemed so distant and surreal. The past weeks had changed his life from that of a happy-go-lucky pimply-faced teenager, enjoying the novelty of military life to one of abject terror, interspersed with periods of uninhibited elation, mixed with alcohol.

Prior to the commencement of his national service, Smith had looked upon the prospect as a necessary but exciting adventure. He had been the star in his personal *Boy's Own*[131] escapade. The training had been great. 1st Phase had been hard, but he was fit and strong and coped well. Then learning new skills, classical war, COIN, shooting, blowing stuff up, all great fun. He recalled the day at SInf when they were requested to state their preferences for posting. The RAR had always been his first choice, ever since the day, as a young boy, he had stood in Cecil

---

129 An aqueous suspension of magnesium hydroxide, $Mg(OH)_2$ in water. Milk of Magnesia is a saline osmotic (hydrating) laxative. The name derives from the suspension's milky white appearance and the magnesium in its composition. It is used as a laxative.

130 Can be used as an antiseptic and protectant to minor cuts and abrasions, chapped skin and lips, bedsores, indolent ulcers, herpes simplex, and gingivitis. Can relieve itching of chilblains, eczema, and urticaria.

131 *The Boy's Own Paper* was a British story paper aimed at young and teenage boys, published from 1879 to 1967.

Avenue in Bulawayo watching the battalion march past. They were led by the regimental mascot, a white goat by the name of Private N'duna. The shiny black faces brimmed with strength and confidence, green uniforms, slouch hats with black ostrich feathers. Pride was on their faces, purpose in their step, they sang the regimental song behind the RAR band.

He reflected on his nervous arrival at 4 Indep, where working with his platoon had been very difficult to start with. His own section had been a real challenge. The troops had been understandably suspicious, naturally very unhappy at yet another inexperienced national serviceman being put in charge of them. They were all older than he was, some nearly ten years older, surly, unhelpful, pretty much refusing to cooperate unless pressed to do so. Smith had been careful not to overreact to their intransigence by behaving like an officious prick, not ordering them about, no needless inspections. He had tried to talk to them as a group to explain how he thought things should be done. This was met with stony silence, the expressions on their faces belying their thoughts … *You young stupid, dumb, idiot, what do you know about anything? You're more likely to get us killed!*

The whole induction into 4 Indep had been a bizarre affair. The previous leaders of his platoon, a NS subbie and sergeant, had spent all of fifteen minutes handing over the platoon to Gibbs and himself. There was no explanations, no advice, just a rapid jumble of statements and observations all in slang that was impossible to follow. Then there was a hurried check of the platoon armoury and equipment storage using an indecipherable handwritten list. Smith subsequently found numerous errors that he was now responsible for. Within minutes of the completion of the final cursory briefing, their predecessors were out of the camp and on a truck back to Bulawayo, their national service over, still alive and happy as pigs in shit.

Smith reflected on the training they had received at SInf, claimed to be the best counter-insurgency training in the world. Yet they were not trained on the simple things, like how to draw rations, how to complete equipment reports, how to draw a vehicle from MT or how to keep records of arms and ammunition. The result was that Smith made mistake after mistake on everything from drawing rations to managing leave and sick-call requests. The worst of it all was that they were not trained on the psychology of working with black soldiers. Smith found himself feeling totally inadequate, losing confidence in his own ability, the constant haranguing by the CSM making things all the more unbearable.

The CSM had latched onto Smith's uncertainty early on, making his life a living hell. Whenever Smith made a mistake, the CSM would give him a good bollocking, but never offering advice or suggestions. It was a game with him, waiting for the new NS NCO to screw up and then taking great pleasure in pointing this out to whoever would listen. In Smith's case, the added fact of him not passing the officer's course gave further ammunition to the CSM's armoury of insults. His first attempt at drawing stores had taken a full day as the CSM made him complete the form, Form 1033[132], over and over again, smiling all the time at his humiliation. This whole learning curve was made even more difficult by the fact that the other regular NCOs made no attempt to assist either. Many of them had taken five years or more to make the rank of Sergeant but here was an eighteen-year old NS wanker, a sergeant in little over six months. Smith could feel their resentment; it felt like a tangible weight on his shoulders. It irked him being trapped between the NS officers and the regular NCOs. The officer's rank provided them with a semblance of protection, protection not afforded to Sergeant Smith.

The first few deployments had been a hopeless mess. The members of Smith's section, with the exception of Fauguneze, were patently not interested. He had liked Fauguneze from the start; he had been the most friendly, always with a ready smile and a joke. The others pretty much ignored him, almost as if he didn't exist. Nkai and Tovakare, the Lance Corporals in his section, kept quiet, speaking only if spoken to, always mindful of not being seen to be too friendly to the new sergeant. Dube was a man of few words anyway, so conversation with him was limited to a few grunts. Moyo followed Dube's lead. The eight-day 'bush-trips' were spent mostly in silence. His only daily conversation was the short evening sitrep to Gibbs who was always positioned some distance away, patrolling a different sector.

The loneliness of the eight-day deployments took a long time to get used to. Some deployments were 'covert' or 'clandestine', meaning that they were required to hide in thick cover during the day, then crawl into ambush position on the River at night. They were issued with a large night-sight that was useful for scanning the opposite bank, well over 400m away. The batteries were hopeless, never lasting more than three days at a time. The routine was repeated each day. No movement at all was allowed so the section stayed hidden during the day, communication with hand signals and very few spoken words. It was purgatory for Smith but much worse for the men who would normally spend the day conversing with each other.

The 'overt' deployments were few and far between; on these occasions noise and movement were encouraged. Campfires were lit

132 Form 1033 was the universal army requisition form. Signing a 1033 passed 'ownership' and responsibility in military property from one person to another.

along the river at night giving the impression that there were many more Rhodesian soldiers along the River than there actually were. The men loved the opportunity to do some fishing; Dube had mastered the art of setting traps for Guinea Fowl. This added some variety to the otherwise hopelessly bland diet contained in the ratpacks.

The early months of being deployed on the River, while lonely, isolated affairs, had their highlights that included the magnificent landscape and abundant wildlife. He had seen everything up close, lions, elephants, hyenas, baboons, hippos, and antelope and of course the famous giant crocodiles. The work had not been demanding, patrolling the River mainly between Chundu Loop and Sansimba Island, looking for crossing points. Nothing of any great excitement had happened. They had not detected any crossings in the sector he had operated in. From time to time a Grey Scout patrol would pass through his sector; they would boil up a cup of tea and have a good bullshit session before they moved off. The Grey Scout patrols had to be stopped after the local pride of lions developed a taste for horsemeat.

On an overt deployment, each day Smith would allocate the sticks in his section an area to patrol. This was in a fan shape so they didn't bump into each other. The idea being that they would slowly traverse the allocated area, meeting back at their small base camp before dark. He spoke to them regularly by radio to make sure that they were progressing well but suspected that some of the corporals just went off into the bush and sat down, waited the whole day, then returned. The unhappiness that his stick expressed each day about having to patrol gave Smith an inkling that this must be true. He nailed it one day, deciding to double back and sure enough, there was LCpl Nkai sitting with his stick under a tree brewing tea, having a great conversation, laughing and joking. Smith and his stick lay down in 'ambush'. He made Fauguneze translate what they were saying. Eventually the four of them sprang up and rushed at Nkai and his men who sat in shocked amazement. Smith decided that this was his opportunity to stamp his authority on the section, so that night he sat them all down and gave them a speech, a team-talk of sorts.

While Smith was very young and inexperienced, he knew enough about the black culture to know that pride and 'face' were very important. He had focused on his disappointment at the day's events, including the fact that some of his section were unreliable and couldn't be trusted to follow orders. He was careful not to mention any names or make personal attacks. He explained how when he had been posted to RAR he was proud to be sent to the best infantry unit in the army of how he expected to work with the bravest and most professional soldiers. They all listened to his story intently. Story-telling in the black tribal culture is important, something to be respected. He told them of his sadness that he could not speak their language. He told them about his childhood and his family, about his school, how his grandfather had fought in Abyssinia, at Sidi Rezegh, at El Alamein and in Italy. They sat in silence, letting him speak, not making any interruptions. When the sun finally set, they crawled into the sleeping positions in all-round defence and Smith overheard a few whispered comments as they settled down.

The next day, Smith detected a small change in attitude. While there was no open friendliness or even attempt at conversation, the next night Dube came across to him and said, 'We have cooked some stew, would you like some *Ishe*?' It was the first time anyone had called him '*Ishe*'.

'*Tatenda* Dube, I would be happy for some stew.' It was a peace offering. Smith had felt like a king. He ate his stew and passed comment that it was the best stew he had ever tasted, to much nodding and shaking of heads from his small group of men.

Smith was initially convinced that he might get through his whole national service without a 'contact'. Strangely, things had changed for the better over the past few weeks since their first contact. The men seemed to be more motivated; they loved the excitement of *hondo*, their status within the Company enhanced as a result. The period operating with *Ingwe* Fullerton had opened Smith's eyes to the other side of the war, what it takes to be a real soldier, the complete soldier.

For the first time Smith started to feel a bond building with the members of his section and in particular, his stick of Dube, Moyo and Sibanda. They had mourned the loss of Fauguneze together, a mutual loss, *he was my brother too*.

Being a Platoon Sergeant did have its perks. He operated largely autonomously and he was not at the absolute bottom of the pecking order. He shared most of the same facilities as the NS officers, who to their great credit treated him very much as an equal. There were no airs and graces. Smith's recent contacts had, to some degree, raised his status, although he did not relish the prospect of being singled out by Fullerton for more 'assignments'.

The operation in Lupane had been a huge eye-opener. He had never seen a Hunter strike or paratroops deployed, or been part of a proper Fireforce. The attack had killed well over fifty terrorists, if the wounded that subsequently died were taken into account. B Company had suffered a broken leg and two dislocated shoulders from the para-drop. 4 Indep had two slightly wounded, one fool got badly burned when a white phos grenade he threw hit a tree branch, a tiny drop of the phosphorous had 'splashed' on him.

B Company and the Selous Scouts were pulled out while 4 Indep spent the next three days following up as many of the blood trails and spoor they could find. Another four CTs were killed on follow-up and more bodies recovered as those with serious wounds had died. At least three CTs were captured. Before they left the Selous Scouts studied all the bodies that had been collected confirming that the CT leader, Brigadier Chabanga, was not one of them. *He was still out there!*

After three days 2 Platoon were allowed to pull out to go on R&R. The feeling of relief and joy at getting out of the bush, the drive to Bulawayo and the excitement of arrival made life feel good again. Smith always drove the platoon right through the centre of town on the way to Brady Barracks. The troops loved shouting out at all the girls, the waves and calls from the passers-by, 'good luck soldier'. Smith always drove the platoon past his mother's offices in town to ask her to fetch him from the gates at Brady Barracks. The people in the office were always delighted to see him; they all crowded round to get the news.

The platoon on R&R always had to run the gauntlet at Brady Barracks. There was a race to the MT yard to avoid the RSM. If he caught them he always made a point of lining them up to tell them what a disgrace they were, long hair, dirty uniforms. It was the time delay that was most frustrating. On this occasion he was nowhere to be seen. They placed their weapons in the armoury, and hit the town.

*

Mike Smith was excited about seeing Jane Williams. He phoned her as soon as he got back, arranging to go to the movies. He borrowed his father's aged Datsun 1500 truck and drove over to her house in Hillside. Mr and Mrs Williams were both there, and he was invited in for a beer. The conversation was stilted and awkward as her parents asked him about the Company and any news. Jane sat on a chair opposite him dressed in a floral dress tied at the waist. He couldn't help looking at her she looked stunning, radiant. She asked questions in a soft voice, but showed no signs of girlish nervousness. She seemed poised, in control. Smith on the other hand was feeling awkward and ham-fisted. He related some of the funny incidents that had happened such as the attack by *Murwisi* on the South African adjutant, the new Lt Light jumping off the booze cruise boat. They all laughed at his stories, and it seemed to break the ice.

Mr Williams brought everyone back to earth when he asked if they had ever caught the group that had killed Charlie. Mike gave a vague answer mentioning that they had hit a very large group in Lupane but there was no way of knowing. The successful attack had been mentioned on the TV news, but the COMOPS press statements were always very general. All the statement had said was that over fifty terrorists were killed in the northwest and that follow-up operations were continuing.

Mike made short work of the beer, quickly getting to his feet. He thanked Mr Williams politely explaining that they shouldn't be late. It was impossible to ignore the great sadness that seemed to pervade the house. Mrs Williams had obvious difficulty in keeping control, her voice often cracked as if she was about to cry. Mike's presence brought back too many memories.

The drive into town was largely in silence; Mike tried desperately to find something to say. Jane had given a short summary of her progress at school, her studies and hockey, but seemed content with her own thoughts. Mike interpreted her silence as being disappointment; he cursed himself inside for being so hopeless at conversation. He desperately wanted to tell her how much her letters had meant to him. He wanted so much to tell her about what had happened to him, the horror of what he had seen and done. He parked outside the Rainbow Vistarama movie theatre. Being back in Civvy Street seemed strangely unreal, almost dreamlike.

Mike loved going to the movies, relishing the opportunity to see another James Bond film, *The Spy Who Loved Me*. The chance to escape while the conniving megalomaniac Stromberg captured nuclear submarines and the fight to the death with 'Jaws'. James Bond falling in love with the Russian spy, laughing at Roger Moore's cryptic comments. Jane gently took Mike's hand in hers as the opening sequence ended, Carly Simons' *Nobody Does it Better*. He looked across at her; she just smiled. He sat back and relaxed for the first time in weeks.

The film ended in the usual James Bond fashion with explosions and mayhem hundreds of people dying but miraculously without any sign of blood. Mike thought about the people he had seen die, the agony of it, the screaming and moaning, the calling out, the help that was never enough. The picture of Charlie Williams' lifeless eyes looking into the evening sky played on his mind. He so wanted to talk about it.

They walked to the car hand in hand. Jane chatted about the film and what she thought. Try as he might he could not concentrate on what she was saying. As they drove out of town she suggested that they stop at Eskimo Hut for an ice cream, Fleetwood Mac's *Don't Stop*[133] was playing on the radio;

---

133 *Don't Stop*, Christine McVie, 1977.

Why not think about times to come,
And not about the things that you've done,
If your life was bad to you,
Just think what tomorrow will do.

Don't stop, thinking about tomorrow,
Don't stop, it'll soon be here,
It'll be, better than before,
Yesterday's gone, yesterday's gone.

The cold ice cream seemed to sooth his jangled nerves. As he looked across at Jane a deep emotional stirring moved within him. He so wanted to hold her and talk to her. His words seemed to echo in his head; they sounded ridiculous, inane. Jane smiled up at him, *she seems to be happy in my company, but she may just be feeling sorry for me.*

The drive home was slow. Mike was happy to have her sitting so close, making the trip take as long as possible. He rolled up to the gate as quietly as possible so as not to wake the folks inside. Then Jane spontaneously kissed him hard on the lips, holding his face in her hands, a tide washed over him, the intensity of the moment overwhelming, stunningly passionate.

'Mike, you are in pain. I can't possibly understand, but if you want to talk to me about it, please do' she said as they walked up to the house.

He turned to her, 'I have never felt this way before, I am sorry if I seem distant. I just have so much stuff going on in my mind. I need you Jane.'

'I enjoyed tonight more than anything' she said, 'I must see you again before you have to go back, maybe you can come for dinner?'

'I want to be with you Jane', he said. Looking at her his heart seemed to miss a beat. She looked up again with the same stunning smile. He had never felt the same raw power of emotion before. His heart was in a twist, filled with an unbelievable longing.

*

Mike Smith called as many of his school friends as be could, but nobody was on R&R at the same time. He managed to play a few rounds of golf with his Dad, which was great, but he seemed to have lost all hand-eye co-ordination. He 'hacked' about in the bush losing innumerable golf balls. His Dad laughed at his difficulty. They had always been fiercely competitive, 'Not to worry, Mike, you will get square next time' he said encouragingly.

Mike always enjoyed having a shower after the game, then sitting on the wide veranda at the Bulawayo Golf Club, overlooking the course. They made the best steak sandwiches and chips in the world. His Dad ordered two beers; he always drank Castle Pilsner, Mike preferred Lion Lager, as it was slightly sweeter.

'You have been in some big scenes Mike?' his Dad asked.

'Yes, Dad … I had five contacts on this last bush trip; I was deployed by chopper four times.' He knew this was information his Dad already had.

'How are you coping with your platoon?'

Mike had told his father all about the difficulty he had when he took over the platoon and the issues with the CSM. 'It's much better now. My stick seems to be working really well together. I trust them.'

Mike gave a summary of the various things that had happened, including his friendship with the Ozzie O'Connell, the now famous *Murwisi* incident and Fullerton's flattening of the South African Major's nose. They both laughed heartily. He had never felt closer to his father. It helped to know that his father knew what was going on, that he had some level of understanding.

Mike's mother had it as a personal mission to put some weight on her son who she felt was far too thin after the last bush trip. No holds were barred, as roast after roast was delivered, with all the vegetables and her masterly puddings.

'We have an invitation to dinner at the Williams' on the night before you are due to go back. I would prefer to be at home …what do think Mike?' his mother declared.

'It might be nice to have dinner with them,' Mike replied, adding, 'Jane has been writing to me, and I really like her.'

He had not had the opportunity to spend very much time with Jane at all. She was still at school, with afternoon activities making late nights during the week out of the question.

On the appointed evening the four of them arrived, Mike's sister in tow, not happy at losing the opportunity to see her new boyfriend. Mike loved his sister but the three-year age gap made conversation with her on anything more than superficial subjects difficult. She was on her own mission, giving her mother hell. There was little Mike could do other than watch as the battle of wills unfolded. His father tried to keep the peace but that was a losing battle.

The Williams were very hospitable and the conversation flowed freely. Of course the talk of political 'settlement' was always a big subject. There were always rumours about peace talks, Britain intervening, secret meetings, South African support. Mike tried in vain to get to sit next to Jane at dinner but instead was placed across the table. When they had sat down he felt a tap on his foot and he looked across at her beautiful smile. She was dressed in a simple dress, with her hair tied on the top of her head with a few strands hanging down, framing her face. He couldn't help but gaze at her, his mind lost in all the buzz of conversation. He missed the enquiry from Mr Williams as to whether he would like another beer.

Mike's sister, who had of course, picked up on the obvious attraction between them, laughed at his discomfort. Jane had made a cake that she brought out after dinner, the inscription drawn on it in icing sugar, 'Happy Birthday Mike'; he had almost forgotten, his birthday was the following week. They all sang *happy birthday*, Mike felt embarrassed by the attention. Jane gave him a present, a writing set with a new writing pad; 'Now you have no excuse but to write to me' she said smiling. Mike's mother made a point at looking across at him; the expression on her face quite clearly asking, *Is there more to this than meets the eye?*

Mike made an excuse to get up to go onto the veranda where Jane joined him.

'Jane I want you to know that I appreciate your letters very much. I am not much of a writer; I hope you don't find my letters boring.'

'No, Mike I love your letters, please write more often … I will too.'

He struggled to find words to describe his feelings as he held her in his arms, looking at her. She gazed up at him her eyes bright and shining.

'I'm going back to the bush tomorrow; my next R&R is more than six weeks away. I will miss you so much,' he said.

She looked at him, tears welling in her eyes. She tried to brush them away.

'Please look after yourself Mike, be careful.'

He instinctively took her into his arms holding her tightly, she sobbed into his shoulder. He just held her tightly, immersed in the familiar smell of her perfume, the texture of her hair, not wanting to let go.

19

Lupane TTL, north Matabeleland

For two days Brigadier Tongerai Chabanga evaded the various SF follow-up teams scouring the area around his Lupane base camp. The Rhodesians, with the help of informers, had discovered the numerous weapons caches that he had built up over the previous two years. Those caches were now completely useless, in fact highly dangerous, as the SF had a penchant for booby-trapping arms caches. The other nasty SF tactic was leaving uniforms laced with Warfarin poison around deserted base camps. Any unwitting cadre who put on the uniform would die a slow, agonising death through massive internal bleeding. Chabanga had also heard of how Thallium, a lethal, heavy-metal toxin similar to rat poison, was injected into tins of corned beef which were then left around for hungry freedom fighters to find.

The initial shock and frustration of the attack had given way to Chabanga's cold hard determination to track down Benkov and kill him in the most painful way possible. He sat with a band of about twenty-five cadres that had survived the attack. The amount of supplies and equipment they carried between them was minimal, as most had dropped their packs in order to get away. All their personal possessions were lost. Chabanga had saved all his own records and codes which included the location of arms caches, as well as the distribution of ZIPRA forces throughout Matabeleland, including the names and locations of all the brigade commanders and political commissars. The options facing Chabanga were once again limited. His forces had been decimated, the survivors spread to the four winds. It would take months to try and regroup the whole force. He decided that his best option was to try and get to the freedom fighter base in the Dett area to the north. He figured he would likely get an idea of where Benkov might be from them.

The days following the attack had given Chabanga more time to reflect on what had happened. The only SF soldiers he had seen in the attack on his base had been black. This did not make sense. He knew of the RAR, their fearsome reputation but he had thought that there were relatively few of them. He was used to seeing Territorial Battalions come through his area and the national servicemen in the Independent Companies. He had successfully evaded them for years. He had lost very few men to SF ambushes and attacks, and then only because his men had been sloppy and unprofessional. The people that had attacked him in Lupane were different. They seemed to be well prepared and knew exactly where his band was. They must have been in the hills watching his camp for days, which meant that they were almost certainly *Skuz'apo*. His decision to move out when he did had saved his brigade from complete annihilation. He shivered at the thought of what could have happened if they had been surprised in their riverbed base.

Chabanga had developed a number of theories around what motivated the black soldiers in the Rhodesian army. From all the accounts that he had read, the intelligence briefings, and interviews with numerous informers, black soldiers actually outnumbered white soldiers by nearly two to one. *Why were they fighting with the Rhodesians, did they not know that defeat was inevitable? They were betraying their own people!* The might of the Soviet Union and China was being brought to bear against the 'Rebel State'. The People were rising up to overthrow the illegal, oppressive regime of Ian Smith. The socialist revolution was underway, and yet these men continued to fight. The presence of so many black soldiers on the other side was a contradiction that was difficult to explain. Chabanga convinced himself that they must have been bribed with money or they had been indoctrinated, brainwashed. In his mind the RAR were just mercenaries who would change their allegiance when the war had been won. That was what mercenaries did.

Chabanga also knew that the British people felt guilty about their colonial past. They wanted to get the 'Rhodesian Question' off the agenda. The granting of independence to their other colonies in Africa had been an easy compromise, avoiding the risk of fighting revolutionary wars as Portugal, Belgium and France had done. The Mau Mau rebellion in Kenya had been enough to frighten Britain into submission; they rapidly granted independence to their African colonies. It was embarrassing for the British Government to have a rebel colony fighting a civil war, a white versus black war. This was politically unacceptable to the British. The ZAPU leadership were convinced that Britain would deliver the country to them when the time came. It was only a matter of time; Britain had capitulated all over Africa. Chabanga was convinced that the maniac Mugabe had no chance of winning power and even if he did, Nkomo and ZAPU would overthrow him. The ZIPRA army would be ready for the final conventional push, with the support of the Soviets, SWAPO, *Umkomto-we-Sizwe* and the Cubans if needs be. Nobody trusted Mugabe and his Chinese handlers.

Chabanga had convinced himself that he needed to kill the Soviet spy, Benkov. Benkov's atrocities were undermining the legitimacy of ZAPU and ZIPRA. His organisation could not be branded as depraved, murderous terrorists. They were legitimate freedom fighters fighting for a just cause against a brutal and oppressive enemy, *who was also white!*

The escape route Chabanga had chosen followed the course of the Gwai River that wound its way to the northwest. It would take him virtually directly to his destination. With every step Chabanga's anger grew, consuming him. *How could the idiots in Lusaka have sent a psychopath into the country? Have they any understanding of the damage that has been done to his organisation that has taken years to build?*

The freedom fighters often hailed busses that plied the many dirt road routes in and out of the tribal areas. As long as they didn't stay on the bus while on the major tar roads this worked well. Chabanga considered this possibility, but he knew the police conducted regular roadblocks on the major roads. The local bus drivers did not mind providing transport to the freedom fighters provided the bus didn't get damaged in any way. In fact, in reciprocation for free transport, the freedom fighters were careful to alert bus drivers to landmines they had laid, mindful of the adverse propaganda impact of killing their own people with landmines.

Comrade Chabanga had found that moving with his fugitive band of freedom fighters was taking too long. They were too slow. He decided to break the band up into three smaller groups, all to follow different routes to the ZIPRA base near Dett. This way his force would move more quickly. Chabanga had felt relieved after he made the decision to split his group. The constant fear of being attacked by SF, what he had seen in Lupane, had rattled him. He was also anxious to get news of Benkov's whereabouts.

He had watched as the other two groups had departed all with strict instructions of where to go and how to get there. They had been warned to stay off the roads and not to 'catch' any transport.

*

Dett, North Matabeleland

Captain Vladimir Benkov, upon arriving in the Dett area, had sent a coded message to the Soviet Base in Lusaka. Dett was a tiny village on a railway siding on the main Bulawayo-Vic Falls railway line. The railway line forms the eastern boundary of the Wankie National Park, while further to the east was a network of heavily populated Tribal Trust Lands. It was in these tribal trust lands that Benkov and his band now took refuge. The Gwai River and its tributaries ran through the TTL providing the only permanent source of water, although at times it was necessary to dig in the riverbed to get to the water running below the surface of the sand. Many of the villages had boreholes and wells, but these were in highly exposed places, not easy to reach undetected.

After the coded communication with Lusaka, Benkov established that the large re-supply group had not yet arrived in the region. This re-supply group had planned to cross in three bands, but Rhodesians had caught one, causing them to lose most of their equipment in the process.

The route between the Zambezi and Dett via the Matetsi Controlled Hunting Area was very dry and inhospitable; water was limited to a few isolated man-made waterholes. The vegetation was mostly sparse thorn scrub, leaving vast open *vleis* to cross. The heat was also a serious limiting factor making walking during daylight hours virtually impossible. The fact that the area was mostly game and hunting reserves meant it was largely uninhabited, so all food and water had to be carried.

Benkov knew he could not sit and wait indefinitely for the re-supply group to arrive. The longer he waited in a single place, being fed by locals, the greater the chances of detection. He was careful to ensure that his interpreter Mlungisi told the locals that they were just passing through, always careful to give a clear, false direction in case the locals were police informers. Benkov had no difficulty making contact with the local ZIPRA sub-region leader. The man had been operating in the area for some time and was well known. He had been careful not to use excessive violent intimidation in his area and that meant that the locals were largely ambivalent to the ZIPRA presence. The network of *mujibas* and informants was extensive in the area. There had been no reports of SF activity for over a month. Importantly the local leader was full of the news of the large-scale attack that had taken place in Lupane TTL. He explained that the SF had used paratroopers and jets and RAR soldiers, and that many freedom fighters were killed. Comrade Chabanga was missing.

The news of the attack in Lupane came as a surprise to Benkov. He felt that his carefully planned diversionary tactics would have worked. The tremor of uncertainty was building in his gut. *Had any cadres been captured? Had any talked about his group? Is my presence in the country known? Had the men he lost at the farm store attack survived to talk about his mission? Where was Chabanga?* These were all the questions that Benkov now considered. *That useless, cowardly bastard Chabanga needed a wake-up call. There are thousands more from where he came from anyway!*

Benkov prepared a lengthy report for his handlers in Lusaka, asking for orders based on this new information. The response came back the next day. He was to continue with the mission, whether he linked up with the reinforcements or not. Lusaka was very clear. The mission must be completed.

*

Police Forensic Laboratory Bulawayo

At the police forensic laboratory in Bulawayo the ballistics results from weapons recovered from the CTs killed in the farm raid were in. The SB Member-in-Charge now had an even better picture. The link was made between, Kamativi, the heavy vehicle convoy, the mission massacre and now the farm raid. He looked at the map on the wall, Kamativi in the north, the convoy attack south, the Kosami Mission attack further southeast and now the farm attack in the north again. *Who are these Gooks? This is not your run of the mill CT raiding party. Where are they going next?*

He picked up the phone to the RIC commander at 1 Brigade, 'Steve, its Bill we need to have another chat about the Gooks who revved the farm near Gwai River last week.'

*

Police Camp Wankie

Sgt Cephas Ngwenya, Selous Scout, had returned to Wankie. He and his stick were given a week's leave after the lengthy OP in Lupane TTL. He had used the time to plough his fields in his home village near the town of Tjolotjo in preparation for the rains. Nobody in his village, including his wife, knew he was a Selous Scout. They all still thought that he was a traffic policeman at Bulawayo Central Police Station. His wife and son always enjoyed his homecoming, as he would bring presents and food with him. The hard manual labour was an enjoyable diversion from the inactive job of sitting in an OP in absolute silence for weeks on end. His life was one of intense boredom punctuated with brief episodes of extreme combat action.

Upon returning from R&R Ngwenya and his stick were given rooms at the main 4 Indep base on a hill overlooking the town of Wankie. The camp had a good canteen and other facilities. There was one other 3 Group Selous Scout stick already in residence. When in the 4 Indep base they were asked to wear civilian clothes, the explanation given was that they were policemen waiting for a posting. The last thing anybody needed was Selous Scout berets and stable belts being seen in town as news travelled fast. Not long after their arrival they were called to a meeting at the Wankie Police Camp.

At the briefing the SB officer introduced them to an old, well travelled bus, a bus just like the standard, common or garden variety 'Shu-Shine' bus used all over the country. It was mainly light green in colour with a darker green stripe down the side. On the top was a roof rack almost the full length of the vehicle, with access provided via two ladders attached to the back of the bus. The suspension looked in need of repair as the bus stood at a slight angle, like an old man leaning on his walking stick. It had all the signs of wear and tear with dents, deep scratches, the odd cracked window and covered in a thick layer of dust. The rear was covered in layers of mud from years of dust mixed with spray from the all too rare rainstorms. Inside the seats were bare metal benches; whatever padding that had originally been in place had long since disappeared. The floor was also metal, scraped of paint, buffed to shining silver in places from heavy foot traffic. The bus looked like it had just returned from a trip, which in fact was the case. The police had only commandeered it that morning.

The SB officer stood on the step of the bus, 'This gentlemen ... is your transport for the next three weeks. You are going to travel the length and breadth of the road network between Vic Falls and Lupane, and with a bit of luck you will pick up a few lazy terrorists who want to hitch a ride. This bus has been used by mineworkers to travel through this area so the locals are familiar with it.'

A buzz of discussion broke out amongst the Selous Scouts.

The policeman continued, 'We need to solve the mystery of the Disappearing Gooks. We have had some major scenes lately where the only way they could have got away is if they caught transport. Your job is to solve this mystery and to try to thin out the local, bus-catching, terrorist community.'

The policeman giggled to himself, happy with his Famous Five metaphor[134].

The Selous Scouts all looked at each other in amazement. They had all heard of this tactic being used, but none of them had actually done it themselves. They circled the bus inspecting it closely.

One asked, 'Where do we hide our weapons?'

The SB officer replied, 'You will all be issued with 9mm pistols with silencers attached and folding-butt AKMs. The bus will be filled with luggage that can be used to hide the weapons. Note that the driver's

---

134 *The Famous Five* is the name of a series of 21 children's novels written by British author Enid Blyton. The first book, *Five on a Treasure Island*, was published in 1942. All the books follow a theme of five child detectives solving mysteries.

seat has a thick armoured metal back to protect the driver from stray bullets. The idea is that you all sit at the back then allow the terrorists onto the bus with them always in front of you. The driver will stop to allow them to get on and will then find an excuse to get off to inspect something. You then shoot the terrorists, maybe capture a few… simple really.'

The next morning, dressed as poor village peasants, the Selous Scouts drove out of Wankie to the south. The bus by this time had a full load of luggage strapped to the roof, large bags, woven baskets and suitcases, bags of mielie meal, a bicycle, even a cage full of chickens. Inside the eight Selous Scouts had taken a seat with a large bag of various possessions on the seat in front of them. From the front of the bus they looked like any other travellers returning to their villages with gifts and provisions. The storage compartments under the bus were full of equipment and provisions including radios and heavy weapons and RPGs. These sticks had been selected on the basis that two of the troopers had heavy vehicle licences; one even knew how to drive a T54 tank … Selous Scouts got around.

They were all in a jovial mood. *How good is this? No walking, ample food and water, we can make as much noise as we like. What a pleasure! Where should we go first?* One of the bachelors asked if they could pick up women. They all laughed and joked about how much fun that would be.

Down the road to Lupane they went, bent on solving 'The Mystery of the Disappearing Gooks'. This was a bus providing one-way tickets only.

*

4 Independent Company (RAR) base camp, Sprayview airfield, Victoria Falls

Sergeant Mike Smith returned to Vic Falls with his Platoon minus 2nd Lt Gibbs who had decided to fly back to Vic Falls directly from his home in Salisbury. They drove back into the camp at Sprayview, which was largely deserted. The next Platoon on R&R, 3 Platoon, had passed them on the road going the other way. 1 Platoon was deployed on the River. It was already getting dark when the trucks pulled up outside their barrack room, everyone was in a sombre mood, always the same depressed feeling after R&R.

'Sergeant bloody Smith,' came the familiar call from Captain Fullerton as the troops started to unpack. Smith looked over to where

Fullerton was standing. *Does this bloke ever go on R&R?*

'Yes Sir?' Smith smiled.

'You owe a round of drinks in the mess. You got a request today … turning into Mr Popular, aren't you?' said Fullerton with his unique brand of sarcasm. Every Sunday the RBC ran a programme called 'Forces Requests' where the announcer, Sally Donaldson, would read out messages sent by wives and girlfriends to their men in the 'bush'. Getting a request cost a round of drinks and, depending on what was said, some serious leg-pulling.

'What did the message say Sir?' enquired Smith, amused at Fullerton's comment.

'O … I don't know exactly … something about you being someone's bush baby or … to the world you're just a guy but to me you're the world. Some crap like that. I bet you it was that married crow[135] you fucked a few weeks ago.'

'What song did they play Sir?'

Fullerton hesitated, '… don't get cute with me Sergeant … I think it was Fleetwood Mac, *Second Hand News*. That makes sense doesn't it?'

Smith knew he was making it all up, so there was no point in arguing or pressing the point further. He resolved to try to give Jane a call on the payphone to find out.

'Thank you Sir … did you get a request Sir?' replied Smith still smiling.

'Nah, if all the birds I fucked sent in a request I would need my own program.' Fullerton laughed loudly, always loving his own jokes. 'It's sundowner time so I think I want my beer now. Go and see if Lieutenant Dawson and Colour O'Connell will join us.'

With that Fullerton turned and went off to the mess expecting everything to fall into place for a good piss-up.

It had been hard leaving home and his mother and sister had cried. He was powerless to comfort them. His mother had cooked an enormous breakfast on the morning of his departure. The family had mostly sat quietly, nobody wanting to raise a subject that could possibly lead to a discussion on Mike's return to the bush.

It was inevitable that he would be nervous about another 'bush trip'. The fear of the unknown he figured was pretty normal, but at least, for the first time, he felt a degree of confidence in what was expected of him. He felt that Fullerton had accepted him, which was a massive confidence builder. Fullerton's acceptance, in turn, seemed to have rubbed off on his section and most importantly on Moyo, Dube and Sibanda. The changes were subtle but Smith was convinced that his men now looked at him in a different light. It made him feel good

135 Rhodesian slang, woman, women of all ages.

inside and he felt a growing pride in his men and the Company as a whole. The feeling of no longer being a total outsider was refreshing, but he had the overall impression that the war was a great deal more serious than people were letting on. The sheer weight of terrorist incursions seemed to be increasing and the fact that elements of the Company were almost constantly in action was alarming.

Mike's father had driven him to Brady Barracks early on the Sunday morning. They had both sat in silence as they drove the short distance. Smith's mind was full of thoughts of Jane and the sudden complex and intense jumble of emotions that she had added to his already cluttered mind.

His father had looked at him when they stopped outside the gates, 'Good luck son', he said, '… be careful.'

'Thanks Dad, I hope to be home for Christmas. Only three more months of national service to go,' he replied, trying not to give away his nervousness at returning to the bush. That was all he could say. He searched for more words but none would come. *How can I be more careful than I already am? … The situation is way out of my control.*

'See you soon Dad.' They shook hands and he walked through the boom gates.

When he took role call only eighteen of his platoon answered their names. He looked down the list again, checking those missing to see if any were AWOL[136] but they were all accounted for, dead, wounded, sick, long leave or VD. While he knew he would only have eighteen men report after R&R the realisation of the fact that there were so few was still confronting. *Shit … how can I deploy with a platoon of only eighteen men?*

*

Wankie Safari Lodge, Wankie National Park, northern Matabeleland

On the northern edge of the Wankie National Park was a luxury tourist resort called the Wankie Safari Lodge. The hotel was Five Star luxury. It was built in the shape of two crescents, back to back, giving each room a panoramic view of the bush including a large floodlit waterhole. This waterhole was kept full of water so it attracted game in huge numbers, particularly in the evening. The resort was a favourite with overseas tourists who were taken into the reserve on game drives. It normally formed one of the stops on the 'Flame Lily Holidays' that included the other major attractions of the Matopo Hills, Zimbabwe Ruins, Kariba and Victoria Falls.

136 Absent without leave.

The Safari Lodge was kept very busy, being a popular venue for meetings and sales conferences. On this particular evening there was a seminar being held that, to the casual observer, would have looked like any other group of executives. The group tended to keep to themselves, not mixing with the other hotel guests. It was the last night of a three-day seminar and the participants looked tired, mostly from too many late nights of heavy drinking. They all looked forward to the end of the session and a good meal in one of the private dining rooms.

One of the assistant managers of the hotel was on front desk duty. He was a neatly dressed young man, his nametag in place, his Southern Sun company tie in a Windsor knot. He had been identified for promotion soon after joining the company, part of their 'integration policy' of advancing black managers. This young man had ambitions way beyond hotel management.

He walked over to his office cubicle next to reception and picked up the telephone. He dialled carefully. Almost instantly someone picked up on the other side. 'The weather is expected to be clear tomorrow, no rain is expected,' he said in English. Not waiting for a reply he replaced the receiver.

*

About 14kms to the east of the Safari Lodge, Comrade Vladimir Benkov once again sat on a dark and lonely hill. He was now looking forward to the end of his mission. He was tired of eating the food supplied by the villagers, he was tired of the heat that was relentless day after day, and he was tired of the company of his band of freedom fighters. He had nothing in common with them. Other than the few short conversations in Russian with his interpreter Mlungisi, he had no other communication.

Benkov contemplated the events planned for the next day, the attack, his escape routes, and his proposed exit from the country. He had sent his evening radio message to Lusaka, he was in position … he was ready. The band he had with him now consisted of twenty cadres divided into two groups. He had been given a few extra men as guides by the local ZIPRA commander. These men were leading the two groups into their correct positions for the attack. All that was needed now was the coming of the dawn; his last radio message from Lusaka had said that 'clear weather' was expected, code for 'Go'.

There was a feeling of overwhelming relief that the mission was so close to completion even though the last phase was by far the most dangerous. Benkov felt very confident. The band he had with him were well trained, dedicated to the cause. They were ruthless killers proven in battle and they could be relied upon. He settled down into a sleeping position, wedged between two rocks, their solid, smooth mass providing a feeling of comfort and security. He lay on his back and looked up at the bright starlit sky. The night skies of Africa always appeared crystal clear. The stars seemed to be so close, so distinct. He watched as a satellite, moved across his field of vision, it seemed to be picking a path through the stars as if trying to avoid them. He thought of the cold Russian skies, the low cloud, the endless blizzards and snow in winter. He felt a sudden pang of homesickness, *I must be getting soft, there should be no room for nostalgia, focus on the mission!* He turned onto his side and tried to get some sleep. A very big day lay ahead.

20

Main Camp Airstrip, Wankie National Park, northern Matabeleland

The African sun pushed up over the horizon, reflecting off the polished aluminium fuselages of the two Douglas DC-4 passenger aircraft parked on the hard-standing at the Wankie Main Camp airstrip. The airstrip, built to service the large number of tourists visiting Wankie National Park and the Wankie Safari Lodge, was long and wide, big enough to take Boeing 737s and the Air Rhodesia Viscounts. It had a small thatched 'passenger lounge' with toilets. There were no other facilities and no control tower. An old fire engine was parked on the edge of the apron. It looked like it would struggle to drive to the end of the runway, let alone rush to an aircraft fire. The fire crew looked as old as their vehicle, sporting well-developed 'beer-bops', testimony to many hours in the pub. An equally old and dilapidated Bedford refuelling truck, blowing clouds of diesel smoke, drove onto the apron to pump fuel into the aircraft.

Both aircraft, built as the military version C-54 at the end of World War II, had participated in the Berlin Airlift. They were converted by SAA to carry passengers in the 1950s and gave long and trouble-free service before being replaced by jet aircraft. They had spent a few years carrying freight around Africa on UN relief missions and had then been lovingly restored by their current owner to their late 1940's glory. A small air-charter company based in Gaborone in Botswana owned them. Both carried Botswana aircraft registration numbers which allowed the 'two old girls' to fly all over Africa on charter work, mainly for well-heeled European and American tourists, looking for an authentic African experience. Rhodesian and South African registered aircraft were not welcome elsewhere in Africa.

The old DC-4 was perfect for landing on rough dirt strips at private game lodges; they were strong and sturdy, perfect for the harsh African conditions. The lack of air-conditioning meant that passengers were always loaded at the last possible minute as the cabin got close to 50°C on a hot day. The seats had been reupholstered in 1947 livery; the cabin even had small curtains that could be drawn across the windows. The crew all wore imitations of 1947 SAA uniforms, which added to the whole ambiance. The tourists loved it. There were very few places left in the world where it was possible to fly in a DC-4.

The owners of the two 'brave old ladies', named Victoria and Elizabeth as befitting of a colonial flying experience, had been supplementing their tourist charter income in other ways. The aircraft were distinguishable only by different colour stripes down the side of the fuselage and their registration numbers. Victoria had a blue stripe with the number A2-DIW, Elizabeth a red stripe, A2-LYL. Their names were stencilled below the cockpit window on the port side. Victoria and Elizabeth had been seen in some very strange and exotic places in Africa and the Middle East. Often their cargo was loaded in the dead of night, by equally strange and exotic people. Sometimes they carried human cargo as well. It was not uncommon for this human cargo to exit the aircraft at their service ceiling of 22,000ft, over countries known to harbour communist insurgents. The two majestic ladies had proved to be very profitable assets for their owners. Their clandestine activities, however, had not gone unnoticed in some circles.

It was a result of a simple twist of fate that both aircraft were sitting together at Main Camp. Elizabeth had developed an engine glitch on a flight from Arusha in Tanzania to Maun in Botswana. The flight carried a group of very wealthy Americans and their families that had got together for the trip of a lifetime. They had flown from Nairobi in Kenya to the Masai Mara to see the Wildebeest migration, then on to the Serengeti, the Gorongoza Crater, and were now on their way to the Okavango Delta. An unexpected diversion to the Wankie Safari Lodge was all part of the adventure. It was purely co-incidental that the other DC-4 was also at Main Camp on a different charter. The flight engineer was concerned that he would not be able to fix the problem before the scheduled departure that morning. The company prided itself on reliability and were not prepared to delay their customers unduly. The flight engineers from the two aircraft had worked all night to fix the problem, uncertain as to how much longer it would take.

The pilots and cabin crew for the two aircraft arrived by bus from the hotel. It was only nine in the morning, but the heat was already building to the forecast high of 40°C. The cabin crew, in their neat, tight-fitting uniforms, removed their jackets, relieved to sit in the shade of the thatched lounge. They chatted away happily without a care in the world.

The four pilots strolled across the apron to the two aircraft to get the latest status from the flight engineers. A hurried discussion ensued under the shade of a wing as they collectively tried to figure out their options. The old refuelling truck stood under the opposite wing pumping in fuel. A decision was made, as most business decisions are made, based on the lowest economic cost in the circumstances. The serviceable aircraft would be allocated to the wealthy Americans while an apology would be issued to the other charter passengers, with the offer of tea and then lunch while they waited.

The pilots then walked back across the apron. The Captain of

Victoria made a call to the hotel. The Americans would leave on time, but on Victoria not Elizabeth. The hotel staff then went about rounding up the guests explaining the delay to those affected. The bus carrying the Americans arrived and the excited passengers hustled and bustled around their copious quantities of luggage. The passengers ranged in age from over sixty to a set of two-year old twins. The passengers all wore various versions of khaki safari outfits with bush hats. They were from Arizona, so the hot weather was not a discomfort for them.

Victoria's two very attractive cabincrew; in their full-length skirts, high heels and forage caps, ushered the jabbering passengers across the apron. The more senior of the two was an inch or two taller than her companion. She had deep penetrating brown eyes and dark auburn hair, wrapped in a tight knot neatly below the forage cap. Her nametag said simply 'Devon' that together with her English accent indicated her family's heritage in the town of Ashburton, in the heart of the South Devon countryside on the southern slopes of Dartmoor. Her accent had a hint of Rhodesian, indicating she had lived in Africa for some time, from the age of fourteen in fact. After finishing school she had been recruited by BOAC but the weather in England and the airline bureaucracy had eventually got too much for her so she resigned, returning to Rhodesia and the flexibility and excitement of charter operations in Africa. English birth meant that she carried a British passport, which was essential for flying charter flights in Africa, most of the continent was hostile to the Rhodesian regime. She spoke in a friendly but instructive manner. There could be no doubt who was in charge. She issued clear instructions to the passengers who seemed to all be talking at once, at the top of their voices, as is typical of excited holidaymakers. They mounted the stairway entering the aircraft through the double rear door. The heat was intense in the aircraft, so the air hostesses did the safety briefing with the door still open, using the original 1940's instruction card. Nobody listened.

Victoria's Captain, an ex-South African Air Force pilot who had flown P-51s in Korea, began the process for firing the Pratt & Whitney R-2000 engines. Bells rang in test, gear horns blared and hands flew to switches and throttles and back again. An APU[137] sounding much like a lawn mower reverberated loudly. The Captain planned to start number three engine first. Cowl flaps opened, oil shutters closed, turn off battery disconnect switches, fuel mixture to takeoff rich, set the throttle at 1,000 rpm …

'Turning! 3! 6! 9! Switches!'

The engine spluttered and coughed, the propeller making two gyrating rotations before stopping. He waited a few seconds and fired

137 Auxiliary Power Unit.

again. This time the old girl turned, a cloud of blue exhaust smoke flew backwards in the prop-wash and she settled into a vibrating idle. Numbers 4, 1 and 2 were then started in succession. The passengers familiar with the routine cheered and clapped. The fuselage shivered with the vibration of all four engines the noise deafening.

The co-pilot had filed a flight plan that morning by phoning Victoria Falls International and Maun from the hotel. The original flight plan for Elizabeth was still in place at Maun and he forgot, in all the confusion, to draw their attention to the aircraft change. Civilian air travel in Africa was always a relatively informal affair. The Captain advanced the engines to build momentum, Victoria moved across the apron, her rudder and control surfaces flapping side to side and up and down like the excited bird she was, fluffing her tail feathers.

Victoria bumped smoothly along the taxiway to the end of runway. The Captain called up the closest civilian air traffic control at Victoria Falls International.

'Victoria Falls Tower this is Alpha Two, Delta India Whisky … departing from Main Camp to the east, runway Zero Eight.'

'Alpha Two, Delta India Whisky, good morning, after departure runway Zero Eight, you are cleared to level nine zero, heading zero five four. Contact Francistown on one two five point seven at top of climb … Victoria Falls Tower.'

The controller at Victoria Falls had an Air Rhodesia Viscount on final approach and, in his haste, he confused himself when he logged the radio call by transposing the two DC-4 registration numbers on the log sheet, A2-LYL for A2-DIW, an easy mistake to make.

'Victoria Falls Tower, cleared to level nine zero, heading zero five four, contact Francistown on one two five point seven, Alpha Two Delta India Whisky, good day to you.'

Victoria reached the end of the runway, performed a neat right angle turn, lining up to the east. The Captain then called up local air traffic on the radio to advise of his departure and that he would be turning out right after take-off. A Cessna 185 was passing to the west on the way to Wankie. It was the only other aircraft in the vicinity.

Victoria was not by any means fully loaded; she had capacity for eighty passengers but only forty were on board. Avgas was expensive in Rhodesia because of sanctions, so the pilots had loaded only enough to get to Maun plus the required minimum to divert to Gaborone or Francistown if that was necessary. The half load of fuel still meant a very gentle climb-out because of the very hot weather.

The Captain looked across at his young co-pilot, just turned thirty with a self-funded commercial pilot's license. The younger man loved Victoria as if she was a maiden aunt; she was the epitome of flying.

He fussed over the take-off checklist. They scanned the instruments to ensure all was correct. Flaps were lowered, trim tabs set, the responsiveness to prop rpms checked, magnetos checked; the co-pilot lifted his thumb and nodded. The Captain glanced back at the flight engineer in his jump-seat, he too nodded his agreement. The engines were advanced to full takeoff power, 47 inches manifold pressure and 2700 rpm, both watching as the revolutions built on the gauges, the brakes still holding the aircraft in place. Both men placed a hand on the throttles to ensure full power was maintained. The aircraft bucked and gyrated violently, as if to tell the pilot that she was now ready to go. He released the brakes and Victoria leapt forward, slowly at first … rapidly gathering pace. There was no wind to speak of, so they were going to need most of the runway to get airborne. She trundled down the runway, the prop-wash sending back curling dust from the edge of the tarmac. Reaching her takeoff speed, the Captain gently rotated and she lifted off the runway in her dignified shallow climb-out. She cleared the threshold; the Captain raised the undercarriage, the distinctive winding noise as the wheels retracted into their bays. Victoria gradually gained altitude maintaining a course directly to the east.

*

From his position on the hill due east of the runway at Main Camp, Captain Benkov could see the DC-4 once it reached 500ft AGL. Aircraft identification at that sort of distance was always difficult. He saw that his target had four engines; it had to be the right one. He lifted the Strela-2M[138] to his shoulder, pointing the launcher at the still distant target. The missile launcher system consisted of a green missile launch tube containing the missile, a grip stock and a cylindrical thermal battery. The Strela has a slant range of about 4.2 km, a ceiling of 2,300m, and a speed of about 500m/second, Mach 1.75. The missile is a tail-chase system; its effectiveness, therefore, depends on its ability to lock onto the engine heat source at the rear of low-flying aircraft.

Benkov waited for the DC-4 to turn onto its new course, that he expected to be to the south. He tracked the target with the iron sights on the launch tube, gently applying half-trigger. The seeker in the missile attempted to track. The heat from the DC-4 engines was still too faint for the missile to register an infra-red signature. He held the missile steadily on the target as it slowly approached on a track virtually directly towards him. He pressed the trigger again; the missile registered the infra-red signature, a green light flashed through the sight and the buzzer sounded. He knew he needed to 'chase' the DC-4. The

138 NATO reporting name SA-7b, SAM7, ground-to-air heat-seeking missile.

aircraft slowly began its turn to the south, its engines clearly audible now, still gently gaining altitude. Benkov then pulled the trigger fully, immediately applying a lead on the target, aiming at a point above the rumbling aircraft. The missile locked on, producing a steady buzzing noise and a red light flashed in the sight mechanism,. He had just 0.8 seconds to provide lead to the target while the missile's on-board power supply was activated and the throw-out motor ignited. The throw-out motor fired the missile out of the launcher at 32m/second, rotating the missile at the same time at 20revs/sec. Benkov continued to hold the launcher on the target. After 0.3 seconds the rocket motor ignited. The heat from the blast buffeted Benkov as he watched the missile climb away, beginning its deadly flight.

The missile's un-cooled, lead sulphide, passive infra-red seeker head can detect infrared radiation at below 2.8 μm in wavelength; the old DC-4 was producing a lot of heat in this band. The missile left a distinctive cloud of white smoke as it streaked through the sky, marking the path to the target. The airliner's heat signature increased as Victoria continued to turn. The missile made minute corrections to its flight.

Nobody on board the DC-4 saw the missile launch. There was no warning just a loud BANG as the missile impacted the starboard main-plane aft of the inner engine manifold. The explosion tore a huge chunk out of the wing which weakened the wing root. The impact forced the wing into a down angle; the old plane began an involuntary turn to starboard.

The Captain did not know what had happened but he knew instantly that he was in trouble … big trouble.

'MAYDAY, Mayday… Mayday, this is Alpha Two … Delta India Whisky, we have an explosion on board, I am returning to Main Camp. Mayday…. Mayday… Alpha Two … Delta India Whisky.'

The controller at Victoria Falls heard the message but did not pick up the c/sign.

'This is Victoria Falls Tower … Last caller, please confirm call-sign …'

The controller called again, more urgently, 'Last caller … please confirm call-sign.'

Pieces of the wing began to flap wildly, tearing off, making the aircraft more difficult to handle.

'We are going in … Geoff,' the Captain said quietly to his co-pilot, then clicked the intercom, 'Cabin crew prepare for emergency landing.'

The big aircraft was rapidly giving up the sky. The Captain had crash-landed his P-51 in Korea on two occasions. Handling Victoria in a rapid, uncontrolled decent was a completely different proposition.

The co-pilot called urgently 'Mayday … Mayday … Mayday … this is Alpha Two … Delta India Whisky; Victoria Falls Tower this is Alpha Two … Delta …'

He never finished the message.

*

Seeing the missile impact the aircraft, Benkov yelled out in triumph, his band of freedom fighters jumped up and down, yelping in excitement. They watched jubilantly as the aircraft rapidly lost altitude, trailing smoke and debris, still turning, the pilot trying desperately to make it back to the airfield. Pieces of wing were breaking off and flames spurted from an engine. The aircraft began to spin, hitting the ground in an abandoned field about four kilometres from the hill that Benkov was standing on.

'Come with me Comrades,' Benkov shouted triumphantly in Russian, they ran down the hill in the direction of the downed plane. A plume of thick black smoke rose into the air, a beacon for all to see. The freedom fighters converged on the smoldering wreck of the airliner. Benkov was anxious to see his handiwork to make sure that he had killed his 'target'.

The DC-4 had made its first impact in a field that had been previously cleared for growing crops. The ground was broken, large tree stumps dotted the field. The aircraft had hit the ground hard, the damaged wing had come off on impact, slewing the fuselage around, sliding it sideways until it struck a tree stump which effectively severed the tail section. The fuselage then spun more violently, throwing many passengers out, still attached to their seats. The severed wing burst into flame as the fuel tank ignited. The fire quickly spread through the grass into the surrounding trees.

Standing on the edge of the field, Benkov surveyed the damage he had caused. The tail section was a good fifty metres from the rest of the fuselage which had ploughed into another set of tree stumps, gouging large holes in the wing and airframe. He could see passengers strapped in their seats in the tail section. It was unclear whether they were alive from where he stood. Between the tail section and the main fuselage he counted eight passengers, still attached to their seats, lying in the dust. The fire had already engulfed one of the stricken passengers, the seat was burning. As he surveyed the scene two people came into view, holding onto each other for support, blood streaming from gashes in their arms and legs.

Signaling for his men to advance across the field Benkov shook out a broad sweep line until they reached the main piece of wreckage. The burning wing was some distance off, the dry vegetation too sparse to burn all the way to the fuselage.

The two surviving passengers standing alone in the field saw the freedom fighters approaching, waved and shouted to them, thinking they were rescuers. Benkov ignored the survivors he pushed past them intent on searching the fuselage, seeking out his target. All he could see inside were women, children and old men. A few of the passengers were still alive, sitting strapped in their seats, too injured or shocked to move. A woman in the rear of the cabin had horrific injuries, her right leg twisted behind her, bleeding profusely from a massive chest wound. She called for help in a weak muffled voice. Benkov held a crumpled photograph of a man in his hand. He studied the passengers carefully. The realisation struck him - *my target is not here!* He ran through the field feverishly moving from passenger to passenger ending up at the tail section – *shit he is not here! How can that be?*

Benkov had not seen or heard the replacement DC-4 land the previous evening; he could not have known that the Rhodesian military commanders, meeting with their South African counterparts together with weapons manufacturers and suppliers, had been moved to another flight. The Commander of COMOPS, the 'target', sat completely unaware on the veranda at the Safari Lodge, drinking tea with his colleagues, waiting for his charter flight to be called.

The two survivors were American girls, sisters, one nineteen and the other twenty; they hobbled over to where Benkov was standing.

'Thank God you are here, please help us … there are more people alive inside.'

The Soviet looked at them, their American accents so distinctive, 'Where are you from?' he asked in his broken, thickly accented English.

'Arizona' one answered looking up at him, confusion in her face at the strange question.

'What are you doing here?'

'We are on vacation with two other families; we were on our way to Botswana. Where are you from … you don't sound English?' the elder of the two girls asked. She looked across at the cadres standing about, studying their AKs, looked at their uniforms, her face paled. She looked back at Benkov; she could tell that he was a white man, covered in black face cream.

'You are not Rhodesians are you?' she said, her voice quavering as the realisation of their predicament set in.

Benkov did not answer; he just looked at her, thinking about the possibilities. He was still trying to come to terms with the fact that his target was not on the plane. The radio message from Lusaka had confirmed the departure time, the fact that the target would be on board. As the situation sank in a whole new opportunity occurred to Benkov. *I have a planeload of Americans here. I can strike a great victory.* His special forces training provided him with the ability to adapt to changing circumstances. He reacted instinctively.

'Comrades, gather all the surviving passengers together,' he shouted in Russian, repeated by Mlungisi. One of the girls began to cry at the sound of the Russian language.

Mlungisi called to Benkov in Russian 'Comrade Vladimir, can we have these two?' he was pointing at the two girls.

'By all means Comrade, they are yours.' Benkov looked up at the men waving them forward.

The two girls saw Mlungisi approach them, realising what was about to happen.

'NO … No you cannot do this … leave us alone, we are American citizens,' the older of the two girls backed away. The younger girl tried to run; Mlungisi swatted her on the back with his AK. She sprawled into the dust. He was bending over to give her another clout, when a shot rang out from the other side of the aircraft.

The Captain, strapped into his seat in the cockpit, had regained consciousness with the presence of mind to lean over and grab his .38 revolver from the safe behind his seat. He had shot a cadre in the face as the man stepped up to the cockpit to look inside.

Benkov signalled the band to take cover and he crept around to the front of the aircraft. Another shot rank out, another cadre screamed in pain. Benkov, loosened a grenade from his webbing belt, stretched up, slipping it through the broken cockpit window. The explosion blew out the remaining glass; a fire extinguisher exploded spraying high pressure CO_2 gas all through the cockpit and cabin.

Benkov walked back to the gaping hole left by the severed tail section and threw another grenade into the fuselage for good measure. The only other survivor not killed by the grenades was the tall cabin supervisor who had been strapped into the tail section. She came hobbling across the field led by one of the cadres. Her skirt was torn and her stockings hung in shreds on her legs, her feet were bare.

'Comrade Mlungisi, we need to leave now. You can gather what ever money and jewellery you can find, but be quick.'

Benkov looked across at the three women; the two young girls were sobbing uncontrollably, their shoulders shaking, the horror of their situation all too clear. The airhostess stumbled across to him, looking up into his face defiantly.

'What are you animals going to do with us?' she demanded. '… you can't take us with you … we will slow you down. The army will be here soon.' She spoke with a clear unwavering voice.

'You will die for the cause of freedom,' Benkov replied in his deeply accented English, laughing loudly, throwing his head back, amused at the obvious contradiction. The freedom fighters all looked on bemusedly; they had not seen Comrade Vladimir laugh before.

'You have an important role to play in current events,' he said, still amused by his private joke.

She showed no sign of fear at his callous remark.

'You are a Russian aren't you? You have been training these terrorists!' she stated accusingly, gesturing at the gawking freedom fighters standing around her.

Benkov dismissed her with a wave of the hand, 'You had better find some shoes in the wreckage or the next few days are going to be more painful than they might otherwise be.' He turned to issue more instructions to Mlungisi, the woman already a distant thought, her fate already decided.

The freedom fighters dragged the dead and dying passengers to the wrecked fuselage, propping them up as best they could. Benkov then ceremoniously instructed them to execute these 'supporters of the oppressive regime'. The cadres let loose with a hail of bullets turning the bodies into a pulpy mess, making them unrecognisable. The sound was deafening, the two American girls stood in shocked silence next to the airhostess, too terrified, too traumatised to speak.

As an after-thought, Benkov called for AP mines. He had three PMN-1s in his pack that he took out. One of the cadres produced an additional POMZ mine. Benkov studied the crash site and worked out the best places to position the mines … less than ten minutes later it was all done.

'Let's move out Comrades,' Benkov called out, his gesture needed no translation.

The cadre that had been shot by the pilot was seriously wounded. The .38 slug had entered his shoulder, must then have travelled down into his chest and punctured a lung because he was coughing up frothy blood. The man stood looking at Benkov, putting on a brave face.

Mlungisi came across to Benkov, 'Comrade Vladimir, we can take him with us, he will recover, it is a small wound.'

'Mlungisi he is coughing blood he needs medical attention which we cannot give.'

'We can take him to a nearby village and they will look after him,' Mlungisi implored.

'No Mlungisi …if he gets found by the army he will tell them about us, about what we have done, and where we are going. He knows too much.'

'You cannot kill him Comrade. He has fought with us … he is one of us. He has family…' Mlungisi's voice trailed off.

The wounded cadre watched the altercation, realising what was being said. When Benkov turned back towards him he began to weep. He was only twenty years old. Sinking to his knees he looked up at Benkov, coughing loudly more blood sprayed from his mouth. His chest was heaving from the exertion of trying to breathe while his lungs filled with fluid, his dark eyes clear and bright, tinged with pain. Tears travelled down his cheeks making streaks through the dust and grime on his face, dripping off the end of his chin onto the dirt in front of him. He made no protest; he simply looked Benkov in the eyes, as if searching for some sign, a sign of hope. Then bowing his head, began to recite Psalm 23,

The Lord is my shepherd I shall not want.
He maketh me to lie down in green pastures:
He leadeth me beside the still waters

The Church of England had educated the young man, like so many others. He had killed and tortured, he had murdered missionaries, raped a nun, yet in his own pending death the atheist communist doctrine he had been taught evaporated. He called on the only God he knew.

He restoreth my soul: …
… Thy rod and thy staff they comfort me.

'You are a brave man Comrade,' Benkov said soothingly in Russian, the man looking up at him uncomprehendingly. 'You shall be remembered as a hero of the revolution, Comrade.'

Mlungisi knelt down next to the doomed man. He placed his arm around his shoulders and finished the prayer with him.

… Surely goodness and mercy shall follow me all the days of my life,
and I will dwell in the house of The Lord forever.

Mlungisi then stood up, shouted his frustration and sorrow to the sky; he pushed past Benkov and called the rest of the band to follow him. As he passed the tall air hostess he gave her a hard slap on the side of her head, venting his anger. They moved off dragging the three women with them. Benkov watched them go, waiting until they reached the edge of the field. He took out his Tokarev pistol and pointed it at the bowed head of the young cadre.

'Sleep well Comrade' he said softly, and shot him in the back of the head, *the price of freedom is great.*

*

Her sister ship did not pick up the distress signal sent out by the downed DC-4 aircraft, Elizabeth still sat on the apron at Main Camp with her radio switched off. The distress signal was, however, picked up by the controllers at Victoria Falls and, by a strange quirk of fate, by the tower at Bulawayo International Airport well to the south. The air traffic controller at Bulawayo did not recognise the aircraft c/sign at first; he was not sure where it was coming from. The controllers at Victoria Falls looked at their logs and noted that the aircraft A2-LYL had departed Main Camp, but the distress call when they played it back on the tape came from A2-DIW. They called Main Camp by telephone and the ranger on duty confirmed that A2-LYL was sitting in front of him on the apron. The two DC-4s from the same company, on the same runway, at the same time created a fatal delay in the response to the disaster.

The Victoria Falls controllers tried to raise Maun and Francistown on their radios, eventually having to resort to a telephone call. Maun confirmed that no aircraft had reported in to them but that A2-LYL was now overdue. More confusion ensued. The controller at Victoria Falls made a decision; he called the sub-JOC at Wankie and reported that he had a distress signal from an aircraft leaving Main Camp and asked if they could search an area about twenty kilometres to the east of the runway.

A further delay resulted as the sub-JOC commander tried to find the pilot of the only aircraft he had available, a Trojan Aeromacchi 260[139]. It was nearly two hours after the DC-4 had been shot down that the lone search aircraft arrived over Main Camp. The pilot lined up the small aircraft with the runway and flew to the east, taking no more than a few seconds to see the pall of smoke from the bush fire, the still smouldering wreckage, in the field below. The pilot circled the crash site while he reported to the sub-JOC. He flew as low as he could looking for survivors but could see no sign of life.

The only SF in the area was a police PATU stick at Dett. They were alerted and drove out in their Land Rovers but it was still a good hour's drive. The crash site was close to the densely populated northern edge of Lupane TTL, but even if someone had wanted to raise

---

139 The Rhodesians had originally intended to buy American T-28 Trojans but the deal was cancelled by the US Government. As the Aeromacchi 260's, a single-engined, high wing liaison aircraft, were smuggled into Rhodesia from France in 1969 they were given the name of Trojan.

the alarm, the nearest telephone was at a trading store 10km away. The sub-JOC commander at Wankie got on the phone to 4 Indep at Vic Falls and asked them to get some troops down to protect the crash site. Ambulances were also sent under police escort from Wankie. The sub-JOC commander had only one helicopter to draw on which he dispatched with a four-man medical team. It was midday and the sun was at its zenith. The weather forecasters were not wrong; it was 40°C outside if it was a degree.

The helicopter arrived over the crash site after only twenty minutes flying time. The pilot pulled the helicopter into an orbit and he and his passengers studied the wreckage below; he didn't want to land and get taken out by a CT ambush. He looked back at the four medics, two doctors and two medical orderlies. They had large bags full of drips and other medical supplies plus a field kit with medical instruments and drugs. He pointed to the ground then circled his hand as he explained that he would drop them and then orbit to provide protection.

The pilot of the Alouette chose his LZ, slowly descended, deliberately choosing a spot far enough away down wind so that he didn't kick dust onto the crash site. The medics exited the helicopter and the pilot immediately lifted off again, the gunner on the twin .303s scanning the bush below. The two doctors and two orderlies picked their way across the rough field, dreading what they might be presented with. They approached the tail section first, quickly establishing that all the passengers in that section were dead. They then moved off in the direction of the main fuselage, checking the bodies that had been thrown clear, still no survivors. Two passengers who had been horribly burned in the fire were still strapped to their seats, smouldering, the smell so distinctive, awful.

The four men approached the main piece of wreckage, looking carefully for any other bodies in the field. One of the young NS medical orderlies, fresh out of his combat medic course, walked to the side of the fuselage, trying to look through one of the windows that was smeared with blood.

The PMN-1 mine is particularly deadly because it contains an unusually large explosive filling. It can destroy a victim's entire leg, often requiring amputation above the knee, in addition to inflicting severe injuries on the adjacent limb which may also require some form of amputation.

As the medic stepped forward the PMN-1 AP mine exploded, taking his right leg off just below the knee. His body was thrown up and back by the blast, sprawled into the dirt. Dust and smoke were thrown up into the air, making it difficult for the others to see him. The blast was so severe that he immediately lost consciousness, lying deathly still. The bone from his severed leg protruding from the thigh, the kneecap still attached but completely blackened, oozing thick red fluid. The three other medics rushed to the injured man's assistance.

The POMZ AP mine consists of a small TNT explosive charge inside a hollow cylindrical cast-iron fragmentation sleeve. The sleeve has large fragments cast into the outside and is open at the bottom to accept the insertion of a wooden mounting stake which leaves the explosive head about 20cm above ground. On top is a weather cap, covering a fuse well, initiated with a tripwire fuse. The effective radius of the mine is often quoted as 4m, but a small number of large fragments may be lethal at ranges far exceeding that.

One of the doctors, rushing from the other side of the wreck, did not see the thin tripwire attached to the POMZ in front of him as he moved around the fuselage to see what had happened. It detonated in a loud thudding blast, throwing him off his feet; three large pieces of shrapnel hit the doctor, one in the leg, one in his hip and the other in his chest below the armpit. He moaned in agony, his arms flopping in the dust, the sudden stupefying shock of the blast, blood covering his whole left side, pumping out of his chest wound. He rolled in the dust trying to get to his feet, then fell back realising instantly that he was mortally wounded. He lay on his back, looking up into the blue sky. The hot sun burned down onto his face, he heard the clapping sound as the helicopter cavitated into another orbit, someway off, the sound seemed to be fading. A Yellowbilled Kite, *uNhloyile*, turned into a thermal above him.

'Don't come any closer,' the doctor groaned in a soft voice. It hurt to speak.

'The place is booby-trapped.'

The doctor died without speaking again, watching the bird circle above him, his blood spreading into the soft soil. The two uninjured medics sat in the dirt looking at him, helpless, paralysed in fear and shock. Lying not more than 30m away was the body of the freedom fighter; his blood too had seeped into the soil, the war ravaged soil of Africa.

21

Wankie TTL, east of the Main Camp Airstrip, northern Matabeleland

Sergeant Mike Smith and his section arrived to a scene of utter confusion at the DC-4 crash site. As he arrived, he watched a Paradak drop a string of paratroops into a nearby field. The police had managed to secure the crash site, but the problem was that it needed to be cleared of mines. The nearest Engineers were on the *Cordon Sanitaire* near Mlibizi on the Zambezi. They had been called but had not yet arrived. A Major from sub-JOC at Wankie had flown in to take charge.

'You must be Sergeant Smith from 4 Indep' he said as Smith presented himself. 'We cannot go into the field. It looks like some Gooks got here before us and have booby-trapped the wreckage. They got a doctor and a medic … the bastards! We've managed to fly them out already.'

The Major looked over at the paratroops now on the ground in the neighbouring field. He saw Smith follow his gaze, 'They are A Company 1RAR, we managed to get them up from Bulawayo, poor sods were waiting to go on R&R.'

'What do you want me to do Sir?' Smith asked.

'I want you to cut for spoor around the perimeter of this field, let me know what you find.' He lifted his binoculars to his eyes, then continued, 'I can see what I think is a dead Gook out in the field. I have no idea how that happened, he could only have been killed by a passenger, but we cannot find any survivors.'

Smith spoke to his section and divided them into two groups. LCpl Nkai took one group to the left and Smith took the other to the right, working carefully on the ground looking for spoor. It took only a very short time.

'*Seg,*' Sibanda called, 'Gooks came this way,' pointing to the ground. Footprints were clearly visible in the ground leading away from the crash site to the west. The rest of the section spread out to take a look, a few comments were exchanged and a stick was used to circle each different footprint.

Smith turned to Dube his most reliable tracker, 'What do you think Dube?'

'There must be twenty or more, but there are women with them.'

'You mean they have girlfriends with them?' Smith asked. It was not uncommon for terrorist bands to take their women with them.

'*Hayi,* No *Ishe*, these are white women.' Dube never elaborated unless pressed.

'How can you tell Dube?' It was always like getting blood out of a stone talking to Dube.

'*Khangela*, look, *Ishe*,' said Dube, slowing his speech down so that his young sergeant could understand, '… you can see these shoes are small and the tread is from shoes too expensive for local women. I have never seen these shoes before.'

'How many are there Dube?'

'There are definitely two, but this one here is difficult, because it is not a terrorist shoe and it is not the same as these women. It could be a young boy.'

The enormity of what Dube had said now sunk in; *fuck these Gooks have kidnapped passengers.*

'The rest of you wait here. Dube and Sibanda come with me.'

Smith hurried back to where the JOC Major had set up a tent. He was talking on a TR48[140]. The A Company sticks had all arrived; a Lieutenant seemed to be in charge. Smith waited for the Major to finish.

'Sir, I think you better come and have a look at what we have found, we think the Gooks have taken hostages,' said Smith confidently, trusting the conclusions drawn by his men.

'Shit! … Sergeant, show me … Lieutenant Jones, you better come along with me,' the Major replied, gesturing to the RAR Lieutenant to follow.

The delegation walked rapidly to where 2 Platoon men were waiting. By this time, Moyo had found two tiny drops of blood in the sand that he marked with sticks. He had also found some drag marks where someone had been dragged for a short way.

The Major and the A Company Lieutenant looked on attentively as Dube explained what he saw on the ground. Dube, looking impressive with the machinegun belts wrapped around his shoulders, warmed to the task of explaining what he saw. The rest of the platoon all nodded their heads and murmured supportive agreement with every sentence, as Dube described the picture he saw on the ground.

'Are you sure that these are the prints of white women, Gunner?' the Major asked.

'They are not black women Ishe,' Dube replied, obtuse as always.

'Do you understand the consequence of what you are saying Gunner?' asked the Major earnestly.

Dube looked at the Major blankly, obviously not sure of the meaning of the word 'consequence'.

Smith jumped in, 'Dube the Major is asking if you are sure that these are white women because, if they are, we need to look for them.'

'*Yebo* yes, *Ishe*, I am sure,' replied Dube confidently, impressed by

140 HF radio, the big-means.

232

the amount of attention he was getting.

Everyone in the section nodded their agreement, reinforcing Dube's conclusions.

'How old is this spoor Gunner?' the Major continued.

'Five hours maybe six hours *Ishe*.'

'Ok, Sergeant Smith, you better get on follow-up immediately. We will support you by leap-frogging[141] with A Company. It looks like they are travelling west … but who knows. We have about three hours of light left, let's make the best of it.'

Leap-frogging is a system that works well if the CTs stayed on the same bearing. Unfortunately for them Benkov was way too smart for that.

Smith gathered his section together and explained what was happening. His section was down to seven men. Three more had returned from R&R with VD, needing treatment. As he prepared to move out the Major called across to him.

'Sergeant Smith, I have called for a troop of Grey Scouts to come down from the Falls to help with the follow-up. We will put them on the spoor as soon as we can. We need speed like never before.'

Sergeant Smith commenced yet another follow-up, his section strung out behind him, with Moyo on the spoor.

*

Further to the south, the survivors of the Chabanga Brigade from Lupane slowly made their way to the freedom fighter base camp near Dett. The three groups had progressed steadily, but of course not being under the control of Chabanga himself, the men were thinking of ways to make their trip a bit easier. They were tired and it was hot; they had seen a few busses passing on the main road that they were using as a guide for their trip to the north. They were travelling in the corridor between the north-south railway line and the main Wankie-Bulawayo road. The area was criss-crossed with minor dirt roads to the various villages and TTLs on the way.

The split into three groups that Chabanga had planned did not eventuate as; no sooner had he departed, than the other two groups re-converged. Safety in numbers was their plan. The leader of this band was a veteran of five years, part of the very earliest insurgencies. He knew the ropes, and he knew the area like the back of his hand. He decided that this walking business was unnecessary and that a short

---

141 The process of flying trackers ahead of follow-up teams to cut for spoor. This speeds up the follow-up as the follow-up teams leapfrog ahead of each other as the spoor is reacquired.

trip in a bus would speed things up considerably. They had done this successfully so many times before.

It was only a matter of time before a bus would come along. Sure enough, within a few hours, a cloud of dust could be seen approaching in the distance. The leader ordered two of his cadres to hail the bus as it approached. They stepped out in the road well in time for the bus driver to see them. The bus could be heard changing down as the driver slowed the bus, double de-clutching, brakes squealing and protesting loudly. The bus slowly came to a halt, then with a sigh, compressed air was released. Dust slowly dissipated. The driver for some reason stopped a good 50m short of where the men stood, the bus sat squarely in the middle of the road. The engine was still running with a loud gyrating idle. Luggage was loaded on the roof of the bus, a bicycle and a cage of chickens, part of a typical rural scene.

The two cadres sauntered down the road, their AKs at the ready, full of bravado and looking menacing.

'*Sawubona umgane*, Hello friend,' a cadre called out to the driver in siNdebele.

'*Ilanga elihle*, good day,' came the prompt reply.

The dust and glare on the windscreen made it difficult for the freedom fighter to see the driver from the front of the vehicle so he walked around to the door.

'*Kunjani ukuphila?* How are you?'

'*Sikona*, I am well,' the driver replied respectfully.

'*Ngiyajabula ukukubona*, I am very pleased to see you. We need a lift to Dett, can you help us Comrade?'

'How many are you?' the driver asked politely.

'We are twenty, have you room?' the freedom fighter stepped onto the first step, craning his neck trying to look inside. All he saw were a few surly faces looking out the windows.

'No problem jump on,' said the driver waving his hand encouragingly.

The freedom fighter called his comrades out of the bush shouting loudly; they all emerged together standing in line to board the bus, jabbering away excitedly. At this point the driver of the bus said he needed to check a rear tyre. Then pushing passed the waiting passengers, he walked around the back of the bus. The new passengers all waited patiently for their turn to climb on. Many had heavy unwieldy packs to manhandle aboard. They were laughing and joking with each other, *What Luck!*

The first few freedom fighters acknowledged the other passengers on the bus, who all sat towards the back looking bored and disinterested. The bus filled up from the front seats. As more climbed on it became necessary to move further back. The leader of the band decided that he wanted to sit towards the back. The AK gave him rights.

'Move out of the way you peasants,' he called out arrogantly in siNdebele, shuffling down the aisle, waving his AK menacingly at them to provide encouragement.

'*Ngilusizi*, Sorry, Comrade,' one of the passengers called out, sliding across the back seat as if intending to move.

The freedom fighter turned his head to call those behind him. In that split second, his head exploded struck by two dum-dum bullets. The headless body stood in the middle of the bus still holding its AK. Pieces of skull and brains sprayed the CTs sitting in front. The new passengers turned in disbelief, met with a stream of bullets.

The Selous Scouts leapt to their feet, spraying bullets from AKMs, the weapons bucking in their hands. Sgt Ngwenya shouted abuse at the CTs as he sprayed bullets left and right down the length of the bus. The windscreen disintegrated into a million pieces. The CTs on the bus died in seconds, their bodies rippled with bullets, blood and gore splattered the inside of the bus smearing the windows. Blood flowed down the aisle, forming rivulets, reaching the door, cascading down the stairs and pouring onto the dirt road. The driver who had waited behind the bus for the shooting to start killed the few CTs that had not yet boarded the bus; their bodies lay in the road. The bus continued to idle loudly, bodywork vibrating, a thick cloud of diesel smoke belching from the exhaust. The headless body standing in the middle of the bus toppled over.

The 'Selous Scout Express', *Free Trips to Hades*, had completed its inaugural journey.

Out towards the north the first thunderstorm of the season was building. A tall African thunderhead stretched high into the stratosphere, its base a thick black churning mass. A boom of thunder rolled across the bush, as if sending a warning for the pending onslaught. The dry, parched bush waited in anticipation, the birds ceased their chattering. The long wait for rain was nearly over.

*

Freedom Fighter Base Camp, north of Dett, northern Matabeleland

Comrade Tongerai Chabanga, pursuing his own follow-up of sorts, had reached the base camp near Dett. He was exhausted from the long walk. His mood was not improved by the news that Benkov had already been through the camp and had left with reinforcements. He had missed Benkov by only one day.

What was disturbing Chabanga was the amount of aircraft activity in the area. Chabanga had seen helicopters, fixed wing aircraft, even a Dakota[142] fly over, all in the same direction. This could only mean that the SF had some operation going on nearby. In the back of Chabanga's mind, he felt that it had to do with Benkov's activities.

What Chabanga had unwittingly walked into was one of the biggest manhunts yet set in motion in the war. The freedom fighter commander sat talking to the leader of the base camp about what SF activities had been going on in his area. The leader could not give any guidance on what Benkov had in mind other than the fact that he carried a strange looking RPG with him.

Chabanga knew that Benkov had Strela missiles; the Soviet had expressed his intention to use the weapon. He had agreed with Benkov that they should only be used against military targets but Chabanga did not trust Benkov one iota. *What has that Soviet psychopath done to stir up the Rhodesians?* The decision as to what to do next was difficult. Chabanga knew Benkov had to be close, but finding him would be like looking for a needle in a haystack.

*

South of Main Camp Airstrip, Wankie National Park, northern Matabeleland

Benkov had made his escape. The confusion caused by his AP mines at the crash site had slowed down the response to such an extent, that the follow-up was at least ten hours behind. Benkov had been careful to constantly change direction, anti-tracking, to make it difficult for the SF to figure out his intended route. He felt exhilarated. He had used the Strela successfully before in Angola, shooting down a Portuguese Fiat G91R. He loved using the weapon. He still had two projectiles left and he intended to use them at the next opportunity.

The three kidnapped women presented him with a range of opportunities. He could murder them brutally, after raping them of course, to maximise the 'terrorist' impact of bringing down the American charter flight. He could kill one and release the others to tell the tale. He could take them with him to Botswana as trophies of war. These were all compelling ideas.

The problem with releasing these women was that they recognised that he was a Soviet 'Advisor'. That was unfortunate … for them. The

142 Douglas DC3, military transport version C47, abridged to "Dak".

fact that the Soviets were supporting ZIPRA was well known, but Soviet Special Forces operating inside the country was another matter. He settled on his only safe and practical course of action ... rape and brutal murder. The important outcome of his mission was to polarise the opposing forces in this conflict to the greatest extent possible, to ensure that there was no prospect of a negotiated peace settlement. Benkov had absolutely no reservations whatsoever as to his course of action, *victory would be accomplished on the battlefield in time, as was inevitable. Horrific events happen in war, that is the very nature of war and civilian deaths are a natural consequence. These three women must pay the price.*

At his scheduled radio communication with Lusaka, Benkov confirmed his successful attack and the identity of his prisoners and then asked for instructions. He waited for the reply that arrived after a long delay. He was surprised at the tone of the message. His handlers in Lusaka were clearly upset that he had shot down the wrong aircraft, that the mission was a failure; the 'target' had escaped. He was given instructions to kill the hostages and to hide the bodies. Lusaka did not want any loose ends. These instructions were made very clearly. He was also told that it was time for him to exit the country. He was to be picked up at a point near Panda-ma-Tenga in Botswana in four days.

Benkov was agitated at the response he had got from Lusaka. The fact that the 'target' was not on the plane was not his fault. Lusaka had confirmed that the strike was on; they had given him the 'Go' message. He went back on the radio, outside of the scheduled communication window, asking that Ambassador Professor Solodovnikov be informed. The more he thought about it the more he blistered with indignation, *this was so typical of the useless staff officers sent from Moscow, no understanding of the sensational opportunity he had presented them, no understanding of the conditions on the ground, they were not Spetsnaz, and they could not improvise to take advantage of changing circumstances. These were Americans, our sworn enemy, supporting the oppressive Rhodesian regime.*

The three women sat huddled together. The airhostess, being older, had taken on a supportive role for the two young sisters. She spoke to them in a soft, gentle voice telling them to be strong, that they would be found by the security forces, *stay strong, it is only a matter of time.* Benkov sat under a tree not far away, disinterestedly looking across at his captives. His blonde beard had grown considerably, so much so that it was difficult to keep it blackened; his hair was also longer, pushing out from under his combat cap. The blonde stubble with streaks of black camo-cream, the dirty hair coupled with his ice blue eyes made him look all the more sinister. He was the stuff of vivid nightmares.

Benkov made up his mind. There was no way that he was going

to follow the ridiculous instructions from Lusaka. These women would die but they *would* be found. The World needed to know that Americans were in the country. The World also needed to know the level of brutality that ZIPRA was capable of. His briefing from Comrade Colonel Kononov had expressly stated that ZIPRA/ZAPU needed to completely alienate itself from the Rhodesian regime to prevent any chance of a peace settlement. The USSR needed to control Zimbabwe as a launch pad for the final assault on the riches of South Africa. That was the briefing that Colonel Kononov had given him … that was his mission!

As Benkov sat in the rapidly fading light, a thunderstorm rolled in. The first large raindrops struck the dry dirt with fierce velocity, throwing dust into the air. As the raindrops increased, a dust cloud was built up ahead of the storm. The trees began to shake as the hot wind ahead of the storm blew through, creating even more dust. Lightning cut the air, followed by bellowing thunder, so loud that it pounded in the chest. The ground seemed to shake in expectation. Finally the rain came, driving away the dust, refreshing the air. Waves of rain driven by the storm wind passed over. Benkov made no attempt to seek shelter. He sat under the small Acacia tree and allowed the rain to wash over him; he licked his lips as the cool, rejuvenating rainwater ran down his face.

Not very far away, surprisingly close, Sergeant Smith and his follow-up team watched the storm approach, stretching their plastic bivvys between trees, tying down the ropes as best as possible. The section sat under the plastic sheets, buffeted by the strong wind thrown up by the storm. The driving rain very quickly drenched everything; the bivvy[143] was no real protection. The wind ripped a few of the bivvies from the trees, blowing them away, never to be seen again, leaving their forlorn owners sitting in the open, crouched over their packs, hugging their rifles into their chests.

The follow-up was effectively over; the rain washed away the spoor. There was nothing else that could be done.

---

143 Short for bivouac, a plastic sheet used for creating a one-man shelter usually by being strung between trees, low to the ground, could be zipped together to create a larger shelter.

22

Wankie Police Camp

The 'Selous Scout Express' rolled back into the Wankie police camp. Blood from the dead CTs was still dripping out of the door as the bus came to a halt outside the Ops room. As the bus stopped, the door opened and the eight Selous Scouts climbed out. The bodies of the twenty or so dead CTs were piled up in the front few rows of seats. Some of the bodies sat rigidly in the seats, their dead faces pushed up against the windows in a macabre horror show, the Selous Scout sense of humour. The bodies were intertwined, *rigor-mortis* freezing them into distorted positions.

The bus was covered in bullet holes, there was no windscreen and the original green paint was almost totally covered in dried, congealed blood. The police crowded around the bus shaking their heads in amazement. The eight Selous Scouts went inside to be debriefed by the local SB Member-in-Charge. This had been a success beyond all expectations. The debriefing was dispensed with quickly. The position that the CTs were picked up was marked on the operations map on the wall. The Scouts were then briefed on the airline disaster, the fact that CTs had kidnapped three female passengers and then disappeared off the face of the earth. The suspicion was that this was the same band that had hit the heavy vehicle convoy and Kosami Mission. The Botswana border was being 'dragged' by trackers but thus far, no crossings into Botswana had been detected. *The Gooks were still in the country.*

It was decided that if this band was in any way related to the other atrocities, then they were quite likely to catch a bus out of the area if they could. Plain-clothes policemen were already travelling on the busses throughout the region, but nothing had turned up.

The next morning, equipped with a replacement bus, this time white with a red racing stripe down the side, the Selous Scouts drove back out of Wankie to the south, looking for more 'passengers' on the road to nowhere.

*

Wankie TTL, northern Matabeleland

The organisation of the response to the airline disaster took a very long time. The investigators were struggling to decide on whether the aircraft had, in fact, been shot down, or whether the old plane had just had a mechanical problem and crashed. The wing impacted by the missile had been burnt by the exploding fuel plus the effect of the grass fire was making things doubly difficult. The DC-4 was on a charter; therefore, the passenger manifest was not as complete as it should have been. It took two full days before the investigators figured out the identities of the two passengers and one crewmember that were missing. The mutilated, bullet-riddled bodies were impossible to identify positively, but the police forensic team were certain that the women were not amongst the bodies. The DC-4 Captain's .38 was recovered, two rounds discharged, but the dead CT had been shot in the back of the head, executed from point blank range, some distance from the wreckage.

The initial conclusion was that the CTs that had attacked the passengers were just opportunists. Strelas had been used against low-flying aircraft before, mainly during external raids but had not been used in the country. There was no conclusive evidence in those critical first hours that the aircraft had been shot down. The fact that the CTs had taken hostages with them, coupled with the fact that they were female, was what got everybody's attention.

The plane had crashed in a densely populated TTL. To the west was the northern section of the Wankie National Park. This was a desolate area with very few roads, where water was scarce, plus there were natural dangers presented by the wild animals themselves. Beyond the national park to the west was the Botswana border. Very few CTs traversed the national park mainly because of the lack of food and water. It was a natural barrier of sorts. The deduction made by the Army commanders was that, while the CTs had moved off to the east, they could be moving either north or south as well. Nobody figured that the CTs would swing around to the west and head for the Botswana border through the national park.

A massive sweep operation began to the east of the crash site from the point that the spoor had been lost. Village after village was searched. The police Ground Coverage and SB teams called on all their informers. Rewards for information were offered. More troops were brought in. Two territorial companies of 9th Battalion RR coupled with two platoons from 4 Indep and the platoon from A Company 1RAR were used to conduct the sweeps. The SF search activity moved further and further out in an increasing arc. The sweeping teams had a few fleeting contacts with CTs they disturbed as they pushed the arc further out, but no helpful information was gained. The CTs that had kidnapped the passengers had disappeared.

News of the intense SF activity reached Chabanga and his small band, hiding near the freedom fighter base camp near Dett, just north of the national park. As the crow flies, Chabanga was only about 30kms from the crash site to the northeast. The news that an airliner had gone down convinced Chabanga that it could only have been Benkov and his band. He knew that it was likely that the SF would sweep through this area eventually, so he made a plan to hide in the national park for a week. He and his group gathered food and water and left.

The contrast between the bush in the national park and the TTL could not have been starker. The TTL was over-grazed, with cleared fields and most of the trees chopped down, leaving the soil exposed to erosion. By contrast, even in the dry season the national park had thick grass, in some places over six feet high with dense tree cover, providing impenetrable protection.

*

Vladimir Benkov had considered all his options. After the rain had eliminated any chance of his tracks being followed, he decided that his best option was to find a bus to take him to the border. The only place that a bus could be found would be in the TTL, so he looped around once again to the north, staying in the populated TTL area to help hide his movement. There was a road directly from Wankie to Panda-ma-Tenga but that would likely be heavily patrolled. He had studied his maps and satellite photographs deciding that the best alternative was to commandeer a bus and then follow the many game viewing roads in the national park that would, by various routes, take him close enough to the border.

He was elated at the prospect of returning to civilisation. His sense of theatre meant that he wanted to make as much of the deaths of the women as possible. He had also been very successful at avoiding the Rhodesians, effectively doing everything he was required to do, largely unheeded. His confidence was restored.

Benkov knew that he needed to keep moving to avoid detection, but heavily wooded deep ravines cut the terrain he had chosen, which made the going slow and hard. He tried to use the course of the Gwai River as it flowed in a northerly direction but it was not always possible because a number of SF patrols were sweeping through the riverbed.

*

Main tar road (A8) between Bulawayo and Wankie

A passenger vehicle convoy from Bulawayo wound its way towards

Wankie. The convoy was made up of about thirty vehicles, small for that time of year. There were only two escort vehicles, one in front and one at the back. The convoy was travelling at a speed of 110km/hr, although some of the older vehicles did slow a little on the hills. The convoy commander in the front vehicle sat with his FN sticking out the window, chatting to the driver. He picked up the radio periodically to speak to the other escort vehicle to check that all was well, that there weren't any stragglers.

The convoy approached a hill after a long straight stretch. The driver changed down to maintain the revs up the hill. As they breasted the top of the hill, the driver of the lead vehicle pointed out a white woman standing on the side of the road, under a shady tree. She seemed to be standing all alone, looking straight across the road. There were no farms or settlements at all nearby. The convoy commander looked at where he had pointed but they were travelling too fast for him to see. *What is she doing out here? Did she wave at us?* He picked up the radio and asked the rear escort vehicle, about a kilometre behind, to investigate. The convoy raced past; many of the civilians in the convoy also saw the woman, not sure what to think. The rear escort vehicle saw her immediately. She was standing well off the road, standing very still.

The police escort pulled off the road onto the shoulder the driver called out, 'Hello, are you ok ….can we help?'

There was no response. The middle aged police reservist got out of the vehicle, calling again, louder this time, 'Have you broken down? Can we help you?'

Still no response, *bloody strange*! He screwed up his eyes shielding them with his hand, trying to see through the glare, the shade under the tree made it difficult to make out any detail.

'You better wait here. Keep a sharp look out. There is something wrong here,' he said to the driver.

'Bill,' he called the gunner on the .303 machinegun in the turret, '… keep me covered with the gun will you". He lifted his FN and walked carefully across the road towards where the woman was standing. As he approached he could see that she wasn't moving, her eyes were closed, she seemed to be asleep.

'Hello,' he called again, increasingly alarmed, her could see her clothes were torn and she was barefoot.

As he edged closer he saw that half her head was missing. She had been tied to the tree facing the road, her brains spattered over the tree behind her. Her long brown hair, sticky with blood, stuck to her face as if she had been caught in a thunderstorm. A neat bullet hole was in the middle of her forehead, a thin trickle of blood oozed from the wound, running down her face dripping off the edge of her chin. The police reservist stood in shock trying to comprehend what he saw in front of him. Then the full realisation struck him.

'Jesus Christ!' he screamed, then turned, dropped to his knees and threw up, coughing and gasping for air. He did not, at that moment, see further into the bush. There was another women tied to a tree, next to her another. They too had been executed. The distraught policeman also did not notice the hand-written note stuck in the pocket of the woman's blouse.

*

Sub-JOC Wankie

To say that the shit had hit the fan was an understatement. The 1 Brigade Commander arrived in Wankie from Bulawayo, immediately letting fly at the Major in command of the sub-JOC, Major Peacock and the TF[144] Lt-Colonel in command of 9th Bat.

'What the fuck are you people doing up here? These Gooks are running rings around you. This is … this is complete bullshit.' He ranted and raved, pacing up and down the cramped Ops room near the Wankie airstrip.

'You people are so busy getting pissed and trying to fuck holidaymakers that you can't do your jobs anymore.' The Brigadier was known for his histrionics.

The political impact of the atrocities in the Operation Tangent area was intense. Questions were being asked in high places.

'I want the area around the crash site searched again. I want roadblocks on every road. I want the area where those women were found combed, look under every rock, search every hut,' the Brigadier bawled. 'I have COMOPS asking me what the fuck is happening in Tangent. I have a bunch of clowns, that's what I've got.' He finished with a rush, 'If you people don't get some results soon, you can fucking go back to Llewellyn[145] and run a fucking training company.'

The bollocking given by the Brigadier very quickly filtered down to the various platoon and section commanders in the field. There was a real sense of desperation. Poor 2nd Lt Gibbs, arriving back from R&R, had no chance of returning to his platoon. Major Peacock latched on to him to help with staff operations and planning. Captain Fullerton had left Vic Falls for the crash site immediately the follow-up began. He was never going to be too far from the action and certainly wasn't

---

144 Territorial Forces, part-time soldiers.
145 Llewellyn Barracks, Depot Rhodesia Regiment, main training base for national servicemen, located northwest of Bulawayo.

available for admin and logistics.

Sergeant Smith and his seriously undermanned section were the closest c/sign to the place where the three woman abductees had been executed. He had received a very garbled incoherent instruction from the sub-JOC via a signals radio relay on top of Kapami Hill, a high point north of the crash site. Smith managed to cover the 8kms in a few hours of hard marching through very rough terrain. He arrived at the site of the murders to find Ingwe Fullerton already there with the balance of 2nd Lt Gibb's section, only six men, a signaller and a medic from 4 Indep. The place was crawling with police who had set up a base with tents and an Ops room. The area around where the bodies had been found had been cordoned off with tape. The bodies had already been removed.

As Smith stood catching his breath after the forced march, 3 Troop Grey Scouts arrived from Vic Falls, all thirty-five of them. Both O'Connell and Lt Dawson were with the Troop, they spent no time in unloading the horses in preparation for the follow-up. There was a sense amongst the men of the harsh reality that faced them; they were up against one of the most ruthless depraved gangs of insurgents that had ever infiltrated the country.

There was an air of nervous tension among the Grey Scouts that Smith had not seen before, everyone going about their business in silent contemplation. There was none of the usual banter when Smith met up with O'Connell. All O'Connell said was, 'This is a fucking disgrace. I am going to rip these Gooks' balls off with my bare hands.' Smith could not remember seeing O'Connell so visibly upset.

Captain Fullerton emerged from the police Ops tent.

'Sergeant Smith you took your bloody time getting here!' he complained in his mocking fashion that Smith was now used to. 'I see your platoon is virtually down to section strength ... not to worry, we will manage.'

'Sir, we have been out for two days on follow-up. I need to get a resupply?' asked Smith in the hope that he might crack a night in Wankie.

'Sorry old fruit but we have more important things to do. We have found the spoor of the savages that killed these women, and we need to get onto it right away,' replied Fullerton, totally focussed on the matter at hand.

They all sat down under a tree and Fullerton explained how he thought the follow-up should be managed. It was agreed that Dawson and his Grey Scouts would get onto the spoor while Smith and Fullerton would follow as closely as possible in vehicles depending on the route the CTs followed. The vehicles would carry provisions and radios and most importantly, would help to cut for spoor on the hundreds of roads and tracks criss-crossing the area.

The horses stood in line, their saddles in place, heavy packs secured in position. Sheila was her normal cantankerous self, attempting to take a bite out of a policeman who ventured too close. She lifted her head when the briefing had finished, letting out a loud grunt as if to say, *come on people, let's get on with this*!

Dube called to Sheila as the troop rode past, 'Go find us *Makandangas*, to kill *Murwisi.*'

She turned her head to look at him, her large brown eyes blinked as if to wink, *don't you worry about that son*!

The general consensus of opinion was that they were following twenty plus CTs; at least the odds were even.

23

Wankie TTL

Benkov knew that the execution of the women would stir up a hornet's nest – that was the whole purpose. He had seen a number of aircraft pass over near his position, clearly part of a search pattern. Tempted to try and shoot one of them down with one of his remaining Strela missiles, he concluded that would be pushing his luck. As it was, he figured he had about eight or nine hours start on the SF follow-up team. What he had not come across as yet was a Grey Scout follow-up that was close to twice as fast as men on foot. In reality the gap was only four hours.

The execution of the women had been his crowning achievement for this deployment. Nothing had been as savage and depraved. *The lengths that ZIPRA would go to for total victory were now clear for all to see. This was total, uncompromising intimidation of the Rhodesian regime and their supporters. Terrorism's aim is to break the will of the civilian population!*

The air hostess had been defiant to the end. She did not show any fear. She did her best to comfort the two young sisters who were both haemorrhaging badly from the repeated rape. The air hostess did have spirit. She stared at Benkov throughout her ordeal, never taking her eyes off him for a second, as if challenging him, the hate in her eyes, her disgust abundantly clear. The older woman had eventually lost her attraction to the cadres because she looked so horrible after the violent beating Mlungisi had given her. Her face was bruised with her hair matted with dried blood after Mlungisi had cracked her on the head with his rifle. The wound bled profusely. Benkov was convinced that her skull was fractured because she remained unconscious for a fair while after the assault. When she finally regained consciousness she wobbled on her feet, vomiting, eventually dry retching, her chest heaving violently and uncontrollably. She seemed to be hallucinating, talked to herself incessantly, her mind lost. In a strange, inexplicable way, Benkov found himself regretting that she had to die.

The two sisters, on the other hand, provided great sport for the cadres, who played with them as a cat would a captured mouse, tormenting them. The cadres watched the two girls beg and plead for mercy in perverse fascination, intrigued by their antics. The injuries to the girls were eventually so severe that they could not be raped any more either. Benkov was convinced that they were about to die from loss of blood. By the time it came to tying the women to the trees for their execution the airhostess had completely lost he mind. She mumbled, shivering, spittle running down her chin. She clearly did not have any idea of what was happening; her mind had long since left her. The bullet in the head was a small mercy. The two sisters, while more lucid, were very weak and had to be carried to their death.

Benkov got Mlungisi to write a note addressed to the American government warning them not to support the Rhodesian regime, to stay out of the fight. He made sure that Mlungisi claimed responsibility for the deaths on behalf of ZIPRA.

They now continued on their northerly course through the TTL knowing that it was only a matter of time before a bus would be found. He was careful to double back on his tracks from time to time, to try to slow and confuse the follow-up. They removed their boots to walk barefoot through riverbeds and watercourses. Often when approaching a village they would bombshell on bare feet to meet up again on the far side. He looked to the sky hoping for rain. It was clear, not a cloud in the sky.

On the first night after the execution Benkov took Mlungisi and worked back along the route that they had taken to look for the follow-up team. He was shocked to find the Grey Scouts so close. He was equally shocked to find his pursuers on horseback. He was forced to make an alteration to his plan.

*

Lt Dawson and his troop were happy with their progress. They kept going until the light faded completely. The horses were corralled and the troop went into all-round defence for the night. The men were exhausted from being in the saddle all day; the horses were also feeling the strain. Fortunately a small stream nearby, swelled by the recent rain, provided water for the horses. Even Sheila didn't complain about being tied up in the horse-lines.

Captain Fullerton and 2 Platoon were not far off. They were following an old mining track running along the banks of the Gwai River. The track was marked on the map but it was completely overgrown, cut by deep gullies that were difficult for the trucks to negotiate. The going was slow but they were still in reasonable proximity to the follow-up team.

The Grey Scouts were up before first light the next morning and were on the spoor as soon as the ground became visible in front of them. There was no talk or chatter, each man aware that if they did well they would likely catch the CTs that day. Each man was alone with his own thoughts.

Lt Dawson called Fullerton on the radio to tell him they were moving out and to confirm the direction. He estimated that the spoor was now a good twelve hours old, but much depended on whether the CTs had walked through the night. Fullerton in turn called sub-JOC on the 'big-means' to bring them up to speed. A 9th Battalion platoon was up ahead of the follow-up trying to cut for spoor across the compass bearing reported by Dawson. The territorial trackers were rusty and out of practice, missing the point at which Benkov had crossed the road they were patrolling along. His band was barefoot and anti-tracking constantly.

Benkov watched the 9th Bat platoon pass by in two files, on each side of the road. He held his breath as the soldiers passed his crossing point. When he had established that they had missed him, Benkov turned and moved his men off at a fast pace. They were fit and strong and could maintain a good steady rhythm. They knew that the SF were behind them that added impetus to their already rapid progress.

Lt Dawson drove the troop hard all day. He had only allowed two short breaks, but the men were not complaining. The tension in the ranks was tangible. The follow-up had crossed the spoor-cut attempted by the 9th Bat platoon; their Colonel could be heard giving his men 'what for' on the radio for missing the crossing point.

The Grey Scout trackers called 'three hours' on the spoor. Dawson looked up ahead at the thick bush. He glanced down at his map which showed that they had entered a steep sided river valley that ran for about 10kms roughly north from their position before opening up again into a cluster of farmed fields and villages. The terrain was too broken for farming, so the bush was thicker, with fewer tracks in evidence. A heavily used footpath ran along the bottom of the valley. This was the route used by the local villagers north and south of the hilly, broken ground. The CTs had used the same path, not making any attempt to hide their spoor. The valley gradually narrowed forcing the horsemen into single file. Dawson rode behind the two trackers while O'Connell had taken up position at the rear of the line.

Dawson had called Fullerton on the radio at the entrance to the valley to confirm that they would not be able to follow in the vehicles but that it would be a good idea to try and get around to the head of the valley to the north, where the ground flattened out again. The Colonel from 9th Bat could be heard sending another platoon on a leapfrog north of the valley. Fresh out of civy-street on a six-week call-up, they were not as operationally fit as they could be. They would be complaining bitterly.

The troop of Grey Scouts wound its way through the narrow valley. The streambed trickled with rain run-off. There were a few deep pools formed in the rocky bottom. The footpath ran along the edge of the steam, well worn from years of use. On the edge of the path the bush was over-grown with tall trees that had miraculously survived the local demand for firewood and building timber. The path meandered, following the streambed, making it difficult to get a good view forward despite being on horseback.

The trackers continued moving fast as the spoor was obvious. If the path had been wider and flatter they could have galloped, not that Grey Scouts ever galloped for fear of losing equipment. A large boulder obstructed the path ahead. It had likely been dislodged from the hillside by some historic thunderstorm. The grass had grown high around its base while the surrounding thorn bush closed in, making it difficult for the trackers to squeeze past. They lifted the thorn thicket away from their faces as they ducked below their horse's heads for protection. The delay caused by the rock obstruction meant the troopers behind started to concertina up closer to each other. The first tracker moved around the rock cursing the thorns digging into his hands. He turned to call the man behind him to watch out as he let the thorny branch go. His horse's front leg tripped a thin wire attached to a POMZ AP mine.

The POMZ, angled up with the rock in support behind it, exploded with a loud smoky thud that reverberated against the steep valley sides. The full force of the blast struck the horse's belly and the rider's right leg in the stirrups. The horse squealed in fright, the force of the grenade from point-blank range ripping open its guts that issued out, as if poured from a bucket onto the path. The horse lost its footing, falling in a terrified panic, its legs kicking out wildly with the natural instinct to regain its feet, throwing its head violently from side to side. The rider was trapped under the horse, his left leg snapped.

The valley walls above erupted in a hail of bullets. RPG-7s were released to hurl their death into the packed horses on the path below. Lt Dawson looked up to see a Soviet stick grenade cartwheeling down above his head, detonating against the rock in front of him, filling his face and chest with deadly splinters. He died instantly in the saddle, most of the top of his skull sliced off to strike the trooper immediately behind him. Dawson's horse, struck by a bullet, spun on her hind legs. She was hit by another and then another. Falling onto her haunches, she collapsed, throwing Dawson's body clear.

The valley was too narrow for escape. The troopers tried to turn around, some urging their horses into the rocky streambed. Unable to find firm footing, the horses fell. The bullets punched through the air from above; a chattering RPD started to find its mark. Horses reared up as the bullets struck their flanks, burning into their flesh. Some of the troopers managed to dismount, running for cover in the valley, trying to shoot up at their attackers.

Colour O'Connell at the rear of the file of horses, kicked Sheila into a gallop, breaking through the horses in front of him, called for the men to dismount, 'Ambush Right … Ambush Right' he yelled. In front of him, riderless horses, most covered in blood from numerous wounds, milled about, whinnying for release from their agony. Sheila showed no fear. She charged, her head held out, shrieking. She jumped a horse lying dead in the path, landing on the other side in perfect balance to race forward. A few of the troopers had managed to get across the stream onto the other side and were blasting away up the hill. A man lay wounded, using his dead horse as cover, firing up at the valley side.

O'Connell, seeing Dawson's body on the side of the path next to his horse, hauled on the reins to bring Sheila to a stop. The bullets cracked above his head, ricocheting off the rocks, whistling in all directions. Sheila reared up as a bullet struck her in the neck. O'Connell could see the blood spurt out but she did not falter, jumping another horse lying on the path. As he approached the rock obstructing the path, O'Connell leapt for the ground rolling under the weight of his pack. He tried to run for the cover of the rock ahead of him but a bullet struck him in the thigh, the impact spinning him off his feet. Bullet strikes appeared in the dirt path ahead of him. He tried to pull himself along with his arms, his leg now a dead weight. The air was knocked out of his lungs as his chest was thumped hard into the ground from the impact of a bullet strike on his pack. Winded, he looked up to see Sheila, her head bent down, gazing at him, her large brown eyes asking - *Are you ok son*? O'Connell tried to call out to her. His lungs were empty, sucking for air.

O'Connell, his chest heaving, crawled along the path desperately seeking the protection of the rock. Still trying to call out, he was making short, laboured sucking sounds as his lungs tried to fill with air. Sheila stayed next to him resolutely throwing her head, as if trying to chase a fly. Another round hit her, the impact forcing her over onto her side. The firing from above stopped as quickly as it started.

The CTs broke off the action and began their escape. Troopers tried to scale the sides of the valley, firing upwards in hopeless desperation but it was way too steep, and rugged.

*

No radio call was necessary; Smith, Fullerton and the rest of 2 Platoon heard the contact clearly in the distance, the thump of exploding grenades and RPGs, the staccato of RPD machineguns. Fullerton yelled at the truck drivers to turn off the road in the direction of the contact.

He could tell on the map roughly where it was. He urged them on. Fullerton tried to raise the Grey Scouts on the radio.

'25Alpha, 25Alpha … this is 44 do you read, Over.'

He knew in his gut that the silence from Dawson and the Grey Scouts was bad news.

'25Alpha … 25Alpha,' he called again and again, only the hissing static came in reply.

Grabbing at the handpiece for the 'big-means' to call sub-JOC, Fullerton called in the contact, gave his own position and the estimated position of 25Alpha. The 4 Indep trucks raced forward, demolishing wood fences and kraals, dodging huts and the few local villagers that were about. The ground was reasonably flat and open from years of cultivation. Ditches needed to be ramped, fences pushed over as Fullerton urged the drivers forward. Eventually the ground became too broken forcing Fullerton to call a halt, the head of the valley lay ahead. Urging the men off the truck, Fullerton sprinted down the path, calling behind him for the platoon to follow.

'Run people …run,' he shouted. Smith had never heard such urgency in *Ingwe* Fullerton's voice before. Smith was struck by a feeling of panic, *what are we going to find up ahead*? He felt true, unadulterated fear.

As they ran along the path dodging obstructions, the first helicopter appeared overhead, flying down the valley. Then another appeared, the sounds of its turbine echoing off the valley sides. The pilots pulled into a tight orbit.

'44 this is Red 1 … we have the contact site visual … two clicks to your south,' came the call from the lead pilot, resounding in Smith's ear. The pilot hesitated, the scene below him was too horrific to imagine. Dead horses lay sprawled along the path; men were waving up at the helicopters some still using their horses as cover.

'We cannot drop our stops there is no place for a Lima Zulu,' called the pilot.

The pilot could be heard calling the sub-JOC, '21 this is Red 1, we see multiple casualties, send Eagles ... Over.' Eagles were the c/signs for four stops in the D Company 1RAR Fireforce in the Paradak, just lifting off from Wankie.

'44, Red 1, we will drop our stops to the south of the contact,' the pilot called to Fullerton.

Up ahead the helicopters were clearly visible now. Fullerton made no attempt to reply. He ran on in silence, the platoon now strung out along the bush path, the gunners starting to fade under the weight of the MAGs and ammunition.

Smith reached the front of the file just behind Fullerton as they saw the first casualty. A horse stood on the path ahead, one of its back legs lifted off the ground, a jagged wound in its rump. The horse watched the soldiers approach, whinnying softly. Behind the wounded horse, the tracker still lay trapped by his dead horse but he was still alive. As Fullerton and Smith pushed around the rock obstructing the path, the sight that met them was appalling. Immediately in front of them was the body of Lt Dawson lying next to his dead horse, both of their bodies covered in blood, still oozing out onto the ground.

Just ahead, Colour O'Connell sat holding Sheila's head cradled in his arms.

O'Connell looked up as the two soldiers approached, 'She's dead,' he said simply. His eyes were clouded with tears. He gently laid her head down on the ground; his wounded leg pushed straight out in front him.

O'Connell leaned over and stroked the horses' neck, 'Goodbye old girl … you were a good Mate … the best Mate any man could have.'

He looked up at Smith and Fullerton, 'She saved my life today, *fair dinkum* she did …' his eyes rolled, he fell backwards, passed out from loss of blood.

> *Hope you are quite prepared to die.*
> *Looks like we're in for nasty weather.*
> *One eye is taken for an eye.*
>
> *Don't go around tonight,*
> *Well, it's bound to take your life,*
> *There's a bad moon on the rise.*

*

Still in stunned shock, Smith looked up to see the Paradak starting to drop the paratroopers to the south. All too late, they were all too late. He turned to see Fullerton sitting on his haunches, looking at their dead friend. Fullerton stretched out to close Dawson's dead, staring eyes, then covered his face with his bush hat.

Fullerton looked up, 'What are you looking at Sergeant Smith? Get a drip into Colour O'Connell. We've got plenty of work to do here.'

The rest of the platoon had now gathered next to the rock, horrified by the death and destruction they saw in front of them. Smith was struggling to get a vein to put the drip into O'Connell. The loss of blood had caused his blood pressure to drop and the arteries were beginning to collapse. Dube and Moyo came and sat next to him. Without being asked Dube took the tourniquet and tightened it, trying to force a vein up. Both the black soldiers looked across at Sheila lying dead in the path.

'*Umgane lisale kuhle*, goodbye friend,' said Dube, in a deep soft voice.

Moyo gently stroked her head. '*UMurwisi hambe kuhle*, Go well *Murwisi*,' he whispered.

Fullerton, instantly back in control, started barking orders at the rest of the Platoon. They moved off to help the stricken Grey Scouts.

*

'We are going to kill these fuckers, Sergeant Smith, if it's the last thing I do on this Earth.'

Ingwe Fullerton had re-gathered himself as they stood on top of the ridge above the deep valley floor. The dead horses could still be seen lying on the path below, there was no chance of them being carried out, so they were to be burnt where they lay. A shuttle of helicopters had casevaced the eight wounded Grey Scouts after an agonising trip by stretcher to the LZ some distance off.

O'Connell had regained consciousness.

'I'm all right. It is just a scratch, … I must get back to my troop.' He complained bitterly that he was able to continue. In reality he was delirious, pupils dilated, his body shivered in shock.

Smith, plunging morphine into him, said, 'Shut up, you stupid Ozzie bastard, you have lost too much blood … you are on your way back to civvy-street for a while.'

The bodies of the three dead Grey Scouts, including Lt Dawson had also been evacuated. Members of Smith's Platoon had taken turns to carry the stretchers. The black soldiers showed the reverence for the dead that was their custom, especially as these men had died as warriors in battle.

Collecting what they could of their kit, the survivors of the shattered Grey Scout troop rounded up the horses to walk out to the road where their vehicles and horseboxes waited. Many of the horses were wounded, a few had to be destroyed. Isolated shots rang out as the troopers put the distressed animals out of their misery. The trauma of the ordeal was so great that the troopers went about their business in complete silence, their eyes empty, faces pale, most trying to settle the injured horses down, *that is what Colour O'Connell would be doing*. The horses stood silently in line, when it was time to move out many limped painfully but not complaining. The troopers talked gently to the horses, stroking their necks, urging them on.

The RAR Fireforce that had been dropped in swept over the surrounding hills. On the top of the ridge the firing positions used by the CTs was clear. Expended cartridges littered the ground. They had used plenty of ammunition.

Fullerton turned to Smith and the waiting platoon, 'These are not ordinary Gooks. I have never seen an ambush like this, the use of the POMZ AP to initiate. This is very bloody strange. This was well planned; they would have known the Grey Scouts were following them.'

It was rare for CTs to initiate an ambush, particularly when outnumbered by a well equipped and organised force. The fact that the ambush was in broad daylight was another indication that this was no ordinary group of communist insurgents. The normal CT tactic was to bombshell; lose the follow-up group, then RV at some point later on. Standing to initiate a fight against security forces was generally not a CT tactic.

'They have left … travelling north. The bastards must have seen us drive right past in the trucks.' Fullerton looked out to the north, his mind momentarily lost in thought. 'We will get onto follow-up, now! It will be dark in two hours,' he said, looking up at the sky.

They discussed their plan and the organisation of the follow-up. In minutes Smith was back in his familiar position at the rear, on another Fullerton follow-up campaign. The difference this time was that there was a steely resolve that Smith had not seen before. The feeling of urgency that Fullerton engendered had been picked up by the rest of the platoon and they were all determined and expectant. The carnage below, the deaths of the Grey Scouts, and the loss of *Murwisi* had affected them all greatly. They too wanted blood.

Smith's emotions were in turmoil. Robert Dawson's death was horrendous. Seeing him lying in the dirt covered in blood seemed surreal, his mind could not comprehend the reality. He had known him so well. They were friends … Now he was dead. Dawson's life snapped off like a twig. The most disturbing of all was the realisation that nobody was safe. They were up against a well-organised and ruthless enemy, these were not a bunch of half-baked tribesman with guns. The propaganda about winning the war seemed hollow and empty. *These people ambushed a whole troop of Grey Scouts in broad daylight, how many more groups like this are there out there?*

The imperative of going out on follow-up immediately was a blessing. Smith felt he needed to concentrate on getting his platoon through the next few days. *Focus on the living.* The time for contemplation would come later. He felt a consuming hate emerging in his chest, hate that felt like a throbbing pain, as if his heart had changed its beat. He had never had such a feeling before. Up to this time the war, the killing of terrorists, had been impersonal, distant. It was as if he had been on the outside looking in, as if gazing through binoculars slightly out of focus, blurred and indistinct. Most of his time had been spent thinking of getting out of the army, of university, more recently of Jane. Smith had felt the deaths of Charlie Williams and Sipho Fauguneze with a profound abiding sadness, a feeling of inadequacy. His emotions were now inexplicably and instantly clear, as if a veil had been lifted from his eyes. This was now deeply personal. He wanted to get into a position to do something about it. He found himself wanting to hurt these people. He wanted to hurt them badly. He wanted to kill them.

As Smith followed Fullerton and his platoon off the side of the kopie, Whitebacked Vultures, *iNqe*, powered by some ancient uncanny instinct, were already circling over the death in the valley below.

*

Benkov had indeed seen the 4 Indep trucks racing to the scene of the contact, and he realised that he had cut the ambush really fine. He also realised that there were a lot more SF chasing him than he thought. The ambush had been textbook perfect. The killing ground had been ideal, made flawless by the fact that the target was on horseback in a confined space. Benkov was certain that he had killed the follow-up commander as he had watched the grenade explode right above the man's head, so obvious with the radio aerial sticking out the top of his pack. The elevation above the killing ground, shooting downwards, had made it almost impossible for the enemy to return fire, much less counter-attack.

As Benkov made his escape, he watched helicopters approach from the west, then a short time later a Dakota. He urged his cadres on; they had another full night's walk ahead of them. They had not had much sleep over the past three days, but that could not be helped. Sleep now would lead to certain death, they all knew it. He didn't need to provide any further motivation.

A bus or rain or both was what Benkov needed and soon. The problem was that he didn't have time to sit on the side of the road to wait for a bus to come along. He looked up at the sky expectantly, not a cloud in sight. He knew he had to keep moving. Deciding that his best chance was to circle back to the base camp near Dett, he and his men set off on a full night and day of forced march. If he could make the base camp, he should be able to rest before the final push to get out of the country. The camp provided the protection with its network of *mujibas* as an early warning system. He turned his band of freedom fighters from a northerly to a westerly course.

*

Comrade Tongerai Chabanga was emerging from his hiding place in the Wankie National Park, chased out by mosquitoes and Mopani flies. The Mopani flies were by far the worst, tiny midges that hover about the head in clouds, seeking moisture from sweaty bodies. They seemed to favour the eyes, sometimes sticking under the eyelid, creating a fearsome irritation. Swatting them away or killing them by wiping with the hand just seemed to attract more of them. There was no relief. At night the mosquitoes took over from where the Mopani flies left off. The TTL, virtually devoid of thick vegetation and standing water, could not sustain these insects in large numbers, but the national park with the pristine environment and numerous manmade waterholes was alive with biting and itching insects that attacked day and night. The insects were driving the men to distraction, and his cadres were ready to revolt. Chabanga had decided that the comfort and protection of the base camp was a good idea.

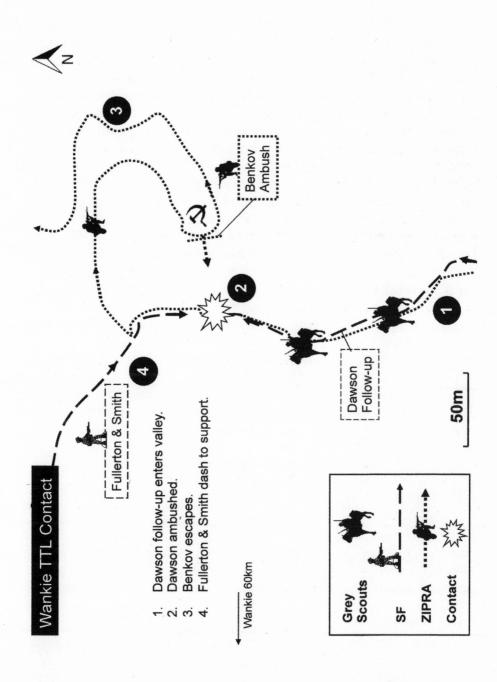

N

③

Benkov
Ambush

②

①

Dawson
Follow-up

50m

④

Fullerton & Smith

Wankie TTL Contact

1. Dawson follow-up enters valley.
2. Dawson ambushed.
3. Benkov escapes.
4. Fullerton & Smith dash to support.

Wankie 60km

Grey
Scouts

SF

ZIPRA

Contact

24

Wankie TTL

Captain Vladimir Benkov pushed his men hard through the night. The early morning light saw them standing on a road intersection with the main Bulawayo road. Their destination was tantalisingly close, only a day's walk away. Benkov signalled his men back into the bush to have a rest before they would start again. He sipped water from his metal canteen, savouring every drop. They were now desperately short of water. Some of the men showed signs of dehydration. Benkov had avoided stopping in the villages for water because he was worried about SF looking for him. The place was crawling with police informers. The day ahead in 38° heat was not a happy prospect.

They had no sooner sat down than the sound of a bus could be heard, crashing through its gears somewhere up the dirt road behind them. Mlungisi called to Benkov excitedly to allow him to stop the bus. Benkov thought for a few seconds deciding that this was an opportunity that needed to be taken. He could now drive all the way to the Botswana border.

Calling for his band to split into two groups, Benkov placed one group in ambush along the road, the other to stop the bus. He did not want to be surprised by another vehicle bumbling into his hijacking. The freedom fighters were suddenly animated. They called out to each other excitedly; the relief of being able to find a means of escape was intense. This was finally the break they had been waiting for. Laughing at their good luck the cadres enthusiastically took up their positions. Benkov moved off further into the bush. He did not want to take any chances. Mlungisi, with his RPD on his shoulder, came across to wait with him. The young cadres knew the drill for hijacking busses. Benkov still carried the Strela missile launcher himself while another man carried the two remaining missiles.

The bus could be heard approaching. Three of the cadres stepped out into the road waving at the bus driver to stop. Benkov could see the men through the trees. The driver started to change down gears when he saw the men on the road waving AKs at him. The bus pulled to a stop well short of where the three cadres stood, so far away that Benkov could not see the bus through the trees. Despite not being able to see the bus, he could hear the loud idling clearly. The freedom fighters, both on the road and in the bush, were forced to walk back along the road in the direction of the bus.

It was difficult to see what was going on, so Benkov and his small group crept along through the trees towards the sound of the bus. Eventually it came into view, a sort of dirty white, creamy colour with a red racing stripe down the side. Most of the group hailing the bus were now walking along the road, totally exposed.

Why did the driver stop so far away? He could hear the voices of his men; they seemed to be joking with the bus driver.

The process is taking too long.

The leader of the band on the road eventually shouted into the trees for the others to come out. He then disappeared into the bus.

The driver climbed off the bus, looked up and down the road, then walked around to the back of the bus.

Something is not right. Benkov hesitated. He ducked down into the bush lifting his binoculars. As he studied the bus Benkov noticed for the first time that one of his men on the road was wearing a distinctive hat. As he focused, an airline pilot's distinctive cap came into view. Mlungisi looked at Benkov quizzically, not sure why he was suddenly so cautious. Up ahead, most of the group waiting on the road were lined up climbing onto the bus. They could be heard laughing and joking with the other passengers.

The driver walked around the rear of the bus, this time carrying an AK. There was no time to call a warning. The bus erupted with gunfire, windows smashed out. The driver mowed down the few cadres still standing on the road. Two men tumbled out of the door screaming. The driver killed one where he stood, the other one managed to dodge around the front of the bus. A shootout began between the man in the front and the driver at the back. Benkov watched in shocked amazement as the driver lay down and shot at the cadre from underneath the bus, hitting him in the ankle. The young cadre screamed in agony then crumpled to the ground clutching at his leg.

The bush in front was too thick to shoot through and the bus too far away for Benkov and his small band to provide support. An unfamiliar feeling of panic gripped Benkov. He looked around to see whether this was part of a broader SF ambush. Panic was not a feeling that Benkov had ever felt before. A few cadres, still hiding in the trees, ran towards where Benkov was standing. The firing on the road ahead stopped abruptly. Benkov watched in horror as four men stepped off the bus, dressed exactly as his band was.

Who are these men, they were all black, dressed as Freedom Fighters? He watched as they walked around the front of the bus and grabbed the wounded freedom fighter by his combat jacket, manhandling him back onto the bus. One of the men gave the wounded man a hard slap on the head, shouted at him in siNdebele. The wounded cadre called out looking into the bush in Benkov's direction. They all ducked down instinctively. The man holding the wounded cadre followed his gaze, shouting at the man again, giving him another hard slap, pointing out into the bush. He was clearly asking if there were any more of his comrades still in the bush. Realising his exposed position next to the bus the man called the others. They quickly loaded the dead bodies onto the bus, the driver jumped back into his seat and the bus pulled off. The whole episode could not have lasted more than five minutes.

For the first time in his life Benkov felt ice-cold fear, his invincibility was under threat. He looked at his watch; it was only 7am in the morning. He had the whole day ahead of him.

That Cadre was going to squeal his lungs out! Benkov snapped some instructions and the men rapidly crossed the tar road going north.

The 'Selous Scout Express' stopped only 3kms up the tar road, under a shady tree. They called up sub-JOC Wankie to report their 'contact'. Sgt Cephas Ngwenya sat the wounded CT down on the step of the bus and knelt down in front of him, speaking to him in a gentle voice. Ngwenya started by asking him how many CTs were in the band.

The young man, while in agonising pain from the wound in his ankle, had the presence of mind to try to provide a misleading answer. He had been trained in the Soviet Union and was part of the ZIPRA elite. Looking around him at the eight black soldiers dressed exactly as he was, he was shocked to hear them speaking his language, joking in the same way that he would have done. One walked across to him and rummaged through his pockets, finding his wallet. Opening it, the man called to the others to look at the photograph of the young man with a very attractive white girl, with some very impressive buildings in the background.

Ngwenya looked at the photograph making no comment. Kneeling down in front of him, he asked the young man about the size of his terrorist band again. He went further by rattling off a few more questions, 'where was he trained, who was his leader, had he ambushed some soldiers, had he seen an aircraft shot down, had he captured any women?'

Ngwenya deliberately gave no opportunity for an answer. The young man looked up at him, bewildered, repeating '*Hayi … Hayi … Hayi …* No … No … No,' to every question.

Suspending his questioning for a moment, Ngwenya, stood up, walking away, took out his water bottle and had a long drink. A short conversation was struck up with one of the other men, too soft for the prisoner to hear. They both laughed, glancing in his direction. Ngwenya then turned back to the young cadre.

'Comrade, we have decided that you are lying to us … I will give you another opportunity to answer correctly … If you do not tell me the truth, I will hurt you badly,' said Ngwenya matter-of-factly.

The young cadre looked up into Ngwenya's deep black eyes. They seemed to be kind, compassionate eyes, not the eyes of a killer. The cadre shook his head again, saying that he had been in Wankie TTL for many months and that he knew nothing of the things being described.

Ngwenya brought out from behind his back the distinctive navy blue cap with gold braid and winged badge and threw it into the lap of the young man.

'Where did you find this Comrade?' he asked.

The young cadre looked down at the cap, the look of recognition on his face showed Ngwenya everything he needed to know. There was no warning, Ngwenya simply pointed his AK at the cadre's right knee and pulled the trigger. The piercing scream could be heard a long way off. It did not carry to where Benkov was standing just to the south, but the gunshot did. Benkov looked up the road from where the shot had been fired. He knew that he was in serious trouble.

The Selous Scouts got back on the radio to sub-JOC Wankie and reported that they had hit the group responsible for the Grey Scout ambush, the airline disaster and the rape and murder of the women passengers. The young cadre was still talking half an hour later, Ngwenya struggling to write down the notes fast enough. While he described his leader as Mlungisi, the young cadre, despite his pain and shock, deliberately omitted the one crucial fact; his true leader was a Soviet Spetsnaz soldier. It was the one question that Ngwenya would never have considered asking.

Sgt Ngwenya and his small Selous Scout detachment waited on the side of the road, listening to the harrowing story being related by the captured CT, interjecting questions, making notes. The quiet of the morning was broken by the arrival overhead of two helicopters. The helicopters circled once before settling onto the tar road, dropping their two sticks, then immediately took off again.

Lt Light and Sgt-Maj Nduku from 3 Platoon, 4 Indep introduced themselves to the Selous Scouts. They all climbed aboard the bus still loaded with dead CTs and drove back the short distance to the contact site. Ngwenya, dragging his now very seriously injured CT with him, asked him to point at where the remainder of the band had been hiding. A short sweep through the thick bush picked up the spoor. Light and Nduku set off immediately, armed with the knowledge that the CTs up ahead had killed Lt Dawson and the other Grey Scouts, had brought down the DC-4, and killed the surviving passengers. They did not wait to get the information on the raid at Kosami Mission or the ambush on the heavy vehicle convoy. There was no shortage of motivation.

The news of the Selous Scout bus ambush and the captured CT reached *Ingwe* Fullerton and 2 Platoon within a half hour of the contact. Fullerton walked them out to the nearest road to be picked up by their trucks. Two hours later they arrived at the police camp at Dett. The fact that the CTs were moving to the west meant that Dett was the best place for a command post. The rest of 3 Platoon had already arrived in their trucks. Fullerton quickly took charge. Radio comms were established with the c/signs on follow-up, 43, Light and 43Alpha, Nduku. D Company 1RAR Fireforce waited at Wankie, only fifteen minutes flying time to the north.

Fullerton sent out four Stop groups to man OPs on high ground along the dirt road between Dett and the main Bulawayo road. This road formed the base of an imaginary triangle stretching out in front of the follow-up group. If the CTs continued west, they would have to cross the road at some point. If they didn't cross the road then the area to search was much more limited.

Another agonising wait began.

*

Comrade Tongerai Chabanga finally reached the relative comfort of the Dett base camp. His men were delighted to be back. The local freedom fighter leader, still in his camp, reported that they had not seen any SF activity. A short time later some *mujibas* reported heavy SF traffic on the road to the village of Dett in the west.

The Dett base camp had been built as a staging area for groups infiltrating the country, for training local *mujibas,* but, most importantly, as a gathering point for volunteers rounded up for training outside the country. Set routes from the camp to the Botswana border had been established to facilitate the efficient movement of men and equipment, going in both directions. The camp was built in an area of thick bush on the top of a low flat hill, broken with large rocky outcrops. The hill was really only a slightly higher elevation than the surrounding countryside so it did not provide a perfect vantage point. The camp was surrounded on all sides by densely packed villages and ploughed land. This was ideal as it provided for an excellent early warning system while providing the men in the camp with their most important needs, access to food and water, *mujibas* and, of course, women.

The camp had been occupied for a very long time, which had given the occupants an opportunity to dig slit trenches and underground bunkers. They had an 82mm mortar in a well-camouflaged pit, plus a B-10 82mm recoilless rifle mounted on its two-wheeled tripod in a dug-in emplacement. The B-10 was a heavy piece of equipment, over 85kg, and had been dragged manually the sixty odd kilometres from the crossing point in the Gwai gorge on the Zambezi in the north. The B-10 was set up on the highest point in the camp to give a reasonable arc of fire. The sleeping positions were all camouflaged with thick jesse bush, cut grass and branches. The camp commander had a strong defensive position in a rocky outcrop that he had built up using the surrounding rocks. Great care had been taken not to create walkways and paths within the camp. From the air, only a single defined path traversed the camp from east to west. The camp was all but invisible from the ground and the air.

At the time of Chabanga's arrival, the camp had about forty occupants that, together with his group, made the total fifty-five in number. Chabanga sat down once again with the camp commander and discussed news that had filtered through from the surrounding villages. They spoke for some time on the news of the aircraft that had been shot down. The commander also had a battery-powered transistor radio that was tuned to a Zambian short-wave radio station. The station had given a comprehensive news account, claiming a great victory over the colonial forces. There was no discussion on the rape and murder of the survivors. There was a much greater focus on the fact that the passengers were all American supporters of the Rhodesian regime.

There had still been no sign of Benkov. Chabanga was fast coming to the conclusion that he might already have left the country. As the day grew progressively hotter, the freedom fighters all retired to sleep under the trees or in the bottom of the slit trenches, where it was much cooler.

*

Captain Benkov and his heavily depleted band, now ten in number, were making fast progress. They carried only the bare essentials, the rest of their surplus kit having been dumped down an abandoned ant-bear hole. Benkov took great pains to backtrack to try to hide his spoor. This made forward progress slower, but he figured that it would likely delay a follow-up group. The area they were walking through was densely populated, so they recruited *mujibas* to go back on their trail to sweep away their spoor.

There was no time for rest or food. The band was constantly on the move. Tension and nervousness was growing amongst the men, mutterings could be heard from the back. Some had concluded that it was now necessary to bombshell, every man for himself, to regroup at the base camp later. Benkov was completely oblivious to the debate going on behind him, until Mlungisi came forward, asking him to stop for just a minute. He listened briefly to the arguments translated by Mlungisi, tempted to dismiss them out of hand. He could see that the men were now very agitated. The ambush at the bus in the morning had severely rattled them. They had all seen the men who had killed their comrades, dressed like ZIPRA freedom fighters. This was something completely unexpected and they jabbered away at each other nervously, their natural superstition coming to the fore. *These men could be evil spirits sent to punish them for what they had done to the white women.*

Taking a short time to consider his position, Benkov eventually agreed to a split of the band into two. The one would loop around to the camp from the north while the other would loop to the south. The plan made sense on the basis that, if a follow-up was close, then a split could lead to confusion and delay. He had a short discussion with Mlungisi using the map that was then explained to the cadres. They could not read a map but could understand the geological features that Mlungisi described. The base camp was only about 15kms away. The two bands were decided upon and the men moved off into the bush. Benkov walked only about 30m before asking his four men to stop. They sat down in the bush while Benkov carefully went back over their trail to sweep it away. His idea was to give the follow-up group an easy choice. The clear trail left by the other men or an indistinct, disguised trail left by his band. For the next 4 kilometres, Benkov took great pains at anti-tracking to hide their trail. They passed through villages barefoot.

It was only two hours later that Light and Nduku reached the point at which Benkov's band had split. They called Fullerton on the radio, reporting their position and what they saw. Nduku was a very accomplished tracker himself, while Light had absolutely no idea. Light was keen to split the two sticks, each to follow a band. Nduku was not at all keen on that idea, bearing in mind that this group of CTs had proved extremely competent anti-trackers, successfully ambushing the Grey Scouts. A four man stick could easily be overwhelmed. Nduku explained to Light that the CTs would likely regroup again anyway. They set off on the clearly marked spoor of the five fast-moving CTs.

As it turned out, the cadre placed in charge of the second of the two bands decided that he was not going to make any detour. On the contrary, he wanted to get to the safety of the base camp as soon as possible. The result was that he set a course straight for the base camp, a course that would take him about four hours or so, while only two hours behind him, catching up all the time, were a very determined Light and Nduku. The young cadre made very little attempt to hide his trail.

*

At the Dett police camp, *Ingwe* Fullerton decided that he needed to get closer to the action, action he knew was almost certain that afternoon. He called Sgt Smith and his platoon and ordered them onto the trucks. C/sign 43, Light, on follow-up, was only about 12km away as the crow flies, but to get to them would need a more circuitous route over some very rough bush tracks. Fortunately, some of the national park roads that they had to use were in better condition.

Fullerton instructed Smith to call sub-JOC Wankie to alert the Fireforce Commander of his intentions. They set off with the midday sun blazing down with its relentless intensity. Smith sat strapped in the lead truck with Fullerton and the TR48 radio operator. There was no breeze at all. The trucks threw up a high cloud of dust that sat in the air suspended above the road. The drivers fought the heavy vehicles over the bush roads, bouncing and crashing along, those in the back being thrown up against their harnesses. The men all held their rifles tightly between their legs to prevent them from hitting the steel sides. Fullerton and Smith held their maps in their hands constantly checking their progress, Fullerton giving directions whenever the track split, which it did very often.

'CONTACT, Contact, Contact, …44 this is 43… we have contact, five Charlie Tangos, Oer.'

It was Lt Light's Yorkshire accent, remarkably calm, as if commentating on cricket.

Fullerton called the driver to stop. The truck shuddered to a halt as the driver killed the engine. They all strained their ears in the sudden airy silence, trying to hear the gunfire.

'43 this is 44, confirm contact … over.'

There was the loud hissing over both Smith and Fullerton's radio. Fullerton did not want to call the sub-JOC unless it was absolutely necessary. They waited anxiously for Light's reply.

Finally it came, '44, 43 … Roger we ave slotted three Charlie Tangos, we are at …' Light gave his map reference in the same tone as a cricket commentator on *a ball driven to the boundary at deep cover*. 'I think that tew others ave escaped to the west …We have a blood trail. I think we winged one of them … Oer.'

'Copied … 43 recommence follow-up … 44, out.'

Fullerton studied the map again. Lt Light was not far away, but not easy to get to by truck. He had to weigh his options, head out on foot and hope to RV with Light or move to the west in a stopping position if that was where the CTs were headed.

Captain Benkov heard the contact clearly, as if it was in an adjacent field. The sound of gunfire was distinct, so much so that it was possible to hear the difference between the MAG and RPD machineguns. The gunfire lasted for less than a minute, then stopped, a fleeting contact. The SF had hit the other band, the decoy.

Now very concerned, Benkov needed time to assess the position he was in. He had no provisions, only four men with him, still anxious to make his escape to Botswana. The base camp was a source of food and provisions, but more importantly, he needed a guide to take him on the best route to the border.

What Benkov needed was for things to settle down. He suspected that if any of his other group had survived the contact; they would definitely bombshell and become almost impossible to find as a result. Alternatively, they could lead the SF directly to the base camp that would be a disaster. He directed his men into an overgrown *kopie*. Then took Mlungisi back along their trail to see if they too were being followed.

The contact with Lt Light was also heard at the CT base camp. Chabanga stood up from where he had been sleeping. The gunfire was only just audible. It stopped as quickly as it started. He called the camp commander, asking him to send *mujibas* urgently in the direction of the gunfire to see what was going on. There was no need to panic. The gunfire was far off. It all depended on what the SF was doing.

'44 … 44, tis 43 do you read,' Light was calling.

'43 go,' Fullerton replied.

'We have found our wounded Terr, unfortunately he has shuffled off this mort'l coil.'

Lt Light's amusement at his witty comment could be heard on the radio.

'Shit,' Fullerton said loudly.

'43 do you still have spoor … Over.'

'Negative. We are cuttin at t'moment but the other Gook has gapped it like the Olympics,' came the reply, Light quite obviously enjoying himself.

'Roger 43 if you cannot find spoor, sweep to your west. See if you can get any locals to talk, we are going to sweep up from the south, we should Romeo Victor at … 44 … out.' Fullerton gave a locstat.

So the cat and mouse game began. Fullerton knew that the CTs had spilt their group up. One had been caught but the other was still out there. They had been moving consistently in a westerly direction, despite anti-tracking. If west was the direction they wanted to go in, Botswana must be their destination. He got back onto the radio and asked the various stop groups on the Dett dirt road, further to the west, to start patrolling up and down the road to check for crossing points. Unless the CTs reversed their course, they should get caught at some point, or, if they were not caught, their trail would be reacquired.

Smith got the platoon off the trucks, arranging them in a broad sweepline that covered about a 100m across. Fortunately the bush was wide open from over-grazing. There were large open fields and villages dotted about. They moved out, Fullerton in the middle, Smith on the extreme right, Dube inside him with Moyo and Sibanda. Smith turned down the squelch on his radio so he could hear more clearly. Fullerton set the pace. It was up to those on the flanks to keep up. This required constant focus on the dressing of the sweepline, to prevent people getting too far ahead or behind. It was difficult because the hand signals from Fullerton came along from the side instead of in front; this meant that those in the sweep line needed to be glancing left and right all the time, repeating the signals as they were received. This was coupled with constant glances to the ground looking for spoor. The management of the sweep line needed intense concentration, which was exhausting in itself.

The platoon progressed reasonably quickly but as the heat grew, the gunners were soon huffing and puffing. When an open field needed to be crossed, it was Smith's stick that made the crossing first, at the trot, covered by the rest of the platoon. Once they were safely across, they provided cover for the rest as they swept over the open ground. This continued for two hours before Fullerton called a halt, calling them all together.

Fullerton whispered his instructions, so softly that they all had to strain their ears.

'Okay people we are within four kilometres of the RV point with Four Three. We need to be very careful now. We may have Gooks to our front as well. I want the sweepline reduced to only four men in front. The rest will follow in single file. Sergeant Smith, I want you to take the lead with your stick.'

The change in the formation had the effect of palpably altering the degree of focus and attention. The men visibly tensioned up, looking more earnestly left and right. They knew that when *Ingwe* spoke a contact was imminent.

Fullerton called Lt Light on the radio to tell him where they were and when he expected to reach the RV point. Smith led the sweep line off in the direction indicated by Fullerton keeping his compass close at hand on a strap around his neck. Fullerton allowed Smith to get out in front by about 40m before he followed.

As Smith started out he glanced left and right at his stick, Moyo nodded, Dube's eyes remained fixed dead ahead, Sibanda smiled as he always did. Smith could not bear to speak, his mind racing. *Gooks up ahead, concentrate, keep quiet, tread carefully, rifle cocked, tracer up the spout, fuck please let me see them first!* They crept forward, each step carefully placed so as not to make any noise. The sound of a twig cracking underfoot can carry a long distance.

The ground started to rise perceptibly. Smith was forced to slow as Dube struggled with the weight he was carrying. The gun, at the ready, was at his waist, held by a sling over his shoulder. A belt of 100 rounds was clipped in place, the end draped across his shoulders. Smith stopped again to take a reassuring glance at the map; the RV point was just up ahead. Fullerton had chosen an area of higher ground for the RV.

Slowing down even more, Smith's stick edged forward with precise steps, searching the ground intently to avoid standing on a crunching tree branch. All he could hear was a few isolated bird calls, a Blackbreasted Snake Eagle, *uKhozi*, turned into a thermal high above, it called out, *kwo-kwo-kwo*. Intensely concentrating on the bush in front of him, Smith could not bear to glance sideways. *Please let me see them first!*

The bush on the hill got progressively denser, thick dry grass, broken by a number of rocky outcrops. Smith glanced back to see how far Fullerton was behind but could not see him. *Should I wait for him to catch up?* Instead he whipped his head forward again, turned the volume up on his radio, the hissing sound increasing as he did so. *I better call Light,* he thought. As his finger pressed down on the transmit button, the earth opened up beneath him.

A lattice of branches with interwoven grass covered the trench so that it could be flipped up in one piece. As Smith stepped forward his front leg disappeared into a void, the side of the trench came up to hit him square in the chest, knocking the wind out of him. His rifle dug into the dirt wall with such force that it was ripped from his hands. The sleeping occupant got Smith's boot straight in the face effectively stifled his shout of surprise. Smith, sucking for breath, toppled over on top of the terrorist lying in the trench.

Dube glanced to his left as Smith disappeared completely from sight. His mind was momentarily disorientated, '*Ishe?*' he hissed.

Smith lay face down on top of the CT in the bottom of the trench, trapping the man completely. The CT let out a blood-curdling scream at the blackened apparition centimetres from his face, his call muffled by the confines of the trench. He tried to wriggle out from under Smith who was still winded, his mouth opening and closing making tiny sucking sounds as his lungs pulled for air with his arms trapped on either side by the narrow trench. The more the man struggled, the more Smith's chest webbing and equipment dug into him, increasing his panic. The man fought fiercely, spitting in Smith's face as he shrieked in terror.

Dube, Moyo and Sibanda went to ground the instant the CT screamed. Dube crawled over to the edge of the trench and looked over the edge. The young terrorist in the bottom of the trench saw another fearsome devil looking down at him, now screaming blue murder on the top of his lungs, violently pushing and struggling to get free.

No more than two metres in front of Dube, a head popped out of the ground then turned to look directly into the barrel of the MAG. His eyes met Dube's. Tilting his head quizzically, he tried to fathom what he was seeing. Dube pulled the trigger exploding the head into a thousand pieces.

Heads now bobbed above the ground in all directions, like a band of Meercats. The CT base camp came instantly to life. Smith had entered the outer edge of the southern side of the camp, passing through the first line of trenches that now effectively encircled his stick. Dube, Moyo and Sibanda started shooting at everything they could see.

Back down the hill, *Ingwe* Fullerton shouted into his radio for Smith to answer. Lt Light, approaching the northern side of the camp answered instead. Fullerton was desperately trying to find out whether his two c/signs had accidentally run into each other. That disturbing thought was partly dispelled when the first 82mm mortar shell exploded immediately behind him, showering him in dust and debris.

The tussle in the slit trench continued as Smith struggled to regain his footing. The CT, with superhuman strength, born of abject terror, pushed Smith upright. With his arms free Smith pummelled the terrorist with his fists, shouting and cursing at him at the same time. The rifle fire, that was now going on all around him drowned out his swearing. Both regained their feet simultaneously, swinging wildly at each other, scratching at each other's faces. Smith was bigger and heavier than the terrorist; his wild flailing blows having more effect. The terrorist, realising his predicament, yelled for Smith to stop, throwing up his hands in capitulation.

'*Hayi ... Hayi ... Ngitshiya ngedwa*! Please stop!' the man called out, his face covered in blood from scratches and gouges.

Smith scrambled for his rifle lying in the bottom of the trench. As he bent down the terrorist kicked him hard in the ribs. Winded again, Smith fell to his knees. The CT gave him another vicious kick and then tried to jump out of the trench, leaping once, then falling back. The brutal desperate struggle had sapped his strength. He turned to kick at Smith again, lifting his fist at the same time. As he turned his head, Dube planted a firm left on his ear, not hard enough to knock him down, but enough to create a momentary diversion. Smith kneeling down, his rifle wedged against the side of the trench, fired, hitting the terrorist in the shin. The man screamed in agony. The impact knocked him back off balance, leaving him leaning against the side of the trench clutching for his leg. Smith regained his feet, desperately kicked out at the CT, bringing his rifle butt over in an arc. With all of the power he could muster, he struck the terrorist on the head, knocking him out cold. Smith hit him again, then again, eventually caving in the skull. He stood over the dead man, panting hard, too shocked and exhausted to think. Gunfire raged, bullets buzzed overhead.

At the base of the hill, Fullerton realised that they had stumbled into a hornet's nest. Rifle fire coming down the hill was intense but fortunately not well directed, most flying high into the trees. He could hear Dube's MAG barking in response. He urgently called sub-JOC Wankie to send Fireforce. The well-entrenched CTs began an accurate mortar barrage in Fullerton's direction that quickly made his position untenable, forcing him to retire into a dry streambed.

Light and Nduku, approaching from the north, also ran into the first line of trenches. They too had to retreat as the fire in their direction was increasingly accurate and well controlled. They set up a stop line at the bottom of the hill in some rocks. Assaulting the well fortified hill with only eight men was not going to work.

'44 ... 44 ... 42Alpha, do you read? Over.' Smith had finally managed to regain his senses.

'42Alpha ... what is your position?' replied Fullerton over the noise of gun and mortar fire, genuine concern in his voice.

'I fell into a slit trench ... we are taking fire from up the hill, no casualties ... over.'

'Where are you now?'

'I am about half way up the hill, in a Gook trench with my call-sign ... Over.' By this time Dube had climbed into the trench with Smith while Moyo and Sibanda were in a neighbouring trench. They had all stopped firing.

'44 ... I am taking heavy fire from further up the hill, I don't want to draw any further fire by throwing smoke ... Over.'

'Roger 42Alpha I am moving to your left up the hill. I will try and flank the CTs. I will call for covering fire ... Out.' Fullerton moved the rest of the platoon off to the left at a trot. The mortar fire, clearly not directed, had stopped. An eerie silence covered the battlefield as both sides tried to figure out what the other was doing.

*

Deep in the base camp, Comrade Chabanga weighed up his situation. The Rhodesians had attacked from both the north and the south, but it seemed that they had small numbers as they had been easily beaten off. He knew that helicopters would be coming soon - *I need to escape.* A Lynx began its orbit overhead. Within a minute three helicopters appeared clattering into an orbit to the north. The base camp was so well camouflaged that the aircraft could not see anything to strike at, they continued to circle, like eagles seeking out prey. The contact area remained silent, nobody wanting to give their position away. Chabanga watched with increasing fear as coloured smoke drifted across the camp. *The Rhodesians are marking their positions.* As he watched a group of five panicked freedom fighters broke cover running down the hill. The helicopter with the big cannon saw them, systematically cutting them down with exploding shells, sending dust high into the air. Chabanga decided that he needed to wait until the men in the camp began to bombshell before he made his move.

A loud drone could be heard from the north, once again Chabanga saw an approaching Paradak. These were men to be feared, devils from the sky. Circling once, Chabanga watched as the wings levelled out in the east, the deadly white mushrooms appeared in the clear blue sky and began rapidly drifting to the ground. He knew then that escape to the east was not an option.

The brave men in the mortar pit had also seen the parachute drop and turned the mortar onto this new target. They dropped bomb after bomb as fast as they could. Their lives were cut short as the K-car eventually picked up their position, turning the mortar pit into a bloody quagmire.

Fear gripped Chabanga as he crouched down in his trench, waiting for the moment to make his escape.

*

Benkov heard the opening contact; he knew it had to be the ZIPRA base camp. His small group sat in the cover of the *kopie*. They all watched the arrival of the Lynx, helicopters and Dakota. The orbiting helicopters were overflying Benkov's position so breaking cover was not a good idea. Despite the arrival of the enemy Fireforce, Benkov was reasonably relaxed. It was obvious that the Rhodesians were focused on the base camp he was in no immediate danger. He looked at the Strela launcher and contemplated having a shot at the helicopters, he had two missiles left.

The Alouette III has a single turbine engine that sits exposed above the fuselage. The turbine exhaust pushed superheated air out just below the main rotors creating an intense heat signature. The Rhodesians had attempted to shroud the engine by directing the exhaust upwards instead of straight out the back. A bath-like shielding, open at the top for maintenance purposes, covered the sides of the engine. The effect was that the heat signature was greatest while the helicopter was in a steep bank, but much reduced in level flight.

Benkov studied the circling helicopters. His strict military training and natural aggression took over. Grabbing the launcher, he slung the pack with the two missiles over his back and dashed out of the *kopie*, leaving instructions for his men to wait for him. He gauged the orbit of the three helicopters, running, dodging as fast as his legs would carry him, adrenaline driving him onwards. This was a deeply personal challenge of his prowess as a soldier. He had the enemy in his sights. The element of surprise was with him. A good sheltered position for a shot appeared in front of him. The contact over the base camp was now in full swing. The gun and mortar fire was intense, incessant. He distinctly heard the familiar CRUMP of the B-10 recoilless rifle. The freedom fighters were putting up a good fight.

The helicopter pilots were concentrating intently on the base camp area, not looking outside their orbit. Benkov picked his target, lifted the launcher to his shoulder, turned on the battery, then waited for the few seconds for the launcher to warm up, then pressed the trigger lightly to get the missile to acquire the heat signature. Following the helicopter with the iron-sight, he waited for it to pass over in front of him. The missile buzzed its acquisition. He hit the trigger. Out shot the missile, igniting in a blinding flash, shooting out over the bush, the clear white smoke trail lifted into the sky, marking the passage of its flight.

The pilot unwittingly saved his life and the others in his helicopter by inexplicably straightening his orbit. The heat signature instantly reduced, the missile lost its way a split second from launch and passed by the canopy of the helicopter. Then climbed up high into the sky finding the intensely hot afternoon sun a more appealing target before self-destructing, leaving a black splodge hanging in the air.

Cursing the missed shot and with no time to deliberate, Benkov set off back in the direction of his band. Glancing back over his shoulder to make sure he hadn't been spotted, he dodged from tree to tree as he went. He knew that the white smoke trail left behind by the missile effectively pinpointed the position of the launch.

The D Company 1RAR K-car Commander saw the missile streak past the G-car flying behind him, the white smoke trail disappearing up into the sky.

'Fuck, did you see that?' he called to the pilot, '… what is that?'

'Strela,' the pilot replied, seemingly unperturbed. 'Green 4 this is Green 1, can you get that fucking Charlie Tango with the Strela to my south.'

Green 4 was the Lynx pilot who was orbiting at a higher altitude waiting to be called onto a target.

'Roger Green 1… I have the smoke trail visual.'

The Lynx dived out of its orbit, the pilot lining up the base of the smoke trail. He could not see the CT that had launched the missile but he had a rough idea where he was. He let go with the roof-mounted 303s shooting blindly, still not seeing a target as he levelled out. The Lynx climbed out scrutinising the bush below but he still could not see anything.

The missile launch forced the helicopters to a higher altitude making close air support more difficult. The four stops dropped by the Paradak had now reached the eastern edge of the base camp, coming under heavy rifle fire. The K-car Commander had decided to use them as the primary attack force plus the two stops dropped by the G-cars. Fullerton was asked to hold the western flank, Light and Nduku the northern flank. Smith was trapped in his position in the trenches to the south.

A process of clearing the trenches now began. The K-car Commander had the presence of mind to call for Hunters as soon as he heard that the CTs were entrenched. They came howling in over the target, in line astern, one releasing frantan, the other Golf Bombs, directly on the highest point of the hill. The frantan roasted the ZIPRA camp commander and his team where they sat in their bunker, also setting off a raging bush fire. The Hunters then flew up to higher altitude to wait for another target.

Smith and Dube stood in the trench together, shoulder to shoulder. Smith called softly to Moyo and Sibanda in their trench nearby. They confirmed that they were uninjured. Dube, shorter than Smith, needed to stand on the dead CT at the bottom of the trench in order to be able to aim the MAG. A thick, caustic cloud of smoke from the frantan and the raging bush fire began to drift down over their position, making it difficult to see.

Rifle and MAG fire was now growing in intensity further up the hill as the Fireforce began to sweep up over the hill. Smith listened to the K-car Commander as he gave instructions helping him to get a mental picture of what was going on. Another loud CRUMP came rolling down the hill. Smith had never seen or heard a B-10 fire before. He had no idea what it was.

Through the smoke haze Smith saw a few fleeting figures darting left and right. The CTs had started to break cover, climbing out of their trenches to get away. The smoke on the ground made it difficult for the K-car Commander to see so he could not give any warning to Smith when a wave of CTs appeared out of the murk in front of him. Dube immediately opened fire with the MAG. The gun, fired only centimetres from Smith's ear, deafened him. He lifted his rifle to take aim using the edge of the trench as support for his elbow; a man came through the smoke right in front of their position. Dube had missed him, not being able to elevate the gun quickly enough. The man was sprinting, looking straight ahead. By the time Smith got a shot off, the man was about to hurdle the trench. Smith's bullet entered just below his rib cage, the impact lifting him up, throwing him back. His forward momentum was enough for him to land on his back on top of the trench, his boot catching Smith on the side of the head. Smith fell back under the weight. Dube cursed, leaned over, grabbed the dead CT by the front of his shirt and with brute strength threw him out the front of the trench. He did not even glance at where Smith sat senseless in the bottom of the trench. Going back to his gun, Dube fired steadily up the hill, TAP TAP … TAP TAP.

Still dazed from the crack on his head Smith called on the radio, 'Sunray this is 42Alpha, we have Charlie Tangos running through our position … Over.'

'I cannot get to you now 42Alpha, shoot the fuckers,' came the immediate and clipped reply, a seemingly practical suggestion.

The K-car orbited back over Smith's position, the smoke now way too thick for the gunner to see the CTs running below. The smoke provided perfect cover for the CTs' escape but also made Smith's stick all but invisible in their trenches. Escaping CTs appeared for only fleeting seconds, Smith found it easier to keep firing steadily into the smoke. He took out the spare belt of MAG ammunition that he carried in his pack and laid it next to Dube. Dube was transfixed in concentration, traversing the gun gently left and right, grunting loudly when he thought he had made a hit. Smith could hear Moyo and Sibanda shooting nearby.

Smith heard the K-car Commander calling Fullerton, giving instructions to move further up the hill. Instant, loud, intense covering fire came from his left.

*

Further up the hill, the smoking bush fire gave Brigade Commander

Chabanga the opportunity he had been waiting for. Whatever breeze there was drifted the smoke to the south. He leapt out of the trench he was hiding in, calling for the few cadres close by to follow him. He ran crouched over into the smoke grateful for the protection it offered. The Lynx put in a Golf bomb strike further up the hill, trying to clear the trenches ahead of the sweep line. Chabanga was careful not to run blindly down the hill. Instead he crept steadily away carefully trying to stay in the thickest smoke. He could hear gunfire further down the hill. Stray rounds were cracking above his head, causing him to duck down instinctively.

Gunfire from down the hill grew more intense, forcing Chabanga to correct the angle that he was moving on more to the right. One of the cadres next to him grunted, falling forward, a broad blood stain spread on the back of his shirt from the exit wound. The man lay in silence, completely still. Bullets, like angry bees clipped tree branches above his head. In front of him, a group of soldiers appeared out of the smoky gloom, spread out in a line. The freedom fighters next to him were spotted, an instant hail of bullets pitched in the ground around him buzzing past his head. The freedom fighters turned back to the left, running wildly down the hill. Chabanga, keeping his composure, steadily moved back to the left, not shooting, trying not to give his position away. The hill behind him erupted into flame as the jets put in another frantan strike. He felt the heat of the exploding fuel mixture on his back, not daring to turn to look.

The jet strike momentarily distracted the Rhodesian sweepline, helping Chabanga to sneak back into the cover of the smoke. Cadres continued to appear in front and from behind, wide eyed, consumed by panic. He tried to rally them but it was useless, they had lost all discipline. Desperate for escape, the instinct to run had overtaken them.

A machinegun thudded into life a short distance to Chabanga's front. He crouched down to look through the whirling smoke, trying to see the firing point. The gun stopped. Chabanga inched forward again, careful not to make any noise, praying that the smoke would continue to hide him. The machinegun blurted out again, closer this time. It seemed close enough to touch. A cadre came running from behind him, the crunching and thudding of his boots through the undergrowth clearly audible. The man did not see Chabanga bent over, creeping forward, instead ran past, going at full tilt. The machinegun fired again, Chabanga saw the man fall, his stifled scream lost in the sound of the gunfire, so very close. He took a stick grenade from his webbing, released the safety pin, and lifted it carefully above his head, aiming at the point the gun had fired from. His arm came forward in a sweeping arc, releasing the grenade. Waiting for the thud of the explosion,

Chabanga sprinted forward. The smoke cleared momentarily. He could not see clearly but he thought he saw men in a trench. He kept running. There were bodies lying at all angles, it was almost impossible not to step on them as he ran. The trench ahead came into view, a man moved, lifting his rifle. Chabanga sidestepped, the bullet passed by his head. There was no option but to jump over the trench in front of him. He fired his AKM from the hip, holding the trigger down, spraying the trench with bullets as he went over the top. He caught a split second glimpse of a blackened face looking up at him with striking green eyes. He was over, enveloped again by the smoke. Focused on the bottom of the hill, Chabanga ran for freedom, he ran for the struggle, he ran for his life, every sinew straining, his legs pounding.

Reaching the bottom of the hill, Chabanga stole a glance back over his shoulder. There was nobody following him. Overhead a helicopter swept past, its machinegun firing at a point up the hill. Chabanga could see the gunner's face encased in a helmet. Next to the gunner he could see a man sitting in the door of the helicopter his one leg resting on the step. Waiting for the helicopter to pass overhead, Chabanga ran forward, trying to stay in the cover provided by the thinning trees. From behind him another helicopter appeared. Chabanga dived under a short, straggly bush – but too late. The pilot corrected his orbit to allow the gunner to bring the machinegun to bear. A line of .303 rounds danced in the dust towards where Chabanga lay. He rolled on his back, swinging his AKM up, firing on full automatic, the rifle bucking in his hands until the magazine emptied. Watching in horror as the helicopter's machinegun strikes raced towards him. Chabanga hopelessly pointed his empty rifle at the helicopter, his finger on the trigger.

Closing his eyes, he waited for his death that must now surely come. '*Sokuyisikhathi sokuhamba, Nkosi.* It is time to go, my God,' he prayed.

As if in slow motion, the helicopter, now virtually directly above Chabanga, dissolved into pieces. A white streaking spear of fire and smoke eviscerated the machine, splitting it in two, turning it into a falling, spinning, disintegrating wreck. Chabanga, still lying on his back, watched as a man was thrown clear of the spiralling helicopter, tumbling to the ground, landing only metres away from him with a loud sickening thud. The impact of the crash was like a thunderclap. Rolling back onto his chest, Chabanga saw the explosion in a nearby field. A rotor-blade lifting clear of the wreck, spinning off into the distance, cartwheeling as it went.

Not waiting to survey the destruction, Chabanga scrambled to his feet and ran to the south, charging from tree to tree.

*

Vladimir Benkov, with the Strela launcher still in his hands, stood at the base of the *kopie,* gazing at the spot where the helicopter had been only seconds before. A thick cloud of smoke rose into the air, marking the crash site. It was now time to make their escape. He had pushed his luck to the limit. His few remaining cadres came out of the thick bush at the base of the *kopje;* all looking over at the black smoke to the north where the attack on the base camp was still in full swing. The sky seemed to be full of aircraft; a helicopter was now orbiting the site of Benkov's kill. He took a few seconds to hide the Strela launcher under a rock, its job done. He then signalled his men to follow him.

His quickly formulated plan was now to continue to the south into the Wankie National Park with the hope of finding a place to rest, so he could figure out his next move. As they moved off stragglers from the base camp started appearing out of the bush running for all they were worth. When they saw Benkov's band they shouted out with joy and relief. In a very short space of time Benkov's band had swollen to fifteen. The gunfire behind them continued unabated.

'Yeka! ... Stop!' came a call from the bush behind the departing band. The rearmost cadres turned to see who had called out.

A man came out of the bush from behind calling in a commanding voice, *'Ubani ukukhuluma?* ... Who is in charge?'

The cadres stared at the man blankly, still suffering from the shock and fright of the attack. The small column came to a stop looking back at the stranger who was demanding answers. Benkov turned to see what was going on, calling out to Mlungisi in Russian to find out.

Mlungisi addressed the newcomer in siNdebele; a chill ran down Benkov's spine, 'Comrade Chabanga! It is good to see you,' said Mlungisi respectfully.

Chabanga walked purposefully up to Mlungisi, his AKM held loosely by his side.

'Comrade Mlungisi, is that Russian bastard still with you?' enquired Chabanga in siNdebele, glowering into the faces along the line. The look on Chabanga's face showed a man under extreme stress. His eyes flicked left and right, his voice strained. Benkov stepped out from the front of the line, looking straight into Chabanga's eyes.

'Welcome Comrade Chabanga,' he whispered in Russian.

Chabanga looked like he had seen a ghost. He was momentarily lost for words, this encounter was so unexpected.

'Have you any idea of the damage you have done to our organisation?' Chabanga stammered, waving his free arm behind him.

Benkov moved forward, his sheer size was intimidating.

'Comrade Chabanga, we are still very close to the colonists, we must escape. Now is not the time to discuss frivolous matters.'

'Now is exactly the time!' Chabanga screeched, now brandishing his AKM in Benkov's direction. 'You animal, how can the deaths of so many of our comrades because of your demented behaviour be described as frivolous?'

The superior tone in Chabanga's voice made Benkov instantly irritated.

Benkov took another step towards the smaller man, then raising his voice slightly, said 'Comrade Chabanga, we can discuss this later. I insist that we move out now!'

'You insist … you insist? … You are in my country, you follow MY orders,' snapped Chabanga.

Then turning to the men, shaking his AKM above his head, Chabanga shouted out in siNdebele, 'Comrades arrest this man, he has betrayed the revolution … he has betrayed our struggle!'

Benkov did not need to understand siNdebele to see what was going on. Mlungisi looked across at him, obviously bewildered, looking for some direction.

Something snapped in Benkov's mind. He did not hesitate any further, lifting his AKM; he aimed it at Chabanga's chest.

'Comrade Chabanga you are confused and frightened, put down your weapon and leave us. Now!'

'You aim your weapon at me! You accuse me of cowardice! Who do you think you are? You white pig … communist heathen? I will tear off your balls with my bare hands,' cried Chabanga, totally flustered.

Chabanga, spittle running down his chin, swung his rifle at the Russian, his eyes wide, the demented eyes of a man that had lost all control, maybe even lost his mind.

Benkov shot Brigadier Chabanga square in the face, the bullet exiting the back of his skull. For a split second Chabanga stood, looking at Benkov his eyes still searching, suddenly empty, the light gone. His knees collapsed toppling him backwards. He died before hitting the ground.

The cadres stood in stunned silence, looking at the body of the most senior ZIPRA man in the region, a man who was a legend, respected by all. They looked at Benkov in horror. Murmurings began as they tried to process what they had seen.

Mlungisi reacted quickly, 'Comrades listen to me, Comrade Chabanga had lost his mind, he was ill … maybe the demons had taken his mind.' He walked carefully down the line of men looking at each one. 'You should forget what you have seen here. Comrade Chabanga was a brave man and a valiant leader, but he was lost to us, his mind was lost, you saw his actions.'

Benkov, saying nothing, turned on his heel and walked into the bush. Mlungisi pointed after him, 'we must get to safety comrades. The colonists will chase us.'

The group reluctantly turned to follow Benkov, the silence broken by a machinegun way in the distance, the reality of their predicament still all too clear.

Tongerai Chabanga's body lay in the parched African dust, in the land of his birth, in the land of his forefathers and the great heroes of the noble Matabele nation, Mzilikazi, Mncumbatha, and Lobengula. The cool light of the late afternoon played on his face, now peaceful in death. The troubles of his country now passed to others to resolve.

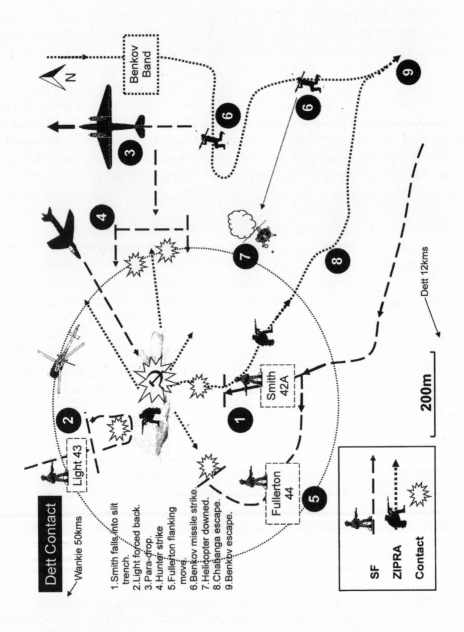

Dett Contact

Wankie 50kms

Light 43

Smith 42A

Fullerton 44

Benkov Band

N

Dett 12kms

200m

1. Smith falls into slit trench.
2. Light forced back.
3. Para-drop.
4. Hunter strike.
5. Fullerton flanking move.
6. Benkov missile strike.
7. Helicopter downed.
8. Chabanga escape.
9. Benkov escape.

SF

ZIPRA

Contact

25

ZIPRA Base Camp, north of Dett, northern Matabeleland

The Fireforce attack group swept over the hill that had housed the ZIPRA base camp. The occupants had either been killed or had escaped. Three who had given themselves up now sat tied up, back to back, on the crest of the hill. The Fireforce leader on the ground, a RAR Lieutenant, sat in a huddle with *Ingwe* Fullerton, Lt Light and Sgt-Maj Nduku, discussing their next move. All the c/signs were accounted for except Smith, 42Alpha. Fullerton called Smith repeatedly on the radio with no response. The silence was disturbing, he now feared the worst.

The sun was rapidly setting; it would be dark in less than half an hour. The helicopters were settling onto a rapidly cut LZ on the hill to extract the dead and wounded. The SF casualties accounted for thus far included the deaths of the two crew of the downed helicopter and four RAR Fireforce riflemen. There were four wounded with two looking very serious, the medics working furiously to stabilise them before casevac.

Fullerton pointed down the hill in the direction that Smith had last been heard. The fire had mostly burnt out, but the atmosphere was still hazy, and the air smelt foul, a combination of frantan, cordite and incinerated flesh.

'We best sweep down to the base of the hill as soon as possible to find Sergeant Smith's stick,' said Fullerton, his voice showing concern.

He stood up, then, followed by the others, shook out a sweepline. Curt instructions and directions were issued, a grim look of unease played across Fullerton's face. The line of men began the careful walk down the hill. It did not take long before they began to find more CT casualties, a few still clinging to life. The sweepline stopped briefly while their weapons were removed, but the bodies were not touched for the time being as CTs were known to pull the pins out of grenades, rolling onto them in their last throws before death. Some would even tuck the live grenade into a pocket or shirt.

Half way down the hill Fullerton called another halt. The trench that Smith and Dube had been trapped in came into view. Through the thick smoke haze, a soldier could be seen working on a wounded man, another kneeling holding up a drip, a third covering the others.

'Sergeant Smith is that you? Sergeant Smith, we are sweeping down towards you,' shouted Fullerton. There was no response. He came forward until he was standing right over the trench. The sight before him was dreadful. There were five dead CTs lying in front of the trench.

Smith sat silently. He looked up at Fullerton with glazed eyes.

'I don't think I can save him … Sir,' Smith whispered, his arms covered in blood to the elbows.

Dube sat across from the body of the wounded man, holding up the drip that was already virtually empty. Blood ran down his cheek from a wound in his scalp from a piece of grenade shrapnel, the side of his head was a mass of matted, blood soaked hair.

'It is Moyo *Ishe* … he is passing,' said Dube softly.

Sibanda sat nearby, casting furtive glances down the hill, powerless to help his wounded friend and mentor.

'Sergeant Major Nduku go up the hill and bring a medic back with you, no arguments, do it now, physically carry him down here if necessary!' demanded Fullerton. Nduku without hesitation turned and jogged back up the hill.

'Let me see what is going on here Smithy,' said Fullerton gently, kneeling down next to Smith. Moyo was lying on his side propped up by Dube, his head resting on a pack. He had been shot in the shoulder as one of the CTs had jumped over the trench to escape. The same CT had shot up Smith's A76 radio in his backpack, the radio probably saving his life. The exit wound was clear, just below Moyo's rib cage. Blood was still oozing from the wound that Smith had attempted to bind with a field dressing. Soaked field dressings lay scattered about, their packing torn into shreds, in the desperation to open them. Moyo was conscious but the morphine that Smith had pumped into him was starting to take effect.

'Moyo, you stay with me, do you hear?' demanded Fullerton loudly in Shona.

'*Ingwe* …' Moyo attempted to turn his head, his voice a hoarse sigh.

'Smith … replace that drip … how much morphine have you given him?'

'Just one ampoule Sir,' croaked Smith, struggling to keep control of his churning emotions. The shock associated with the contact was starting to set in.

'That is enough for the moment. He needs to fight for his life … He is not coughing blood so the bullet may not have hit a lung,' said Fullerton encouragingly.

Fullerton stood up and ordered the men to make up a stretcher using some cut branches and a bivvy. He then took the handset of his radio, 'Sunray this is 44 I need space on a chopper before dark, I have another casualty … Over.' The helicopters could still be heard taking off and landing up the hill. The K-car continued its protective orbit above.

The small group of men lifted Moyo's litter onto their shoulders and started struggling up the hill, scrambling to keep their footing in the rapidly fading light. Smith, Dube and Sibanda followed behind, Sibanda carrying Moyo's rifle and pack over his shoulders. The medic led by Nduku met them on the way up the hill and quickly listened to Moyo's chest with his stethoscope; the pulse was desperately faint.

The medic looked up shaking his head, 'It's not good,' he murmured.

It was virtually dark by the time they reached the top of the hill. Not all of the Fireforce had been able to get out. They had taken up a position of all-round defence on the LZ.

'44 this is Sunray, you will need to light up the LZ if you want to get your man out,' called the Fireforce Commander.

'Copied Sunray ... what is casevac ETA?'

'Green 2 is expected in five minutes.'

The medic went to work on Moyo, pulling off the field dressings and replacing them. A third drip was attached to the catheter in his arm. He was fighting hard, moaning quietly. Someone lit a flare to help the medic see what he was doing; it lit up the surrounding bush brightly,

'Watch your front people,' shouted Fullerton to the men in all-round defence.

'44 ... Green 2, I am approaching from your east, over.'

'Roger Green 2, I hear you ... standby.'

Fullerton, took out an Icarus para-illuminating flare, then pulling the release, it shot up into the night sky, bathing the LZ in a milky light.

'Green 2, I have torch light to the east and west of the LZ, you may land in the middle,' the men with the torches pointed them in the direction of the approaching helicopter.

'Roger 44 I have your LZ visual,' the helicopter pilot responded.

Out in the distance, green tracer lifted from the trees, streaking up towards the approaching helicopter. The CTs were shooting at it. The G-car gunner went into action trying to suppress the attackers on the ground.

'44 ... I have incoming fire to my left, I need to go round again,' called the pilot. Landing on a forested hill under fire at night was a very dangerous maneuverer.

Fullerton ran across the LZ to the east mustering MAG gunners including Dube.

He shouted desperately to the men gathered there, 'When that chopper comes around again I want you to shoot with everything you have in the direction of that tracer,' ordered Fullerton pointing out into the darkness, once again cool under pressure. The Icarus flare suddenly extinguished turning out the light as if someone had flicked a switch.

The helicopter spun around again. As the green tracer lifted, the men on the hill opened fire, a wave of red tracer spread out in response. The CTs were a long way off, probably way out of range but the barrage seemed to do the trick. The helicopter flared to land on the LZ, now almost invisible in the dark with only a faint beam of torchlight to focus on. The men instinctively ducked down waiting for it to settle. Dust spat up into their faces, Smith held his hat over Moyo's face to protect it. Moyo moaned loudly as the makeshift stretcher twisted, the bearers struggling under the weight. As the helicopter touched the uneven ground the group scraped forward, bent almost double under the whirling blades. The engine was still screaming at almost full power and Smith closed his eyes as they filled with sand and dust.

As they shoved Moyo into the helicopter, Smith lent forward and shouted into his ear, '*Hamba kahle* ... go well.'

The medic jumped in beside Moyo holding the drip in his hand and the helicopter lifted up and away. Sudden silence returned, bright starlight lit the crest of the hill as the remaining men took up their positions for the night.

In the distance the sounds of trucks could be heard, their engines revving loudly as they pushed through the bush. The police from Dett were coming in to help with the recovery and clean-up.

'We are going to have to base up on this hill tonight,' called out Fullerton to no one in particular.

Mike Smith rolled out his sleeping bag and lay down on it. Looking up into the night sky, he began to shiver from the delayed reaction from the terrifying contact he had just experienced.

*

Benkov's band of survivors rapidly swelled to nineteen. One of these men had a nasty jagged arm wound which had been bleeding badly. He had attempted to bind it up but it still dripped blood through the bandage. Benkov made them walk for the first few hours, travelling south, back into the populated TTL for protection. They stopped on the edge of a village. Mlungisi took a few men to collect food and water. Benkov contemplated splitting the group up again but decided against it. He calculated that he might need the numbers for another diversion if the SF caught up with them.

The radio, still being carried by one of the cadres, was down to the end of its battery life. Benkov calculated that he would get one or maybe two more messages through to Lusaka before it gave in. He took the opportunity to formulate a message and turned the radio back on to send it. Panda-ma-Tenga in Botswana was still about 130km due west from his position, over relatively flat featureless terrain, with no permanent water and virtually devoid of local population. Most of the route would be through either national park or controlled hunting area. This was to be a four-day walk at the very least, tough and demanding, in intense heat.

The band of freedom fighters walked through the remainder of the night. Benkov swung in a westerly direction and, when the sun came up, they were a good 20kms from the site of the contact, to the west, on the extreme outer edge of the populated TTL. Fortunately the area was well known to the cadres that had been based in the ZIPRA camp and most importantly, Benkov established that at least two were familiar with the best route to the Botswana border and the location of a nearby arms cache. This gave the group the opportunity to refill AK magazines. Benkov took a few rifle grenades. Through discussion with Mlungisi, Benkov established that the two cadres had made the trip to Panda-ma-Tenga recently escorting ZIPRA recruits to Botswana for onward transportation to training camps. The men knew the best route to take, but they emphasised the need to carry plenty of water. They also indicated that water was available in two places along the way. A fair amount of time was wasted after sunrise as the freedom fighters went into the villages to collect as much food and water as they could carry. Benkov carried six water bottles of his own and still had a few tins of bully beef. The wounded cadre was left behind and told to make his way to Lukozi Mission, south of Wankie, where he should get some medical attention. All was set for the final leg of Benkov's mission.

*

Sergeant Mike Smith slept fitfully; he lay on his back looking up at the stars, perfectly distinct in the night sky. He had managed to brew some tea in the dark that he shared with Ingwe Fullerton. The hot sweet liquid calmed his jangled nerves. He still had a vision of the CT running at him, through the smoke, firing at him on automatic, leaping over the trench. He could hear the distinctive grunt from Moyo as he was hit. The scene played over and over in his mind, the CT shooting, Moyo's grunt when he was hit. He felt physically and mentally drained but still could not sleep. He could hear the other men in their sleeping positions moving about, facing their own demons. A guard had been set on a rotation, but the number of men on the hill meant that his services were not required, the benefit of rank. It made no difference he was wide-awake anyway.

The moon was yet to rise but the Milky Way, seemingly so close, bathed the hill in a magical light. The dark had always frightened him as a young child, but the army had changed all that, to the extent that he now looked forward to the night. The knowledge that he could not be seen, gave a feeling of safety. The stars provided a strange, inexplicable comfort to him. He had no knowledge of the stars, capable of finding the only feature used in training, the Southern Cross. On his many deployments along the River, he had counted the number of satellites travelling across the sky at the same time every night. He imagined the Apollo astronauts walking on the moon looking down at the Earth. He had watched so many documentaries on the Moon landings on television, he could recite the names of each of the Apollo crews by heart; Apollo 1, the oxygen fire, Gus Grissom, Ed White and Roger Chaffee; Apollo 17, Eugene Cernan, Ronald Evans and Harrison Schmitt. He had built a plastic *Airfix* model of the Saturn V rocket; it was still on his desk at home. The memory of the first Moon landing was burnt into his mind, he could recite the words used by the Astronauts as they approached the landing site, 'Houston ... Tranquillity Base here ... The Eagle has landed'. As a youngster he had dreamed of being an Astronaut, *Would Rhodesia send a man to the Moon, Mom?*

Rolling over, Smith looked at the luminous dial of his Timex watch. It was 4:30 in the morning, first light in only forty-five minutes or so. He could still smell Moyo's dried blood on his combat shirt. His hands and arms had been caked in blood; he had tried in vain to wash but the blood was very difficult to get off. He did not carry a spare shirt on deployment, only a spare pair of socks.

The horror of seeing Moyo wounded was indescribable. He had panicked at first, calling out for help, tearing at the field dressing, his mind numb trying to think of the best thing to do. His medical training at SInf had been rudimentary in the extreme limited to administering morphine, putting in a drip and applying first field dressings. It had taken what felt like an age to get control of his mind, to focus on trying to help Moyo as best he could.

Moyo had spoken to him, 'It's okay *Ishe* ... I will lay still for the drip.'

It was hard to see the vein in the wounded man's forearm arm, despite the fact that Dube held the tourniquet tightly on the upper arm. On a white man, the blue vein is easy to see, but on a black man, in fading light, the bulge of the vein was the only indication. As Moyo's blood pressure dropped, the veins started to collapse. He missed the vein on the right arm with the first three attempts, causing too much damage, so he had to switch to the left arm. He steadied himself, a silent prayer, *please God help me*. He got the vein in the left arm on the first attempt and the drip immediately began running strongly. He had yelped with success, slapped Dube on the back as he sat up. Moyo had smiled up at him, his eyes glazed, close to losing consciousness, the morphine taking effect.

Looking at the stars, Smith wondered whether there was another star up there, Moyo's star. Not a particularly religious person, Smith made a silent prayer for Moyo, *Please God make him be all right*.

At 5am he heard Fullerton stirring nearby. Time to stand-to for first light. The time-honoured infantry routine is stand-to at first light and last light, the most vulnerable time for an ambush. The sun's crescent on the eastern horizon rapidly expanded until the ground came into view.

The hill held the only remaining members of 2 and 3 Platoons, a police PATU stick and four other police SB members and two sticks of D Company RAR Fireforce. The large number of CT casualties in the contact meant that the police were going to need a long time to clean up. The sun was no sooner over the horizon that the helicopters returned, carrying more SB personnel and to uplift the RAR Fireforce sticks.

Fullerton was back in charge again, the previous days events seemingly already forgotten, 'Sergeant Smith, I want you to sweep back down the hill to the south and try to pick up Gook spoor. Lieutenant Light, I want you to sweep for spoor at the base of the hill from the north, eastwards around to the south.'

Fullerton stood at the apex of the hill silhouetted against the sunrise, once again in his element. Without any further comment or discussion he demanded, '… Move out people!' His rifle sweeping up and down indicating the direction he wanted Smith to go in.

As he led his depleted platoon down the hill, Smith overhead Fullerton shout, 'Sergeant Major Nduku, take inventory of men, weapons and ammunition up here … call for vehicles to pick us up, I have a feeling we are in for another eventful day.'

The remains of 2 Platoon clustered around Sgt Smith, a forlorn group of twelve, decimated by disease and enemy action. The platoon had once again reorganised itself without reference to Smith. He was relieved, one less thing to think about.

'*Ishe*, I have asked Mpofu to join our stick,' said Dube in his usual offhanded manner. It appeared that Dube had now taken Moyo's place as the head of human resources in 2 Platoon. He had a bandage around his head from the shrapnel wound, a bloodstain spread through the material. Smith had offered for Dube to stay with Fullerton for medical attention but got a curt response, 'It is nothing,' was all Dube said.

'Thank you, Dube, Rifleman Mpofu, make sure you stay close to Dube on patrol,' replied Smith, trying to smile encouragingly at the young replacement beaming at him. Mpofu also came from a long line of old RAR soldiers his father was CSM of Support Company. Mpofu was ready.

'Move out people! We haven't got all day!' bellowed Fullerton at them from the top of the hill.

Smith spread his platoon out, about three or four metres apart and they slowly walked down the hill to the south. Sibanda took up his position on Smith's right shoulder, Dube and Mpofu to his left. At the bottom of the hill, the bush was largely open from years of over-grazing and wood chopping for firewood and hut building. The still smouldering wreckage of the downed G-car could be seen through the bush away to the left. Policemen, who were no doubt waiting for an air force recovery team to come in and collect what they could from the wreckage, surrounded it.

'Blood spoor *Ishe*,' someone called out from Smith's left.

Sure enough, a few splatters of blood could be seen in the fine dust.

'Just one Gook *Ishe*,' said someone else. As they continued to the south, a few more CT tracks were discovered all on a roughly parallel heading.

'Over here *Ishe*,' called Cpl Tovakare.

Smith moved over to where Tovakare stood over the body of a dead CT.

'Be careful, watch out for a booby trap!' shouted Smith, pulling his men away from the body.

The platoon went down on their knees waiting while Smith approached the body. Tovakare threw him a piece of thin rope about five metres long. Smith carefully tied it to the man's belt and then withdrew. He lay down, and then gently pulled the body over onto its stomach; nothing fell out. Smith stood up and walked slowly back to take a closer look. He gingerly pushed the body back onto its back, searching the reis-fleck combat jacket. A thick wad of documents, rapped in a clear plastic bag fell out. Smith knew instantly that this was no ordinary CT.

'44 ... this is 42Alpha; I am approximately two kilometres due south of your position. I have found a dead CT that I think you should look at ... Over,' called Smith.

'Roger 42Alpha, wait there for me ...out,' replied Fullerton, excitement in his voice.

Dube pointed out at least nine other CT spoor including a wounded man still bleeding slightly. Smith signalled for the men to go into all-round defence while they waited for Fullerton.

'Jesus, Sergeant Smith, you have found yourself a *makonia makandanga*[146],' exclaimed Fullerton when he looked at the documents.

---

146 Shona, Terrorist, Communist Insurgent. *Makonia* in Shona means important or big. In this case an important terrorist.

'I bet you this is the Gook that took out Lieutenant Dawson's troop. Check this out, the bloke is a brigadier or something.' Fullerton pointed at the small black diary, Brigadier Chabanga's diary, his neat handwriting was easy to read.

Fullerton hesitated while he considered the enormity of this find, 'Fuck ... I bet you this is the same Gook that took out the DC-4 and killed the passengers! ... This is the prick we have been chasing on and off for three weeks!'

'*Ishe*, look at this,' a rifleman held up the Strela missile launcher that had been hastily hidden in the nearby *kopie*.

'Fuck me gently,' sighed Fullerton incredulously. 'Look ... this Gook has been shot between the eyes, what a lucky shot!' He turned, 'Sergeant Smith did your section shoot this Gook?'

'No way Sir, we were stuck up on the hill. We were only shooting up the hill. There were no other call signs behind us, except you.'

'Well it definitely wasn't me. He must have been shot from the helicopter before he brought it down.' Then the ridiculousness of that statement dawned on him. 'It could have been a stray shot from up the hill when Fireforce came over ... that must be it,' concluded Fullerton unconvincingly.

Looking down at the body again, Smith was not game to question how it was that he was shot in the front of the head and not the back, *who gives a shit, he's dead anyway.*

'Sergeant Smith you had better carry on with the follow-up, my guess is that this Gook's *mukkas*[147] will RV up ahead. Give me a sitrep every half an hour, more often if they change direction. Right ... move out,' said Fullerton eagerly, still holding the pack of documents. Smith, once again shook his head at the amazing resilience of the man, he was back in the zone, all business; ready for anything the war could throw at him. Fullerton's indomitable spirit was so infectious that Smith felt completely ready to seize the day. *Shit am I actually getting used to this?*

Sibanda positioned himself over the tracks left by Benkov's band as they had headed off to the south, pointing in the direction they were headed. He did not need to say anything. The loss of Moyo now placed more responsibility on the young man. He was now lead tracker. Smith positioned himself behind Sibanda, sending him off on the spoor. He looked back at his ragged platoon as they filed in behind. Nobody was talking, the prospect of a hard day's march in extreme heat, with very little chance of replenishing water, not at all appealing.

The sun in the clear, cloudless sky was vicious, despite the fact that

---

147 Rhodesian slang, friend, friends. In this case Fullerton is referring to the Freedom Fighter's friends.

it was only seven in the morning. Smith could feel the burning on the back of his neck instinctively reaching behind his head repositioning his face-veil to protect his neck. He thought of reapplying the black camo-cream to his face and arms as it had mostly worn off, *bugger that, it's too bloody hot.*

The number of CTs they were following steadily increased through the day, as Benkov's band mopped up more fleeing cadres. Smith reported that the group had swung around to the west. The density and number of villages rapidly decreased as they travelled further to the west. By late afternoon they passed through the last of the villages. The spoor was still clear on the ground. The few local tribesmen they passed stood sullenly by, watching, always nervous at the presence of security forces. There was no point in stopping to question the locals. The trail was obvious, the distance they were behind all too clear. The number they were following twenty or so – give or take.

Smith walked his men until last light. He identified some thick scrub on the edge of a deep *donga* and doglegged, in the usual way, into the sleeping position. They waited patiently for half an hour after dark to see whether they had been followed. The hunters too could be hunted. Smith put the men into their sleeping positions and made his last sitrep to Fullerton. They had covered a very respectable twenty-five kilometres during the day. Smith took out his ruler and measured another +-100 kilometres to the Botswana border, *shit I hope I don't have to walk the whole way!* Smith figured that there was no way that he would catch them if they kept walking through the night. His map reading skills were going to be sorely tested as the 1:50,000 map showed precious few contour lines and very few hills or landmarks of any consequence. Fortunately a few tracks were marked, and a few very isolated boreholes.

*

Police Camp, Dett, northern Matabeleland

After the clean up of the CT base camp, *Ingwe* Fullerton returned to the police camp at Dett. He had Nduku and Light with him and the three of them sat around the map figuring out their next move. It was obvious to them that the CTs would not possibly keep their present heading unless they were heading for the Botswana border. The area was part national park and part controlled hunting area. There were no villages at all.

The terrain was mostly flat, cut by river lines and ridges running east-west. There were a good many hunting roads and tracks that criss-crossed the area with two main gravel roads: one from the south, and one from the north near Wankie, to Panda-ma-Tenga on the border. 4 Indep had been based at Panda-ma-Tenga in the past, and the older hands in the Company knew the area reasonably well. The bush itself was mostly dry acacia, not densely wooded. The dry riverbeds would contain water if it were possible to dig deep enough. Elephants were very adept at digging in the right places; they could smell the water beneath.

Fullerton knew that they were going to have to work quickly if they were to catch the CTs before they reached the border. Smith and 2 Platoon were never going to be able to do it on their own. He worked out a leapfrog using the few tracks that the departing CTs would likely cross, in the hope that they could gain some time, hoping too that the CTs would get lazy and walk down one of the roads. Fullerton had already requested helicopters, but none were available, as Fireforce had been redeployed elsewhere. If they made contact there would be no air support; if they were lucky, they might be able to call in a Lynx from Wankie. When Fullerton had called sub-JOC at Wankie to ask if there were any other units available in the area, he was told that there were none. 1 Platoon had returned from R&R but had immediately been sucked into a follow-up of another large CT insurgent group that had crossed the *Cordon Sanitaire* near the Gwai gorge. Recent history was repeating itself. Fullerton would have the help of three PATU sticks, one from Dett and two from Wankie. He had the use of forty men, including cooks and bottle-washers, to cover an area close to 1,000 square kilometres, *no problem!*

Sgt-Maj Nduku was sent directly to Panda-ma-Tenga, with two vehicles, five men in each. Their job was to cut along the border track, north and south of the abandoned customs post. As the follow-up neared the border, they could be positioned as stop groups. Lt Light, with the remainder of 3 Platoon, would take up a position on a track nearest to the follow-up team, ready to react if contact was made. He would also relieve the follow-up team on the spoor the next day. Fullerton with his HQ detachment would traverse the main dirt road between Dett and Panda-ma-Tenga, looking for spoor and ready to support a contact. The three PATU sticks with their trackers would traverse ahead of the follow-up team in their Land Rovers, cutting for spoor, hopefully to leapfrog ahead.

Fullerton called Sgt Smith, 42Alpha and told him the plan and that Lt Light would relieve him at the end of the following day … unless things changed.

Before first light the next morning Sgt Smith and his platoon were already up and ready to start the day. As the milky sunlight touched the spoor in the sandy soil, they set off.

*

Matetsi Controlled Hunting area, West of Wankie, northern Matabeleland

Vladimir Benkov had tried to push his band through the night, but it proved too difficult. It was pitch dark, the lack of moonlight made the going very slow. He used his luminous compass to keep his bearings but found the way blocked by *dongas* and steep rocky ridges. The complete absence of light meant men were falling into holes, being snagged by obstructions and complaining bitterly. The few men he had collected from the base camp knew the route well, but they relied on following landmarks that they could not see in the dark.

In desperation, to increase speed, Benkov walked along a track that was mostly westerly in direction. He knew where he was from checking the satellite photo he had with him. The track led them to an abandoned hunting lodge where the name *Nyala* hung forlornly from the broken gate hanging on its hinges. The lodge had a water tank with a tap attached that the experienced cadres had used before. The cadres indicated another abandoned hunting camp was about thirty-five kilometres further west that also had water tanks. Benkov looked at his map and satellite photo to pick it out. The Botswana border would then be a further forty-five kilometres to the west. The hunting tracks in the area spiralled in all directions, meaning that the route to the next camp could not be directly by road.

As they started off the next morning, Benkov drew confidence from the fact that he heard one of the cadres pointing out two hills to the east, *Karunda* and *Surichenji*, which confirmed that they knew exactly where they were.

*

Fullerton's first break came at 11am the next morning when one of the PATU sticks picked up Benkov's trail on the track to the Nyala Hunting Lodge. They called up excitedly to report their find, a clear path of nineteen-odd men traipsed along in single file. The police reservists drove carefully along the road to the hunting lodge wary of being ambushed. The camp was a large complex with at least ten thatched bungalows, a central dining area and other outbuildings, workers' accommodation and a large water tank attached to a borehole with a wind-pump. The CT activity around the water tank was clear to see.

Looking at his map, Fullerton drew a line with his finger to the west as far as the border. He called up Lt Light and told him to take up the follow-up from the Nyala hunting camp and send his vehicles to pick up Smith and his platoon. His gaze fell on another hunting camp approximately thirty clicks almost due west; *the bastards are going from camp to camp for water!*

The radio instruction to walk out to the track 4kms to his north came as a great relief to Smith and his men. They were tired, water supplies virtually finished, it was excruciatingly hot, the heat, perceptibly sapping everyone's strength. The men's spirits lifted with the news; there was no need to urge them forward to the road. The trucks were waiting for them when they arrived; they climbed aboard in silence totally exhausted. With energy levels completely depleted, there was no boisterous chatter, just the rumble of the trucks as they lurched and bumped along the rough track to their RV with Fullerton further to the west.

Any thought of a chance to rest were quickly dispelled by Fullerton when they met up.

'Sergeant Smith I want you to lay an ambush at this hunting camp here,' he said stabbing the map with his forefinger. 'I think these Gooks are travelling from camp to camp because they know that there is water in the boreholes and rainwater tanks.'

The 1:50,000 map had little detail although a number of buildings were marked. A tributary of the Deka River circled around to the north of the camp, completely dry at that time of the year.

'Have you set up claymores before?' enquired Fullerton, fixing Smith with his usual piercing stare.

'Only in training Sir,' replied Smith, trying to anticipate Fullerton's idea.

'Piece-a-cake, just point them in the direction of your chosen killing ground, place the det in the hole in the top and then run the electrical cables back to your position.'

Fullerton carried on in the same vein as if he was discussing the weather.

'A few things to watch out for, make sure you use a new radio battery, clean the contacts, and make sure that the positive and negative wires are kept well apart at all times. You don't want these things going off prematurely … could spoil your day.'

Fullerton studied Smith's face after this rudimentary set of instructions. 'Oh yes, make sure that your ambush position is a good twenty or so metres back from the claymores.' Then his final thoughts,

'… yes, also it would be a good idea to bury the cables or disguise them as your gooks could arrive during daylight. You'll find a box of four claymores in my truck with dets and cable … any questions?'

Smith marvelled at the brevity of his instructions, he had a thousand questions. He looked at Fullerton, the man's confidence and focus, a constant source of admiration. He resolved that any questions would simply irritate Fullerton so he would have to figure it out as he went along.

'No Sir, no questions … where will you be, Sir?'

'I will position myself further to the west. The border is less than twenty clicks from the lodge along this river line.' He pointed at the map once again. 'If these Gooks bypass your position, or if you miss them, then I hope to catch them somewhere in this river line. I have positioned Sergeant Major Nduku on the border track … he's our last line.'

Finishing his brief explanation, another thought occurred to Fullerton.

'One last thing, we have no idea where these gooks are, so they may be planning to ambush us as they did to the Grey Scouts. I suggest that you debus the vehicles well short of the hunting camp and recce it carefully before you enter.'

Just as succinctly Fullerton turned away, Smith's briefing was complete, his mind now on other things.

The A76 radios came to life, '44 … 44 this is 43, confirm CTs still movin in a west'ly direction … we are at …' Lt Light gave his locstat. 'Confirm CTs moving on bearin two, six, zero, degrees … Oer.'

Smith heard Fullerton reply, 'Copied 43, 44, Out.'

Fullerton then bellowed across the road in Smith's direction, 'Sergeant Smith, you better get your arse into gear, those gooks are heading directly for your ambush position.'

The faces of the men showed the physical strain they were under. They were too tired to complain. The platoon crowded around a water bowser towed by one of the vehicles to refill water bottles. Many stripped off and splashed the cool water over their bodies. Smith looked on, wishing he could have a shower or a swim, anything to remove the grime that had built up on his body; camo-cream, blood, sweat and dust was all caked on his skin. He was too tired to bother.

With a few more playfully sarcastic comments from Fullerton ringing in his ears, Smith ushered his reluctant platoon onto the trucks and set off on the circuitous route to the abandoned hunting lodge. He noted it was called *Kande-le-Nyati* on the map, named after a hill 9kms to the southeast. The approach road to the camp was from the north, the turn-off on the main road from Wankie to Panda-ma-Tenga. Smith stopped the vehicles a good 5kms short of the camp and got everybody off. He then called Fullerton to let him know he was moving into position. Smith had given his men a short briefing before they left but he knew that it was useless until he could see the lay of the land.

2 Platoon walked down the road until they got to the point that it crossed the dry Deka tributary, they then left the road moving along the river line until they reached a point due north of the camp. The bush was very open, dry as tinder and the ground was virtually devoid of grass cover. The shallow riverbed was about five hundred metres from the camp, clearly visible through the sparse trees. It was a large complex; he could count at least ten chalets, a large corrugated iron shed, and a rambling old farmhouse with wrap-around verandas. The place looked completely deserted. Smith scanned the buildings with his binoculars for a good twenty minutes. His men, stretched out left and right also studied the camp closely, everybody critically aware of what this band of CTs had done to the Grey Scouts. They did not wish to suffer the same fate.

Smith called Fullerton on the radio to confirm that he had the camp 'visual'; he saw no movement and was now advancing into the camp. Smith then briefed his men in more detail, pointing out that the riverbed was to be the RV point in the event of an ambush. They all nodded, there was no talking; the tension starting to build as the reality of a possible contact sunk in.

Smith positioned Dube with the MAG next to him on the right, Sibanda and Mpofu on his left with LCpl Tovakare with his stick further to the right, LCpl Nkai to the extreme left. They all stood up in a sweepline and began a fast walk towards the camp, carefully keeping a set distance apart. They covered the ground quickly. As they entered the compound Smith felt uneasy as the men were funnelled through the buildings. He kept the sweepline moving as fast as possible until they swept right through the lodge buildings to the other side. There was no sign of life.

As he walked through the complex, Smith identified a large rainwater tank attached to the main farmhouse; another tank was attached to a wind-pump borehole. He tested the taps. The rainwater tank had water in it while the other tank was dry. There was no fresh spoor in the camp, but Dube pointed out that people had definitely been through the camp in the last week or two. An eight-foot high security fence surrounded the farmhouse with a large gate on the eastern side that was standing open.

The water tank attached to the side of the house was on a brick plinth about half a metre off the ground. It was positioned on the western side of the house in a ten-metre gap between the house and the large corrugated iron storage shed. There was no place to conceal his men for the ambush. There was also no way of knowing which direction the CTs would approach from. They would have to literally step over the men in the ambush to get to the tank and the killing ground. It was getting late. He needed to make a decision fast.

The nearest cover to the water tank was a low garden wall about thirty metres to the south. The garden was now over-grown; a few large bougainvilleas had spread out over the wall. It seemed unlikely that the CTs would approach through the garden as it would be difficult to negotiate at night. Smith figured that, if they approached from the east, they would walk through the open gate, and then around the front of the house to the water tank. He glanced furtively into the bush beyond the gate, *they may be watching me right now!* Inside the security fence both he and the CTs would be trapped in a 'hen house' with only one way out. He contemplated setting the ambush at the security fence gate but there was no cover to hide in.

Smith decided the garden wall was his best bet. To hedge his bet, he sent Tovakare to cut a hole through the security fence on the edge of the garden to the south so that they could escape if things got out of hand. He then set about laying out the claymores.

The claymores were modeled on the US M18A1 mine consisting of a horizontally convex, olive green, plastic case which is vertically concave. Smith contemplated the raised words on the front of the case 'Front Toward Enemy'. He decided to lay the mines in a daisychain along the edge of the steel shed where some tufts of grass had grown up. The side of the shed would also be in deep shadow at night.

The distance between the edge of the house and the shed was so narrow that aiming the mines with the open sight on the top wasn't necessary. Smith unpacked all four mines, placing them equal distances apart along the full length of the shed. That way, if a few CTs hung around the front of the house, he would get them too. The claymore mine contained a layer of C-4 explosive on top of which was a matrix of hundreds of 1/8th inch diametre steel balls, set into an epoxy resin. It had a killing range of up to 100 metres but was completely lethal at 30 metres - 10 metres would turn people into mincemeat.

Starting at the extreme left of his chosen killing-ground Smith unfolded the two pairs of scissor legs attached to the bottom to support the mine, allowing it to be aimed vertically. He rolled out the electrical wire pushing it right up against the edge of the shed in the grass. Dube worked behind him pushing sand over the wire. He left the detonators out of the mines until he was finished, then rolled the cable with the firing switch attached to the garden wall. The problem was that the garden wall was at right angles to the line of claymores, which the instruction manual warned against, in big fat letters. Anybody looking over the wall at the time of detonation would likely get hit.

As the sun began to set Smith walked down the line of mines, pushing the detonators into position, then went back over the wall. Nkai took a few men and carefully swept the ground with cut branches to remove their spoor. Smith decided that splitting his men into two stop groups was too dangerous. Ideally he should have the gate covered to get any escaping CTs that survived the claymore blast. Instead he put them all behind the wall in a line, sending Tovakare with one man to guard their escape route through the wire fence. The plan was to initiate the ambush with the claymores. The men were then to sit up and shoot over the wall at any survivors, *piece-a-cake*, Smith recalling Fullerton's immortal words.

Careful not to allow the two detonation wires to touch, Smith layed out the trigger switch and battery in the position he would take up. Smith then worked along the line of men behind the wall, methodically explaining the plan over and over again. The men all nodded their understanding, but Smith still felt uneasy. Being trapped inside the security fence really worried him. Just before sunset he called Fullerton to confirm they were in position. Lt Light also came up on the radio to confirm that the CTs were still maintaining the same bearing at last light. The Evening Star[148] was already shining brightly on the western horizon.

Lying in his ambush position, Smith looked at the electrical contacts, questioning in his mind whether he had prepared everything correctly. He momentarily reflected on one of O'Connell's favourite songs from Vietnam, Buffalo Springfield[149].

> *There's something happening here*
> *What it is ain't exactly clear*
> *There's a man with a gun over there*
> *Telling me I got to beware*

Sometimes once a song gets in the mind it just plays over and over again. It is indeed strange how the mind works when stress is combined with numbing fatigue.

> *I think it's time we stop, children, what's that sound*
> *Everybody look what's going down*
> *There's battle lines being drawn*
> *Nobody's right if everybody's wrong*

---

148 The planet Venus as it appears in the west at sunset.
149 *For What its Worth*, Stephen Stills, recorded in 1968 by Buffalo Springfield.

*

Comrade Benkov and his band arrived outside Kande-le-Nyati just before last light; he too studied the abandoned buildings in the fast fading light but could not see any movement. He decided to wait an hour or so just in case any SF or a hunting party had taken up residence.

The cadres were anxious to get water and they agitated to get going, chattering loudly. Benkov could hear Mlungisi telling them to be patient. He felt tired, exhausted really. The heat was indescribable, which, coupled with his poor diet was taking its toll, the pace that they had kept up for two days had been relentless with food intake meagre at best, he was down to one tin of bully-beef. He still could not face the gruel that the cadres prepared for themselves. He was happy in the knowledge that he had only one more day to go.

As prearranged, Mlungisi took half the men forward to the gate. They would take turns the first group would go in, replenish their water, wash if they wanted to, and then the second group would go in. Creeping forward, Mlungisi hesitated at the gate. The starlight was bright enough to see the buildings clearly. There was no cloud cover. The new crescent moon was up, but not providing much assistance. Mlungisi waited a few more minutes peering into the dark, seeking out any signs of movement. When he was satisfied, he moved the group of ten men through the gate. The experienced cadres knew the water tank was on the far side of the farmhouse, they led the way.

Stepped up onto the veranda of the house, Mlungisi tried the front door, it was locked. The freedom fighters that had traversed this infiltration route so many times had amazingly never broken into the house. None of the windows were smashed. Mlungisi momentarily contemplated breaking in; he stepped around the veranda onto the eastern side where an old wooden rocking chair sat, a lone piece of furniture. He propped his AK up against the wall and sat down on the chair. It felt really good; he put his head back and closed his eyes, gently rocking the chair with his feet. *When the struggle is over, I must get a house like this with a rocking chair,* he thought to himself.

An AK opened fire on the other side of the house. The window to Mlungisi's right exploded outwards in a deafening roar. The sound of thunder beat at his chest, the blast of glass fragments sprayed all over him. His mind was fleetingly confused, *there's somebody in the house!* He touched his cheek; the right hand side of his face was a mass of tiny cuts.

The night erupted into gunfire. Red tracer rounds sprayed into the night. Ambush! Mlungisi jumped to his feet, grabbing for his AK but he couldn't see it clearly, his hand knocking it over. Fear burst through his numbed mind. On all fours he scrambled for his rifle. Trying to regain his footing he slipped on the smooth, dust covered cement veranda. In front of him he saw a comrade walking in circles. The air was thick with dust. As he took a breath it made him cough uncontrollably. He could not see who it was. Gunfire continued from the other side of the house. Mlungisi ran towards the man, he tried to grab the man's arm - there was no arm. His hand felt the slippery wetness of blood. The man made no noise. Mlungisi tried to push the man towards the gate, but he collapsed onto his knees. In blind panic, Mlungisi ran for the gate.

His eyes closed, Benkov leaned up against a tree thinking of a winter in Moscow, the bitter, familiar cold, drinking Vodka. He longed to be cold again.

The claymore blast wave hit him in the chest; Benkov knew instantly that the first group had been ambushed. He did not panic. He got to his feet as he saw a man running through the gate towards him. The cadres around him broke into an agitated babble. They wanted to run. Benkov called out to them in Russian to be still.

Mlungisi ran up to him, waving his arms, '...we must get away Comrade!' he called out in terror. He was still coughing hoarsely.

The gunfire in the hunting lodge compound stopped. The night was again deadly quiet. Mlungisi was too shocked to comprehend, jabbering way to the other men.

'Shut up Mlungisi,' Benkov hissed in Russian, '... we don't know how many there are or where they are.'

Benkov needed to establish if there were Rhodesians in stop groups outside the fence. He grabbed Mlungisi by the shirt and pulled him towards him, 'Comrade, you must be quiet, our lives depend on it,' he spat. He slapped Mlungisi on the side of the head; it seemed to get the message across.

Benkov made the men lie down facing the compound. He needed to make an assessment. He still could not see any movement, in or outside the compound. Still needing about eight or nine hours to get to the border, he weighed up his options. His training and natural aggression once again kicked in. Mlungisi had settled down, a drink of water had stopped his coughing. He made Mlungisi explain to the surviving cadres that they were going to skirt around the south of the compound, then head for the riverline and finally to walk rapidly to the safety of Botswana. The talk of Botswana seemed to do the trick, calming the men down, the deaths of their comrades temporarily forgotten. The survival instinct, self-preservation, came to the fore.

Leading the men around to the south, Benkov kept the hunting lodge in sight. As they crept along trying to be as quiet as possible,

Benkov saw movement at the security fence. He stopped and pointed. The others froze, looking into the dark. Benkov knelt down bringing his rifle into his shoulder. The others followed his lead. The RPD gunner lay down and opened the bipod. Benkov tapped Mlungisi on the shoulder and called out to fire.

A hail of bullets split the night. Green tracer shot across towards the farmhouse, disappearing into the dark. Tracer split upwards, ricocheting off solid objects. Initially no fire was returned. Then a single rifle shot from somewhere near the fence. Benkov got back to his feet, indicating for the men to follow. They moved rapidly for another 50 metres, the fusillade was repeated, but this time, the crack of MAG and FN returned fire. The freedom fighters ceased fire and melting back into the dark. Benkov thought he heard a truck changing gears somewhere in the distance.

*

Sgt Smith leopard-crawled towards the gap that Tovakare had cut in the fence. The RPD chattered on the outside of the fence, green tracer thumping over his head. Dube was returning fire from the garden wall with the MAG, belt after belt. The shock of being attacked from behind had disorientated the men, plus the massive ear-slitting explosion of four claymores, three kilograms of C4, was deafening. Smith's ears were still ringing.

In front of him Smith heard a rifle returning fire, 'Tovakare … is that you?' he called out.

'Yes *Ishe*, Ndlamini has been hit.'

The CT rifle fire from Smith's right had now stopped, so had the return fire. Smith crawled further forward until he reached Tovakare who was under a bush just inside the security fence. Next to him was the body of Ndlamini, a young recruit only four months out of Depot.

'He was standing next to the fence when the CTs opened fire *Ishe*. He went down straight away.'

Smith put his still ringing ears next to Ndlamini's mouth. It was no use, he could not hear him breathing. He felt for a pulse at the neck, nothing. It was too dark to see the wounds that the man had sustained but he could feel the blood on his skin.

'Help me carry him to the farmhouse Tovakare.'

The two men climbed to their feet, Ndlamini was a tall man. They strained trying to lift him, a shoulder under each arm. They stumbled forward, Ndlamini's feet dragged behind. Smith could feel blood once again soaking into his uniform. At the garden wall the men were silent, waiting for another attack. Smith made sure to call out so that he wasn't shot at; the men were highly agitated, jumpy and nervous.

'Nkai, check all the men for wounded, check every man yourself,' Smith called out. After he had initiated the ambush Smith had reported to Fullerton on the radio. Fullerton had confirmed that he would drive to the hunting lodge himself. Lt Light had heard the massive explosion over 12kms away.

Smith did not want to risk shining a light in case the CTs were still waiting out in the dark. There was no way of knowing how many. He called Fullerton to confirm he had a casualty and needed casevac. It was not long before he could hear the vehicles approaching.

*

The ambush had nearly gone horribly wrong; the CTs had arrived so soon after dark that Smith was taken completely by surprise. They announced their arrival with loud talking and joking. Smith could hear the tap being opened and water splattering onto the concrete. He had pressed the switch on the trigger mechanism, but it didn't go off. Feverishly feeling around in the dark, he found one of the wires was loose and he had to reconnect it. It took agonising seconds to screw the wire back in place. The clicking sound of the trigger being pressed was heard by one of the CTs, who panicked, opening fire in the direction of the wall. It was only then that Smith managed to get the claymores to detonate. The deadening shockwave buffeted the wall; thick dust tumbled over the top, covering everything in a fine film, including the ambush team. The dust hung in the air like an impenetrable cloud. Shooting over the top of the wall was impossible. Nothing was visible. It was also difficult to breath in the dust. The men simply blazed away into the dust cloud until Smith's shouting stopped them.

When Fullerton arrived at the Kande-le-Nyati hunting lodge it was still early, 8pm. He rigged up a few gaslights from his trailer and set up a map on the farmhouse veranda. Every window of the house had been blown out. Fine glass fragments covered the concrete that crunched loudly underfoot. Dust covered everything. Fullerton positioned one of the trucks next to the shed to illuminate the killing ground.

The sight was indescribable. The CTs standing next to the water tank were reduced to pieces of tissue, literally vapourised. The bodies were unrecognisable, shredded to smithereens. The wall of the house was pocked-marked, covered, as if spray-painted, in faded red dust-laden blood. The water tank was like a colander, water spraying out from a million tiny holes. It was impossible even to tell how many men had been standing next to the tank. In the front of the house, further away from the blast, two bodies lay on the driveway.

Fullerton stood on the veranda, surveying the scene, 'Well Smithy, your ambush seems to have been very successful,' he commented approvingly, '… pity the CTs left some people outside, you would have definitely got all of them if they had come in here.'

Then thinking out-loud, gazing out to the east, he said 'The CTs are gapping it to the border for sure.'

Ndlamini's body, wrapped in his bivy, was carried across the driveway to be placed carefully in the back of Fullerton's truck. Smith watched Fullerton's eyes following the body as it was carried past, not even a blink, no sign of emotion, just a steady gaze as if thinking about something else.

Still looking in the direction of the body being loaded, Fullerton stated to no one in particular, 'It's no use waiting here to commence a follow-up in the morning. The gooks will be drinking beer in Francistown by then.' He turned to Smith who stood looking up at him, 'we will have to take our chances at the border crossing. We just have to hope that one of our stop groups picks them up.' He seemed resigned, 'I think we may have lost this lot Smithy … the bastards!'

> *Paranoia strikes deep*
> *Into your life it will creep*
> *It starts when you're always afraid*
> *… , hey, what's that sound*
> *Everybody look what's going down*

*

Border Track, south of Panda-ma-Tenga, Northern Matabeleland

The men were loaded on the trucks and headed off on the short trip to the Botswana border. The Police PATU sticks had already arrived at the abandoned customs post at the border crossing to Panda-ma-Tenga. The police still maintained a detachment at the local police station. A truck was sent to pick up Lt Light who was still bumbling through the dark, completely lost. Map reading in the Rhodesian bush at night was a little different to windswept Salisbury Plains on conventional exercises. He eventually resorted to shooting up mini-flares so the trucks could find him.

The terrain south of Panda-ma-Tenga is flat, dry and cut by large wide *vleis* that fill in the rainy season. These swampy areas overflow to feed the Deka and Matetsi rivers that flow northeast to the Zambezi. The bush is open and sparse other than in the very narrow river lines. The *vlei*-lines are virtually devoid of vegetation in the dry season. There were no vantage points upon which to set up OPs.

The border itself, in most places, was a three-strand barbed-wire fence, followed on both sides by dirt tracks. On the Rhodesian side the track was used by national parks rangers and professional hunters - not too many of them these days. On the Botswana side, the Botswana Defence Force patrolled. The wild game migrated freely across the border; the area on both sides is virtually devoid of permanent human habitation besides the small village of Panda-ma-Tenga itself, which is inside Botswana.

By midnight Fullerton had everybody assembled on the Rhodesian side of the border crossing. In the interests of time he rigged up a gas light on the back of his Four-Five truck with the double tail doors open so that everyone could see him. He had cellotaped a 1:50,000 map to one of the doors and held a tree branch in his hand.

'All right ... everybody listen up. These CTs are moving from Kande-le-Nyati to the border. The poor light will mean that they will not be going as fast as they would normally do. My guess is that they will reach the border at or just before first light. They will check carefully for SF on our side and BDF[150] on the other side before crossing.'

Fullerton paused to make sure he had everyone's attention. He had the PATU sticks and all of 2 and 3 Platoons sticks sitting together in their c/signs.

He continued in quick clipped sentences, 'this is one seriously smart gook we are dealing with here. He is not afraid to take us on. He will run but only when he absolutely has to. If he has the opportunity to kill you, he will.' Pointing to the map, waving the stick in a circle to the south of Panda-ma-Tenga, he emphasised ' ... the most direct route will mean the CTs will cross in this area. Their primary aim is to cross the border. Once they have crossed, they will walk to the Francistown road hoping to get a lift from a BDF patrol.'

Fullerton then allocated sectors to each c/sign. The extreme southerly sector was allocated to Smith, and then each c/sign was marked going north, in roughly one-kilometre intervals.

After he was finished the briefing Fullerton summed up, 'If you make contact give your c/sign on the radio. All other c/signs should converge on the contact area along the border road. We will position trucks on the road for this purpose. You need to be careful; with so many of us in a small area the risk of friendly fire is high. Keep your radios on at all times.'

150 Botswana Defense Force.

Fullerton surveyed the men in front of him to make sure his briefing had sunk in. 'Do not, I repeat NOT, follow the CTs into Botswana … Is that clear?' he demanded, pointing expansively towards Botswana.

Everybody nodded. The last thing on their minds was crossing into Botswana.

'Unfortunately there is no Fireforce and no air support at this time. Sub-JOC Wankie said that we may get a Lynx at first light, but we know that the Blue Jobs don't like getting out of bed too early.' There was a stifled laugh from a few. 'Move out people. Remember this gook will kill you if he gets half a chance.'

Nobody needed any reminding.

Everyone piled back onto the trucks and set off down the border track. They travelled in silence, Fullerton's warning ringing in their ears. The track itself was in good condition as the police regularly 'dragged' it with tyres to check for CT spoor.

Smith sat in the front of the first truck, his platoon making up the last three stop groups, 42Charlie - Tovakare, 42Bravo - Nyati, and his own, 42Alpha. The death of Ndlamini was momentarily forgotten as they keyed themselves up for yet another contact.

Smith's mind felt completely numb, the emotional roller coaster of contact after contact was just too intense to cope with. Concentrating on the job at hand was all that Smith could focus on. One thing was for sure, Smith was now convinced that the overall situation was completely out of control. The CTs seemed to be everywhere, *is this what it is like in the whole country? If so, we are in deep shit.*

The headlights of the Four-Five picked up animals all along the road, impala, elephant, kudu and a lone hyena. He had measured the distance he needed to go using the truck's tachometre in conjunction with his map. The problem was there were no obvious features on the map to identify. He dropped off his other two c/signs and then travelled another kilometre before stopping. They left the truck on the road then followed a dry *vlei* for about four hundred metres; he needed to find some cover to lay-up in.

The area was dead flat, completely open. Eventually he settled on a small clump of trees where the four of them lay down in all-round defence, feet almost touching. The starlight reflected off the parched, almost white, sandy soil. Visibility was crystal clear for at least a hundred metres. They lay in pretty much the only clump of trees for some distance. A lion roared in the distance. The cicadas were buzzing, newly hatched after the first rains. A bullfrog barked loudly from a waterhole somewhere off to Smith's left. Each man would do an hour's watch with everybody awake an hour before first light. Smith lay down on the hard packed ground, his mind frozen from fatigue and lack of sleep. Dube took first watch and Smith was asleep almost instantly, the dreamless sleep of the totally exhausted.

26

Border Track, south of Panda-ma-Tenga, Northern Matabeleland

Mike Smith did not wake after the first shake from Sibanda. Sibanda had to lean over and place his hand on the back of Smith's head to shake him awake. Smith awoke slightly disorientated, trying to get his mind in focus. He looked at the luminous dial on his watch, 4:30am, one hour to first light. Smith checked that all four of them were awake. They lay waiting in complete silence, each man alone with his own thoughts. The real possibility of contact with the enemy meant that there was little fear of anybody nodding off. If they did not contact the CTs before 6am, it was almost certain that they had missed them in the night. They would have crossed into Botswana successfully. There was always the possibility, of course, that Fullerton's guesswork was completely wrong and that the CTs were either further south or further north.

By 5am the light on the horizon was a clear band of orange, the ground still in darkness. Smith watched as the light slowly improved to the extent that he could see across the wide *vlei*. They were lying in the midst of four stunted acacia trees, in the middle of a wide expanse of nothing, as if on an island in the ocean. The edge of the *vlei* was at least two hundred metres in any direction. Nobody would be able to approach their position without being seen; similarly even the most inexperienced of CTs would not cross such an open area. Smith cursed under his breath.

CRACK, crack, crack, gunfire opened up to Smith's left, north of his position. It sounded like an RPD, definitely not an MAG. The radio was silent. A bang from a grenade rolled across the *vlei*.

'44 this is 42Alpha, I have gunfire to my north.'

'42Alpha, copied … move up from your position,' came Fullerton's instant reply.

'Let's go,' Smith shouted to his stick.

The four of them got to their feet trotting across the open *vlei* in the direction of the gunfire. They were dead men if the CTs saw them before they could make the edge of the *vlei*. The gunfire stopped and then started again, sporadically, it seemed to be coming closer. Still no call on the radio, *where are Nkai and Tovakare?* Smith's stick made the thin tree line on the edge of the *vlei*; game trails spiralling out from the muddy waterhole in the middle. He searched the ground ahead looking for signs of movement. They stopped running … walking forward, vigilant … rifles at the ready. Smith was concerned that Nkai or Tovakare would be chasing forward, with the risk of being caught up in friendly fire.

Is that movement in the distance? Smith peered through the trees, blinking to clear his eyes.

'CTs *Ishe*,' said Dube quietly, pointing out in front; the men automatically went down onto their knees.

'How many can you see?' whispered Smith, he could not see, his eyes nowhere near as sharp as Dube's.

'I can see four. They are walking,' replied Dube almost inaudibly, calmly pointing his hand to show the direction.

'44 this is 42 Alpha, I have four Charlie Tangos visual … too far to engage,' called Smith as quietly as possible, holding his hand over the mouthpiece. He then gave an estimate for the grid reference of his position.

'Copied, 42 Alpha, stay in your position, I am calling for an air strike, you talk them in … Over.' Fullerton's voice came back so loud and clear that Smith jumped with fright, frantically turning the volume down.

'I can see nine CTs now *Ishe*,' murmured Dube, pointing once again in the direction of the enemy.

Smith stared through the trees, concentrating hard, following Dube's indication. He could now see the CTs very clearly, walking across his front, about 400m away. They had their rifles at the ready, obviously alert. As he watched he counted two RPD gunners and one CT had an RPG launcher with a projectile in place. The CT leading the band was a good foot taller than all the rest.

Out to the north Smith heard the engines of the Lynx as it approached. The familiar sound was strangely comforting. The CTs also heard the Lynx. They went to ground hiding under the low trees. Even though the acacia trees were small and stunted, they still had a thick green canopy. *Where are Nkai and Tovakare?*

The Lynx pilot called Smith's c/sign, '42Alpha …Yellow 1.'

With the volume turned down Smith had to hold the handset tight against his ear.

'Yellow 1 this is 42Alpha I read you fives you are to my north,' Smith whispered into the handset. He could not see the Lynx, but he could hear it rapidly getting closer. The CTs remained in their cover, unaware that they had been spotted. Smith carefully unfolded his map and laid it out in front of him, pushing sand onto the edges to hold it in place. He lifted his floppy hat and turned it inside out to reveal the day-glo[151] panel stitched inside. The others followed his lead.

---

151 All SF had an orange day-glo panel stitched into the inside of their combat cap or hat. The bright panel could be seen clearly from the air and helped to ensure the correct identification of friend or foe. Many a SF c/sign was on the receiving end of .303 or

The Lynx passed overhead at about 2,000 feet.

'Roger 42Alpha I have you visual…. you need to mark target over.'

So as not to give the CTs an indication that they had been spotted the Lynx pilot continued on his course only banking into a left-hand turn some distance away. Smith heard the change in the engine note as the pilot clawed for more altitude for his attack run.

'Roger Yellow 1, nine Charlie Tangos to my east approximately 500 metres, I will mark target with a red mini-flare … over.'

'42Alpha, I am throwing fran. Fire a mini-flare on my mark … over.'

On the road behind Smith's position, trucks could be heard arriving, bringing men in from the north. The sound of diesel engines racing was clear in the still early morning air.

The engine note from the Lynx changed again as the pilot brought the aircraft around onto the attack run.

'42Alpha … standby,' called the pilot.

Smith held his mini-flare projector in his hand, trying to figure the correct trajectory so as to land the flare as close as possible. The flare was pushed into the top of the tube with a spring-loaded trigger, to be pushed over letting the firing pin impact the bottom of the flare. The engines of the Lynx increased in intensity.

'42Alpha … standby,' the pilot's voice now more urgent, '… standby … steady … MARK!'

Smith released the firing pin; the flare cracked and shot out in an arc towards the CT position, a thin trail of smoke marking the direction.

'Roger 42Alpha I have your target visual.'

The engines began to howl as the pilot accelerated into the dive. From where Smith lay he could not see the Lynx, its attack run coming in from the south. He heard the twin, roof-mounted .303 Brownings open up as the pilot attempted to suppress any thought the CTs may have had to break and run for it.

The Lynx come into view, the engines screeching loudly. A single fran canister was released and the pilot instantly pulled up. The canister tumbled, then disappeared from view … CRUMP. It exploded in a flash of bright orange flame, throwing the green petroleum gel forward in a cloud of superheated gas.

'UP, UP,' Smith shouted, scrambling to his feet, running instinctively towards the CT position. He stopped next to a tree, fired three rounds, taking off again. He heard firing from either side as his men spread out to skirmish forward. No return fire. Smith could see a few trees on fire; he could hear the crackle of the flames, the smoke churning up.

The four men ran through the open ground, there was no cover to protect their approach. Firing and running, firing and running, tap…

20mm cannon as a result of forgetting to turn their caps inside out.

tap, tap… tap. It seemed to take forever to cover the four hundred or so metres, completely exposed the whole way. If the CTs had seen them coming it would have been disastrous.

Dirt spurted up in front of Smith, his mind trying to comprehend, a round passed his ear, *I am being shot at!* He dived into the dirt, lifted his rifle, and fired out in front of him, *where is it coming from?*

Dube dived to his left and opened up with the MAG.

Rounds were buzzing in close by. Still no cover, nowhere to hide, *we have to move or we die!* The rule of skirmishing is fire and movement – *move or you die!*

'Move Dube!' Smith screamed, '… skirmish forward, I will cover you!'

Jumping to his feet again, Smith dashed towards the burning trees only thirty metres ahead. He looked around for Sibanda and Mpofu but could not see them.

The two men rushed forward, firing as they went, Dube firing the MAG from the hip, running through the area of the airstrike. Smith saw a smouldering body and instinctively shot at it, but kept on running through. They stopped on the far side of the air-strike zone and turned, both their chests heaving with the exertion of the sprint across the open ground. Smith knelt down next to a tree, rapidly scanning the bush in front of him. Dube did the same. Still out of breath, Smith again scanned the bush for signs of movement, he could not see anything. The rifle fire had stopped.

'Did you see Sibanda and Mpofu?' asked Smith.

'They were next to you *Ishe*,' replied Dube as he scanned the bush ahead.

Smith looked back through the contact area seeing two charred bodies. A thin trail of smoke swirled above one, something was burning in the chest pocket. A few trees smouldered, burnt to a crisp. The Lynx passed back overhead.

'42Alpha I have CTs visual to your south,' instructed the pilot.

'*Ishe*, help me,' someone called. Smith looked back; out in the open ground he saw his other two men approaching. Sibanda was supporting Mpofu who was limping painfully. He and Dube stood up and walked back to where they stood.

'The gooks shot from over there … *Ishe*,' said Sibanda pointed towards the southern flank. 'I saw them and shot back. They stopped shooting and ran.' He continued in his clipped and succinct fashion, 'Mpofu has been shot in the leg, below the knee.'

'It is nothing *Ishe*,' added Mpofu quickly.

Another firefight began, further to the south, not far off. Smith heard Fullerton on the radio calling in the contact. He had Light and

Nduku with him. The Lynx pilot chimed in as he saw CTs breaking cover to the south.

'SEG!' shouted Sibanda pointing out to the right, 'It is Corporal Tovakare *Ishe*.'

Smith called out, 'Tovakare we are over here.' Through the trees Smith could see the stick of four men approaching. Tovakare walked straight up to him, his face ashen.

'Corporal Nkai is dead *Ishe*,' said Tovakare, his face grey with shock. 'They are over there, about a click,' he added pointing in the direction from which he had come. 'They were lying together, *Ishe*, Nkai is shot many times. ... I could not call you *Ishe*, my radio is US.' Tovakare was shaking, his voice broken with emotion. Nkai and Tovakare had been close friends; they had been together since training. 'I have told his men to carry him to the road,' sighed Tovakare, drained from the shock of what he had seen happen to his friend.

Smith stood in front of the men, dumbfounded. He had no idea what to say. They looked at him expectantly, as if he could bring Nkai back.

'The contact is still going on,' said Smith, trying to remain in control. The sound of rifle fire was continuing sporadically from the south. He could not find words to say; he did not know what to do. *Don't show any emotion, be strong. They need you to hold it together.* 'We may be needed by Captain Fullerton. We should go back to the vehicles. I need a medic to look at Mpofu. We will fetch Nkai and his men later.'

Two men slung Mpofu between them; the rest began the short walk to the border track. The radio still crackled as Fullerton barked instructions to the other c/signs as they tried to stop the CTs from crossing to safety.

'44 this is 42Alpha, I have 42Charlie with me ... 42Bravo has been killed ...' called Smith, struggling to finish; he released his finger from the handset.

'42Alpha, 44, confirm 42Bravo is Kilo, India, Alpha... Over.'

'44, affirmative, 42Bravo is KIA, I have one wounded, I am returning to the vehicles ... Over.'

'42Alpha, copied, 44 out,' came the metallic voice, so impersonal, so matter of fact, like asking the time. Smith had lost two men in one day.

*

Comrade Vladimir Benkov had seen the Lynx fly over. He was pretty sure that he had not been seen. Despite the very thin ground cover, the acacia trees were relatively close to the ground providing a thick canopy. The chance encounter with the SF c/sign as they crept forward to the border fence had been unfortunate. He was concerned about the border being patrolled, but they had literally walked on top of the four sleeping men in the half-light of early morning. A cadre had panicked when one of the sleeping soldiers had moved and shot him up with his RPD before anyone else could react. Benkov had been hoping to slip past in the dark safety was so close.

The Lynx airstrike on his position had been equally unexpected; fortunately he had heard the crack of the mini-flare projector seeing the flare for a split second. He had just enough time to scream for the men to break cover and run. A few had been too slow. The presence of other SF was a real worry. He watched four of them skirmishing onto the position of the airstrike. His enthusiastic RPD gunner had a go at them from long range, unsure of the result.

Benkov had split the group, sending half to the south as a diversion, with orders to cross as soon as they outflanked the SF, while he would double back to the north to do the same. Benkov and four freedom fighters now moved back to the north. They could hear gunfire continuing to the south. It sounded like the other group had been caught. That was good news; *let's hope the Rhodesians are held up long enough for me to cross.*

The border fence was now just in front of him. He scanned the bush on either side. The dragged area was a good twenty metres wide, swept clean, then the fence, then Botswana. So tantalisingly, close. They could not see the SF Four-five pulled into the trees, some 300m to the south.

Benkov called Mlungisi, 'Comrade, tell the men that we are going to run to the fence, two men must place their rifles on the barbed wire to hold it down for the others, then the others will help them.' He waited while Mlungisi repeated the instructions. The men listened intently, life and death in the balance.

'There must be no hesitation. Run to the fence, climb over and run for the cover of the trees on the other side.' Nobody spoke, they just focussed on the fence so enticingly close.

'GO' Benkov shouted. The men ran out to the fence, two men immediately pushed down on it with their rifles. A bullet struck the ground next to Benkov's foot. He looked up; Rhodesians were shooting at them from further down the road. The rifle fire intensified, more dirt was thrown up all close to where they stood. Bullets passed overhead, thump … thump … thump. Benkov jumped over the fence. Mlungisi was next. He lifted his leg to climb over. As he did so, he gave a grunt and fell back. Bullet strikes were now all about, the thump, thump, thump as bullets zipped and hissed overhead.

'Comrade Vladimir … I am hit … help me,' implored Mlungisi, lying on his back next to the fence.

Another man went down. Pressure released, the fence sprang back up. The other men tried to jump over it, but with their packs on it was too high to hurdle. Stuck on the fence, the barbed wire dragged at their clothing.

Benkov blinked, a flash of raw terror gripped his chest; the Lynx was again overhead. Mlungisi was trying to crawl under the lower strand, his pack snagging on the wire. Another round hit him, his body jerked violently from the impact.

'Comrade please!' begged Mlungisi, his head and torso stuck halfway under the fence.

The Rhodesians were running towards them, a machinegun was firing. The air seemed to be alive with bullets. Benkov turned to run into the bush so close behind him.

'Don't leave me, Comrade! … Please … Comrade,' Mlungisi beseeched, his voice fading as his strength began to ebb away.

Benkov looked down at his man with the realisation that he could not help him. He turned and ran for the cover of the Botswana bush, not looking back. Mlungisi's desperate cries faded, further bullet strikes sucking his life away. No other cadre followed, all were trapped at the fence, dead or dying.

Smith, Dube and Sibanda saw the man jump the fence; watched as he hesitated for a second then dashed for the shelter of the bush. Smith watched him, the distance was still over fifty metres, *that is one hellova big gook, has that gook got blonde hair? … Blonde hair!*

Without thinking, Smith rolled under the fence, calling the others to follow. Dube handed the MAG over and too slipped under the fence. Instantly the bush ahead erupted in gunfire.

'42Alpha this is Yellow 1 … I have Bravo, Delta, Foxtrot visual in the bush to your front. Get back across the fence NOW… Over,' called the Lynx pilot, seeing the danger.

Bravo, Delta, Foxtrot, what the fuck is that? In the heat of the moment Smith's mind would not register.

A Botswana Defence Force patrol, alerted by the gunfire along the border, had come to investigate. When they saw Rhodesians cross the fence, they opened fire themselves.

Smith heard the radio call in his ear, but the in-coming fire was too intense to reply; they sprinted for the cover of the bush on the Botswana side. A drainage channel had been cut off the border track, creating a shallow trench. The three men dived into it, instantly pinned down.

'Yellow 1, 44, we are in hot-pursuit[152] ... provide air support ... Over,' interjected Fullerton. '42Alpha, 44 ... throw smoke so I can see you ...'

Smith complied by throwing a red smoke grenade to his right. That just excited the BDF patrol more, as they increased the accuracy and intensity of their fire.

'Roger 42Alpha I have you visual, we are coming up from your south.'

Fullerton, Nduku and Light had crossed the fence and were coming up in support of the trapped men. The bush was so open that the red smoke in the still morning air was clear to see.

The Lynx dived out of the sun firing 37mm SNEB rockets onto the BDF position. The exploding rockets were enough to suppress the fire from the inexperienced BDF soldiers. The BDF firing stopped instantly.

Benkov had dived into cover as soon as he entered the line of trees. He did not see the soldiers pursue him across the fence. He also did not see the BDF patrol until they opened fire on the Rhodesians chasing him. He was trapped between the two groups. Crawling forward, away from the border fence, he tried to get out of the line of fire. The bush was still relatively open with very little cover. He crawled from tree to tree, fighting the urge to get up and run.

'42Alpha, I have a CT visual ... he is two hundred metres to your west ... crawling away,' came the call from the Lynx pilot. Benkov was clear to see from the air, crawling through the open ground.

'Yellow 1 copied,' replied Smith, thinking about what to do next.

'Come on let's get this bastard,' called Smith to his men, getting to his feet. They looked up at him incredulously. Smith didn't wait for any reply; he crouched down and moved off in the direction indicated by the pilot. The others scrambled to follow.

Benkov, sensing the presence of the Lynx above him and his exposed position, decided to make a break for it. He got to his feet and began to run, in the long loping strides that had always been his strength.

'42Alpha, your CT is now running ... standby ... I am going to throw fran.' The Lynx pilot watched Benkov running below him.

The aircraft turned onto its attack run and began to dive. Smith watched the Lynx turn. Looking out across the open bush, he could see the CT running in the distance. He was a tall man, athletic, running freely. The Lynx opened up with the twin .303 Brownings, the path of bullet strikes racing towards the man.

Inexplicably the man stopped. He turned, raised his rifle and fired defiantly back at the Lynx as it dived towards him. He continued to fire,

152 The Rhodesians claimed that they were legally entitled to cross international borders in hot-pursuit of terrorists.

the AKM bucking in his hands. The man's right hand, holding down the trigger, was as white as day. The shock realisation hit Smith. *That is a white man!* The Lynx passed overhead, the man, standing his ground, disappeared in a cloud of flame and smoke.

Standing in awe, Smith watched the plume of smoke and flame billowing up into the sky, mesmerised by the sight of the man engulfed in fire.

Hesitating for only a split-second more, Smith urged his men, 'Let's get out of here … quickly.' They turned and ran back to the safety of the border fence.

Fullerton, flanked by Light and Nduku, was standing at the border fence his foot leaning on the centre strand. His FN was tucked into his waist while the familiar disarming smile played accross his face. As Smith approached Fullerton called out to him.

'Where the fuck have you been Sergeant Smith? … Looking to take a safari in Botswana … or are we all victims of a giant hoax?' He threw his head back and laughed loudly, both Nduku and Light smiled with him.

Smith, suddenly completely drained, looked blankly up at Fullerton.

'Oh … by the way, Smithy, I have some excellent news for you …' His face still covered with his trademark mischievous smile.

'Yes Sir?'

Fullerton stretched it out for dramatic effect, 'Your intake's national service has been extended by six months …'

> *Mama put my guns in the ground*
> *I can't shoot them anymore*
> *That cold black cloud is comin' down*
> *Feels like I'm knockin' on heaven's door*
>
> *Knock-knock-knockin' on heaven's door*

*

In front of a thatched mud hut deep in the Lupane TTL, a Sangoma looked up from his early morning meal. He felt a shift in the breeze; the leaves of a lone Mopani tree rustled, the spirits of the dead were restless. He felt the presence of the spirit of the young girl, so brutally murdered. She had news for him. He studied the tree for a few seconds then smiled to himself, revenge had been taken. She could now rest in peace. Her brothers and sisters left behind could not.

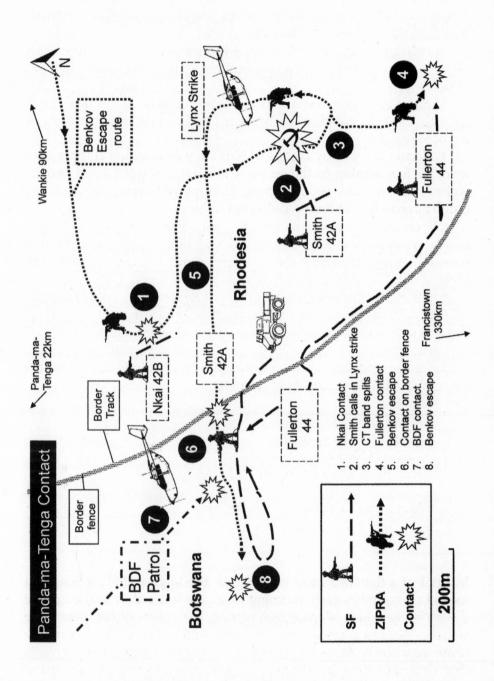

Panda-ma-Tenga Contact

Rhodesia

Botswana

Wankie 90km

Panda-ma-Tenga 22km

Benkov Escape route

Lynx Strike

Smith 42A

Smith 42A

Nkai 42B

Fullerton 44

Fullerton 44

Francistown 330km

Border Track

Border fence

BDF Patrol

1. Nkai Contact
2. Smith calls in Lynx strike
3. CT band splits
4. Fullerton contact
5. Benkov escape
6. Contact on border fence
7. BDF contact.
8. Benkov escape

SF
ZIPRA
Contact

200m

Postscript

Whether the Soviet Union allowed its operatives to infiltrate Rhodesia in support of ZIPRA has never been proved. Certainly, Soviet Advisors were present in the ZIPRA training camps in Zambia, Tanzania and Angola. The first military training for ZIPRA cadres in the Soviet Union began in the northern summer of 1964 and continued throughout the conflict[153]. It was not until a formal request by Joshua Nkomo on 4 January 1977 that the Soviets agreed to send advisors and military instructors to Africa to support ZIPRA operations[154]. The first group of twelve Soviet officers arrived at the ZIPRA camp near Lueno (formally Vila Luso) in Angola in July 1977 under the command of Lt Col Vladimir Pekin. Col Pekin's deputy for political affairs was Captain Anatoly Burenko who has written extensively on his experiences in Africa in support of ZIPRA[155]. The second Soviet advisory team was sent to Zambia on 13 July 1978 under the command of Col Lev Kononov[156].

The logistical support for the training at Lueno was provided by the Cubans, who also acted as platoon and company commanders on field exercises. On 26 February 1979, after the second Air Rhodesia Viscount disaster, the Rhodesian Air Force, supported by Canberras from the South African Air Force, attacked Lueno. In that attack, 192 ZIPRA cadres were killed with approximately 1,000 wounded. In the same attack, Alpha bouncing bombs killed six Cuban instructors and a Soviet Warrant Officer, Grigory Skakun[157]. Incredibly, despite the repeated attacks by Rhodesian forces on ZIPRA training camps in Zambia and Angola there are no other confirmed reports of Soviet casualties.

Joshua Nkomo, in his memoirs, played down the role of the Soviet military advisors, he states, '… there was never any question of sending combat troops, or even advisors, from the Soviet Union or any other country to help us fight our war'.[158] One can only ascribe Nkomo's denial of Soviet support in his book as a political expedient necessary at the time.

An estimated 37 missionaries were murdered by both ZIPRA and ZANLA during the course of the war. The most publicised atrocity was the attack on Elim Pentecostal Mission in the Vumba Mountains

---

153 Vladimir Shubin, *The Hot Cold War - The USSR in Southern Africa*, Pluto Press 2008, at 155.
154 Shubin supra at 171, Joshua Nkomo made the request at a meeting with the USSR Ministry of Defense.
155 A. Burenko, *A Hard Exclusively Important Period of Life* (2006).
156 Shubin supra at 173.
157 Shubin supra at 173, quoting A. Burenko.
158 J Nkomo, *The Story of my Life*, Methuen 1984, at 175.

near Umtali. In that attack twelve missionaries, eight adults and four children, were, raped, hacked and bludgeoned to death[159].

Two civilian airliners were shot down by ZIPRA using Strela (SAM-7) ground-to-air heat-seeking missiles. The first was on 3 September 1978 when an Air Rhodesia Viscount was shot down soon after taking off from Kariba. Of the 53 on board, 18 survived the crash but ZIPRA guerrillas massacred 10 of them, including 6 women. A second Air Rhodesia Viscount was shot down coming out of Kariba on 12 February 1979 with the deaths of 54 passengers and 5 crew. The plane came down only 50km from the spot where the first aircraft crashed. Joshua Nkomo accepted responsibility for both attacks but claimed that the second aircraft was supposed to be carrying Gen Peter Walls, the commander of COMOPS. ZIPRA had planned to bring down a civilian airliner during the referendum for the internal settlement in January 1979. Shooting down airliners was seen as a means of creating an emotional backlash by the white electorate, and in so doing, derailing the internal settlement negotiations.[160]

---

159 Paul Moorcraft and Peter McLaughlin, *The Rhodesian War – A Military History*, Pen & Sword (2008), at 152.
160 Moorcraft and McLaughlin supra at 156-157.